Life Happens

on the

Stairs

AWARD-WINNING AUTHOR

AMY J. MARKSTAHLER

www.breakthroughnovelawards.com

LIFE HAPPENS ON THE STAIRS

Copyright © 2018 Amy J. Markstahler

Amy J. Markstahler

www.amyjmarkstahler.com

Edited by Eeva Lancaster
Cover and Book Design by The Book Khaleesi
www.thebookkhaleesi.com

10 9 8 7 6 5 4 3 2 1

To my daughter, Emily
and my parents, Hank and Barbara Rothermel

Table of Contents

Life gave her an assignment
One she didn't choose
Lost for answers
She felt beaten and bruised...
The days dragged on
Hopeless and dark
Until she met the one
Who lit a spark...
She needed a place
Somewhere to hide
He professed his devotion
Yet, she lied and lied...
She was stuck in adulting
Forced to be strong
Time was ticking
Her dad didn't have long...
Ashamed and embarrassed
She could barely breathe
Torn between family
And a companion she needs.

Faith is taking the first step even when you don't see the whole staircase.

– Martin Luther King Jr.

Chapter

1

I followed Dad toward the Fourth of July festival, carrying a portfolio full of drawings and a folding table. Hundreds of people wandered through downtown. The aroma of kettle corn moved with the breeze, carnies ran neon-pink and green rides, alongside game booths piled high with oversized stuffed animals. I stopped on the sidewalk and wiped the sweat off my face, unsure if the perspiration was from the stifling Tennessee sun or the possibility of hearing negative opinions about my artwork.

Calm down, I told myself. *No one would be cruel to a seventeen-year-old.*

Dad was setting up the pop-up tent in our rented vendor space and waved at me to hurry. Ten minutes later, we set out the pastel and charcoal drawings I'd prepared. We stepped back to examine our work.

"Relax. Enjoy the day." Dad wrapped his arm around my shoulder. "You got this, Elsie."

The security of his embrace stilled my jitters.

"Have you sent your application to Memphis yet?" he asked.

I had my heart set on Memphis College of Art. "I'll mail it tomorrow."

"You'd better. Don't miss your chance." He squeezed me tight. "I'm gonna get a lemon shake-up. Want one?"

"Please. I'm dying of thirst."

When he walked away, I noticed him dragging his left foot as if it was weighed down with a cinderblock. He took a staggered step to readjust then moved on with a more confident stride.

I started to follow but changed my mind. He'd be fine. Then, the thought of him falling down made my heart skip. What if he loses his sense of direction and couldn't find his way back? He'd been acting weird lately – starting a sentence but never finishing, and sometimes slurring his words. A twitch here or there, and the other day when we were walking the pepper field, he almost collapsed from the heat.

I had to call Mom and tell her how odd he was acting. The doctor said the brain tumor was in remission, but the threat of it returning loomed over us like the smog from the paper mill. *Maybe he was only dehydrated,* I assured myself. The lemon shake-up would help.

My best friend, Emma, hurried down the sidewalk wearing a Nirvana T-shirt and dark skinny jeans. She held out her arms with a big smile.

Yes. She promised me she'd make it. We gave each other

a quick hug.

"I was afraid you left for Florida already," I said.

"No. Dad's coming to get me tomorrow." She glanced around the booth. "Everything looks great, but where's your momma?"

"Working."

"On the Fourth of July?"

"Mrs. Vaughn's going to Houston. The old woman wanted Mom to pack her suitcase."

"When you've got that kind of money, I reckon you can have someone else do it."

"I suppose."

She looked down the street. "Y'all need something to bring people in."

"Like what?"

"Sketch me." She grinned, propping her hand on her hip. "People will totally notice, then they'd want you to draw them too. For a fee, of course."

"Works for me."

I grabbed a folding chair for her, set up my flimsy, three-legged easel, and began drawing her likeness on a 12x16 sketchpad. Charcoal worked perfectly for her choppy, black hair which contrasted with her pale skin. I'd been in the sun all summer, helping Dad with his crops. Long days walking the fields had bleached my hair almost white. Emma and I were like yin and yang, from our looks to our thoughts. She was a math guru, me an artist. She was outspoken and bold. I was quiet and preferred to be at home. I was tall and tan, she was petite and goth. But just as the symbol represented, we were in perfect balance.

After a few minutes, several people stopped to watch, and then a few more gathered around. *Where was Dad?* I needed him to help buffer the attention. I looked over my shoulder. *He should've been back already.*

"Elsie," Emma whispered. "There is this hot guy standing outside the booth."

"I'm busy." I rubbed the paper, shadowing in her prominent cheekbones.

"You gotta look."

I took a quick glance. A heavyset man whose hairy belly hung out from underneath his T-shirt stood on the sidewalk, eating popcorn. *Yuck.* I went back to my sketch. After a few more strokes and Emma's incessant expressions, I had to look again. Several yards up the sidewalk, a guy with light brown hair, wearing a navy Polo and dark jeans, stared my way. I hadn't seen him before, and with a face like his, I'd have remembered.

I turned back to the drawing. "The guy in the Polo?"

She giggled. "Did you see him?"

A plump lady in a garish floral blouse stepped beside me. "Miss, I love the portrait you're drawin'. I'd like one of my son. How much do y'all charge?"

"Ten dollars," I said. "I'll be done with her in just a minute."

"Sounds good."

I grinned at Emma. She smiled back, then looked over my shoulder.

"Oh my gosh, Elsie. He's coming this way."

"Would you stop? I have to focus."

I waved for the lady to bring her son over. Just as I flipped to a clean page, someone touched my shoulder. I jumped. *Dad. Thank God, he made it back.*

Dad handed me a Styrofoam cup. I took a sip of the tart lemon drink and started a sketch of the blond-haired, blue-eyed boy with round cheeks.

"How are you, Emma?" Dad asked. "We haven't seen you much this summer."

"I'm good, Mr. Richardson. How've you been?"

"Better than I deserve. Ready for your senior year?"

"Sure am."

"Will you graduate early with El... El... Elsie?"

"Yes," Emma drawled, eyeing him with concern.

I stopped sketching. Dad's words slurred and stuttered like he'd been at the bar all day. He scrunched his forehead and rubbed his right eye.

"So, where y'all from?" the lady asked him. "Ya don't sound Southern."

Dad and I chuckled. The question followed us everywhere in Hardin County. We'd moved to Tennessee five years earlier from Central Illinois, and the locals were always baffled at why we polluted the air with our Northern accent.

"Illinois," Dad said as he swayed to the right. "Whew, it's hot out."

"Are you feeling okay?" I asked.

He nodded. I didn't buy it.

Trying to shake off my worry, I gave the lady her drawing.

"I love it." She handed me a twenty-dollar bill. "Thanks so much."

"I'll get your change."

"No, you keep that, darling. You earned it." She smiled and walked away with her son.

As I flipped the page back to Emma's portrait, a musky, cedar-laced scent moved through the air. The guy in the Polo had stepped inside the booth. I moved closer to Dad. He noticed the guy and held out his right hand.

"Brandon Richardson."

The guy tilted his head, as if our name triggered a thought, and then he returned the handshake. "Nice to meet you, sir. This is some mighty fine work."

"She's quite talented. Would you like your portrait drawn?"

I nudged Dad with my elbow.

"No, thank you, sir—"

Dad's arms had started to shake, and a massive tremor rolled through him. Then, he collapsed like he'd been hit with a bolt of lightning. The guy grabbed Dad under the arms, following him to the ground, helping break the fall. Terrified, I plunged to my knees beside them.

"Dad!" I grabbed his trembling arm. "Oh God, someone call 911!"

The guy pulled out his iPhone and pushed the numbers. "What's wrong with him?"

"It's a seizure."

Emma rushed to my side. "Elsie, what can I do?"

"Find Woodrow. He's at the barbecue stand."

Emma jumped up and sprinted out of the tent. The guy spoke into the phone, telling emergency where we were. I grabbed Dad by the shoulders and tried to roll him over. He wouldn't budge. Tense and balled up from the convulsions, his weight pressed against the concrete, scraping his skin.

No, no, no... not again. I yanked on his shoulder and he finally flopped on his back.

I gasped.

He looked like a man being executed in an electric chair. His eyes rolled in the back of his head, exposing only the whites.

"The ambulance is on the way," the guy said.

"I need my mom!"

"Where is she?"

"Working at Vaughn's."

"Um... okay. I got that, too."

"Who are you?" I asked, more annoyed than I intended.

"Tyler."

He stood up and pressed the phone to his ear. Emma ran back to my side.

"I found Woodrow," her voice quivering. "He's on his way."

Woodrow was Dad's closest friend, but at seventy years old, it would take him more than a few minutes to get through the crowd.

Tyler turned around. "Your mom will meet you at the hospital."

I recoiled. How did he get hold of her? Whatever. I didn't have the time or patience to care. Everyone knew the Vaughns.

I turned back to Dad. Blood was now trickling out of the corner of his mouth. More tears clouded my sight.

"Why is he bleeding?" I cried out.

Tyler dropped to his knees and gently tilted Dad's chin upward. Calm and collected, he then reached in his back pocket and slipped his wallet between Dad's teeth. He did it so fast I barely had time to comprehend what he was doing. Dad clenched his teeth down on the leather. Chills ran up my arms.

"He bit his tongue," Tyler said. "He needed something to bite down on."

"This is awful."

"The ambulance is almost here."

Bells from the carnival games echoed off the buildings.

People chattered outside the booth as they watched the spectacle of my father convulsing on the ground. Music blared in the distance, and then the ambulance sirens overpowered all the noise.

How could this happen in front of all these people? Ashamed, my cheeks burned underneath my tears. I wasn't embarrassed by Dad, but the horror of a grand mal seizure was better experienced in the privacy of home.

Emma wrapped her arm around me and pulled me close. I buried my face in her shoulder. *Why? Why wouldn't the damn brain tumor go away?*

Paramedics rushed at us, offering their aid with precision. Emma and I moved out of the way, and Tyler stepped back into the crowd. I wanted to thank him, but I didn't have time.

A female paramedic led me toward the ambulance, saying words I completely tuned out. I looked back over my shoulder and saw a medic handing Tyler his wallet.

Our eyes met. I hoped he understood how much I appreciated his help. He slowly inclined his head, concern written all over his face. I took another long look at the compassion in his eyes, and then I climbed inside the back of the ambulance.

Chapter

2

I paced the lobby of the emergency room, chewing on the side of my thumb. I shouldn't have nudged Dad. I should've known better. Mom had warned me that the littlest thing could trigger a seizure. *Where was she, anyway?* It shouldn't have taken her so long to get across town.

I turned to go to the front desk, but then I heard the doors to the entrance slide open. *Mom.* Just the sight of her made me sob. She hurried toward me and I ran into her embrace.

"Are you okay?" she asked.

"Oh, Mom... I elbowed him, and then he just dropped. It's all my fault."

She pulled back, her blue eyes fixed to mine. "This is not your fault."

Wrapping her arms around me again, we cried on each other's shoulder.

Moments later, we gathered our composure, and she headed to the nurse's station.

I sat down in the waiting room, still riddled with guilt.

The doors to the ER slid open and Woodrow limped inside, his bum hip slowing him down. Lines from years of working in the hot sun softened his worried eyes.

I stood up and gave him a hug.

"Y'all be okay." He patted my back. "Brandon's a strong man."

A few minutes later, Emma rushed in and sat down with us.

"I packed up your booth and ran it by the house," she said.

"Thank you."

Memphis College of Art... goodbye. If the tumor was back, I couldn't just leave Mom and go to college. I laid my head on Emma's shoulder, feeling selfish for even thinking about it. She lovingly pressed her head to mine. My girl. She always helped me feel better.

Mom returned, her face streaked from tears. "They're prepping him for emergency surgery. I didn't even get to see him."

Woodrow stood and wrapped his arm around her. "He'll be all right. God's got this."

"I hope so."

Hope. Hope was all we had. A futile attempt to wish the tumor away. After seeing how that seizure ripped through Dad's body, I'd lost hope.

"Why don't we go to the cafeteria and get something to eat?" Woodrow asked.

Mom agreed and we all started walking through the lobby. A motor hummed and the entrance doors whooshed open. I glanced up.

Tyler.

Tall and confident, he walked straight toward me, expression still full of concern.

His arrival stopped me in my tracks.

"Hey, I'm glad I caught you. I found these on the ground near your booth." Tyler held out the truck keys. "Are they yours?"

"Yeah, they're my dad's," I said as I took them. "They must've fallen out of his pocket."

"How's he doing?"

"We don't know anything yet."

"I hope he's okay." Tyler pushed his hands in his pockets, scrunched his shoulders, then shifted from side to side. "Um, well..."

"Thanks for everything you did," I said. "I was scared to death."

"No problem. It freaked me out, too." Tanned cheeks turning red, he waved his hand and took a step backward. "Just wanted to make sure you got your keys. Hope y'all are okay."

"Thanks."

He hesitated like there was something else to say. His dark eyes met mine and my stomach filled with butterflies. But then he gave a sincere nod and turned and walked out.

"Who in the world is that guy?" Emma asked.

"Tyler." I shrugged. "That's all I know."

"Maybe your summer won't be so bad, after all."

"I'm not holding my breath."

"Girl, he's totally into you."

The last thing on my mind was a boy. "I'll never see him again," I said.

"Fifty bucks says you're wrong."

I smirked. "I could use fifty bucks."

For the next six hours, we rotated from the cafeteria to the surgery waiting room, to the bathroom, and back. By six o'clock, Emma went home to finishing packing for Florida. I gave her a hug goodbye, dreading the rest of the summer alone. Woodrow read about the latest gossip in the Hardin County newspaper, as Mom's spirit dwindled with every passing minute.

At seven-thirty, Dr. Wood walked into the waiting room. Anxious to hear his news, Mom and I hurried across the room to talk to him.

"Hello, Mrs. Richardson."

"How is he?"

"He made it through surgery. He'll be in recovery for a few hours."

We both let out a sigh of relief. Woodrow stepped up behind us.

"We did our best to remove as much of the mass as we could. But... if you think of the tumor like it's an octopus, the tendrils had twisted their way through the crevasses of the brain, making it impossible for us to reach all of it." He pursed his lips as if he'd failed somehow. "The nurse will let you know when he's settled in the ICU. You can see him then."

"Thank you," Mom said.

Dr. Wood's defeated manner left me feeling unsettled and even more skeptical.

After the doctor walked out, Mom said, "I need to call Mark."

"Does he know what happened?"

"I talked to him earlier. He's driving here tomorrow."

I hadn't seen my big brother for almost a year, and we weren't exactly on good terms when he left. Mark hated Tennessee as much as I loved it. So, in his typical way of making Mom's life hell, he'd started drinking and partying until she finally had to ask my grandparents for help.

"Sure hope that boy has his head on straight, now," Woodrow said.

"Me, too," Mom agreed.

An hour later, a slender brunette in Scooby-Doo scrubs stepped inside the waiting room.

"Are you Claire Richardson?" she asked Mom.

"Yes."

"You can see Brandon now. He's in room 311."

"Thank you."

I followed Mom into the low lit hallway of the ICU. The first room I saw had a neon yellow sign on the door, warning outsiders: *Do Not Enter If Pregnant.* I bristled. *Why?*

I scanned the rest of the hall. All the rooms had glass outer walls with curtains – some stood wide open, others were shut. Beeps and low voices haunted the sunless corridor.

I glanced to my right. A middle-aged man lay in bed with tubes attached to his face. A plump woman sat next to him. As she raised her tired, heavy eyes to mine, a lump tightened my throat. Her hopeless expression deeply disturbed me and I quickly looked to my left.

A woman paced back and forth, holding a rosary in her hand as she murmured prayers. She stopped beside the bed. A small child hooked to tubes and machines lay motionless in front of her. The little one was no older than six, bald and pale, genderless under the veil of disease.

I stopped in the middle of the hallway. *A child?* My stomach dropped.

Mom touched my shoulder. "Elsie, come on, sweetie."

"Oh my gosh," I said, looking at the woman consumed with worry. "I can't imagine."

"Me, either. Just don't look."

I fixed my eyes on the back of Mom's head. A few doors later, she stopped in front of a glass wall with Dad's name and a chart written in erasable marker. A young, dark-haired man wearing blue scrubs sat at a computer station by the entrance.

He stood. "Mrs. Richardson?"

"Yes."

"I'm Aaron." He shook Mom's hand, then smiled at me. "Brandon's been resting quite peacefully. Y'all need to put on a gown and gloves before you go inside." He pointed at a plastic rack behind us.

I thought that once inside Dad's room, I'd feel better. But as we followed Aaron's instructions, all I wanted to do was run away from the place. I slid into the gown, then smoothed out the folds of the awkward, yellow paper. Mom handed me a pair of purple gloves. I pulled the soft rubber over my right hand, trembling with anxiety. As I put on the other glove, I looked into Mom's eyes.

"I don't think I can do this."

"Yes, you can," she said.

"I'm scared."

"In other words, you wanna run."

I lowered my head and looked at the white-tiled floor.

My family used to joke and call me "The Runner," but after my last attempt to flee from my fears, the joke wasn't funny anymore.

"Get it reeled in," she said in a firm tone. "You need to be with your dad."

I nodded. Easier said than done.

She stood taller and headed into the room.

I held my breath, about to burst from the pressure inside. The only man I'd ever loved was lying in bed, fighting for his life behind the curtained glass. I wanted to be there for him, but the thought of escaping was just as attractive. I wanted to hold his hand and tell him how much I loved him, but the last thing I wanted was to accept that he'd been classified to sleep next to the dying.

Aaron stepped beside me and placed his hand on my shoulder.

"It's not as scary as you think. If you need someone to talk to, I'm here all night."

"Thanks."

Tucking my chin, I moved past the curtain.

Mom sat beside the bed, holding Dad's hand, tears streaming down her cheeks. A clear tube ran to his mouth, each breath being pushed into his lungs by a machine beside the bed. His chest rising and falling in sync with the harsh clicking sound. Beeps and hisses filled the air, like a Willie Wonka invention, minus the chocolate. More tubes ran up Dad's arms, disappearing under the sheets, while another came from the back of his head, funneling fluid into some mysterious place.

Mom stood up and held out her arms. She hadn't been harsh to hurt me. She knew that if I ran, I'd never forgive myself, and she was the only one who could convince me not to.

For the next two hours, we listened to the symphony of machines without saying a word. We weren't there just for Dad... Mom needed to be there, too. She stroked his cheek and held his hand. I didn't really know what to do with myself, until I spotted a pen and paper next to the telephone. Instead of staring at my parents, I stayed busy by drawing caricatures of the space-age machines hovering above Dad. He would've loved my silly cartoons, influenced by years of watching Bugs Bunny together. Even in the worst of moods, Dad would roll with laughter when that silly rabbit did something clever.

One more time... all I wanted was one more time to laugh together, to talk. A tear rolled down my cheek, landing on the notepad. *Relent, God, please relent.*

The glass door opened with a gust of cooler air and Dr. Wood stepped inside. He smiled at Mom and then me. Gentleness had replaced his matter-of-fact approach after surgery.

I relaxed in the chair, relieved a human being had operated on Dad, and not some cold robot posing as one.

"Hello again, Mrs. Richardson."

"Please, call me Claire."

"Of course." He sat in the chair beside her. "Brandon's going to be here for a while. He's stable, but his brain is already starting to swell. The staff will monitor him overnight, but if the swelling continues, I'll induce a coma to help him heal with less stress. Do you have any questions?"

"Um, yes. What are we supposed to do?"

"Well, after the damage from the seizure, on top of the stress from the surgery... we're going to have to wait and see." He gave her a sympathetic smile. "Claire, I suggest you start preparing for the worst. I'm sorry to say this, but his chances of a full recovery are slim." She closed her eyes and shook her head, like she didn't want to accept the words. He patted her hand. "We never know, though. He's a strong man. I'll keep you updated, okay?"

"Thank you."

He acknowledged me with a kind smile and walked out.

A deafening silence filled the room. There were no words to ease the moment. Mom covered her face with both hands and cried. I bowed my head, begging for God's help.

After sitting that way for close to an hour, she let out a sigh. "Go ahead and go home, sweetie. Woodrow said he'd wait for you. I'm gonna stay here tonight."

"Are you sure? I can stay."

"No. Go home and get a good night's sleep. I'm going to need your help tomorrow at the Vaughns' house. She wants me to do a bunch of extra work while she's in Houston. If you help, I can get back here sooner."

"Okay." I gave her a hug. "Call me if anything changes."

"I will. Love you."

"I love you."

Chapter

3

I woke the next morning, gasping from a nightmare about Dad's seizure. Pulling the covers over my head, I cried until I heard Mom's footsteps. She was home. I jumped out of bed.

When I stepped into the kitchen, she was sitting at the dining room table, talking on the phone. I poured a cup of coffee, fighting off the dread of spending the day at the Vaughns'. I admired Mom for how hard she worked, cleaning the estate and several other homes in Savannah. But the job felt demeaning to me... like I wasn't worthy of a better life.

As I went back to my room to change, Mom dialed another number. I left the door open a crack so I could listen to her conversation.

"Hi, Daddy, how's everything going?" she said. "Has Mark left yet?... Oh, okay. I don't know if Brandon's going to be able to fight it this time... I know. I just talked to his sister. His vitals crashed in the middle of the night."

Hearing that bit of news, I burst out of my room.

"Okay, love you, too." She hung the phone on the wall.

"Is Mark on his way?"

"He left a few hours ago."

"What about Dad?"

"It's not good. They induced a coma this morning."

Determined not to cry, I walked away without a word. The disappointing news didn't surprise me anymore. I was expecting it.

Ten minutes later, Mom hollered that it was time to leave.

As we drove across the Harrison-McGarity Bridge into Savannah, the air shifted to the smell of burnt broccoli and sulfur. The stench preceded every storm moving toward the Tennessee River Valley. A wonderful byproduct of Pickwick Paper Mill—it complemented my stinky mood. Nevertheless, I actually loved the Vaughn estate. Built in the early 1800s, it was what one would imagine when the word "plantation" was mentioned. But, I despised Mrs. Vaughn. The first and only time I met her, she had sized me up and pointed at a stain on my shirt.

Mom parked the truck on the asphalt driveway and climbed out. She looked exhausted, as we walked up the steps to the front porch. She unlocked the mahogany door and pushed it open.

A grand staircase divided the second level into separate wings, like Beast's Castle in *Beauty and The Beast*. I stepped on the red-and-black Oriental rug, in complete awe of the pristine, white-walled foyer.

Mom rounded the staircase, eager to get to work.

I slowly climbed the stairs. The glossy, walnut handrail felt cool and smooth under my touch. Tiny rainbows sparkled off the walls from the chandelier above and plush carpeting cushioned each of my unworthy steps. Mom passed me, running on pure adrenaline. I worried about her almost as much as Dad. If she didn't chill and get some rest, she'd end up in the hospital, too.

When I caught up with her in the hallway, I said under my breath, "This house."

"What about it?"

"It's so beautiful, and perfect."

"Yeah, well." She pushed Mrs. Vaughn's bedroom door open. "Everything isn't perfect just because it's beautiful."

Whatever. I would've killed to wake up every morning in such luxury. Soft gray walls outlined in white crown molding, a king-sized, cherry poster-bed covered in spotless white linens and plush pillows. Even the blooms on the mimosa tree outside danced in the breeze, like little pink fairies curiously peeking through the full-length windows.

"Pull out the bedside table," Mom said. "We have to wipe the walls."

"Why?"

I've never had to wipe walls at our house before.

"Because she's paying me to do it," she said, deadpan. "Now, come on. I wanna get this done. I hate not being at the hospital."

After ten minutes of wrestling with the cumbersome furniture, I flopped on the mattress.

Mom didn't slow down a beat. Heading straight to the

navy drapes, she pulled one side shut. The room darkened, and muted shadows fell across the white carpeting.

"We have to steam clean these." She yanked the fabric again. "There's a steamer down in the basement. It stands upright, kind of looks like a vacuum. Think you can find it?"

"Sure."

Anything to get out of wiping walls.

I headed downstairs and took a right toward the kitchen. Thinking nothing of it, I detoured to the polished stainless-steel refrigerator, yanked the double doors open, and scoffed out loud. An array of fresh fruits was stocked in the drawers, while milk, power drinks, and bottled water filled the shelves next to stacks of packaged fresh meat. Why would the woman need so much food? Leaning forward, I buried my head inside.

"Anything good in there?" a guy's voice resonated from my right.

I jumped back and slammed the doors. Staring at the floor, I quickly blurted, "I'm sorry. I didn't take anything." Then, I looked up and gasped. "Tyler?"

"Elsie." He smiled. "What a nice surprise."

He stood at the doorway, wearing black Adidas warm-ups and a white tank top, his tan skin glistening with sweat. My heart pounded. Absolutely breathtaking.

"Are you related to the Vaughns?" I asked.

He bit his bottom lip for a brief moment, then said, "I am a Vaughn. I apologize. I should've told you that yesterday. How's your dad doing?"

Well, that made more sense, considering his speedy phone call to Mom.

"He's stable. Thanks for asking."

I stared at his Nikes, unsure of what to say. Tyler

scratched the side of his head, as if he was struggling with the same thing. Then, he took a step closer.

"Why don't we start over?" He held out his right hand. "I'm Tyler Vaughn. It's a pleasure to meet you again."

"Nice to meet you, Tyler Vaughn." When I took his warm hand, goosebumps tingled up my arm. "Elsie Richardson."

"And Elsie's short for?"

"Elizabeth."

"Nice. I wondered if it was a nickname."

"It is, but I prefer Elsie."

"Elsie it is, then." He released my hand. "I never had the chance to tell you why I came into your booth. I really love your work. You certainly are talented."

I'd forgotten all about that part of the horrible day.

"Thank you. It was the first time I'd tried to sell anything."

"I'm sure that under different circumstances, you would've done well."

I took a step back. The last thing I wanted was the subject to shift to Dad's seizure.

"I need to go to the basement. Mom wants me to get some steamer thingy. Could you maybe send me in the right direction? I have no idea where it is."

"The door's in the foyer." He motioned over his shoulder. "It blends in with the wall."

"Cool. Thanks."

Moments later, I stood in the entry, staring at the thirty-foot walls. Tyler stepped beside me, looking amused.

"Where the heck is it?" I asked.

He pointed at the wall to my left. "It's there."

I still didn't see it. His muscular arm moved past my face, then he pressed the panel right in front of me. Click. The secret door cracked open, disguised behind the white, molded trim.

"Nana had these walls resurfaced years ago. Did you know..." he started, exaggerating his Southern drawl, "it isn't lady-like to have a basement? One must cover such atrocities with something more appealing."

I laughed. "Thank you. I never would've found that."

He stepped backward, pulling the door open with him. "You've never been down there?"

I shook my head. The hesitant look in his eyes made me nervous.

"Why don't I help you find it, then?"

"Okay."

I followed him down the narrow stairwell – a far cry from the staircase in the foyer – and the pungent smell of red-clay dirt punched me in the nose, exposing the true age of the mansion.

He flipped on the light at the bottom of the stairs. A soft yellow glow from bulbs hanging off the rafters illuminated the brick floors. Across the room, he opened a door and flipped another switch. The fluorescent lights flickered, before a full-service laundry room appeared. The workroom had a center folding table and two sets of washers and dryers.

"So, what's this thingy you're looking for?" Tyler asked.

"It's a steamer for the drapes. Mom said it looks like a vacuum."

We both spotted the appliances at the same time. Five different machines resembling vacuums were lined up against the wall.

"Which one is it?" I asked.

Tyler turned to me with a baffled look. "You're talkin' to the wrong guy. I don't use steamer thingies."

"I don't either." I laughed, then I looked closer at the brand names on the labels. "Okay, this one's definitely a vacuum. I don't know what that one does... This one's a steamer, but for hardwood floors. And—"

"Ooh, it's the one on the end," he said, like he'd found a golden egg.

"How do you know?"

He pointed at the bulkiest hunk of metal in the group and smiled. "It says 'Steam Cleaner,' right there."

I giggled, and started to reach for the handle. He caught my hand to stop me.

"I'll get it," he said.

"Thanks."

Within minutes, we were headed back upstairs.

"Are you home for the summer?" he asked.

"No. I live outside Morris Chapel."

"How old are you?"

"I'll be eighteen in November. It's my senior year."

"Oh. You seem older than that," he said. "So, you'll graduate in May?"

"No. December, if everything goes right. Are you in Savannah long?"

"Six weeks." He pulled in a heavy breath and stepped in the foyer. "Six, long-ass weeks."

The tone in his voice took me off guard. I shut the basement door, certain I should leave the subject alone. He set down the steamer and gave a me a warm smile.

"Any chance you like to jog?" he asked.

"I've been known to run, but I rarely jog."

"You should try it."

"Do you run a lot?"

"Yeah, close to twenty miles a day."

"Seriously?" I exaggerated my tone. "Why?"

"I, um... run cross country for Vanderbilt University, so I train a lot."

"Yeah?"

"Elsie!" Mom's voice echoed from upstairs.

My cheeks burned. Her bellow reminded me of the old milk commercials Dad always teased me about when Elsie the Cow was called home.

"I gotta go."

"Sounds like it," Tyler said with a smile. "You want me to carry that upstairs for you?"

"No, thank you. I can take it from here."

"I'll be at Shiloh Park around seven. You're welcome to join me."

I cringed. "Seven in the morning?"

"You're lucky. I usually go at five. It's not as hot then. Have you been out to Shiloh?"

"Sure. Dad loves Civil War stuff. It's a beautiful park, but... "

I didn't know how to answer. When I "ran" it was out of fear... not exercise. But an offer to hang out *was* tempting. He flashed a flirty grin, almost as if he liked the challenge that I might say no.

"Come on... You know you wanna meet me. Besides, I'd like to figure out where this Yankee accent I'm hearin' comes from."

"Yankee?" I repeated. "What are you talking about?"

He chuckled. "Oh, okay. You wanna play that way, huh? I can roll with that." Pleading with his eyes, he said, "Meet me, please."

My heartbeat pounded in my ears. I wanted to say yes. I had to say yes.

"I... I'll try."

"Great! I'll see you in the morning."

"Where in the park? That place is huge."

"Oh, yeah. Just follow Confederate Road. I'll be outside my car. You won't miss me."

"Okay."

"Do you have a cell number, just in case?"

I frowned. "No. I don't have one yet."

"That sucks. Oh well. Hope to see you tomorrow."

I hurried up the steps with the steamer before Mom yelled my name again. What did I just agree to? I hated jogging and sweating. Hell... exercise, in general. And he was a college athlete. I'd make a total ass of myself within minutes.

When I stepped inside Mrs. Vaughn's room, Mom was wiping the baseboard.

"Where have you been?" she asked.

"Sorry." I set down the steamer. "I ran into Tyler downstairs."

"Oh, I forgot he was back for the summer. He was the one who called the house when your dad had the seizure. Thank God I answered the phone."

"Yeah, he helped us out. He was amazing, actually."

"Really?" Her shoulders slumped. "That's nice of him and all, but it kind of sucks."

"What's the big deal?"

"I haven't told Mrs. Vaughn about your dad."

"Why?"

Mom could be ridiculously private sometimes. I didn't understand why she wanted to carry everything by herself. *Stubborn German* was the only thing that came to mind.

"It's none of her business," she said. "Besides, she doesn't care. I keep my life private, and she likes it that way."

"Do you think Tyler will say something?"

"I hope not. He's pretty reserved for the most part."

I grabbed a rag and joined her on the floor. "He didn't seem very reserved to me."

"What does that mean?" she snapped.

I flinched. "Nothing. Wow. You need some sleep, Mom."

"Sorry. I really want to get to the hospital. Finish wiping these baseboards and I'll start steaming the drapes."

After three hours of cleaning a room that was already clean, we were finishing the windows when Mom's cell phone rang.

"Hello... yes, this is she... okay... Thank you." She slapped the phone shut.

"Who was that?"

"The nurse. Dr. Wood's doing his rounds soon, and he wants to talk to me."

Within minutes, we were putting the furniture back, and hurried out of the house.

Driving across town, her knuckles bled white from gripping the steering wheel.

"What did you and Tyler talk about?" she asked out of nowhere.

"Nothing, really. He helped me get the steamer."

After her reaction in the bedroom over Tyler being a good Samaritan, I decided to wait to tell her about his invitation.

"He's a nice kid."

"Where's he from, anyway?"

"Memphis area. Comes here for five or six weeks every summer."

"He didn't seem too thrilled about it."

"Would you be? You've met his grandmother."

"She's terrible, isn't she?"

Mom shrugged. "It doesn't matter how I feel about her. We need the money."

I knew I should keep my mouth shut, but I couldn't let it go.

"Why is she so rich?"

"They're old money from logging the forests. They owned the paper mill for years. I think her son's still an executive of some sort, but after Mr. Vaughn died, they sold the business to a subsidiary company. I can't imagine what she's worth now."

"How old is he?"

"Who? Her son?"

"No. Tyler."

"I'm not sure... around your age." She turned onto Main Street, then she gave me a hard glance. "I know he's a handsome boy. But he's off limits. We're the staff and nothing more."

"Jeez, Mom. All I asked was how old he is."

"And where he lives... and why they're so rich."

I sat silent.

"You have to understand how important this job is."

"I do, but would she really fire you over a boy?"

"He's not a boy. He's her grandson. I'm serious, Elsie. You have no idea how protective she is. I need this job, especially now."

"Okay... I get it."

Crap. I was screwed. If I meet Tyler in the morning, I'd have to lie to her. And I sucked at lying. Backing out wasn't an option, though. I wanted to go, but telling the truth wasn't an option either. She'd just given me the answer to that route.

I took a deep breath. No matter... It wasn't a big deal. We were only going jogging. I'd just change a few minor details, like name and gender.

Mom parked the truck and turned in the seat. She had something else to tell me, something I didn't want to hear. God, please don't let it be about Dad.

"I hate to ask this of you," she said. "But I need you to start cleaning a few houses by yourself." I let out a huff and slumped in the seat. She held up her hands. "I'm sorry, but I can't be in two places at once. It'll only be Mrs. Baltic and Mr. Smith."

"Mom—"

"Mom, what?" Her tone was calm but firm. "I need your help, Elizabeth."

"I know, but I hate Jack Smith. He's a sleazebag who reminds me of Jabba the Hutt."

She pushed back a smile. "He's not that bad."

"Yes, he is," I said in a dry tone. "When?"

"Every week. Mrs. Baltic's house is easy. All she really wants is someone to talk to. Jack goes to breakfast most mornings. If you're there by nine, you'll be done before he gets back."

"Where will you be?"

"With your dad. Where do you think?"

I wanted to help her, but cleaning houses wasn't my gig. Why couldn't I go to the hospital and sit with Dad while she worked? A pain of guilt stabbed my stomach. I had to think about both of them. What if Dad didn't make it? If he didn't, I'd be the only person Mom could rely on.

I looked into her desperate, deep-blue eyes.

"Yeah. I'll do it."

"Thank you."

Chapter

4

Mom dozed off while we were sitting in the waiting room. The doctor was attending to Dad, and the nurse wouldn't let us go in. I grabbed a magazine and started flipping through the gossip articles. Fifteen minutes later, Dr. Wood appeared. I nudged Mom.

She woke, and sat up. "Dr. Wood?"

He pulled up a chair next to her. I sensed he had bad news by the way he hesitated. "I've upgraded Brandon to critical condition," he said. "I'm afraid Brandon's still taking on fluid. Some fluid is normal, but this isn't what we wanted."

Mom pressed her hand to her lips.

"Let's see what the next few days bring," he said. "I've contacted the cancer center in Nashville. The doctors there think they can help. If I see some improvement in the next twenty-four hours, I'll take him off the meds, and hopefully he'll wake up."

"Okay."

"You can see him soon. Do you have any questions?"

"I have a thousand questions," Mom said.

"I understand. I've already contacted Hospice. If you go to the second floor, they'll be happy to go over everything with you."

"Thank you."

He stood. "We'll talk soon, okay?"

"Yes. Thanks."

As Dr. Wood walked out, my brother, Mark, stepped inside the waiting room.

I froze. Mark looked so much like Dad it took me a second to realize who he was. Six-foot-tall, thick blond hair... he'd gained a few pounds but he was still lean and lanky.

Instantly, I began to shake. I had no idea what to say to him. He moved across the room, tense-lipped, nose flared.

"Here we go," Mom muttered.

She pushed out of the chair and held out her arms. Mark's shoulders stiffened, then he leaned in for a brief hug. She tried to lovingly touch his face. An immediate flinch, his eyes filled with tears, before he looked away like he was ashamed.

I swallowed the tight lump in my throat. Mom stepped back, disappointment written all over her face. I hated the tension between them. Mark had built a wall as thick as East Berlin, and it hadn't been torn down. The fortress helped him cope. Brick by brick, he had stacked his defense ever since we moved to Tennessee. Dad had chosen to scrape by, farming peppers. Mark couldn't understand why we'd move away from a life of privilege offered by Mom's parents. Of course,

Mom took it personally. She'd built her own hedge and wouldn't admit it. Granted, I didn't have to climb her thorny wall, but Mark did. Her inability to relate to my brother had resulted in a war of wills. I'd learned to accept Mark for who he was. At least, until the accident.

While we waited out the silence, memories of falling down the ravine flashed in my mind. The pain in my shoulder and arm. My throbbing head. He'd ditched me, and I'd never forgive him for it. He'd chosen drugs over all of us. Anger welled inside of me at the memory.

He sniffled and wiped his face, then he made eye contact with me. Neither of us smiled or spoke.

Asshole.

"How was the drive?" Mom asked.

"Hot. Grandpa's car doesn't have air conditioning."

"Did you stop by the house?"

"Yeah. I'm gonna head home. I'm beat."

"But you just got here."

"Mom," his tone was laced with attitude already. "I just drove seven hours."

"Well. I think you should at least see him before you go."

"Fine."

Mom looked hurt.

I felt her defenses like we were attached by wire. The conversation would only escalate if someone didn't buffer.

"Are you staying at the hospital tonight?" I asked Mom.

"I'd planned on it."

Mark glanced from her to the floor.

"Okay," I said. "We'll go see Dad, and then Mark can take me home."

"Sounds good," she said. "I'll wait here."

Walking down the ICU hallway, I didn't look to the right

or the left. Mark's head bobbed from side to side, huffing at the sight of each room we passed.

"Shit... " he breathed out. "This is fuckin' nuts."

"Wait until you see Dad," I said, dryly.

"Whatever, Elsie."

"Just sayin'."

"Fuck off."

"You fuck off, Mark."

Taking longer strides, I made a beeline for Aaron.

He stood up from the computer desk and smiled. "Elsie. Good to see you again."

I forced myself to return his kind greeting. "You too, Aaron. This is my brother, Mark."

"Nice to meet you, Mark."

Mark grunted but didn't make eye contact. His demeanor didn't seem to faze Aaron.

"You two can go in and see Brandon whenever you're ready."

"Thanks." Turning to Mark, I pointed at the rack. "You have to wear a gown and gloves."

"Great."

His sarcastic tone pushed my launch button.

"You're really pissing me off," I quickly whispered, then stepped away.

"What did I do?" his voice cracked.

"Seriously?" I hissed. "You're freakin' rude, coming in here with a chip on your shoulder. You think Mom and I are enjoying ourselves?"

"Whatever. I just got here. Give me a minute, okay?"

I gritted my teeth. "No."

Our blue eyes locked.

"Back off," he growled.

"You ditched me."

"You fucking ran, you little baby."

"Druggie."

"Nark."

"Bite my ass."

I snapped the glove on my hand and stomped into the room. Unable to calm down, I paced beside Dad's bed. As if things weren't hard enough, Mark had to come back like it was all about him. I wanted to scream. *Stop. Breathe. Get it together, Elsie.*

After a few minutes, I walked out. Mark passed me, lightly side-swiping my shoulder. By the time I pulled the paper gown over my head, he'd disappeared inside Dad's room. I tossed the garment in the trash can and went back to the waiting room.

Mom sat alone in the massive space full of empty chairs, an uncanny metaphor to her current circumstances. I flopped in the seat next to her and went off about Mark.

"I should've waited to call him," Mom said in a weary tone.

I'd made her feel even worse. My stomach bottomed out. "He needs to be here."

"I have to go talk to Hospice. Will you at least get a ride home from him?"

"Of course."

She stood up. "Throw in some laundry?"

"Sure." I remembered I wanted to leave early in the morning. "Oh. By the way, I'm meeting Jenna in the morning to go jogging, if that's okay."

"Who's Jenna?"

I hated lying, but I couldn't tell her about Tyler.

"She's in my class. You've met her before."

That part wasn't a lie. Technically, Mom had met Jenna. My freshman year at a football game, Mom bought a box of chocolates from Jenna for a fundraiser.

"Okay," she said.

"I'll leave before seven."

"Why so early?"

"It isn't as hot then."

She smirked. "You hate exercise."

"Maybe we'll just walk. I don't know."

She leaned down and kissed my cheek. "I love you. I'll be home at some point."

"Love you, too."

She waved at me as she left the room. I waved back. Guilt stabbed me. Lying wasn't my style at all.

Minutes later, Mark stepped into the waiting room and shrugged at me like I'd been making him wait, and then he walked out.

On the way home, we sat in silence, refusing to be the first to forfeit. When we arrived, I went straight to my room and slammed the door. He slammed his seconds later. Flopping on my bed, I glared at the ceiling. *Fuck Mark. Fuck cancer. Fuck everything.* Nothing could help me. I had no one to turn to but Mom, and she didn't need something else weighing her down. I was on my own.

Exhausted, I turned on my side and fell asleep.

At six the next morning, I woke to Mom shaking my shoulder. Light poured through the window, highlighting her long, blonde hair.

"Hey, sweetie." She sat down on the edge of my bed, holding a plastic bag in her hands. "I stopped by the store on my way home this morning and bought you a gift."

Snuggling my pillow, I couldn't hide my excitement.

She pulled out a box. "It's a dumb phone, not a smart one, but it has unlimited text."

I softly clapped my hands with a cheesy smile. "Thank you."

"You're going to need one when you're cleaning. I don't want you stuck out on the road or at a house without a way to call me." She handed me the box. I gave her a hug and a kiss on the cheek. "Please, don't be one of those teenagers who's always looking at a phone."

Ignoring the comment, I opened the box and pulled out the device.

Chapter

5

At six-thirty, I pulled on a pair of gym shorts, my navy Chicago Bears T-shirt, and a pair of my cleanest tennis shoes. I couldn't wait to see Tyler, even if it required jogging.

I grabbed a bottle of water out of the refrigerator, and hurried toward the front door. Mom had fallen asleep on the couch with the TV on.

"Elsie. Where are you going?"

I spun around. *Dang it...* I'd almost made it out.

"I'm meeting Jenna, remember?"

"I need you to go to Mr. Smith's at nine."

"Really? You didn't tell me that last night."

"Sorry. I forgot. I have to go to Vaughn's and finish up

before she gets back from Houston, but I'd like to get to the hospital by two."

"Okay," I said, as I headed out the door.

Ten minutes late, I turned into the park. The place was beautifully kept; acres of forests adorned with patina cannons, pyramid stacks made of shiny black cannon balls, alongside monuments dedicated to the various states that fought in the battle – Ohio, Indiana, and others I couldn't read because of years of weathering. Dad had told me about the Battle of Shiloh, but I always dismissed his extensive knowledge of the Civil War, tuning him out like I did history class. He'd tried to share so many things with me, why hadn't I listened?

Within the next mile, I spotted Tyler standing next to a polished, silver, two-door Mercedes sports car. Arms crossed, he watched me pull up. I started shaking, nerves on high alert. *Oh my gosh.* He looked like he'd been posing for a photo shoot; dressed in long, navy shorts and a light gray T-shirt, his dark hair damp and clean-cut.

"This is crazy, " I whispered as I parked the car.

Deep breaths, Elsie. You can do this.

He opened my door. "Mornin', nice you made it."

"Sorry. I didn't mean to be late." I climbed out and nodded toward his car. "Nice ride."

"Thanks."

"I've never seen a Mercedes like that."

"Yeah, it's a 2015 CL63. Dad drove it for a while, but then he gave it to me." He shrugged, as if everyone had a Dad that gave them a Mercedes. "Bears, huh?"

"What?"

He pointed at my T-shirt. "You might get hot in that. You

ready?" He motioned to a tree line several yards away. "I like jogging this trail. It's called The Sunken Road."

We walked toward a split-rail fence dividing the woodlands from the acres of open battlefield. He waved for me to follow as he started slowly jogging down the trail.

"It's a beautiful morning," he said. "Be careful. This trail can trip you up."

We started at a slow pace and for the first few hundred yards, I actually enjoyed the peaceful setting. The morning breeze was cool, balancing the hot July sun. Birds were singing, and the breeze rustled through the trees. Despite the scenery, I couldn't stop watching Tyler. Jogging with perfect posture, his torso solid against his fitted shirt, and his tan arms rippling with muscle.

As we crossed a small wooden bridge, sweat began to trickle down my face and my head tingled with perspiration. Not good. Once my face lit up from the heat, I'd look like a drowned cat. After a few more strides, a sharp pain pierced my side. I cringed, trying to ignore it. But then my lungs started to burn.

"Y'all right back there?" he asked over his shoulder.

I forced out the word, "Sure."

The next step, I stumbled forward, my legs wobbling like a baby giraffe's. Regaining my footing, I thought I could recover gracefully, but then the stitch stabbed me again. I stopped. Hands to knees, I gasped for air. I heard gravel shifting, and then his Nikes stepped inside my small perspective of the ground.

"You okay?" he asked, offering his hand.

"Hell, no," I panted. "I think I'm gonna die."

I took his hand and stood straight. We both burst out laughing. Another stitch wrenched my ribs and I hissed and grabbed my side.

"You need to walk. I shouldn't let you stop like this." He put his hand between my shoulders, guiding me forward. "Damn, girl, your face is really red."

"Great." At least it covered how embarrassed I felt. "Sorry. I'm not very athletic."

"You don't have to apologize. It's just something I do, and I thought it would be great to have you join me."

"Don't get me wrong, I'm glad to be here. I just didn't plan on making an ass out of myself. Not that quickly, anyway."

"You didn't make an ass of yourself. It's all good." He turned around and started walking backward with a slight bounce. "So, that Bears T-shirt..."

I looked down at the orange Bears logo across my chest. "What about it?"

"You're a Bears fan, huh?"

"Yeah, they're my team."

"Okay. I like football. More of a N'Orleans fan myself."

"Not the Saints!" I let my head fall back, pretending to be disgusted. "What about the Titans? You're a Tennessean."

He winced. "Titans? I like to win. That's not where I'm going with this though. Miss Elsie, I believe you've given yourself away."

"About what?"

"No one around here likes the Bears. That accent, that shirt, you're totally from Illinois."

I eyed him. "You aren't going to let this go, are you?" He shook his head to confirm. "Yes, I'm from Illinois. Fighting Illini country."

He jumped in front of me, pumping his arms above his head, and then he jogged in a circle to imitate a crowd cheering.

"Whatever." I laughed.

After another exaggerated cheer, he let his victory dance go, and we continued down the trail.

"Why are you so private about it?" he asked.

"I don't know. We've been here for five years. I guess I haven't picked up the accent."

"You and your mom. Claire definitely doesn't sound Southern." He dropped his drawl for a candid northern inflection. "Midwesterners have such enunciated words. Your English is very proper." He switched back to his silky, Southern drawl. "Mind you, we don't use the word 'very' 'round here. 'Mighty' or 'awfully,' yes. But never 'very.'"

He could charm a rattle snake into a firepit with that voice.

"Note taken." I giggled, face burning even more. "Everyone doesn't talk that way. Mom's always correcting our English, it's so annoying."

"My mom does, too. She claims I'm better than a Southern twang, as she calls it."

"You definitely don't sound like the boys around here. They still blow me crap about my stupid accent. Such jerks."

The locals in the area had bloodlines that ran deep into American history. Rebel flags and Southern pride spilled across the region, reminding all trespassers they'd better tread lightly. Tyler's grandmother's house was no exception. The place was filled with priceless Confederate artifacts. I had to assume he felt the same way as everyone else.

He must've sensed my insecurity because he stopped walking as we approached a white-stone memorial of the Iowa Regiment. He stepped toward me and gently touched my chin.

"Hey... I could care less where you're from," he said. I lifted my eyes to his. "I'm glad you don't run around with jerks. If you did, I'd have to question what kind of guy I am."

"You aren't very shy."

"I'm usually not this forward, if that's what you mean."

He stepped away, and then he asked if I knew anything about the battle at Shiloh. Of course, I hadn't listened to Dad, so I let Tyler explain it to me again.

The Sunken Road was where the Union troops retreated, fighting against the surge of Confederate soldiers who later called the area The Hornet's Nest. After the Confederates withdrew, Shiloh was labeled the bloodiest battle of the Civil War. Tyler also told me about the different states that fought (including Illinois), reciting dates, the number of men who died, and both sides' strategies. His intelligence was invigorating. He animated his stories, hands moving in the air, walking with an enthusiastic bounce in his step. Pure passion for the subject flashed across his face, and he made normally boring facts sound fascinating.

We'd come to the end of the trail when he took my hand, lacing his fingers between mine. Smiling, he whispered, "Let me show you something."

My head spun at the feel of his touch. He led me across a paved road toward an area of dense trees. We gazed through the canopy of a massive oak, then he pointed toward the top of the tree next to it. I tilted my head and scanned the branches. He bent down to share my perspective, his face less than an inch from mine.

"You see it?" he asked, moving his arm a little to the left.

Then I saw a huge nest, near the peak of the tree, where an enormous white-headed bird was watching us from above.

I gasped and pressed my hand over my smile. "Oh my

gosh, it's a bald eagle."

The bird eyed us, stretching out its massive wings.

"I saw her the other day," Tyler said. "Isn't she amazing?"

"Yes. I've never seen one before. So beautiful."

"I bet her wingspan's over five feet. She was circling the peach orchard when I saw her, and then I watched her swoop down and grab a snake out of the field. I love this place. It's one of the few things that makes being at Nana's tolerable."

"Why do you stay with her if you hate it so much?"

"They insist on it."

He stared at the nest, waiting for the bird to fly. I watched him instead. His intense focus held an underlying tone, almost as if he were jealous. He wanted to fly, too.

"Let's go over here. Maybe she'll take off soon," he said, leading me across the lawn to another split-rail fence.

"So, if they insisted you come here, maybe you should rebel," I teased. "Do something drastic. Get a tattoo, or better yet, go goth. That'll get their attention."

"Yeah. That's never gonna happen." He laughed. "You have a twisted mind."

"Ooh, I know! How 'bout we trade cars? You can drive the Honda, and I'll drive yours."

"Good try," he said as he leaned against the fence. "No one drives my car but me."

"Oh, really? Well, I'm gonna have to change your mind on that one."

"Good luck with that," he said. "How's your dad doing?"

I leaned against the fence beside him, nerves prickling from the question. "Not great."

"I've thought about him a lot since the other day."

"That's nice of you to say."

"I mean it. That has to be really hard for you. Why is he

43

sick?"

I swallowed. *Please don't cry in front of him. Please.* "He has a brain tumor."

"Oh." He gave me a concerned look. "How long has he had it?"

"Five years. The doctor told us to prepare for the worst. Translated: He's dying."

"I'm sorry," he said, and then he gently took my hand in his again. "If there's anything I can do, please tell me."

"Thanks." I had to change the topic. Tears threatened me, the pre-sting before the burn. Blinking my eyes, I looked up. "Can we talk about something else?"

"Of course. I didn't mean to upset you."

"You didn't. It's just... well. It's hard."

He squeezed my fingers between his.

"Do you like school?" I asked.

"Sure. I like being on my own, mostly."

"Was Vanderbilt your first choice?"

I'd noticed several Vanderbilt diplomas in Mrs. Vaughn's den, as if it was some kind of family tradition to attend the college.

"No, I wanted to go to Stanford, but I didn't have a choice. All Vaughns go to Vanderbilt. Nana had five of her kids attend, so the University loves us."

"What's with Vanderbilt?" I held up my hand. "Don't get me wrong, I realize it's an excellent school, but why can't you choose?"

"Like I said, they insisted. My great-grandfather had been a board member, and since then, it had become a family tradition. Nana's adamant about keeping the Southern customs in place. That includes the overall belief system of how the North stole the South. She says every generation after forgets more about where we come from. I understand not forgetting, but the rest of it borders on bigotry. I refuse to have anything to do with it."

"Oh. That's kind of crazy. So, Vanderbilt's just a label? It's all about tradition."

"Exactly. Just like coming to Savannah. They've sent me here every summer since I was three, so now it's required. Sometimes, I don't mind. I can chill and study, the solitude doesn't bother me. I'm just ready to move on. Do my own thing, you know?"

"Makes sense. How old are you, anyway?"

"Nineteen. But they won't let me go until the trust fund's opened. That happens when I turn twenty. Until then, they think I'm incapable of supporting myself." He shook his head. "Maybe they're right, but they hover over me like I'm a little kid or something."

"I'm sorry to hear that." I tried to resist my curiosity, but deep inside I had to know. "I have to ask you something, and maybe I'm a jerk for doing so, but... What's it like?"

"What's 'what' like?" he asked. "School?"

"No, not school."

I shouldn't have said anything... such a thoughtless question.

"The money?" he asked.

I nodded. He slowly swayed his head back and forth like he couldn't decide which item to order off a menu.

"It's all right, I guess. I know people think it makes everything perfect, but there's a lot... well, it comes with a lot of pressure. Don't get me wrong, it does make life easier, but it depends on how a person handles it." He smirked. "I know so many snobs. They ruin everything because of the way they act. I refuse to ever be that kind of person."

I wanted to hug him for saying that. Assuming money made his life perfect was easy to do since our family didn't have any at the moment. Clearly, he hadn't been given a pass from normal problems just because of his bank account.

"Do you have any brothers or sisters?" he asked.

"Yeah, I have an older brother, Mark. You?"

"No, it's just me."

"What are you studying?"

"Business."

"Is that what you want?"

"Not at all."

"What do you want then?"

He lifted our hands and pressed his lips just below my knuckles. I held my breath, savoring his cool kiss against my hot skin. Lightheaded, I slowly exhaled as he lowered our hands.

"You're standing in it," he said, and then he pushed off the fence and turned to me. "I spend a lot of time out here when I'm in Savannah. I read about the wars – the Revolutionary War, Civil War, and World War I and II. It's what I do. Well, during the summers, at least since I'm too busy during school. But I think I'd be a good teacher. I'd love to talk about history all day, make it interesting for kids, especially teenagers. They just need someone who'll teach it in a thought-provoking way." He stopped talking, as if something interrupted his enthusiasm for the idea. "But it doesn't matter what I want. To my family, teaching is a service job."

As I listened, I realized how much we actually had in common. Living in polar opposite worlds, we were fighting against the same currents. We were stuck; expected to behave in the proper way, do as we're told and suck it up. He didn't have any more control over his life than I did over mine. At least I had my art to escape to. I had to wonder how he handled the pressure.

He ran his hand through his hair, and looked at me with curious eyes.

"Do you ever feel like you're being pushed by something bigger? Not by your family, but something more? Our circumstances are so random. I didn't ask to be born into money, any more than you asked to move to Tennessee. We're at the mercy of our parents, but then we have to find our own way, and one bad decision, one missed step will send us tumbling backwards. It's like we're on a staircase. We're desperate to reach a goal, so we skip a step or maybe two, hoping to get there faster, and then we get kicked back to learn the lessons we missed. That's the hard part... finding the courage to keep trying. We have to accept what we've been given and embrace our circumstances, even if we don't like them. After that, we have to try to make them our own. You know? Reinvent."

"My family's enslaved in circumstances. Have you talked to your parents about it?"

"Kind of. Dad's cool. He listens, but Mom and Nana think I have more potential than being a teacher."

"You can definitely make more money doing something else."

"I know, but that isn't my concern," he said, dismissively. "I assume you want to study art. You'd be crazy not to."

He leaned against the fence again, this time a little closer to me. I liked his unabashed affection, but I sensed he wouldn't move too fast. His approach was temperate. A gentleman who understood the art of treating a girl with respect. There was a kind of pureness about him. I had to question if he was the player he could've easily been, yet nothing about him implied he was playing around.

"Yeah, I'd really like to go to art school."

"What colleges have you looked at?"

"Not many. Memphis College of Art has been the goal. I haven't applied though."

"Why not?"

I shrugged. "Circumstances, I guess."

My enthusiasm for school had dwindled since Dad's seizure. But I didn't want to talk about that. I wanted Tyler to get to know me for me, not out of sympathy or even obligation. I could handle the chaos in my life on my own. What I wanted was to be with someone who would help me forget about it all, even if it was only for a few hours.

"Okay, you got me there," he said. "But you have to make your own circumstances, too."

"I'm not even sure what I'd do with an art degree."

He chuckled. "Make art."

"Right." I smiled. "I guess it's easier to say what I don't want than what I do want."

"What don't you want, then?"

I lightly bumped against his shoulder. "To never clean another person's house again."

"It's weird, isn't it?"

"It's so uncomfortable. You have no idea."

"You're right, I don't. It has to suck."

"Pretty much. But I have to help, we're broke."

"What does your dad do for a living?"

"He farms, but it isn't exactly pulling in the cash. We come from the Heartland of rich, black soil. Corn and beans, you know? It's not the same down here."

"He isn't farming corn and beans, is he? That's a terrible crop for this area."

"Pimentos."

"The little red thing inside an olive?"

"Yes, the little red thing in an olive, which is actually a red pepper." My cheeks burned. Pimento farming sounded ridiculous when I said it out loud. "If we don't figure out something, all our work would be wasted. Five acres is too much to farm by hand, and I have no idea how we're going to harvest it all."

I pushed off the railing. "Let's walk... " He didn't hesitate to follow. I continued, "See, Mom comes from a family similar to yours. Well, they're not millionaires, but old German blood that runs back to the homeland. My great-grandfather never learned English, that's how embedded they were in old tradition. So, I understand what you mean about your grandmother. It isn't any different up North – it's just a different settlement of people. Anyway, they had high expectations for who Mom married. I still don't exactly understand what happened. Dad and I talked about it once and he said he needed to be his own man, whatever that means."

"Money doesn't make the man," Tyler said.

As we walked across the road back to The Sunken Trail, his comment lingered in my mind. He wasn't self-conscious of how his affluence made him appear, but every time we talked about money, his demeanor would change, as if he carried some secret knowledge about the burdens of wealth. Whether it was by his father or someone else, he had obviously been groomed to understand the responsibility that came with privilege.

"Can I ask you something?" he said.

"Sure."

"Is Nana awful to your mom?"

I bristled. "Um... I plead the Fifth."

"Seriously, I know what kind of woman she is. *And* she

hates everything from the North. You seemed freaked out when we first met."

"I had no idea you were there!" I laughed. "That was so embarrassing."

"No, that was hilarious."

"You scared the shit out of me," I said. "Anyway, I don't think your grandmother likes me. Just being there puts me on edge. I feel like if I look at something the wrong way, it'll break."

"I hear ya. I still won't touch anything in the great room."

"I know, right?"

We walked a little further in silence. Even though I'd lied to Mom, I was compelled to make sure he knew the truth about my situation. Telling him might not have been fair, but deep down, I guess I sought absolution from someone.

"Mom doesn't know I'm with you. She's afraid that if we hang out, she'll get fired."

"Really?" He sounded surprised. "I'm sorry. I'm not trying to put you in a bad position."

"You don't have to apologize. I wanna be here. I've had a great time."

"Me, too. I understand Claire needs her job. I won't threaten that, not on purpose, anyway. Nana's just... stuck in her old ways."

"We know we're the staff or whatever, but she... " I couldn't get the words out. He had no idea what Mom went through almost every day.

"Go ahead, tell me. She, what?"

"She likes to mess with Mom. She'll leave money lying around – like wads of cash. Mom thinks she's being tested, so she puts it back where it should be or doesn't touch it at all. Mrs. Vaughn even docked Mom's pay once because she accidentally broke a jar of pickles. The woman, literally, counted the money – to the penny – in Mom's hand. She just belittles her all the time, like Mom's some sort of idiot or something."

"That's ridiculous. Nana's a snob. I've said it for years."

I stopped in the middle of the trail. "Please keep this between us. Mom will kill me for saying something. She's already told me to stay away from you."

He flinched. "Why? She hardly knows me."

"Not because of you. We're, you know... just housekeepers. It's not hard to figure out."

He stepped back. "I must be slow because I don't see a housekeeper. I see a fine young lady I'd like to get to know better. And maybe, help her get in better shape."

I laughed, looking down. "I could use some exercise."

"I don't mean your figure. You're gorgeous. But maybe we could build your strength while I'm here." He pointed down the trail. "You made it just past the bridge over there, not far, I must say. So tomorrow, I expect you to make it here." He turned around, picked up a stick, and pushed it into the ground next to the trail. "There, now we know your goal."

"I can do that," I said, and then I gasped and grabbed his arm. His watch read 9:30. I'd forgotten all about Mr. Smith. "I'm late!"

"Where do you have to go?"

"I was supposed to be at Mr. Smith's at nine. Mom's going to freak out if he calls her."

"Jack Smith in Savannah?"

I glanced over my shoulder. "Yeah, you know him?"

"Sure, I know Jack." He took an extra-long stride to catch up with me. "He gets coffee up at the restaurant. Kind of sleazy. You'll be there by yourself?"

"I've been going with Mom for over a year. I'll be all right.

His house is gross, though. I think he has Mom clean just to ogle her."

"Ogle, huh? That's creepy. Hey, if you ever need..." He put his hand on my shoulder to stop me. I turned around. "If you ever need someone, you can call me."

"Seriously? You want to help me clean?"

"You're stubborn. "

"I know what you mean." I waved my hand. "It'll be fine. He's old."

"He's a perv."

"I have to go." I jogged across the road, slipped in my car, and rolled down the window. "Hey, Mom gave me a cell phone last night. Let me give you my number." I rattled off my digits. "Text me, then I'll have yours."

"Will do," he said as he typed on his iPhone. "Meet me tomorrow at seven?"

I hesitated like I had to think about it, then giggled and said, "Yeah. I'd love to."

"Good," he said with a wave goodbye. A few seconds later, he disappeared behind the black tinted windows of his Mercedes.

What an amazing morning. I couldn't wait to get back.

As I drove down Confederate Road, a shadow on the concrete caught my eye. I slowed down to look out my window. The eagle soared high above the tree line, circling the battlefield like a watchman in the sky. A perfect ending to a perfect morning.

Chapter

6

I slid through the back door of Mr. Smith's house almost an hour late. Hurrying to the sink, I flipped on the hot water. Then, I bounced from task to task – washing the dishes, straightening the counters, sweeping the floors. Normally, I hated the work, but Mr. Smith was gone, and I was flying high. The way Tyler kissed the back of my hand... my heart still skipped at the thought. I shouldn't read too much into it, but he did it right after I asked him what he wanted.

Two hours later, I grabbed Mom's paycheck off of the table and headed outside. The front door slammed. I froze on the back step.

"It's me, Mr. Smith," I squeaked. "Elsie."

"Ell—Sie," he yowled out my name like the cow commercial. "Y'all get in here."

"I'm all done, sir," I shouted through the screen. "I have to meet Mom."

"Ya know," he said, appearing out of the shadows, "you's late this morning."

"Yes, sir, I'm sorry about that. I lost track of time."

"I called your momma. She said you'd be here soon. Staying out of trouble?"

His leathered cheeks, dotted with age spots, jiggled around his beady eyes. Whiskey wafted off his breath, tainting my nose.

"Great," I said, stepping back. "I'm sure she isn't happy with me."

"Na, she's fine," he slurred. "Come in and have some tea. I gots a special treat I add."

"No, thank you. I definitely need to go."

"Didn't mean to get youse in trouble. Let me mend it for you."

I started down the steps. "It's okay, Mr. Smith. I'm good."

"Your daddy doing all right?" he shouted.

"Um, not that great. I'll see you next time."

I hurried around the house and climbed in the car. Mom expected me at the hospital no later than eleven. Glancing at the clock, it was almost a quarter after twelve. I grabbed my cell phone. No missed calls. Why didn't she call me? I knew she would chew me out for being late. The first time I meet Tyler and I almost blow my cover. What was I thinking?

Ten minutes later, I stood in the elevator, taking deep breaths to calm my nerves. *Ding.* The doors slid open. Walking down the stark white hallway, I braced myself for Mom's lecture. I stepped in the waiting room and scanned the faces.

Woodrow's wife, Ruby, was sitting next to Mark in the far

corner, running her fingers through his hair like he was one of her own. She and Woodrow never had children, a residual effect of her brutal childhood. Regardless of her cruel upbringing, she had more love to offer than both of my grandparents combined.

She motioned me over with a hurried wave. Almost seventy-years-old, the woman still turned heads. Her chestnut hair was always set, layered around her face, her figure slender and fit from working and training the horses they kept in their stables. I'd never seen her without her makeup, and I'd put money down that Woodrow hadn't either.

"Hi, Ruby."

Mark stared at the floor.

"You need to go in there and see your daddy." She waved her hand. "Go on... Go inside, now. He's been asking for you."

"He's awake?"

"Don't know for how long, honey. You'd better get going."

I spun around and hurried out of the room.

After suiting up in a yellow gown and purple gloves, I stepped inside Dad's room to the sound of machines beating their rhythm of life. Mom met me halfway inside. I could sense her urgency as she approached.

"Oh, thank God you're here. Is Mark here, too?"

"Yeah, he's in the waiting room with Ruby."

"Good. I want both of you to see him. We don't know if he'll stay this coherent."

"How long has he been awake?" I whispered.

"An hour or so. Go talk to him. I'll get Mark."

She hurried out the door. Turning around, I assessed the scene. Dad's head was wrapped in bandages, skin gray and dry. They'd removed the tube attached to his mouth, but his face looked emaciated, and his eyes were closed.

I sat in the chair next to him and placed my hand on his. He slowly turned his head at the feel of my touch and opened his crystal-blue eyes.

Thank you, God, for not changing his beautiful eyes.

He tried to smile, but only the right side of his face would cooperate.

"My sweet girl." His voice low and raspy.

"Hi, Daddy."

His lids went heavy again, shutting me out.

I stared at our hands, doubt pushing down on my spirit. The reality of our future was clear. The tumor had won. All poetic ideals of death were gone. His pain and suffering was cruel, and I craved the power to stop it. He had to wake back up. I needed to say I love you. I needed him to know. Taking a deep breath, I closed my eyes.

"Elsie, you're here," I heard. "I've been waiting for you."

I immediately opened my eyes. "Hi, Daddy. I'm here."

"Guess I'm down for the count." He swallowed, then a tear dropped from the corner of his eye. "I'm so sorry."

I'd never seen Dad cry. My eyes welled along with his. He'd always been so strong, confident, determined, but he'd been transformed into a broken soul in no time.

"I'm sorry this is happening to you," I said.

"It's happening to you, too."

"We'll be okay." My voice cracked. A tear fell. "I just want you to get better."

"My sweet girl... " he said, "that's not going to happen."

"Oh, Dad, don't leave us. Please."

I stood up and sat on the bed next to him, and laid my head on his chest.

All the possibilities being robbed from us flooded my

mind. He wouldn't get to scare a boy taking me out on a date. He'd never see me graduate. He wouldn't get to walk me down the aisle in my wedding dress. He'd never meet his grandchildren.

He gently stroked my hair with his right hand. "You're so talented, Elsie. Don't ever stop dreaming. Even when your dreams seem impossible, you have to believe in yourself."

I sat up and wiped my face. "Thank you."

"I love you, my sweet girl."

His face was blurred behind my tears.

"I love you, Dad. I love you so much."

He let out a quiet sigh, and then he closed his eyes. My stomach flipped in fear that he'd died, but that only happens in movies or cheesy books. I sat next to him until I saw Mom through the glass door. Taking her signal, I went outside.

"Are you okay?" she asked.

I nodded, wiping my wet face.

"Mark needs a ride home after he sees your dad. Please wait for him."

I slumped. I'd rather she chewed me out for being late to Smith's.

"Elsie, I love you. Cut me some slack."

Mom looked a hot mess, and I wasn't helping. She needed a shower and a good night's sleep, but she had me to contend with, plus Mark, *and* the brain tumor killing her husband.

"I'm sorry," I said. "That was so hard. I think it was the hardest thing I've ever done."

I broke down and started to cry again. She pulled me into her arms.

"I know it was. I'm sorry, sweetie. I know."

A few minutes later, I tossed my gown and gloves in the trash can across the hallway. As I started toward the waiting room, I stopped outside Dad's door. Mark sat beside the bed with his head hung, tears streaming down his cheeks. Dad lay motionless with his eyes closed. A pang of guilt stabbed me that he'd given all his energy to me and didn't have enough left for his son. Maybe if Mark waited, Dad would wake up again. The last thing I wanted was for either of them to miss the chance to talk. I could barely breathe watching my brother's pain. Hurrying out to the lobby, I waited until he was ready.

When we got home, I rummaged the refrigerator while Mark went straight to his room. We still hadn't spoken, stubborn as two bulls. I'd sworn to myself that I wouldn't be the first to give in.

I sat on my bed, staring at my sketchpad, wishing for some inspiration. I was too preoccupied thinking about Dad to even attempt to draw.

I remembered how I used to ride on the tractor with him while he tilled the fields. I'd hold his strong arm, watching the dust fly around us. The first few years after his diagnosis, I thought the cancer would lose. Dad was a fighter. But all of my hopes had gone into the trash with the yellow gown and purple gloves.

Last summer came back to me like I'd pressed replay on a movie. Dad and I had just finished walking the rows and we were surveying our hard work. The plants were healthy, and small peppers had started to show. The sun sat low on the horizon, casting golden rays over the treetops. Cedar filled the evening air. I'd helped Dad all day, pride swelling inside me for completing the job. Arms crossed, Dad looked across the weeded crops.

LIFE HAPPENS ON THE STAIRS

"Elsie, you need to understand why we came down here," he'd spoken without looking at me. "I had to get away from your mother's family. A lot of people accuse me of running, but I don't see it that way. I'm my own man, and your grandparents refuse to accept it."

Mom's maiden name was Diefenbach. Off-the-boat German heritage and devoted to Martin Luther, her parents had insisted Dad convert from Catholicism to Lutheranism before they could marry. Dad always laughed and said it was a lateral move as far as his faith was concerned. Regardless, he'd done what they'd asked – learned their religion, and attempted to fit in. The Diefenbach dynasty of corn and beans had more power than the modest, well-manicured farmstead conveyed. In the flatlands of Illinois, Mom had grown up in a complex web of farm families that thrived and prospered in traditions. Many of the older generation still spoke Low and/or High German, secretly plotting and controlling the politics of the area in their native language. Nobody dared set themselves apart from the inheritance of the generations that came before. There was plenty to respect of such privilege, but Dad was an outsider who fell in love with the family's prize daughter. They'd wanted Mom to marry a tool, preferably a German tool. Someone who would do as he was told and be grateful they were willing to let him in. But Dad was a mutt, Irish/English of sorts, and most of all, he wasn't a tool.

He was an independent thinker who wanted to provide for his family in a different way. Mom had stood by him through all his choices, and I'd never heard her complain. Their love was all that mattered. Everyone could see it... with the exception of my grandparents. They didn't care about love. They cared about what everyone thought, and how it made them look. Dad always said that was their problem, not his.

When we moved to a different community, he started farming on his own, and then he found God in a new way. Despite the detriment to his future, he walked away from the family farm and the church, and they shunned him faster than a criminal.

By the time I'd turned twelve, he'd packed us up again and washed his hands of Illinois for good. Sadly, within weeks of settling in our new home in Tennessee, he was diagnosed with a brain tumor. No matter how hard he'd tried, he just couldn't win.

"You're a descendant of things you don't understand," he had said, kicking the dry dirt. "The wills are written, practically set in stone. No matter what happens, Elsie, you'll be taken care of. Your grandparents own half the farmland in the County, and one day it will be passed on to you and Mark. But I need you to understand, no matter what anyone says about me, I walked away because I couldn't let them control our lives anymore."

"Mark hates it here," I'd said. "He's making everyone miserable."

"I know. I'm hoping that'll get better in time. I think we'll see some big changes soon. You'll see." He'd put his arm around me and squeezed me close. "I love you, my sweet girl."

Even though he'd tried to explain, I still didn't understand why he'd traded a life of privilege for hard work and struggle. I thought of how he'd kissed the top of my head, and how I'd wrapped my arms around his waist, squeezing him tight.

Slumping back on my pillows, I wiped away my tears. How in the world would I ever go on without him? We'd worked together all spring, planting the fields, making sure to clear out any weeds as the crops matured. I needed to get out there and see if it was overgrown. Even if he hadn't asked, I knew he relied on me to pick up the slack.

Talking to him was a good sign. Maybe there was still a chance he'd get better. I didn't want him to come home to a field full of weeds, smothering the pepper plants.

Chapter

7

The next morning, I sat in the car, heavy-eyed, waiting for Tyler. Part of me was glad he was late. I wanted to see him, but I wasn't looking forward to jogging. Just as I started to doze off, the purr of his car whizzed by. I sat up, rubbing my eyes. Seconds later, he opened my door.

"Good morning," he said, offering his hand.

I accepted his help, and stepped out. We stood inches apart.

"Oh, wow," he said. "Your eyes are incredible this morning."

I looked down at his navy T-shirt. "They're swollen and puffy."

"Not at all. Look at me." His fingertips brushed the side

of my cheek. I glanced up. "They're practically silver instead of blue. Just beautiful."

"Thank you," I said, shyly turning away.

He shut the door and leaned against the car. "Are you okay?"

The morning sun warmed my cheeks, casting light on the mask I hoped he wouldn't see through. But it was hard to keep it all inside. The way he patiently waited for me to answer, the compassionate look in his eyes... I needed to talk to someone. "Not really," I said. "Yesterday morning was great, but it was all downhill from there."

"Your dad?"

"Yeah. But I *did* get to talk to him."

"Is he getting better?"

"He won't get better. There's really no other way to look at it."

"Aw, Elsie." Tyler stepped forward and gently pulled me into his arms. I surrendered, pressing my face against his chest. His breath was warm against my cheek as he whispered, "You don't have to go through this alone."

I agreed with a sniffle, rubbing my cheek on his chest.

He eased away, then looked into my eyes for several heart-pounding seconds. He wanted to kiss me. I wanted him to kiss me. Instead, he smiled, and stepped away.

Damn it.

"Are you in the mood to jog?" he asked. "We can always walk."

I followed him across the road, still reeling that he didn't go for it.

The trail looked cool and shady in the morning light. Running didn't sound so bad after that emotional rollercoaster.

"Jogging sounds good, actually."

We started every day for the next three weeks that way.

Me: exhausted from cleaning and staying late at the hospital.

Him: full of energy and ready to run.

He never pushed for information, but when I wanted to talk, he'd stop jogging, and we'd walk together. His attention astounded me. He was never condescending or dismissive of my feelings. He offered advice if he had some, but mostly, he'd just listen.

I couldn't wait to see him each morning. I'd get up early and hurry out before anyone else woke up. Even though I grew stronger each day, I still struggled to keep up with him, but he'd always fall back and run along with me when he noticed I was lagging behind.

While jogging the roads and trails around the park, Tyler charmed me with his knowledge of the Civil War and personal stories about the men who'd died there. He knew about the Federal and Confederate troops, explained the generals' strategies, The Bloody Pond, Pittsburg Landing, Grant's last line, and how the battle began at Fraley Field.

His intelligence, his passion, the way he sought and expressed knowledge, fascinated me. I gave him the same respect he afforded me by listening to his insight, and considering his ideas. Like a curtain had been pulled back, Tyler had revealed a whole new view of the past, pointing out where history repeated itself by renaming the evil and replacing the men in power to implement it. He'd rattle off the names of authors like Steinbeck and Hawthorne, or artists such as Millet, recording the realism of everyday workers, and how the Post-Impressionist movement responded to industrialism at the turn of the nineteenth century.

He taught me more in three weeks than I'd learned in all my years of history class.

At night, Mom and I would sit in the hospital room with Dad, but knowing I would meet Tyler in the morning pulled me through the long evenings. I went out of my way to keep Mom from becoming suspicious. I was always on time, never mentioning his name or the Vaughns' in general. Despite the fact that my lie was only one of omission, for me, it grew.

The lie empowered me.

It became my private world. A place I could go and forget about everything. Tyler was my secret, and nobody knew where I took shelter. Except for him. He understood. He'd hold my hand, sometimes wrapping his arm around me as we walked and talked. Several times, he pulled me into his embrace when I spoke of Dad's worsening condition, and then I cried, buried in his arms. He still hadn't kissed me, and I yearned for him to take the next step. But I resisted making the first move, obliged to return his respect and behave like a lady. Regardless, he showed me enough affection that I knew it wasn't just about me. It was about his character and integrity, about being a gentleman.

And so, my lie grew.

I was willing to sacrifice everything to keep our world safe.

Every day that I grew closer to Tyler, Dad grew weaker and further away from me. The idea of him coming home seemed impossible. Mom said we'd surely kill him if we brought him back, given all the care he required. It wasn't an option at that point anyway.

After the day I talked to him, he'd taken a turn for the worse. The medical team induced another coma to relieve the continued swelling. When the doctor reported the diagnosis, Mom and I cried in each other's arms again. Our staircase of circumstances kept crumbling beneath us. Instead of learning a lesson, like Tyler suggested, my expectations were being smashed under the pressure of my weight. As if my staircase had wood rot.

In the morning, I'd start my day feeling strong and in-spired, but by nightfall, the reality of my existence would hit me – I will soon lose the man I'd loved my whole life.

Each night, I sat in the hospital room with my parents. Dad didn't wake, but we talked to him as if he could hear us. Ruby and Woodrow would stop by throughout the week and help lighten the mood for a while. Mom had lost at least ten pounds (weight she couldn't afford to lose), especially since she hadn't had a home-cooked meal in weeks. I tried to keep her fed by running to the cafeteria to get her dinner. She was thankful but rarely ate more than a few bites.

Around ten, we'd head home like zombies and go to our rooms. I'd call Tyler, and talk until I couldn't stay awake any longer.

He'd become my refuge, my hope, my only solace when everything else around me was uncertain.

Chapter

8

Cicadas buzzed the air, a clear indication that school would start soon. I hated the thought of summer ending, not only because it meant I had to go back to Hardin High, but most of all, Tyler would be leaving for Nashville. I tried not to dwell on it. I only had one semester of classes, but the more important fact was... I only had two weeks left with him. I'd go back to high school as a student with a dying father. He'd go back to being Tyler Vaughn.

With these thoughts rolling through my head, we jogged near the river at a slow pace. Turning south, we followed the curve of the road. A little cabin and a white church sat in the distance. I slowed down and started walking. He slowed with me.

"You okay?" he asked.

"Yeah, I'm just having a bad morning. Bummed it's August. You have to leave soon."

"I know."

He took my hand, lacing his fingers between mine as we walked toward the cabin near the woodlands. A cemetery occupied the other side of the road. We stopped and read the plaque that said the log cabin was the original Shiloh Church. *A Methodist meeting place from which the battle was named.*

"Place of Peace," Tyler read, then he grinned at me. "Maybe we should make this our place of peace, too."

We walked across the lawn and stepped inside the one-room church. The cabin was constructed in hand-carved wood with the exception of the built-in stone fireplace. Two rows of hewed benches lined either side of the space. Weathered, uneven, plank flooring under our feet. I thought about how many people had stepped where I stood. We looked around for a few minutes, and then I sat down in the front bench. Tyler sat down next to me.

"Am I making all of this harder on you?" he asked. "You have enough on your plate."

"Not at all. You're the only thing I have to look forward to. I mean, well, don't think I'm latching on to you. You know, I'm—"

"Yeah, I get it," he said. His cheeks reddened, and then he said, "Can I see your dad?"

"Really? Um, yeah. We can arrange that."

Tyler looked down at his lap, almost as if he was embarrassed for asking. "If I don't see him now, I may not get another chance."

The guy never ceased to amaze me. My eyes filled with tears. He looked up. I quickly looked away.

"Aw, it's no big deal," he said.

I tried to smile, but a tear fell in spite of me. Tyler wiped it away with the back of his fingers. Then, he slid his hand into my hair, leaned in and brushed his lips across mine. I'd never been kissed. I'd been waiting my whole life for this moment. Slowly pulling away, he looked into my eyes as if seeking my approval. We both smiled, and then he pressed his lips to mine again, pouring more passion into me than my senses knew how to handle.

Finally. He'd been such a gentleman, so respectful. I thought he'd never try. He moved his lips over mine, then pulled back just enough to look me in the eyes again.

"I've never felt the way I do when I'm with you," he said. "I don't want this to end."

"Me, either."

"Will you let me take you out this weekend? It's driving me crazy that you're keeping this secret. Will you please let me pick you up and see where you live?"

"Yes."

"Really?"

I smiled.

"Who would've thought the girl I'd fall for would have to lie to be with me?"

"I bet." I giggled, then I gasped. "That's what it is... you like the challenge."

"It doesn't hurt," he snickered. "But that isn't what it is at all. I like you for who you are. From your smile to your eyes, to how hard you work, and the love you give your parents. Your talent, and the way you make me feel when we're together. I could keep going."

"Keep going," I joked.

"You're a beautiful person, Elsie. Inside and out," he said, and then he gently kissed me again. After he pulled away, he asked, "Do you have to work today?"

"No, Mom's at your house. It's a good time to go to the hospital if you want. She won't be there until late in the afternoon."

"Works for me."

He stood up and offered me both of his hands. Pulling me to my feet, he caught my lips with his. He was claiming me, that much was clear. Clutching my face with one hand, he pressed our bodies tight, infusing me with his energy, exploring me with his touch, filling me with his taste and his irresistible scent. He kissed me deeper, running his hand through my hair, and then he slowed, letting the moment linger before pulling away.

"Damn... I've been waiting weeks to do that. Now that I've succeeded in my conquest," his eyes danced, "let's run."

He understood my language. Taking my hand, he led me outside to the paved road. The cool morning had shifted and heat and humidity smothered the atmosphere. After a few hundred yards, I couldn't take the sultry air any longer. I pulled off my T-shirt, exposing my cami underneath. The breeze was cool on my sweaty skin. I wiped my face with the shirt without giving it a thought. Tyler glanced my way.

Oh no, my scar... I'd totally forgotten! Then, like a vice had clamped onto my right calf, a piercing pain shot through the back of my leg.

"Damn it," I shouted.

I started to pace in a circle, trying to work it out, but I could feel the knot tightening with every step. Tyler stopped and turned around.

"You'll get it," he said. "Keep walking."

I moved toward him with my hands on my hips, sucking

in short breaths. A black Cadillac passed us on the road, distracting me as I limped out of the way. Tyler ignored the driver, chuckling at my sudden attack.

Panic and pain wrestled for my attention. I knew what was coming next.

He nodded at my shoulder. "What's that from?"

"What?"

"You know what I'm talking about."

My calf pounded with a misplaced heartbeat.

"Um, it's from an accident I had a few years back."

"What kind of accident?"

"A stupid one."

"You can't do that now!" His voice cracked. "We've come so far. You can't avoid questions anymore."

"It's a long story. Can I tell you later? I have to go home and change if you want to go to the hospital."

"You're a pro at avoiding a direct question. How about I meet you at Wally's gas station?"

"Um, your Mercedes at Wally's, and me climbing inside, isn't the way I want Mom to find out we're seeing each other. Meet me at the hospital. You'll blend better there. You look like a doctor in that car."

"Dr. Vaughn." Tyler grinned. "I can still go that route."

"I'm sure you're smart enough to."

As I drove home, I replayed the morning over and over in my mind. My first kiss. An amazingly perfect first kiss. Every time I thought about how his lips felt against mine, my stomach flipped with joy. I wanted to shout from the hilltops, *Tyler Vaughn is my guy!* Glancing in the rearview mirror, I looked the same with the exception of the cheesy smile I couldn't wipe off my face. Inside, I didn't feel the same. In the midst of all the pain hammering down on my family, I never thought I'd find an ounce of joy. If Tyler felt half as comfortable in my embrace as I did in his, the stars had finally aligned, allowing me to feel hopeful again.

Chapter

9

I managed to look, in my opinion, better than I ever had in front of Tyler. I showered and dressed in my best jeans and a fitted, cornflower-blue Henley. Feeling rather confident, I climbed out of the car and stopped in my tracks. There he was, looking like he'd just stepped off a catwalk. His hair still damp, he was wearing dark jeans and a white, Ralph Lauren button-up, the fabric practically glowing next to his tan skin, sleeves rolled up, unbuttoned just enough for me to see his smooth chest. If this was his hospital look, what in the world would he wear on a date?

"I didn't think you could get any more beautiful." He shook his head, smiling. "Once again, you've proven me wrong."

"I could say the same thing about you..."

After a long walk through the hospital, we found Aaron at his normal post outside Dads room. He looked up and smiled, and then he did a double take when he saw who I was with. Standing up, Aaron's eyes brightened as he sized Tyler up.

"Well, who's your friend, Elsie?" Aaron asked, holding out his hand.

"Tyler," my guy said, returning Aaron's handshake. "Nice to meet you."

"Heaven have mercy!" Aaron blurted out, followed with an awkward laugh. He cleared his throat as his face turned crimson. "Y'all are welcome to go on in. He's stable."

"Thanks," I said.

Aaron quickly darted across the hall into another room as we walked into Dad's room.

"What was that all about?" I asked Tyler.

"He plays for the other team, darling."

"Oh."

Tyler stopped at the foot of the bed as I approached Dad and looked him over. His head was wrapped in gauze, eyes closed, and with the exception of his chest rising and falling, he didn't move.

"Well, here we are." I leaned down and gave him a kiss on his cheek. "Daddy, I brought someone to see you. You've met before, but he wanted to see you again."

I sat down in the chair next to the bed. Tyler stood back, looking over the scene, and then he sat in the chair on the opposite side. He took a breath like he was going to say something, but he turned to me instead.

"I'm going to talk to him, is that okay with you?"

"Of course. They say he can hear us."

LIFE HAPPENS ON THE STAIRS

Tyler scooted the chair closer to Dad then leaned forward, supporting himself on his forearms. We made eye contact. He gave me a shy smile, and then he turned to Dad.

"Mr. Richardson, I'm Tyler Vaughn. We met about a month ago at the festival, but I wanted to properly introduce myself. I'm sorry it has to be under these circumstances." He glanced at me again. "I've been spending a lot of time with Elsie. You've raised a fine young woman, if I may say so, sir. I wanted to tell you how much she means to me. It's only right. If a father has a chance to know, a man should tell him what his intentions are."

I sat straighter. Intentions? Where was he going with this?

"Sir, I won't disrespect her, or you. I just want you to know that you can trust me, and I'll treat her right."

I wanted to scream like the Bears had just won the Super Bowl. Tyler looked up and his dark eyes found mine. My stomach fluttered as I held my breath.

"Elizabeth." Dad's voice rolled through the silence. "Does your mother know about this?"

I jumped. Tyler gasped and sat up.

"Dad!" I said, slapping my hand to my lips.

He coughed out a laugh.

"That's crazy," Tyler said, leaning back in his chair, pressing his hand to his chest.

"I thought you were in a coma! Oh my gosh, you scared the crap out of us."

"Little girl," Dad said, "you should know by now you can't sneak nothin' past me."

Dad always caught me. Whenever I was doing something wrong, he loved to bust me. He'd say, *Whatcha think you're doing?* I'd let out a screech, and he'd grab me up in his arms, bellowing laughter as he hugged me and kissed my cheek.

"How long have you been awake?" I asked, hoping my heart would slow down.

"I woke to my little girl telling me she'd brought someone to see me. I heard a man introduce himself, so I thought I'd listen." Dad pushed his eyes open further, and then he rolled his head toward Tyler. "It takes a hell of a man to come talk to a corpse. I know your family. Do you realize what you're getting into?"

"Yes, sir."

Getting into? I glanced at both of them. What the heck did that mean?

"Nice to meet you again," Tyler said, looking Dad directly in the eyes.

"Likewise," Dad said. "You wouldn't bullshit a man on his deathbed, would you?"

"You have my word."

"Good." Dad slowly turned to me. "Now Elsie, you'd better tell your mom about this. Don't get yourself in a mess. Okay? And don't drag me down with you. If she finds out you came to me first, we'll both be in big trouble."

"I'll talk to her soon," I said, reaching out to take his hand.

He tried to talk some more, but his words slurred together. We sat with him for a few more minutes, and then it was clear he needed to sleep.

As we headed out of ICU, Aaron was at the main nurse's station.

"He's having a good day, isn't he?" he said. "The doctor took him off his medication this morning. Did he wake up for y'all?"

"Yeah, he woke up," I said. "See you soon, Aaron."

"Yep, I'll be here, Elsie. Nice to meet you, Tyler."

Tyler waved. Panic surged through me. Mom would be

here in a few hours. What if Aaron said something about Tyler? I let go of his hand and darted to the nurse's station.

Tyler stopped and waited.

I leaned against the counter. "Hey," I whispered to Aaron. "Don't say anything to Mom about Tyler, please?" His eyes sparkled like he loved a good secret. I continued, "I haven't exactly told her I'm seeing someone. Can we keep this between us?"

"Keep what between us?" He grinned. "I never see anything but my patients."

"You rock, Aaron."

He winked, then took a quick glimpse of Tyler. "Enjoy your evening."

"You, too."

When I returned, Tyler took hold of my hand and led me out of the hospital. Deep in thought, we walked in silence, both at a loss for words. After we stepped outside, he let me go and threw his arms in the air.

"I almost had a heart attack!"

"I know, right?" I laughed. "It's totally like Dad to do something like that."

"I'll never forget it," Tyler said, shaking his head.

For the next hour, we talked like time didn't matter.

"I'll let you go," Tyler eventually said. "Will Saturday night work for you?"

Relief flooded me for having an extra day to find an outfit. "Yeah, sounds good."

"Saturday it is. Six o'clock. What's your address?"

"The back hills."

"Elsie... "

"All right. 1708 West McAllister Road. Do you know how to get back there?"

He pulled out his iPhone. "This can get me anywhere I need to go. When you enter this part of the twenty-first century, I'll explain more."

He gave me one last kiss goodbye, and then we both climbed into our cars.

All the way home, I thought about the day. Tyler's declaration to Dad spoke volumes about his character. What nineteen-year-old would be willing to say those things to a girl's father, one on his deathbed, no less? Tyler's willingness to commit had been remarkable from the start, and our first kiss had finalized the deal. He'd confessed his feelings to me, but I never thought he'd declare them to Dad. After telling Dad I would talk to Mom, my conscience swelled with a whole new pressure. I'd promised him. I had to talk to her.

When I walked inside the house, Mark was sitting in the recliner, eating ice cream from the carton.

"That's gross," I said. "You'd better finish it or throw it away."

He scooped the spoon from the container, exaggerating his next bite.

"I know what you're up to," he said with a mouthful. "You can fool Mom, but you're not fooling me."

"What do you mean?"

"You probably aren't even fooling Mom. She's just too busy to care. Who are you meeting? I know it ain't some girl. Who is he?"

I gave him my best "wouldn't you like to know look" and left the room.

Churning over his comment, I knocked off each task on Mom's list – scrubbing the bathroom, throwing in a load of laundry, washing the dishes. I stopped at the window in the dining room and scanned the five acres behind the house. I couldn't even see the peppers. The weeds had grown higher than the crop. My stomach rolled over. I had to get out there.

I went to the living room and picked up a handful of Mark's trash, while he continued to sit in the chair watching TV. When I couldn't take another second, I grabbed the paper plate and cup he'd ditched on the end table and threw them on his lap.

"What the hell?" he yelled, jumping up, dropping the trash onto the floor.

"Clean up your own mess," I shouted. "You suck, Mark. You won't do anything, and then you sit there letting me clean up your mess. At least get out in the field and pull some weeds. The crops are going to shit!"

He gaped at me, pants soaked in soda pop and spaghetti.

I huffed and went to the bathroom.

Rule of the house: The bathroom was a safe place. No busting in on someone else's bathroom time. I locked the door as rage welled inside me. My inability to forgive him, and his insistence on being the laziest person in the county, made it impossible for me to show him any kindness. I paced from one end of the room to the other, a total of three steps each way. I counted each one, turned, and counted again. I wanted to run. I wanted to run and hide.

I stopped and looked in the mirror. I hadn't thought about running since Tyler and I'd started jogging together. Of course, Mark could provoke all of my childish ways to rear up again. I took a few deep breaths and thought about Saturday night. I needed something to wear. Determined to be the bigger person, I headed to the kitchen and grabbed my car keys.

"Where are you going now?" Mark asked as he cleaned up the plate I threw.

"None ya business."

Twenty minutes later, I parked in front of The High End Thrift Store in downtown Savannah. The not-so-clever name of the boutique was where I hoped to find a dress. I'd been inside with Mom once, but I'd never tried to find anything for myself before.

The shop was clean, organized by color and size. The racks were packed with various dresses, women's jeans, blouses, and pretty much anything a girl would wear. I found the right size rack and after searching for a few minutes, I pulled a simple black dress off the hanger. In the dressing room, the silky fabric felt soft as it fell over my skin. A V-neck cut, it covered my scar and came over the shoulders just enough to hide the one on the back of my arm. I liked how it stopped right above my knees, showing off my toned legs. Finally, the benefit of jogging showed. I had awesome-looking legs. The dress was perfect.

I needed shoes too, but this part was a bit out of my comfort zone. My personal policy: Don't wear other people's shoes. But these were desperate times – little time, little money. I scanned the shelves for a clean pair of black heels. The selection was good, most of them were nice, but I didn't like any of the styles.

Hidden on the top shelf was a pair of red-bottomed, black pumps. The scarlet soles were barely scratched, a good indication they'd hardly been worn. I grabbed them. They were exquisite – smooth black leather, three-and-a-half-inch heels. I ran my finger over the print on the ivory lining. It read *Christian* connected to a swirling script spelling out *Louboutin*.

Lou, who? I flipped them over and the price tag read ninety dollars. I thought I was at a thrift store... I had a hundred and sixty dollars and the dress was fifty-five. I could do it, and it was totally worth it if they fit.

I sat on a bench, slipped on both shoes, and slowly stood up. Perfect. A bit painful, but perfect. I gathered my items and headed to the cashier.

"Ooh," the young lady said. "You found some gems here. Special occasion?"

"Yes." I smiled. "A date."

"Well, you're gonna be gorgeous in this."

She folded the dress and placed it in the bag.

As I walked to the car, I couldn't stop smiling. I'd found the perfect outfit and couldn't wait to spend my evening with Tyler, hidden in my private world.

Chapter

10

Tyler and I met Friday morning for a quick run. I had to be at Mrs. Baltic's house by nine, then go to Smith's. Our morning jog and the thought of going on a date the next day helped me endure the idea of cleaning, but it took everything in me to leave him. After a long kiss goodbye, he stayed to run a few more miles, and I pouted all the way to Savannah. All I wanted was to have a day to myself, to do whatever I wanted. Then guilt overrode my pity party. I couldn't imagine how Mom yearned for a normal day, too, so I sucked it up and drove on.

I pulled into Mrs. Baltic's driveway at nine. She stood on the step, holding the door open. The plump contours of her body pushed the seams of her pink robe. Her hair was twisted in curlers, and cheap Avon perfume mixed with the hint of mothballs rolled off her as I stepped inside. Mrs. Baltic meant well, but she required a lot of patience. She waddled behind me, while I grabbed the rags, wood polish, and toilet cleaner. Then, she followed me from room to room, talking the entire time. I'd smile and shake my head yes or no, trying not to sigh or roll my eyes (she might have caught me once), but if she asked a direct question, which was rare, I'd force myself to answer in a neutral tone. After ten minutes, I tuned her out and screamed in my head: Why don't you clean your own house if you can follow me around?

A half hour later, she finally wore herself out and went to get a glass of tea. A twinge of guilt twisted inside of me for being annoyed. People probably thought I was too quiet, maybe even rude, but if I said what I was thinking, they would've despised me. Before I left, she gave me an awkward hug and handed me a check written to Mom. I said goodbye and headed across town to Mr. Smith's.

Mr. Smith sat at the kitchen table, eyes drooping, head swaying back and forth. Drunk already and it wasn't even noon yet. I wanted to avoid him, but he kept the cleaning supplies under the sink in the kitchen. Tiptoeing to the cabinet, I quietly gathered what I needed. I clutched them to my chest and started across the room. The bathroom was a safe place, right? If I could make it there, maybe he'd leave me alone.

"Miss, El... Elsie," he slurred.

I stiffened and slowly turned around. "Hello, Mr. Smith."

"You's late again."

"No, sir. Mom called you yesterday," I said, inching toward the hallway. "I had to clean another house before yours."

"Come on in here."

I bolted to the bathroom, shut the door, and locked it. Panting, I pressed my back to the wall. He'll fall asleep. Calm down, he'll fall asleep. My arms shook as I set the cleaners on the counter. Get it done and get out, that was my best option.

I tried not to skimp, moving as fast as I could. I had to do a good job for Mom; her reputation was on the line. But the bathroom was nasty. I gagged three times as I scrubbed the toilet. While wiping down the counter, I had to stop and pick toothpaste out of the sink, and then I polished the faucet. His teeth sat next to the soap and cringing, I wiped around them.

The bathroom alone was worth the sixty-dollar paycheck.

Forty minutes later, I stood by the door, contemplating how to clean the kitchen. I pulled out my phone and texted Mom.

Me: Mr. Smith's drunk. I'm a little freaked out. Do I have to clean the whole house?

Several minutes later...

Mom: Please finish. He will take a nap soon. I need the $60.

I groaned and texted her back.

Me: Seriously? I told you he's drunk. You can keep my $10 from Baltic.

I sucked in a deep breath, walked down the hall, and grabbed the vacuum cleaner out of the closet. Ten minutes later...

Mom: How's it going?

I ignored her until I finished vacuuming the floor. Tiptoeing toward the entrance, I glanced in the kitchen. Mr. Smith had his head cradled in his arms on the table. A gargling sound echoed from the room.

Me: He's asleep. I'll get it done.

Thirty-seconds later...

LIFE HAPPENS ON THE STAIRS

Mom: Thank you. Will you stop by Vaughn's and drop off the pay checks?

Me: Sure.

She had no idea how happy I was to read that text. I'd do anything to get a glimpse of Tyler. I flew through the rest of my chores, glancing over my shoulder every few seconds to make sure Mr. Smith wasn't lurking. Then, I returned the supplies, grabbed the check, and hustled out the front door.

After ordering a meal at Jack's drive-thru, I drove to the Vaughns'. A chicken sandwich and a pop helped me perk up. Driving down Main Street, I turned on Riverside Drive. The estate spread several acres to the west, trumping every other house near them. Tyler's Mercedes was parked in front of the garage. I slowed to give myself time to calm the butterflies in my stomach.

The driver's side door of Tyler's car opened. He stepped out. I rolled a little closer, feeling a bit like a creepy stalker. He walked around the front of the car, opened the passenger's side door, and offered his hand. A beautiful, blonde woman stepped out beside him.

Who the hell was that? My stomach flipped, threatening to reject the chicken sandwich. I pulled over on the side of the road and watched.

She stood a few inches shorter than Tyler, golden hair spilling over her shoulders, dark jeans covering the entire heel of her spiky pumps. She carried an oversized handbag that annoyingly matched her printed blouse. She turned my way and I gasped. Absolutely stunning. Jealousy consumed me. They followed the sidewalk toward the front steps, his arms wrapped around her shoulder. She leaned closer to show her affection and he squeezed her close. Ever the gentleman, he pulled the front door open, holding it for her, and then they stepped inside.

I wiped away the tears clouding my eyes and texted Mom.

Me: I don't feel good. Ate a nasty chicken sandwich. Gotta go home.

I waited for her to answer, tears streaming down my face. A beep alerted me to a text.

Mom: Okay. I'll run home before I go to the hospital.

Me: Thanks.

Attempting a U-turn, I couldn't get the car turned around without backing up. Forward then backward. Rage boiling inside, I slammed the little Honda on drive and stomped the gas.

I had to get away from that house.

Who was she? I was an idiot to think I could have a guy like him. Filthy rich, dressed in designer clothes even when jogging, Tyler's world was light-years beyond mine, a world I'd never belong in. Why had I gotten close to a guy so out of my class? Of course, he had girls breaking down the door. That woman looked incredible. Not a hair out of place, her ensemble perfect, accentuated by proper posture, she practically floated when she walked. And the way he put his arm around her! *Who was she?*

I followed Coffee Landing Road into Morris Chapel. At the last second, I whipped the wheel to the right, pulling into Ruby and Woodrow's driveway. I turned off the car and looked in the rear-view mirror.

Ugh, I thought. I looked like a peasant.

Ripping my hair out of my ponytail, I moved it around to cover my red face.

LIFE HAPPENS ON THE STAIRS

When I walked up to the front porch, Woodrow sat in his chair, picking ticks off his dog, Ranger. He'd pull the insects off and throw them down, popping their swollen bodies with the toe of his boot into a bloody mess on the decking. Ruby stood at the screen door.

"Hey, y'all okay?" she asked, wiping her hands on her blue apron.

"Your daddy all right?" Woodrow asked.

"Yeah, everyone's fine." I sounded pathetic.

"You're upset about something," Ruby said, stepping outside and letting the screen door slam. "What's the matter, honey?" She wrapped her arm around me. "Come over here and sit."

She pointed to the swing and we walked across the porch and sat down. She pushed the swing back and forth with her toes.

"You want some tea?" she asked, then she shouted, "Woodrow get us some tea, an' quit pickin' them ticks off that ole' dog."

"It's okay, Ruby," I said. "I don't need anything."

"Now," she said, ignoring my comment, "you sit here and tell me what's on your mind."

She turned in the swing so she could look at me. Woodrow attempted to stand several times before his legs cooperated, and then he limped inside.

"Ruby, I've met a boy," I said, starting to cry.

She sat up straight. "Y'all ain't pregnant, is you?"

"No way! He's... I saw him with someone else."

"Mm, hmm." She eyed me. "Who's this boy belong to?"

"I can't say yet," I said. "I'm sorry, Ruby. I haven't told Mom. Please don't tell her."

"Mm," she hummed. "I won't. He's not hurtin' you, is he?

I mean, physically?"

"Oh, no. He's not like that, he's... he's too good for me."

"What the hell do you mean by that?" she blurted. I flinched. "I've never heard such nonsense in my life. Nobody's too good for you. You're the finest girl in Hardin County."

"Gee, thanks, Ruby," I said, dryly.

"Okay, that's not a good example. In the whole state of Tennessee, then. Any boy would be lucky to have you as his girl. What's got you thinkin' this way?"

"I saw him with a beautiful girl." I shook my head. "No. She's a woman... I don't know what to think. I'm supposed to go out with him tomorrow night, but now, I don't know."

Woodrow returned with sweet tea in each hand. I said thank you. He went back to his chair and started picking ticks off the dog again.

"Miss Elsie," Ruby said, "don't go gettin' ahead of yourself. You don't know what you saw. Go out, have a good time, and ask him about her. That's all it takes. Now, more importantly, why haven't you told your momma?"

I stared at my glass. "Um, she's not going to be happy about it," I said, and then I looked at her and smiled. "He met Dad yesterday, though."

"How'd y'all do that when your momma don't know?"

"We went in the afternoon when she was at work. He asked if he could go to the hospital and see Dad because he might not get another chance, so after our jog—"

"Jog!" she squawked. "When did you start jogging?"

"Early July." I shrugged, and then I told her about us going to the hospital.

"I never thought they'd get a chance to talk." I slumped back in the swing. "Oh, Ruby... he said the sweetest things, and then I had to see him today with that Victoria's Secret model."

"You need to tame this crazy imagination of yours." She waved her hand at me. "If that boy is willing to go talk to your daddy, I think he deserves a chance to explain." Ruby bobbed her head once as if to put a period at the end of her sentence, and then she sealed it with another opinion. "Sounds like good people to me."

She put her arm around me and I let her squeeze me close. "Thanks, Ruby."

"You need to go on home," she said. "Take a long shower and a good look in the mirror. I don't ever want to hear you say you're not good enough again. Understood? You're a beautiful, smart, and talented girl. If a boy can't see that, he's as blind as that ole' dog over there."

"Thank you for listening." I said, giving her a hug.

"All right, you go on now." She patted my back. "And cheer up."

I said goodbye and headed home. Ruby always made me feel better, but I was nervous I'd told her about Tyler. I'd gotten too bold. I had to end the lie before it blew up in my face.

Chapter

11

I tossed and turned all night, nightmares in full color, waking me every two hours. I hadn't talked to Tyler, and I swore I wouldn't text or call him.

I heard a tap on my door around nine the next morning. "Come in."

Mom stepped inside and sat on the edge of my bed.

"I'm headed to the hospital. I probably won't be home until late. Your dad, well, it's hard to say what will happen, but he's not doing well this morning."

"What?" I sat up. "I just saw him last Thursday. He woke up and talked to me. I thought it had been a good sign."

The ache of constant uncertainty plagued my stomach.

Her eyes brightened. "You talked to him?"

"Yeah, Aaron said they took him off his medication."

"I don't know what to think," she said. "The swelling won't go down. They're talking like they want to transfer him to Nashville. If they do, you're going to have to work my jobs for me, especially at the Vaughn's. I haven't told her about your dad yet, but I can't afford for her to use the time off against me."

"What kind of person holds your husband dying against you?"

"She's... well." She raised her eyebrows and shrugged. "She's a bitch. There's no other way to say it."

I pressed my hand over my mouth to cover my smile. I couldn't believe Mom said it. She never spoke that way about anyone, especially her clients.

"I don't want to send you, but I think it'll only be for a few days." She gave me a stern look. "You have to ignore her and her snide remarks. She doesn't have a filter. To be honest, I think she loves to patronize me because I'm not Southern."

I remembered Tyler saying how she hated Northerners. It didn't make any sense. It was almost as stupid as hating a person because of their skin color.

"Hopefully, they'll tell me today if they're transferring Dad," she said, patting my leg with an exhausted look.

I didn't refuse to help or give her any attitude. Complaining might've broken any spirit she had left. She walked across the room and opened the door.

"Thanks for all you do, Elsie. It helps to know I can trust you. I love you."

"Love you, too."

Guilt pierced my stomach. I couldn't tell her about Tyler (even though my lie might have been irrelevant after seeing him with that woman). Mom was under too much stress already. After all the crap Mark and I'd put her through, she still trusted me. But it had taken over a year of isolation and self-punishment to regain her regard. I sunk back on my pillows and stared at the ceiling.

My phone beeped.

Tyler: I missed you this morning.

Sure, you did...

Me: Yeah, right.

No, I couldn't send that. Delete, delete...

Me: Me too.

I pressed send.

Tyler: 6, right?

Me: Yes.

Tyler: You okay?

Me: Sure.

Tyler: Good. See u soon.

Me:

I had nothing to say. I let the phone drop on the bed, and then I grabbed my sketchpad. A tornado had just ripped through my secret world of happiness. I needed to forget about Tyler and focus on something else. All I could imagine was him sitting at his grandmother's, talking about the poor girl he'd taken pity on. I turned the page, shaking off that horrible thought.

The sketch was of Dad. I'd been working on a twenty-three-portrait series of him from the age of eighteen to present. I'd gathered photos from each year and affixed them to separate pages. The problem was, I wasn't sure how I should portray his current "look." He'd drastically changed, and it wasn't flattering compared to how handsome he once was. I wanted to honor him, not record the way he'd deteriorated. That part I wanted to forget.

LIFE HAPPENS ON THE STAIRS

For the rest of my life, I'd question why people died the way they did. Some people passed in their sleep, peacefully without pain, while others were ripped away within seconds, and then there were those who had to endure a long, slow, and painful death. What qualified one person to get a peaceful, quiet passing and another to be tortured until their last breath? It would never make sense, and as a simple human being, I'd never understand. The thought made me wonder what fate held for me. I turned the page, shaking off the awful idea.

Tyler. *Damn.* I'd actually stopped thinking about him for a minute. Looking over the pages, I'd drawn several versions of him, but there was something about him I couldn't capture – something internal, an aspect that I didn't understand yet.

Tyler challenged me. He defied my charcoal and my talent. I had to try harder.

I flipped to a blank page and snatched up my charcoal, determined to do it right. I started with a collage of Dad depicting his different expressions over the years, positioning each version in opposite corners. Smiling brightly; rubbing his forehead (something he did often); staring into the distance, and a sketch of him laughing. At the center, I drew a larger version of him, copied from a photo I'd found, where he had a look of pure love that I knew was directed at Mom. Recreating that one hurt. I loved the way Mom and Dad could communicate with just a simple look.

Tears started rolling down my cheeks.

When I was eight years old, I had asked Dad if he would take me to get ice cream.

"Elsie, I don't have a penny to my name."

I thought I was brilliant as I ran around the house, gathering all the pennies I could find. When I handed him my pile, he stared at his palm, and then looked at me with stoic blue eyes.

"I stand corrected," he'd said. "I have seven."

He'd taken a deep breath, closed his hand around the change as he ruffled my hair with his other. Then he'd pulled me close to give me a hug. I'd squeezed him around the waist in return.

"Let's see what we have in the deep freeze," he'd said.

Five minutes later, we were sitting on the back step together, eating a fudge pop in the afternoon sun. Dad always found a way. I didn't have a clue how I'd move forward without him.

I wiped my face, yearning for him to get better.

I flipped to a clean page and tackled Tyler's profile. I started sketching his shy smile when he'd kissed me in the log cabin church. By the time I'd finished, I gasped when I looked at the clock.

Four-thirty!

I dropped my stuff and ran to the bathroom. At ten till five, I hurried out of the shower, performing all my usual rituals to get ready. By five forty-five, I'd managed to put myself together enough to slip into my new dress and shoes. I stood in front of the full-length mirror, impressed with the person reflected back. In the past few weeks, my jogging had transformed any fat I had into muscle. My arms and legs were defined, and the shoes jacked me up another three and a half inches. Even if I had to throw him out because of the beautiful blonde, at least I had a new dress and shoes that were clearly meant for me.

A knock boomed from the front door. I walked to the living room, took a deep breath, and opened the door. My heart skipped a beat. Tyler wore black on black, standing tall with both hands in his slacks pockets.

He smiled. "You look amazing."

"Thank you."

As he stepped inside, his earthy-cedar scent filled the air. The top two buttons of his shirt were undone, and his sleeves were rolled halfway up his forearms. I tried to remember how mad I was at him, but his cologne clouded my judgment, and he had turned to me with his dark eyes. Sliding his hand into my hair, he pressed his lips to mine. I clutched his strong shoulders, completely incapable of resisting him.

"Nice, I like you up here," he responded to my newfound height.

"You look really good in black."

He flashed an adorable smile. I stepped away and headed toward my room to grab my purse. My sketchpad with his face drawn across it was lying on the bed. I snagged the book and flipped it over. When I turned around, he was leaning against the doorway, looking around the room.

"You have a lovely home," Tyler said.

"Thank you. It's not that great, but it's home."

"It's you. I just want to know about you." He nodded toward my bed. "I'm hoping you'll share what's inside that sketchbook one of these days, as well."

I looked at him straight-faced, unable to discern his wishes. Those particular sets of drawings were for me alone. He wouldn't get near that book until I knew the truth about the girl.

"Something wrong?" he asked, perceptive as always. "You seem... tense."

"Um... I have something to ask you."

"Anything." He pushed off the door and moved closer.

"Mom asked me to come by your house yesterday. I, um...

I saw you get out of your car, and, well, you were with a woman. And she certainly wasn't your grandmother," I blurted, and then I took a deep breath to reel in my anxiety. "Can I ask who she is?"

An amused smile broached his lips as he stepped toward me and took my hands in his. Heart pounding, palms sweating, it was the first time I'd ever wanted to pull away from him. I waited. His hesitation was unbearable. Maybe he was trying to decide if he should tell me the truth. If I had to, I'd show him to the door. I wasn't in this to get jerked around.

"Miss Elizabeth, if I may be so bold as to use your given name, you're more beautiful right now than I've ever seen you. Seriously. Amazing." He let the statement linger for a few seconds, then he looked at me with the sincerest expression. "The woman you saw yesterday is my mother. My parents are in town for the weekend."

"Who has a mom who looks like *that*?"

"I guess I do." He chuckled. "Elsie, you have nothing to worry about."

He leaned in and kissed me so tenderly I thought my knees would fold. Thankfully, he held me around the waist as he deepened his embrace. After he pulled away, my cheeks felt like they were on fire.

"I feel pretty stupid," I whispered.

"Don't. Can I take you out for dinner now?"

I smiled. "Yes."

Tyler took my hand, and within minutes, I was sitting in another world – his world. The Mercedes had black-leather bucket seats with white stitching lining the leather, chrome highlighted the dash without a speck of dirt in sight, and it still smelled brand-new. When he closed the door, it didn't slam with a bang or piercing squeak, like the Honda, but with a quiet and demure *click.* I strapped on the seatbelt as he started the engine. The dash lit up in fluorescent blue, and then the soft sound of a classical piece filled the air.

"I think you'll like where we're going," he said. "It's a bit of a drive, but it's worth it."

"Anywhere but here sounds good to me."

Tyler drove north out of Savannah through the valley and into the high hills, maybe a tad too fast, but the car rolled over the bumps on the road like they didn't exist. After weeks of stress, I finally felt like I could relax and enjoy myself. He reached over and took my hand. The music changed, and the sound of Jeff Buckley's aching electric guitar filled the air with the slow tempo of *Hallelujah*. The first time I heard the song was in the movie *Shrek*. Buckley's version was different, but it was definitely my favorite. Tyler's warm touch, his unwavering confidence, the erotic sounds of the haunting music – made me wish the evening could last forever.

Thirty minutes later, Tyler turned onto a country road and followed the curves, gradually climbing in elevation through the dense woodlands. Within a half mile, he drove down an asphalt driveway to a small brick building with twenty-foot, black iron gates guarding the entrance. He rolled down his tinted window.

"Good evening, Mr. Vaughn," a bald, plump guard said. "How are you?"

"Very well, sir," Tyler said with a nod.

"Enjoy your evening."

"Same to you, Philip."

The gates opened to a lane that led to a two-story, log cabin lodge that was settled in the center of a vast, green lawn, overlooking the mountain valley. On both sides were one-story wings with full-length windows facing the tranquil view of the forests.

"Oh my gosh, it's beautiful," I said. "It's in the middle of nowhere."

"Yeah, not many people know about it." He smiled. "Only the ones who know. You know?"

I smirked at his corny remark as we drove up to the front entrance. A young man, wearing black slacks and a white dress shirt, ran around the car to open the door. Tyler gave him the keys and then shook the guy's hand, leaving some cash in his palm. Nerves prickled my arms as I watched Tyler walk around the car and open my door. He offered me his hand. Standing up, I paused to compose myself.

He smiled, giving my hand a squeeze. "You're perfect. Follow me."

Tyler held the door open, and I stepped inside a lodge meant for Aspen, Colorado. The maître d' immediately rushed to greet Tyler. The man acknowledged me with a nod, and led us through the low-lit dining room, past the tables of people enjoying dinner. The tall ceilings were stamped copper, outlined in mahogany wood trim. Deep-burgundy walls complemented the dark woodwork. Brown leather booths lined the space, tables covered in white linen filled the center of the dining room as the chandeliers twinkled above. The maître d' presented us a booth next to a long window overlooking the serene forest.

Tyler thanked him, and then he said something in French. I did a double-take – *French*? The man nodded and walked away. Tyler settled in across from me.

"You know French?" I asked in disbelief.

He shyly smiled. Within a minute, a male server approached with two glasses.

"Ah... Mr. Vaughn," the man said. "I heard you would be

here tonight. Very nice to see you again."

"Nice to see you, Alto. I'd like to introduce you to Elsie."

Alto smiled and bowed his head. "My pleasure to meet you, Miss." His obsidian eyes glimmered under the light. "Would you like a glass of sparkling water?"

"Yes, thank you," I said.

He set a glass in front of us, presented the menus, and walked away.

Tyler held up his glass. "Would you like a toast?"

"I'd love one."

"To you, Elsie," he said, dark eyes set on mine. "Meeting you has changed my life."

Our glasses clinked, as my heart skipped a beat. That was a loaded statement...

"Likewise," I said.

We took a sip and started looking over the menu. To my surprise, all of the entrées were in foreign languages.

I whispered across the table, "I have no idea what any of this says."

He grinned and turned on the charm, pronouncing each French and Italian dish with expertise, as if he ate in Europe every night. Overwhelmed by the choices, I told him I liked a rare steak. Tyler took it from there when the server returned to take our orders.

"Where are we, exactly?" I asked after we were alone again.

"My family's country club. They built it in the late nineties."

"It's amazing." Then I realized what he'd said. "What do you mean 'they' built it?"

"We don't own it anymore. Nana sold it after Grandpa died. She's liquidated everything. On some levels, I understand, but something like this... I'd love to own it again some-day."

"I can see why."

The place was remarkable, shrouded in low amber light-ing that made me want to curl up on a winter's night in front of the grand stone fireplace at the far side of the dining room.

"Grandpa logged the forests locally and chose every piece they used in the project. He said it took four years to build. All the mahogany was brought in from an antebellum man-sion they were disassembling near Knoxville. The booths are covered in leather from a ranch near Jacksonville, and the chandeliers were shipped in from an artisan in Gatlinburg." He smiled. "That's what I loved about the old man. He had so much pride for Tennessee."

"What would you do with it if you ever got it back?"

Tyler glanced around the dining room. "I always thought it would be a cool house."

"More like a mansion... "

The server approached and placed our appetizer at the center of the table. Tyler said it was bruschetta and tomato salad with crumbled blue cheese. He scooped a piece of toast on his fork and set it on my plate. When I took a bite, the sa-vory tomato and basil, tart cheese, and crisp garlic bread de-liciously melded together.

Ten minutes later, the server brought a plate of something fried. Tyler called it calamari. I loved the name and the flavor of the breaded delicacy. After I'd tasted a few of them with approval, he explained it was squid. I had to compliment his proper timing (squid sounded awful), but I actually loved the taste.

Then, our server brought a third dish of thin slices of rare beef layered around the plate, with a garnish of arugula salad.

LIFE HAPPENS ON THE STAIRS

An odd, toadstool aroma lifted from the appetizer.

Tyler curiously watched me. I eyed him, then picked up a piece with my fork, daring myself to try the paper-thin meat. I took a bite. The rich flavor melted over my tongue.

"What is this?" I asked.

"Carpaccio. Thinly sliced, raw tenderloin coated in white truffle oil. You said you like rare steak," he chuckled.

"It's fantastic. It smells weird, but I love it."

"It's the truffle oil. It has an odd scent, one only a wild boar can appreciate."

I giggled at the comment, and then he proceeded to tell me how truffles were harvested.

Shortly after we finished, the server returned with our entrées. Tyler had ordered a rare filet for both of us. The flavor of the beef trumped every other dish we'd been served.

When we were done with our dinner, the server returned once more to remove our plates, leaving us alone in our private world.

"You're absolutely stunning tonight," Tyler said, leaning back in his chair.

"Thank you. Look at you," I said, teasingly. "You should be on the cover of *GQ*."

"That's funny. I'll have to make that my pet project." He propped his elbows on the table and leaned in closer. "What I've been wondering all night is... for such a simple girl... where in the world did you get the *Louboutins*?"

"The what?" I shook my head. The name sounded familiar, but his pronunciation in French didn't make any sense.

"*Louboutin*," he repeated. "I assume you didn't pay hundreds of dollars for those."

"Paid hundreds for what?"

"Your shoes. They average near seven hundred dollars."

"What?" I glanced at my feet. "How do you know so much about shoes?"

"The red bottoms. That's Christian Louboutin's signature. Mom's closet is filled with red-bottomed shoes."

"People pay that much for shoes? That's insane. I got a bargain, then."

"You have good taste."

"Yeah, cashmere taste on a polyester budget."

As we waited for dessert, we joked about how much money was in his mom's closet, determining I could buy the house I lived in and still have cash for years. In the midst of our giggles, the server placed a bowl on the table, and then he flicked a lighter, setting the top of the dish on fire. When the brief flame dissipated, the top was golden brown. I wanted to clap my hands like a little girl watching fireworks. Tyler said the dish was called crème brûlée. The combination of the crunchy sugar and creamy vanilla filling was the perfect finish to our meal.

I sat back in the booth, my taste buds on flavor overload.

"Thank you for dinner. Everything was fantastic."

"My pleasure. I'm glad you enjoyed it." He took a sip of his water, then set down his glass. "So. Are you going to tell me about your scar?"

I gave him my best "really" look.

Pleading with his eyes, he said, "You promised."

I liked his determination for some reason, but I had to take a minute to find the courage to say it. I hated recounting that night, and I didn't want to ruin my perfect evening. I fidgeted with the cloth napkin in my lap. He smiled. I scanned the dining room. He waited. We were one of three tables remaining. The conversation and noise from earlier had faded, and the soft sound of a piano piece complemented the ambiance. The fluid melody stole my attention. I listened, ignoring his unnerving patience, but he couldn't take the silence any longer.

"It's Rachmaninov," he said like he read my mind. *"Rhapsody on a Theme of Paganini."*

"It's beautiful."

"You're avoiding questions again," he teased.

"Okay, well... I was fifteen. Dad had a seizure that day and it scared us pretty bad. Mom rode in the ambulance and Mark and I followed them in the truck."

I leaned in closer so I could speak in hushed tones.

"Later that night, Mom had told us to go home because she needed to stay the night at the hospital. Instead of doing what she said, Mark had driven to Bobby's, one of his drinkin' buddies. He told me to keep my mouth shut and just go for the ride. I didn't argue with him. I did whatever he wanted at the time. So, he picked Bobby up, and we went north of Saltillo toward Dog Creek. Then, he pulled into a small bar tucked in the woods. Mark had been so stupid to get mixed up with that crowd. He kept going out and getting drunk. Mom had been mad at him all the time. By the time it was all over, he'd lost his football scholarship at the University of Tennessee."

"I remember your brother." Tyler's face lit up like he'd finally connected some of the missing dots. "He went All State, didn't he?"

"Yeah, played tight end... and he was good, too. Anyway, he told me to stay in the truck and that they'd only be a few minutes. So... there I was, sitting in front of a biker bar in the middle of nowhere. People kept coming and going and all of them looked shady in their leather jackets and long hair. I started freaking out. They'd been inside for way longer than a few minutes. So... I ran."

"You were serious that day, then?" he asked. "You actually run away?"

My face burned. "Yes. That wasn't my proudest moment. I really screwed up that time."

"What do you mean 'that time'?"

I quickly looked away. How much did I need to confess? Letting him in on my senseless reactions in the past was a risk I wasn't sure I should take, and running was only half of it. I had hiding places all over our property, and if I still needed to use one, I would.

"It wasn't the first time," I continued. "I get... well, irrational is one way to put it. I really thought I was in danger, though. Mark had scared me. I wanted to go to the marina and call Mom, Ruby, somebody. But I was stupid and had run through the woods, instead of following the hills and curves. I thought it would be a shortcut and thought I'd find the road on the other side. Well, it might have worked in the daylight, but I couldn't see a thing. I was pushing through the thicket, but then I lost my footing and had fallen down a ravine." I looked up at the ceiling to stop the tears threatening me. "I'm sorry, this is hard to admit."

"Take your time," he said. "I don't want to upset you."

I took a deep breath to suck in my embarrassment. I wasn't sure why it was important for him to know where my scar came from, but he had an empathetic air about him... as if he understood what it meant to go through something terrifying.

"Talk about being an idiot," I said. "I got first prize that night. I was out there for sixteen hours – my collarbone had been shattered, and my upper left arm broken. I'd hit my head several times, so I kept slipping in and out of consciousness. I don't remember much, thank God. After Mark realized he couldn't find me, he had called the police, who then turned around and arrested him for underage drinking. Bobby ran like the spineless creep he was, and of course, he didn't get caught. I was in the hospital for a week. I had to undergo a couple of surgeries – one on my collarbone and the other under here."

I lifted my arm to show him the four-inch scar down my left triceps. He acknowledged my battle wound with a nod.

"While all this was happening, Dad was in critical condition. Mark had been busted not only for underage drinking, but for the bag of cocaine in his pocket. I had *no* idea that's what they were after. He had inevitably lost his scholarship and everything he'd worked for. My poor mom had to deal with both Mark's mess and a full-out search and rescue for me by the police and people from church. By the time she had accounted for her whole family, two of us were in the hospital, and the other one needed to be bailed out of jail."

The end of the story floated around us, dense as smoke, clouding my mood. Tyler had propped his elbow on the table, his chin resting in his palm, with his fingers curled around his lips. Shame overwhelmed me. I started to regret my honesty, unsure of how to read him.

"That's where my scar came from," I whispered.

He stayed silent as he contemplated his response, and then he said, "I was in a car accident a few years ago. I understand how hard it can be to get over something traumatic." He took a sharp breath like it was just as hard for him to talk about as it had been for me. "I was with my grandfather and he died at the scene. He probably didn't know what hit him."

"You were with him? I'm so sorry." I could feel his pain from across the table. His dark eyes said it all. That night haunted him every day. "It's so random, isn't it?"

"What is?"

"How we die. Dad won't go without a fight, but your grandpa had been ripped away from life in seconds. It's hard to wrap your brain around it."

"There is no rhyme or reason."

Tyler gently took my hand in his, staring down at our fingers intertwined together. The intensity of his gaze, his gentle touch, his hesitancy – everything he did held me in suspense, waiting for what he might say next. His eyes met mine.

"Let's change the subject. We're having way too nice of an evening to recount our worst moments. Thank you for telling me where your scar came from. I'm sure you hate it. However, be assured that it's quite sexy."

I smiled, glancing away. He squeezed my fingers between his. I looked back at him still fighting my embarrassment.

"More than that," he continued, "what happened that night doesn't define you. It's just one of those times when you were knocked back a few steps, and you had a lesson to learn."

His words took me by surprise. I hadn't thought of it that way. Letting that night rule my feelings and self-esteem was exactly what I'd been doing.

"Thank you for saying that," I said. "I really do need to let it go."

"Just forgive yourself. We all screw up sometimes."

I nodded in agreement, even though forgiveness wasn't one of my strengths.

"Elsie, I have my own confession to make." He paused, leaving me in suspense again. "I think about you constantly. Since the first day I saw you, I cannot get you off my mind. No one has ever fascinated me the way you do. As complicated as your family is, so is mine." He hesitated. "When I want something, I have to be discreet in the way I pursue it, but when I know what I want, I go after it. I'm not exactly sure how to make everything work out right now. I have a lot of commitments and a few obstacles in the way, but what I *do* know is that each night, all I can think about is being with you the next morning. Now, granted, you've stroked my ego, listening to all my talk about Shiloh and the Civil War. But if reciting interesting facts keeps you coming back, I'll talk until I pass out." Then, he abruptly flipped his hands in the air and exaggerated his expression. "You have no idea how crazy this is making me. If I could just focus on something other than you."

His words shocked me. I sat there speechless while he waited for my response.

"Tyler, I, um... Thank you."

He recoiled. "Thank you? What are you thanking me for?"

"I don't know." I laughed. "I'm sorry. It's hard for me to let my feelings out like that. I know it would sound stupid to say I agree, but I agree. Ever since my accident, I've become a hermit. Like I'm afraid of myself or something. I don't want to take chances, and here you're the biggest chance I've ever taken." My heart was racing and my voice didn't sound familiar. It was like someone else was talking for me. I took a deep breath, and continued, "I've never needed someone so much, but at the same time, I'm trying like hell not to need you. You make me want to get up and go jogging, of all things! You talk about stuff I've never considered before, and most of all, you make me laugh. But the truth is," I pointed between us, "I know this is impossible. I'm setting myself up, sabotaging my heart, but I can't say no. I should run from you like I run from everything else, but you're so damn charming."

"That's exactly what I'm banking on. Being so damn charming, you can't say no."

I smiled, deeply amused that he would find me challenging. He had no idea of the lengths I would go to be with him. He didn't need to bank on anything, he already had me.

"Elsie, what you see is what you get. I'm not playing you. I will never bullshit you, and you have no idea how sincere I am. Please don't think we're impossible. Nothing's impossible."

I still wasn't convinced. He had too much going for him, and I hadn't even graduated high school yet. I loved what he'd confessed that he wanted us to be together. But "nothing's impossible?" What exactly was he expecting?

"Aren't you afraid of telling your parents about me?" I asked.

"No."

"Really? I'm not from your world."

"I'll give you my world. I don't care where you're from."

That was a tall offer. He didn't even flinch. I looked him over, trying to process his conviction.

"Let's get out of here," he said, and then he slid out of the booth, offering his hands. Standing firm, he pulled me toward him. "Please, don't think this is impossible. Anything's possible. We just have to figure out how to make it work."

He leaned in and brushed his lips over mine.

"Just trust me, okay?" he whispered.

"Okay."

With a satisfied smile, he grasped my hand and led me past the empty tables toward the door. We were almost through the lobby when a red-haired man with glasses and a round face stepped out of the bathroom.

"Tyler," he said. "How are you, son?"

"Mighty fine, sir," Tyler said, releasing me to shake hands. "How's your family?"

Tyler immediately found my hand again, lacing his fingers between mine.

"Rebecca's great. She starts Vanderbilt this fall. How was your year?"

"Fine, thank you."

The man's eyes darted towards me. His arrogant air, along with the snide smirk on his face, didn't set well with me at all.

The man nodded. "Who's your friend?"

"Oh, I'm sorry." Tyler stepped aside. "This is Elsie. Elsie, Jonathan Rockwell."

I accepted his proffered hand. "Nice to meet you."

"Likewise," he said, looking me over before he eyed Tyler. "Is your grandmother out of town?"

"No, she just returned from Houston. I'll tell her you asked about her. Nice to see you, Jon. Please tell everyone hello."

"I will."

Jon stepped away, but then he reached out and put his hand on Tyler's shoulder. I felt Tyler's tension all the way to his fingers.

"You know, Tyler. It would be good for Rebecca to have someone she knows when she gets to Nashville. Maybe you could show her around campus when you get there?"

Tyler pushed the door open. I stepped outside, relieved to get away from the man.

"Yeah, sure. Have a good evening, sir," Tyler said, letting the door close in the pretentious man's face. The valet immediately took Tyler's ticket, hustling off to get the car.

"Are you okay?" I asked.

"The guy's a jackass. He's calling Dad right now to tell him he ran into me."

"Are you surprised? We're at your family's former country club."

"I don't mind that we ran into someone, but Jon... He's always trying to get me to take his daughter out. It's so annoying."

"He's really arrogant."

"Yeah, that's a nice way of putting it."

After the valet pulled up, I climbed inside the car. As Tyler drove out of the parking lot, lightning flashed across the southern sky as muted sounds of thunder rumbled outside. The track on the stereo changed and a soft melody filled the car, sending goosebumps over my arms.

"What is this?" I asked.

"Delibes, *The Flower Duet*."

The harmony of the instruments rose and fell with the rhythm of the road. The symphony, fading softer then gradually building, rising and descending, was a perfect accompaniment to our drive through the hills and curves.

"How do you know so much about classical music? Do you play?"

"No, I never took to it. Mom's a benefactor to the Cultural Center in Memphis, so they get season tickets every year. The symphony was about all I could stand growing up. Most of the other stuff – musicals, ballet, especially any kind of dance, are not my thing. Mom wanted to make sure I had plenty of culture or whatever. But the symphony, that's different. When something's that beautiful, there's no denying it."

He looked over at me and smiled. I smiled back, face

burning at the idea that his words were meant for me and not the music.

When we pulled into the driveway, the lights were off in the house. I tried to shake off my fear of being caught as fat raindrops started slapping the windshield. This was the riskiest part of the night. I knew Mom would be gone when Tyler picked me up, but as far as returning, I had no idea what time she'd be back. Tyler hurried around the car and opened my door. When I stepped out, the smell of the paper mill lingered in the air, as lightning illuminated our path to the back steps.

I turned around at the front door. "Mom might be inside."

"I understand," he said. "Miss Elsie, I've had a wonderful time with you tonight."

"Me too," I said. "Thank you for everything."

Lightning crackled across the sky again, as if our energy shot straight to the heavens. He leaned down and swept his lips over mine, then slowly pulled away just enough that I could still feel his breath on my mouth. Tension brewed as he paused and held his lips so close... yet not close enough to touch mine. Rain started to pour, pounding the ground, bouncing off the metal overhang. Then, he came in strong like the sound of the rumbling thunder, kissing me deep, sending currents through my entire body. I wanted him more than the earth needed the rain. His musky scent, his sweet taste, the sound of his eager breath. I ran my hands through his hair as he pushed his hands over the curves of my hips. Slowing our rhythm, he breathed me in and pulled away.

Ever the gentleman, he stepped back and ran both hands through his hair.

"I have to go now, or I'll never leave. Thank you for an amazing night."

"Thank you." I touched my tingling lips, unable to control

my smile.

"Goodnight," he said, looking at me like he wanted to say something more profound. He shook it off with a wave good-bye and stepped away, but then he turned around. "You're meeting me tomorrow, right?"

"Of course."

"I'll text you when I know what time."

I nodded. He took two long strides back to me, grasped my face in both hands, and pressed his lips hard against mine. I clutched his shoulders. He held steady like he couldn't let me go. My heartbeat erupted in my chest. I touched his smooth face. He didn't move, and then slowly... he pulled away. Still cupping my face, he stared deep in my eyes.

"I cannot get enough of you," he whispered. "I'll see you tomorrow."

"Goodnight, Tyler." I said, quivering underneath his touch.

He stepped away, then gracefully moved through the rain and climbed into his car.

I wanted to scream, "I love you!" I wanted to run to him, jump in the passenger's seat and shout, "Go, drive as fast as you can!" Instead, I watched him back out and disappear down the road. He'd stolen my heart, and I didn't have a clue what to do about it.

Thinking I'd pulled off the perfect night, I shut the door with a quiet click and started to tiptoe through the dark living room.

"You're so busted," I heard from the shadows.

I gasped.

"Mom came home two hours ago," Mark said.

"Oh my gosh, you scared me," I whispered. "Where is she?"

He snickered. "She went to bed."

"I wanna talk, but let me change my clothes first."

A few minutes later, I whisper-shouted for him to come to my room.

"Okay, tell me what she said," I insisted, as I shut the door behind him.

"She just wanted to know where you were. I had a feeling you were out with your mystery person, so I told her you were with Josie, or whatever her name is... "

"Did she believe you?"

"Yeah, I think so." He shrugged. "She looked like shit. Who is he, anyway? Was he driving a freaking Mercedes?"

"Keep your voice down." I flopped on my bed, crisscrossing my legs. "Mark, you can't say anything to anyone. I'll tell Mom soon, but not yet."

"Why would she care? What, did she keep you locked up while I was gone?"

"I can't talk about it, so forget it. Anyway, wouldn't it make your day to know Mom tortured me while you were in Illinois."

"Why are you being such a bitch? Whatever, you owe me for not busting you out. Don't forget it." He turned to walk out.

"Mark, I'm sorry. I didn't mean for it to come out that way. Seriously, I can't talk about it. He's a good guy, believe me."

Mark stopped at the door, shifting his stance back and forth. I wasn't sure if he would accept my apology. No matter how hard we tried, we couldn't get back to where we were before the accident. He'd been my buddy my whole life, and

I genuinely missed my friend. He turned around and let out another anxious huff.

"I'm sorry I left you in the truck that night, Elsie. I never should've taken you along. But you... you screwed me when you ran off. What the hell were you thinking?"

Looking down at my hands, I had no idea what to say. I never thought he'd get in that kind of trouble. It was a survival instinct for me, but it ended up ruining his opportunity for a great education – an education that he truly deserved. Regardless, I had no idea he had been messing around with drugs. That part was his to own.

"I'm sorry, too, Mark. I was scared. I thought I could find the marina and call Mom or something. I trusted you."

"Yeah, I know. I need to forget about it," he said. "Don't worry about Mom. She was beat when she got home. She said they're transferring Dad to Nashville, but she doesn't want us to go." He shrugged. "I guess we're on our own next week."

"Okay," I said. "Thanks for covering for me."

He nodded and shut the door.

After a perfect evening, I should've known I'd come home to terrible news. For the hospital to transfer Dad to a cancer center, that meant the doctors here had done what they could. I wanted to talk to Mom, but waking her up would've been selfish. I laid back on my pillow. Butterflies swarmed my belly. I'd have to clean houses for her all week, including the Vaughns' house. Resigning to my fate, I rolled on my side and thought about Tyler until I fell asleep.

Chapter

12

I woke up the next morning to the sound of my phone

Tyler: Shiloh at 4? Meet me by the big cemetery

Me: ok c u then

I rolled out of bed and headed to the kitchen. Mom stood at the sink, washing the dishes.

"Good morning," she said over her shoulder. "Did you and Josie have a good time? I didn't even hear you come home."

"Who's Josie?" I asked. Oh no, Mark told her the wrong name. "Oh, you mean Jenna. Yeah, we had a nice time. Went out and ate, that's about all."

Damn, the lie just grew. I held my breath, hoping she'd drop the subject. She turned around and leaned against the counter, drying her hands with a dishtowel.

"I'm leaving at three-thirty for Nashville. They're transferring Dad to Sarah Cannon Cancer Center, so I'd have to be there all week. I spoke with Mrs. Vaughn this morning and told her everything about your dad's condition. The schedule's simple enough. Vaughns' from nine until two, Monday, Wednesday, Friday. Be professional and dress nicely." She gave me her "mom" warning look. "Don't go in your sweatpants and Bears shirt, okay?"

"Okay."

"Mrs. Baltic's on Tuesday, and Mr. Smith's house on Thursday. I arranged for separate days so you don't become overwhelmed."

"What about your other houses?"

"Everyone's been amazing. Mrs. Ackerman and the Johnsons offered to pay me even if I can't make it. I hate to accept it, but they insisted. Such kind people."

Tears welled in her eyes. She looked exhausted, and I wasn't sure how long she could do everything on her own. What if she wanted to go back to Illinois? What an awful thought. I didn't want her to resort to such a crazy idea, which meant, I had to stay strong for her.

Moving across the kitchen, I held out my arms. She clung to me as we embraced.

"It's okay, Mom. I can handle the work. Mrs. Vaughn can't be that bad. No worse than Mr. Smith."

She stepped back with a concerned look. "He really bothers you, doesn't he?"

"He's creepy."

"I'm sorry you feel that way. That's why I moved him to Thursday. He meets his sister for breakfast. If you get there by nine, he's usually at the restaurant until eleven or so."

"Okay."

She gently patted my face and then kissed my cheek. "I can't thank you enough."

"It's okay. What do you think will happen with Dad?"

"I honestly don't know. They've done everything they can for him here. If this doesn't help, I guess he comes home."

I narrowed my eyes. "And then what?"

"We take care of him. Well... until, you know."

Her words stole my breath. I couldn't imagine what that situation would feel like.

"Will they let us do that?"

"Of course. People die in the comfort of their homes all the time." Her tone softened like the idea tore her up inside, too. She started to walk away. "I need to start packing."

"Let me help."

We spent the morning together, drinking coffee and chatting. Around noon, she decided to make stuffed green peppers for lunch, so we headed out to the field behind the house.

The sweltering midday sun beat down on us. I stopped at the edge of the field and slumped my shoulders. Weeds. So many weeds. All of our hard work had been taken over by buckhorn and bull thistles, and many of the peppers were already turning red. We needed to start picking soon.

"What are we going to do about the harvest?" I asked.

"I have no idea. I'll let them go if I have to," Mom said as she scanned the field. "Picking five acres isn't a small job. I just can't worry about it right now."

There had to be another way.

"Dad and I worked our butts off last spring," I said. "I'll talk to Mark. There has to be something we can do."

Dad and I had walked the rows for countless hours over the early summer days, and because the peppers are a food product, we couldn't use pesticides or herbicides to combat insects and weeds. Tending to each row, we carried along our pointed hoes, clearing out anything that trespassed on our potential harvest. Staring across the once pristine field, remorse and guilt filled me for neglecting our hard work.

"It is what it is," Mom said.

At three-thirty, Mark helped us pack her bags in the car. We reassured her that we'd be fine. She hugged us goodbye and waved from the car window as she drove away.

I hurried inside and changed clothes, with just enough time to make it to Shiloh by four.

After I parked the truck, I waited for Tyler, watching the cars pass by. Dread filled me as I plotted my day at the estate. I hated the idea of him seeing me as the cleaning lady again. Maybe he would run most of the morning, and I could slip out before he got back. I could hide in the basement most of the day, doing laundry. Maybe I should just tell him. No, that wasn't what I wanted either. What I wanted was to remain as the girl in the little black dress and overpriced heels.

A black Cadillac slowed in front of the truck, bringing me out of my internal banter. It stopped in the middle of the road, then the tinted window rolled down. A square-faced, heavy-set man held up his phone like he was going to take a picture. I glanced in the rearview mirror. There was a monument in the courtyard behind me. He must be taking a photo of that. I looked back at the guy. We made eye contact as a light flashed from his device. A chill through me. Then, he rolled up his window and sped away.

Something caught the corner of my eye. I gasped. Tyler. He was standing outside the truck. I turned off the engine and climbed out.

"You scared me," I said.

"You look good in a truck."

I gave him a quick kiss, forgetting all about the man in the Cadillac.

He took my hand in his and asked, "Do you have to be anywhere?"

"No."

"Let's check out the river then. It's too hot to jog."

We walked across the parking lot to a monument of two cannons. A sign marked the area "The Left Flank." I followed him down a steep slope to the rocky shoreline. Kneeling, I ran my fingers through the cool water as Tyler sat on the ground next to me and rubbed his hand up and down my back.

"How's your dad doing?" he asked.

I sat down and laid my head on his shoulder, staring across the river.

"Not good."

"I'm sorry. You okay?"

"No."

"You feel like talkin' about it?"

"Not so much."

His arm tightened around me and he pressed his head to mine. As if our touch merged into one, I sank into him. Complete. Whole. Fulfilled. No one had ever made me feel like I'd been missing a piece of myself. We stared across the river in silence, listening to the water whoosh to the shore.

"Do you have a heavy load this semester?" I asked.

"Yeah. Sixteen credit hours. I'm not looking forward to it."

"Do you like your classes?"

"They're okay. Mostly advanced business and math."

"You're like physics-and-calculus smart, aren't you?"

"No. Well, yeah, I've taken them. Did you ever mail in your application to the art school?"

"No. It's in the car. I keep forgetting about it."

He recoiled. "Why haven't you sent it?"

"I just said, I keep forgetting. I've been busy."

"You're procrastinating."

"Whatever." I scooted away to look him in the eyes. "I don't know if I can go anyway. I can't just leave Mom and Dad. I have no idea what's going to happen before I graduate."

"No one knows what's going to happen at any given minute—"

"Circumstances, right?" I scoffed. My circumstances sucked, and he knew it.

"Yes. Let me help you."

"Whatever you want. It probably doesn't matter anyway."

He hopped up and held out his hands. I accepted, letting him pull me to my feet.

"Sorry," I said. "I'm not seeing the brighter side of things today."

"I can tell," he said, brushing the back of his fingers over my cheek. "Don't let what's going on make you cynical. You know you can handle all the bullshit that's thrown at you." He kissed my forehead. "Be confident in who you are. You've helped me have more confidence, do that for yourself, too."

"*You* needed more confidence?" I said in a dry tone. "That doesn't seem possible."

"Yeah, well... You've helped me more than you understand." He leaned in and gave me a long kiss.

LIFE HAPPENS ON THE STAIRS

For the next few hours, we strolled by the river, making our way back to the National Cemetery. Wandering past the limestone grave markers, we'd gotten on the subject of how Dad's tumor grew and why it affected his motor skills. Tyler started rattling off about how the brain worked and communicated with the rest of the body; neurons, neurotransmitters, nervous systems, comparing the effects of the tumor to other diseases.

After he concluded his point, I said, "I can barely comprehend everything you just said. You're freaking brilliant."

A cool evening breeze replaced the heat of the day as the sky changed to amber and pink.

Tyler placed his hand on my arm. "Elsie, I have something to tell you. I probably should've said something already. But—"

"Excuse me!" A deep voice echoed through the air.

We looked toward the sound. A stout man, wearing a black uniform, was walking our way.

"Y'all's gonna have to head out for the night," he said. "Park closes at sunset."

Damn. The guy squashed my progress. Tyler waved. "Sorry, sir. We'll get out of here."

The man approached with a proffered hand. Tyler stepped toward him, and they started talking. I followed, pretending to listen, smiling and nodding like I cared, as he rambled on about vandals invading the park.

I shifted my weight from side to side, pressing out fake smiles. I needed to talk to Tyler. What was he getting ready to tell me?

"Well, y'all enjoy the evening," the man finally said, walking away.

"You too, sir," Tyler said, and then he turned to me. "Jeez, he can talk."

"What were you going to tell me back there?"

"Ah." He waved his hand. "It's no big deal."

"It seemed like a big deal."

"It's not. I hate to end the evening, but Mom and Dad are leaving tomorrow. I told them I'd be back early."

"Okay."

"See you in the morning?"

I grinned. "Maybe."

"You'd better be here."

Chapter

13

The next morning, we met at seven and jogged for a couple of miles. He stopped only to give me a kiss, then went on to finish his workout.

As I drove out of the park, I passed the Cadillac I saw the day before. We made eye contact through the windshields. A chill ran over my skin again. Why would he be back at eight-thirty on a Monday morning? Something's not right.

But as I drove toward Savannah, the man in the Caddy became irrelevant as regret overwhelmed me. I should've told Tyler I'd be at their house. If I could make it through the day without getting caught, then I would tell him I'd be there on Wednesday. Avoiding the subject felt right, yesterday. Today, it felt like a total mistake. What in the world was I thinking?

I drove to the gas station off Main Street, hurried to the bathroom, and changed into khakis and a white button up blouse. Minutes later, I pulled into the driveway of the Vaughns'. A black BMW sat where Tyler normally parked. I turned off the ignition and gasped. The truck! Tyler already saw I was driving it.

"Damn it!" I smacked the steering wheel with my palm, then looked in the mirror and took a deep breath. "You can do this," I said to my reflection. "Just relax."

I gathered my nerves and headed toward the house, entering through the garage like Mom said. All I had to do was make it to the secret basement door and disappear in the laundry room.

I quietly stepped in the mudroom. Muffled voices came from the kitchen. I cracked the door open and peeked around the corner.

Tyler's stunning mother walked my way, clutching a cup of coffee. She glanced up.

"Oh. You startled me," she said, and then she looked at her coffee as though I'd interrupted their quiet time together.

"Hi," I whispered.

"Is that Elizabeth?" A long, drawn-out accent resonated from the depths of the kitchen.

I stepped around the corner. The elder Mrs. Vaughn narrowed her eyes, staring me down.

Dark auburn hair, full of layers around her face. Her hands were folded together at her waist, as she waited for me to approach.

I glanced at the floor, then back at her. Floor. Mrs. Vaughn. Floor.

"Yes, ma'am, it's me." My voice trembled. "Please, call me Elsie."

"I prefer Elizabeth," she stated.

I bristled. Mom's words rang through my head, *"Be polite."*

"Yes, ma'am."

"Did Claire tell you the duties of the house?" She raised her brows and stared down her nose. "I hope you're capable of the same excellence she provides."

"Yes. She gave me a schedule and a list."

Footsteps echoed through the foyer. I held my breath. Please don't be Tyler, please...

My heart skipped. A man who looked like a preview of Tyler in twenty years walked our way. He stood over six feet, dark, feathery hair, with the same gentle eyes as his son. He stepped beside the old woman and offered his hand to me. I accepted, returning his firm shake.

"Hello, I'm Gregory. You can call me Greg." He glanced at his mother with pursed lips. "You're Elsie, correct?"

I smiled at his subtle jab at his mother. "Yes, sir. Nice to meet you."

"It's my pleasure. Katherine and I are leaving for Memphis soon, but I'm glad I had a chance to say hello—"

"Oh, yes," Mrs. Vaughn interjected. "Katherine is my daughter-in-law. This is my son, Gregory. You may or may not see Tyler, my grandson. He's in and out all day. Where *is* Tyler?"

"He's out for a run," Greg answered, walking away.

"I reckon he needs to train," Mrs. Vaughn said. "Okay, good enough. You should tend to your duties. I'm sure your mother instructed you well enough for you to figure it out."

"Yes, ma'am," I said, stepping around her to go to the foyer.

Before I'd made it out of the kitchen, she piped up again.

"Oh, Elizabeth!" she practically sang my name. "Don't forget, the linens need to be stripped off the beds and pressed before y'all leave."

"Yes, ma'am."

I hurried to the basement and grabbed a laundry basket, then hustled back upstairs to gather the sheets. Starting in the guest room, I tugged and pulled as fast as I could, throwing the pillows back on the bare mattress. I wanted to run down the hallway, but instead, I clutched the basket tight, and quickly walked to Mrs. Vaughn's bedroom. After stripping her bed, Tyler's room was next.

I glanced inside. His room was almost as big as Mrs. Vaughn's. Soft gray walls, a king-sized bed nestled under a line of windows spilling warm sunlight throughout the space. I slowly stepped in. To the left were French doors leading out to a balcony. Built-in walnut bookshelves filled the wall to my right. On the other side of the room, a door stood open to a bathroom.

Next to his bed were a stack of books. The top one was titled *Shiloh*, by Shelby Foote. On the floor next to them, a textbook lay open to a page full of math equations. I looked closer. Calculus III. Wincing, I stepped back. Way too many numbers for a girl who loved art.

Turning to his bed, I yanked the navy comforter back. A hint of his woody scent blew through the air. I wanted to dive face first into his pillows, but knew I was crazy to even consider it. So, I quickly finished, and shoved the sheets in the basket.

As I pivoted to leave, I spotted a brown leather journal on the nightstand. It would be so wrong to look. Maybe it was another history book. I bit my lip. Just a peek wouldn't hurt. Glancing out the door, no one was in the hallway. I took two steps backwards, angling myself to see the doorway and the book. I reached out my shaking hand and pulled back a chunk of pages. Words written in precise blue print filled the page.

I used to go out to Shiloh to get away. To feel the history, not just study it. I wanted to be a part of the scene as I recounted the war strategies, but Elsie has changed everything. When she leaves, I feel haunted by her presence, not just the ghosts from the past. I've forgotten why I love the place. I only want to be there with her.

Smack! I slammed the book shut, heart pounding, I hurried out of the room.

Oh my gosh, I shouldn't have read that. Haunted by her presence... I only want to be there with her... she's changed everything. I rushed down the stairs, lost in my thoughts. When I stepped on the main floor, Greg walked out of the kitchen.

"Elsie," he said. "I want to apologize for my mother. She's, well... She thinks she's the only one with manners when all along she's the rudest person in the room. Thank you for filling in for your mother. Life is much smoother around here if we don't rock Mom's boat." He took a sip from his coffee cup. "I'm sorry to hear about your dad, by the way. I hope he gets well soon."

I stood there in awe of how much he reminded me of Tyler – the gentle look in his dark eyes, his subtle nod of compassion.

"Thank you, Mr. Vaughn. It's okay."

"Please, call me Greg. Mr. Vaughn was my dad's name." He smiled. "Relax. The old bird will leave you alone. She's too busy getting her hair and nails redone to notice anything else." He chuckled and stepped away. "Have a good day."

"Same to you," I said, walking to the basement door.

When I pushed on the panel, it wouldn't open. I tried

again. It still didn't budge. Katherine exited the kitchen. I pushed again. Nothing. She moved to my side and smacked the upper corner with her palm.

Click. It opened.

"It sticks," she said, and then she turned and walked away like nothing had happened.

Okay... that was weird.

"Thank you," I called out.

I made my way to the laundry room and stayed there all day. The workstation was organized with every need right at my fingertips. I was content and comfortable. No one came down to talk or check on me – it was as if I wasn't even there. After a few hours, I found a routine, dancing around the room, folding clothes as I sang.

Around one-thirty, the laundry was folded and ready to go. I started up the basement stairs and peered into the foyer. All looked clear. Dashing out, I trotted up the staircase and slipped in the guest room. I made the bed, then scurried down the hall toward Mrs. Vaughn's room. Her huge mattress took twice as long to make. I pulled the sheet tight on one side, crossed to the other, and pulled again. I moved to the end and yanked. Back and forth, I tugged and jerked until the sheets were smooth. Panting, I glanced at the clock. Two-eleven! I was supposed to leave at two, but all I had left to do was make Tyler's bed.

This time, when I got to his door, it was shut. I froze. I had to knock. What if he answered? I lifted my trembling hand.

Tap. Tap. Tap. No answer. *Tap.* Nothing. I quietly pushed it open and stepped inside. Water was running, but I couldn't place where it was coming from. I crossed the room to the French doors and stepped out on the balcony. Water spilled over an obelisk fountain at the center of the patio. Inhaling the spicy air from the mimosa trees, I walked back inside.

His journal caught my eye again. Guilt stabbed me for invading his privacy. Who does something like that? Mom's first rule was to keep my nose out of other people's business. She never snooped, and if she did see something personal, she'd take it to her grave. I began tucking the fitted sheet at each corner of the bed, moving from side to side to smooth out the fabric.

A door clicked. I glanced up. The bedroom door stood open but no one was in the hall.

The bathroom. I gasped and spun around.

Tyler stepped out, wearing only a white towel wrapped low around his waist, face partially covered as he dried his hair with another towel. He had no idea I was standing there.

I pressed my hand to my mouth. I was a complete idiot! The water was from the shower.

He looked up. Shock erupted all over his face, and he took a step back.

"Well, this is a nice surprise," he said with a big smile when he recovered.

"Oh, my gosh," my words muffled behind my hand. "I'm so sorry."

His smooth skin and muscular chest led to cut abs that rippled down to defined hipbones, hinting at other unknown places. Golden from head to toe, the only tan line was on his left wrist where he wore his watch. His bicep bulged, as he held the towel to his hair with an amused grin.

I darted toward the door, and hurried down the hallway.

"Hey, you haven't finished making my bed," he called out.

I turned around and gave him a joking glare. If anyone else had said that to me, I would've screamed, "Bite my ass."

But he was so adorably sexy, leaning out the door, all I could do was laugh.

He blew me a kiss. My face burned with embarrassment, and I bolted down the stairs.

Minutes later, I flopped against the washing machine, covering my ridiculous smile with my hands. He was flawless. Lean and muscular, not an ounce of fat on him. My body ached just remembering. Seriously, it should be illegal to be that fine.

After a few minutes, I realized I was giggling to myself in an empty room. I had to get out of the house before Tyler came downstairs. I'd explain everything to him later. Tiptoeing back upstairs, I checked the foyer again. All was clear, so I headed through the kitchen, into the mudroom, then let out a long sigh of relief as I stepped into the garage.

"I knew you'd try to sneak out," Tyler said from across the room.

I gasped. "Tyler, you keep scaring the crap out of me!"

He was leaning against the hood of his car, barefooted, dressed in dark jeans and a black T-shirt with white writing that read, *Running takes balls. Other sports just play with them.*

"Me?" his voice cracked. "You're damn lucky I had a towel on."

I laughed, blood rushing to my cheeks as I walked toward him. Arms crossed, he looked at me. I could tell by the heaviness in his eyes that he was upset with me.

"Why didn't you tell me you were working here today?"

"I'm sorry. I didn't want to talk about it. I was hoping you wouldn't see me."

"You're the one that got the eyeful." He chuckled. "That'll teach you."

I attempted to sound prissy. "I'm working. Mom insisted

I be professional and keep my mouth shut. I've achieved my goals." I bowed with a curtsy. He lightened up and smiled. "I met your parents. Well, kind of. Your dad's really nice. All your mom said to me was that I startled her, and 'It sticks.'"

"What sticks?"

"The basement door."

"Oh, yeah, it does stick," he said. "Dad told me Nana was rude to you."

"You knew I was here?"

"Yeah. I saw the truck when I pulled in the driveway, that pretty much gave you away. But when I came inside, Dad told me Claire's daughter was here, and that Nana was in one of her moods when she talked to you. Just ignore her. She's a pompous ass. She'll come rolling in here soon, insisting I eat her diet food for dinner. You can't imagine how painful the evenings are. Every year Dad says, 'This is the last summer, son,'" Tyler mocked. "I don't know. I'll turn twenty in April. It's just a matter of time, I guess."

"Your dad even made a comment about how no one wants to rock her boat."

"Yeah, that's one way of putting it. We just try to keep her happy."

"Why? Because of the money?"

"No... Dad has his own money. It's because she'll make his life hell. He's the baby of the bunch. Mom and I have to endure the ride."

"I can understand that, she *is* his mom. You said you'll turn twenty in April. April what?"

"Twenty-fifth. I'm so fuckin' ready to move on. So, what did you think of Dad?"

"I think you're his clone."

He smiled. "Yeah, maybe. He's pretty cool. It irritates me

that he insists I come here, but he has my back for the most part."

"He has kind eyes like yours."

Tyler bashfully looked me over. Pushing off the car, he grabbed my waist and pressed our bodies close.

"You even make cleaning house look good," he said, leaning in to kiss me.

Just as his lips touched mine, the motor to the garage door hummed to life. I jumped back.

"Damn it," he said, stepping away.

"I have to go." I hurried to the side door, then I heard, "Bye... " as I slipped outside.

I pressed my body against the bricks. Mrs. Vaughn's car drove off and the garage door hummed to life again. I waited. The humming stopped. Hurrying across the side yard, I climbed into the truck and backed out.

On the way home, I relaxed for the first time all day. Tyler seemed irritated with his grandmother more than with me. Maybe I had pissed him off. I couldn't be sure. He'd given me so many mixed signals. Something weighed on him... something he wouldn't admit. Hopefully, he wasn't mad. It'd be my luck to screw everything up because of my stupid pride.

As I drove around the curve to our house, my phone rang in my pocket.

I flipped it open. "Hello?"

"Hi," Mom said. "How did it go today?"

"Um, I think okay."

"You think?"

"Yeah, it was fine." I pulled into the driveway and parked. "I spent most of the day in the basement doing laundry. I had to wash all the sheets. How's Dad?"

"He's having a pretty good day. How did Mildred treat you?"

"Mildred?" I repeated. "That's her first name? Oh, it's so awful, it fits perfectly!"

"Did you behave?"

"Of course. It really wasn't that bad. She was cold and a little rude. Insisted on calling me 'Elizabeth.' I met Ty—Greg and Katherine. He was nice. She's beautiful but a little odd."

"Greg seems pleasant. I haven't met his wife, though. Did you get the laundry all done? What's this about sheets?"

"She wanted them stripped and washed. I did the upstairs bedrooms."

"Really?" Mom scoffed. "Okay."

"What?" Then I mocked Mrs. Vaughn's drawn-out accent. "She told me not to forget."

"Yeah, well, she doesn't know squat. I did that before I left. She's just messing with you. It's only for the week, sweetie. We should be home by Saturday."

"Don't worry, it'll all be here when you get back. Mildred and her empire."

We talked for a little longer, then said I love you and hung up.

When I stepped inside the house, I heard Mark rustling around in his room, cussing to himself. His door flew open, hitting the wall with a loud smack. He stomped out and looked at me, red-faced and fuming, and then he headed down the hall.

What the hell now?

The bathroom door slammed, reverberating through the house.

Cardinal rule: No busting in on someone in the bathroom.

"What's going on?" I demanded from the hallway.

"I can't find my damn Social Security card," Mark shouted. "I need it for an interview."

"You're mad over a Social Security card?" I crossed my arms. "I'm not buying it."

Mark was well known for his tantrums. They usually weren't directed at anyone in particular. They were meant for the invisible force that tried to ruin his life by sabotaging everything he went after. He'd curse the sky, flailing his fists while stomping his feet. From afar, the spectacle was quite entertaining, but when too close, he looked like a madman arguing with imaginary friends. He tried to explain it to me once, claiming he felt like every path he chose wound to a dead end. I somewhat understood what he meant, but his underlying pain was the red thread woven through his tapestry of life. The rebellion, the alcohol, the drugs, his response to Dad's illness – it all stemmed back to his inability to control his emotions.

"What the hell happened, Mark? I know you're not mad about your card."

"Have you talked to Mom?"

"Yeah, I just got off the phone with her."

"Did she tell you about Dad?"

"She'll know more on Wednesday, she said. Will you open the door?" I wiggled the knob. It twisted, but I didn't push it open. "Come out here, for crying out loud. What's going on?"

Mark jerked the door open. His eyes were red and swollen.

"There's nothing else that can be done. They're sending Dad home to die."

I winced. "Why didn't she tell me?"

"She's probably afraid you'll fucking run."

"Would you freaking drop it, already?" I snapped back, and then fear struck me like a blast of cold air. "How are we going to take care of him?"

"Hell if I know. I feel like an asshole for being pissed about it, but I thought we were going to take him back to Illinois."

"Why? That's the last place he wants to be."

"How else are we going to do it? We're broke, and the crops are going to rot in the field. We'll never get them harvested."

"We can at least try. Jeez, Mark, it isn't brain surgery." I cringed. "Excuse the pun. But seriously, all we have to do is start picking."

I needed his help. If he'd just walk the fields with me, we could save the crops.

He let out a long sigh. "I guess. God... I hate working crops in this shitty red dirt. I swear I'll never eat another pepper again in my life."

"I know, right? I'm so sick of them, too." I laughed. "Let's try. Help me. Dad and I had worked like crazy, and if we don't do something, Mom's going to let them go. It'll all go to waste."

Mark hated farming, even in the hundred-thousand-dollar John Deere tractors Grandpa owned. Mark didn't want anything to do with it. All we had was a small scoop tractor that Dad used to plant the field, but as far as harvesting was concerned, we were back to the days of hand picking. It would take us weeks with only the two of us, but if we could take some of the peppers to the processing plant, then at least all of our work wouldn't be in vain.

"You're right. We can get some of it done," he said. "I still need this other job, though. Do you know where Mom keeps all the legal stuff?"

I pointed toward the dining room. "In the hutch."

"Cool, thanks."

My phone alerted me to a text. I pulled it out of my pocket.

Tyler: Meet me at 6 instead of 7

Me: Is the sun even up at that time?

Tyler: Yes ☺

Me: Ok

Mark walked through the living room and out the front door. I went to the kitchen, made ramen noodles, and sat at the table to eat.

Around nine, exhausted and devoid of any inspiration to draw, I crawled in bed. Tyler hadn't called like he usually did. I double-checked my phone just to make sure, and set it on the nightstand. Too tired to worry about it, I closed my eyes.

A few hours later, I woke to rustling sounds in the kitchen. The red numbers on my clock glowed, twelve forty-two. I stepped out of my room.

Mark staggered toward the refrigerator. He looked at me with bloodshot eyes, swayed a little, and then grabbed the counter for balance. No. Freaking. Way.

"Are you drunk?" I snapped.

"What's it to you?" he slurred back.

"Great, Mark. This is your plan, drink it all away?"

"For... the... " He hiccupped. "Moment."

"Where's the truck?"

"I think," he squinted like he was trying really hard. "I think... I left it outside."

He swayed backwards, taking a step to steady himself. I hurried to the living room window. He'd parked in the grass at an angle in the front yard.

"Mark, are you crazy?" I yelled through the house. "It's so stupid to drink and drive!"

"Yeah, well," he shouted back, "so are you."

Ignoring his childish taunt, I went to the bathroom, fuming on the inside.

That self-indulgent bastard. Just what I needed, one more thing to worry about.

On my way back to bed, I spotted the truck keys on the counter. Quietly scooping them up, I kept them with me so he couldn't leave again.

Chapter

14

I woke to a text at five-fifteen.

Tyler: Meet me at the Indian mounds

Sitting up, I rubbed my eyes. The Indian Mounds? Oh yeah, they're in the park.

Me: Ok

Forty-five minutes later, I climbed out of the truck, inhaling the crisp, cypress air. Rounded, green mounds preserved by the National Park were shaded by the towering pine trees. Tyler had told me the Indian Mounds were found in the late 1800s, dating back almost 800 years. The brilliant craftsmanship of the Native Americans had even withstood the war.

LIFE HAPPENS ON THE STAIRS

Tyler stood outside his car, staring across the grass hills. He gave me a weak smile when I stepped beside him.

"Everything okay?" I asked.

"Yeah. I didn't sleep much last night. You ready?"

"Sure."

We walked to the road and started jogging at an easy pace. After a few hundred yards, he picked up his speed. I pushed my stride to keep up. Elbow to elbow, I glanced at him. Sweat rolled down his face, and his shirt was already soaked. A few seconds later, he fell back to slow us down. Relieved, I stayed with him, refocusing on the rhythm of us jogging as one.

Suddenly, the sound of his pounding footsteps stopped. I looked over my shoulder. He was bent over with his hands on his knees, gasping for air. I turned around in the middle of the road. What the hell? He never burned out.

"Are you okay?" I shouted.

He took a few more breaths. "Do you trust me?"

"What do you mean?"

"Do you trust me?" he said, emphasizing the words this time.

"Of course, I trust you. I run in the woods alone with you." I chuckled. "You could've killed me a long time ago."

He stood straight and stared me down. Clearly, he hadn't found my joke funny.

"You met me here, yesterday. No, wait." He waved his hands as if he was erasing the words. "First, you spend Sunday evening with me, then you came out here the next morning, and not once did you say a word about having to clean at the house. Do. You. Trust me?"

"I thought you understood. Why are you so mad?"

"I'm not mad. I'm confused, a little freaked out, and now

I'm starting to doubt. I'm not this fucking emotional," he insisted. "You're so damn guarded, Elsie. I need to know that you trust me, that you'll tell me when you have to do shitty work, and you won't dodge me."

I took a step back. "You're angry because I didn't want to tell you how embarrassed I am that I washed and pressed your sheets yesterday, or folded your clothes? That I hate admitting that I have to do my mom's job while she's gone?"

"Why is that so embarrassing?"

I gaped at him like he was crazy. Did I really have to explain it?

"Whatever," I said, then a surge of anger welled inside. "Don't question if I trust you. I don't know shit about you outside this park or your grandmother's house. I have nothing to offer you. So, I have to wonder, Tyler, why are you here, wasting your time with me?"

He cringed. "You seriously believe that?"

"Yes. I do. You're freaking gorgeous, and you have everything going for you. So, why are you messing around with me? I'm just the housekeeper's daughter."

"Elsie." He ran his hands through his hair like he always did when he had a rush of emotion. "I'm not messing around. And not a second of my time has been wasted when I'm with you. I can't read. I can't sleep. I can't even comprehend how fucked up I feel. Every morning, I can't wait to see you, and I hate it when you have to leave. You have no idea the guy you see is the man I want to be. You do that, not me. Everything I know about myself is changing, and it's freaking me out. No one has ever made me feel this way. And I'm trying like hell to be a gentleman, but my thoughts are killing me." He took a sharp breath. "You have no idea... But the worst part is, we both know our time is running out."

I stood there, speechless, trying to process his confession. His words made my head spin.

"Are you willing to be my girl, and can we trust each other?" he asked, firmly. "Because if we don't trust each other, then it's pointless for us to be together. I could care less about anything else but the answer to those two questions."

Be his girl? He wasn't playing around.

"Tyler. I want to be your girl more than anything, and honestly, I trust you with my life."

"Okay, good," he said, but he still wasn't satisfied. "I have to be sure that no matter what happens, no matter who tries to tell us we're wrong, you and I know we're together. This is between us. It doesn't matter what Nana, your mom, or anyone else thinks." Stepping forward, he touched my face, then pressed his forehead to mine. "I've fallen... " He squeezed his eyes shut for a moment, like he had to force himself to stop, then he breathed out, "Are you with me?"

"Yes. I'm with you."

Brushing his cheek against mine, he found my lips with his. Slow and tender, I sank into his embrace. Fallen? Yes. I'd completely fallen, too.

After he let me go, his sour mood immediately dissipated. Taking my hand in his, we walked toward the parking lot.

"Why are you so afraid that I don't trust you?" I asked.

"I'm not afraid. It just... hurt. I'm not used to feeling that way."

"I'm sorry. I didn't mean to do that. This week really sucks for me. I'm at your house Wednesday and Friday, another house today, and then Smith's on Thursday." I let my head fall back, looking up at the sky. "I can't stand it. I keep telling myself it's only for a little while."

"It's not forever." He squeezed my hand. "Where are

your parents? You never told me."

"They transferred Dad to Nashville."

"Really?" he sounded optimistic.

"They're sending him home. I guess there's nothing else they can do."

"Oh, I'm sorry. Are you okay?"

"Not really. Especially, when I came home yesterday, Mark was throwing one of his fits. I tried to help him calm down, but then he goes out and gets drunk last night."

"What a dumbass. But what do you mean, he threw a fit?"

"Everyone in my family deals with stress in their own way. Mark gets mad. Mom shuts down. I run. It's been a weird web of emotions in our house these past few years."

"Do you still think about running?"

"Not really. Well, sometimes. But jogging with you has helped."

"Where do you go?"

"I used to go to the barn and hide in the hayloft, until Dad figured out my spot. But... I still have one place no one knows about."

He grinned. "Where is it?"

"No, way. I'm not telling."

"If you don't think about it anymore, what does it matter?"

"It matters to me. I have to have a place no one else knows about." "I can relate, but how can you keep everything bottled up?"

"I don't know. How do you deal with everything?"

He narrowed his eyes at my challenge. "I'll tell you, but only if you tell me."

"You go first."

"No way! I refuse to let you change the subject. Focus, my

beautiful girl."

"All right, all right. Promise, you won't cheat?"

"Darling, I don't cheat," he said, with a cocky grin and mischievous eyes. "I don't need to cheat."

"Ugh. Why do you have to look at me like that? Okay, let me get my mind straight." I took a deep breath. "You have to take this to your grave, okay?"

"I promise, if you promise to never run and hide again."

"Fine, I promise. There's an old, abandoned house by the curve up the road from us. You can get inside from the back door. I like the Victorian couch in the living room. I'll just sit there until I feel better. But I don't want to be that person anymore. After my accident, I swore I wouldn't run again, and I haven't. But like I said, jogging with you helps. Okay, I told you. Now I can never go back there, so the information is useless. Your turn."

Letting out a low growl, he stared forward. "Besides running, I write."

A pang of guilt stabbed my gut. I looked up at the sky. Lying to Mom, I had exceeded my dishonesty quota. I couldn't hold another one, especially to Tyler.

"I guess, I kinda knew that already," I said. "You have a journal by your bed."

"Yes, I do." He glanced at me out of the corner of his eye. "Have you looked?"

"Um, well—"

He gasped. "You have!"

He pushed his arms in a V formation, and started skipping backwards in front of me.

"That's a violation," he shouted. "You are in violation of cleaning law!"

I laughed. "I'm so sorry. I couldn't resist. It was only a

glance."

He froze in the middle of the road and lowered his arms. "Seriously, you really looked? What did you read?"

"Only like... one sentence." I fluttered my eyes. "Something about a girl haunting you. I have to wonder who else you bring out here. I'm not very ghostly."

He let out a relieved sigh and stepped toward me. "It's all you, Elise." Then he leaned down and kissed me.

I drew back. "You're not mad?"

"No. I don't have anything to hide, not in that journal anyway."

"Damn, I should've read more."

By the time we made it to the parking lot, I had to leave for Mrs. Baltic's. After several playful attempts to get away from him, he gave me a long kiss goodbye, then let me go. Driving out of the park, I realized that I'd never understood what yearning for someone felt like. For whatever reason, I thought of my parents.

Chapter

15

When I pulled into Mrs. Baltic's drive, the door wasn't opened by a happy, plump lady in her pink robe. I walked up the steps and knocked. No answer. I wiggled the knob. Locked. I stood there confused for a second, with a bad feeling, so I walked around to the back door. The knob turned without a problem, and I stepped inside the kitchen.

A low moan came from the belly of the house.

"Mrs. Baltic?" I called out.

Another moan. I froze. The hairs on my arms stood on end. I looked around the corner down the long hallway. All the bedroom doors were open.

Another moan came from the end of the hall.

"Mrs. Baltic? It's Elsie." I began to shake, walking toward her room. "Are you okay?"

I stopped outside her door and peeked inside. She was lying in the middle of her bed, curled in a fetal position. Panic surged through me and I dashed to her side. She tried to look up but couldn't even raise her head.

"Oh my gosh, Mrs. Baltic!"

She didn't react to my overreaction, which freaked me out even more. I grabbed my phone and dialed emergency, reciting her name and address as fast as I could. I didn't know what to do after I hung up.

I asked her what was wrong. She moaned. I asked if she wanted water, or a blanket, or anything. A scarier moan. I jogged down the hall to the front door and pulled it open, listening for the sirens over my pounding heart. Finally, I sighed with relief when I caught the faint sound of an ambulance. I ran back to Mrs. Baltic's room. She was rocking back and forth, groaning. Feeling faint, I grabbed the doorjamb to keep myself upright. The next moan sent me running down the hall again. Loud sirens echoed outside as the ambulance pulled up in front of the house. A fire engine parked behind it, then three men stepped out of each vehicle. Overwhelmed at the sight of them, I backed away from the door.

A firefighter approached the screen. I waved him inside.

"Where's the emergency, miss?" he asked.

"Down the hall." I pointed. "The last bedroom on the right."

Dizzy and stunned, I flopped down on the couch, relieved someone could help the poor woman.

A slender, young woman with brown hair pulled in a low ponytail walked my way. "Are you okay, Miss?" she asked, kneeling beside me.

I nodded.

"Is she a relative of yours?"

"No, I'm the housekeeper's daughter. I'm cleaning for my mom." Tears rolled down my cheek. "Is she okay? It sounded bad."

"She'll be all right." She patted my knee and stood. "If you're willing, since there's no one else here, will you follow us to the hospital? It'll be helpful if someone could speak to the hospital staff about the incident."

"Incident?" I flinched. "She was like this when I got here."

"I understand." She smiled. "It's not like that. It's only so they have someone to reference until we can get a family member here, okay?"

"Yes, of course."

She turned and walked toward the bedroom. I pulled out my phone and called Mom.

"Hi, how's it going?" she answered.

"Oh, Mom!"

"What's wrong? Are you okay?"

"It's Mrs. Baltic." I sniffled. "The ambulance is here. It's awful! She's in so much pain."

"Take a deep breath." She waited a few seconds. "Now, tell me what happened."

I explained everything, and then I asked, "Who do I call?"

"Give me a minute, I'll call her sister. Go ahead and go to the hospital."

"Okay. Let me know."

"I will. You'll have to come back later to clean."

"Are you serious?" I wanted to scream at her, but I kept my cool.

"Elsie, she's going to need all the help she can get. Please, let me know what you find out. I hope she's okay."

"Thanks, don't worry. I'm fine."

She didn't get it. I was horrified and wanted to go home.

"You did great. I'm proud of you. Please don't get upset about the job. People rely on us. Okay, I'm gonna go. I need to call Betsy."

"Call me tonight, please. I need to talk to you."

"I'll try," she said. "Love you."

"Yeah." I flipped the phone shut, instantly feeling guilty for being a brat.

I scanned the house to see how bad it was. The place wasn't filthy, but I worried what the bathrooms looked like. The paramedics came down the hall, pushing her on a gurney.

"We're heading to HMC. Will you follow?" the female paramedic asked.

"Yes. I called my mom, she's going to call Mrs. Baltic's sister."

"Great. Thanks for your help."

"Is she okay?"

"Yes, they have her sedated. We'll know more when we get her to the ER."

"Thank you," I said, then a wave of exhaustion flooded me.

Not another ER stint. I'll be there for hours.

When I arrived at the emergency room, I went straight to the counter. A girl pointed me to a lobby full of chairs. I found a cold seat and tried to relax. Fifteen minutes later, a nurse came out and asked questions about Mrs. Baltic's condition when I found her. The nurse took my name and told me it was a good thing I showed up at the house because Mrs. Baltic's appendix was on the verge of rupturing.

I pulled out my phone to text Tyler but a call interrupted me.

"Betsy's on her way," Mom said. "Now Elsie, I hate to tell you this, but she's in Chattanooga. It's going to be a while."

"Moooomm," I whined. "I don't want to sit here for hours."

"Wait until she gets there, then run back, and at least scrub the bathrooms. I'm sure they need it. Make sure the kitchen's wiped down, too. She'd want that done. Have they told you what's wrong yet?"

"Kind of." I forced myself to sound kind. "Something about an appendix."

"Oh, wow. Good thing you found her."

"That almost sounded like a compliment."

"It is. " She sighed. "You did well, sweetie."

"Mm... "

"I have to go. I'll call you tonight, okay?"

"Yep."

I slapped the phone shut. Nurturing people wasn't my gig. It was Mom's.

I texted Tyler.

Me: I'm stuck at hospital what r you doing?

It took a few minutes before my phone vibrated in my hand.

Tyler: Is it your dad? Where are you?

Me: HMC. The lady I clean for is sick. Called ambulance.

Tyler: Why are you there?

Me: Waiting for her sister.

Tyler: Sit tight.

Me: What?

He didn't text back.

I sat there for thirty minutes, staring... watching... bored. Slouching in the corner of the chair, I surrendered and closed my eyes. Over the next few minutes, I sensed twenty people walk by, but then the air shifted, and Tyler's woody scent drifted my way.

I opened an eye.

"Thought you could use some company," he said, settling into the seat beside mine.

"It's about time," I whispered. "I'm going crazy here."

"Trouble seems to find you everywhere you go."

"I have to get your attention somehow."

"That, you have... " he said, relaxing back in the chair. "So, now what?"

"Mom wants me to wait for Mrs. Baltic's sister. It could be a while." I laid my head back, and stretched out my arms. Tyler's warm touch started at my elbow, running all the way down to my hand, lacing our fingers together. "Thank you for coming. You didn't have to."

"What? And miss a chance to sit in a hospital?" He waved his other hand. "I do this all the time. I love spending my afternoons here."

I laughed, and for the next hour, we joked about the outlandish clothes people wore. But after two hours, time slowed to a crawl. Tyler didn't seem to notice, Mr. Cool and Collected. I fidgeted in my seat, about to come unglued.

He tossed down a magazine and smiled. "Are you okay?"

"No. I'm ready to get the hell out of here."

"She can't be too much longer."

"I hope not. Mom didn't let me off the hook, either. I still have to clean."

His eyes darted to mine. "That almost sounded like you were whining. Your mom just wants you to have the same work ethic as she does."

"I was not whining," I said, trying not to smile.

"I said, 'almost.' Want some help?"

I recoiled. "No. I'd never ask you to do that."

"You didn't."

"Okay, well, that's nice of you and all, but it shouldn't take me long."

"Fine. Your loss. I have mad skills with a dust rag."

"Yeah, right." I laughed.

An elderly couple approached the front desk. We watched them talk to the receptionist for a few moments, then Tyler looked at me.

"Will you have to take care of your dad?"

"I don't know. All I know is what Mark said."

"How long? I mean... " He shook his head. "I guess you wouldn't know that. Will you have a nurse to help out?"

"I have no idea. If not, we'll just have to get through it." I shrugged. "All of it scares me, and then I feel guilty. On top of everything, we have five acres of peppers to harvest. Mark and I plan on picking some, but that's a lot to do with only two people."

"Yeah, it is. You have some kind of machinery, right?"

"Not at all. We have to handpick."

He coughed. "Are you serious? That's insane."

"I know. We've done it since I was thirteen, just the four of us. Of course, Dad did more than the rest of us combined, so it seems impossible to do it with only Mark and me."

"You only need two more people?"

"No, I need two days and fifty people. Then it wouldn't be a nightmare. With the four of us, it took at least two weeks. There's no way we can get them out before they rot."

"I can help."

"You've completely lost your mind. The work sucks."

"Why do people think I can't handle physical labor?" His voice cracked. "Jeez. I run over twenty miles a day in the blazing hot sun. I can handle picking a few peppers."

I chuckled at his comment. He could handle the work, but who would sign up for something like that if they didn't have to? But two more hands always made a difference. If we could get an early start on harvest, and a full load delivered to the processing plant, the money would really help Mom.

"Thank you," I said. "Let me see what's ready to pick. Most of the crop won't come on until after we start school, but anything helps."

"Well, I have ten days until I have to leave. I'm sure we can do something."

"You have no idea how much I appreciate that."

He nodded with a smile. I leaned forward, letting out a sigh.

"If I could have one wish," I said, rubbing the tension in my forehead, "it would be that everything would go back to the way it was. I'd even welcome the old Mark who loved to make our lives hell, just to have Dad back."

"Elsie." Tyler leaned forward so he could look me in the eyes. "I believe you were given more character and strength than the average person. I don't know what's going to happen, but I do know you're a tenacious girl who'll persevere. You just need to believe that, too."

His words took my breath away. I was not feeling strong and tenacious at all.

"How will I ever get through this when you leave?" I whispered.

The whole world disappeared around us as we stared into each other's eyes. Then, he leaned in with a shy smile and kissed me like no one else existed.

An hour later, the spitting image of Mrs. Baltic hurried into the waiting room. She scanned the seats, wild-eyed and pan-icked-looking. I stood to get her attention. She waved and scurried my way.

"Are you Elsie?" she asked with a high-pitched Southern drawl.

"Yes, ma'am. Nice to meet you." I offered my hand. She placed her floppy, soft fingers in mine.

"Yes, you too," she said. "Do you know anything about Betty?"

Betsy and Betty? That had to be confusing growing up.

I squinted at her. "Are you twins?"

"Yes, yes, miss, since birth. Now, do you know where I can find her?"

"Sure, follow that red line on the floor." I pointed over her shoulder. "It will lead you back to the nurses. They wouldn't allow me back there since I'm not her kin."

"Oh, thank you," she said, reaching out to give me a hug. She stepped back and grabbed my hand. "Now, your momma told me all about what's going on. You take that and keep it for your troubles. It's mighty nice of you to sit here like this waiting for me."

I looked at what she'd left in my hand. A hundred-dollar bill.

"Oh no, Mrs.—Betsy, this isn't necessary."

I tried to hand it back. She shook her head once, turned, and followed the red line through the steel doors.

"Thank you," I said, too late.

Tyler stepped behind me and put his hands on my shoulders. "What was that about?"

I flashed the bill at him. "She gave me a hundred bucks."

"That's cool," he said. "Let's get out of here."

Chapter

16

Tyler wanted to follow me to Mrs. Baltic's house. Thankfully, I had talked him out of it. I appreciated the offer, but taking him along would've only distracted me.

When I got there, I couldn't even bring myself to do the short-list Mom gave me. But the bathrooms were a wreck, and Mrs. Baltic deserved to come home to a house cleaner than when she left.

Three hours later, I was backing out of the driveway, numb and exhausted. I rolled down the window and headed west toward home.

The sun breached the canopy of the trees, casting red, yellow, and orange across the sky. A barge tinted in the warm hues of the evening chugged down the placid Tennessee River. The fresh air felt cool on my sticky skin, and I breathed in the earthy smell of the water. It'd been a long day, but I felt good. Mom would be proud that I'd finished the job.

Later that night, a text arrived.

Tyler: Meet in the morning?

Me: Of course.

Tyler: Wanna pick a peck of pimentoed peppers?

Me: LMAO you've lost your mind.

Tyler: Seriously. I'll be there at six. What' cha think?

Me: I'm not going to refuse.

Tyler: Good. I'll see you then.

Me: I wouldn't dress in your usual clothing.

Tyler: I can handle it...

Me: The work isn't exactly fun.

Tyler: We'll make it fun.

Me: Once again you've lost your mind.

Tyler: Once again, I'll see you at six. Get some rest. You deserve it.

Me: :)

At six sharp the next morning, Tyler pulled into the driveway. I met him outside in my favorite worn-out Levi jeans and Bears T-shirt. He stepped out of the car in dark blue designer jeans and a navy Under Armour shirt.

"That isn't exactly dressing for field work," I said.

He shook his head. "Well, good morning to you, too. Is there a dress code?"

"No." I chuckled and waved my hand. "Follow me."

I led him behind the house, then down the steep hill toward our whitewashed barn. When we stepped inside, the dry scent of red dirt and hay filled the air. He grabbed my wrist, pulled me to him, then pressed his forehead to mine.

"You haven't given me a kiss," he said.

I laid a long one on his lips and pulled away. "Better?"

"It definitely gives me more incentive to work."

His willingness to come along on my rollercoaster ride was almost too much to handle. Don't get sappy. Suck it up. He doesn't want praise. He just wants to help.

I crossed the wooden plank floor and grabbed two canvas bags off of a hook on the wall, then handed one to Tyler.

"Here's an apple bag for you."

He chuckled. "I thought we were picking peppers."

"Luckily, apple bags will hold anything you put inside them."

"True."

"I'll drive the tractor to the field so we can empty our bags in the scoop as we go."

He pointed at the scoop tractor parked at the far end of the barn.

"You're going to drive that?"

"Yes. If you can, I'll be happy to let you."

"Um, no. Feel free to show me how it's done."

"My pleasure, city boy."

"That's nice. Insult the help before we get started."

I grinned over my shoulder. "You can handle it, right?"

I grabbed the handle to the barn door and pulled the heavy wooden wall open. Sunlight spilled onto the floor, dust billowing in my face. I waved my hand in the air so I could breathe, and climbed up on the tractor seat.

"You look damn good up there," Tyler said.

"You think?" I loved it when he said things like that. "Don't get used it. I'm done farming after this. I'm thinkin' the city will fit me pretty well, too."

I turned the ignition and she fired up without a cough. Running the tractor wasn't that big of a deal. It drove just like a car. Nevertheless, I was proud that Dad had taught me. Tyler trotted over, hopped up the step, and plopped down on the fender next to me.

"Show me how it works," he said over the rumble of the engine.

I pointed at the throttle and pushed it to max, then shifted it into drive and let my foot off the brake. We rolled toward the open door. The blazing hot sun had broken over the tree line, warming the stagnant air. Bumping across the dirt lane, Tyler scanned the scene as I drove to the furthest row by the woodlands. Cypress and cedar trees framed a thick border around the five acres. At the far end of the rows was a pond overgrown with brush. Dad told me to never go back there. Copperhead and rattle snake nests were all I needed to hear to stay away.

A few hundred yards later, I parked under the tree line in the shade, before I pushed the lever to lower the scoop.

"I counted forty-five rows," Tyler said over the cackling motor. He pointed down the field. "How far is that?"

I turned the key, killing the rumbling vibration.

"Quarter of a mile. Dad told me last spring that there are roughly three hundred and thirty plants per row. You can figure out the rest."

"Fourteen thousand eight hundred fifty plants?"

"Wow. You did the math that fast? I was just kidding, but thanks for the info."

I stared across the field at the weeds that prevented me from seeing how many peppers were ripe. I pointed at an ancient oak tree near the thicket line.

"If we work the front section of the field, we can cover at least fifteen rows on this side of the tree. The sun beats this corner, so there should be plenty of them ready to pick, and we won't have to walk as far to unload our sacks."

"You sure? We could knock out the whole row so you don't have to go back."

"Sections are fine. I have to be at your house by nine. Besides, we'll walk it again as they continue to ripen."

"Whew, that's a ton of work."

He hopped off the tractor and held out his hands to help me.

Part of me wanted to be sassy and jump the other way just to show my independence, but he was so sweet I couldn't insult him. I grabbed his hands and jumped down. He had both canvas bags over one shoulder. I took one and hung it across my chest as we headed toward the first row.

Tyler seemed content, hanging out with my impossible mission, and me. But fourteen thousand plants? Why did he have to say that number? Overwhelmed, I scanned the field.

"This may be pointless," I said. "It's just too early."

"Let's see what we can find," he reassured me. "We can cover several rows, can't we?"

"Yeah, that works best. Take three rows on each side of you, and I'll do the same."

He moved up field, leaving six rows between us.

"So, I just pull off the red ones?" he asked.

"Yep, but if there's too much green on it, don't pick it."

"Okay. Too much green... " he repeated under his breath.

He was lost. Adorably lost. I watched him for a moment. His face brightened when he pulled the first red pepper, then he held it up with a big smile. I gave him a nod of approval and started searching for signs of red, pushing weeds aside, lifting the leaves.

"There's more here than I thought," I said, grabbing several myself. "I think they're turning red as we go."

"There's a ton over here." He pushed both hands full in his sack. "It's kinda like a treasure hunt."

His giddiness filled my heart. He had no idea how much his effort meant to me.

We worked for almost two hours, gathering twenty total loads. After we emptied our last sack, I spread the stock inside the scoop.

"Thank you so much," I said. "This is a really good start. If I can get two scoops in the back of the pickup, Mark can take them to the processing plant."

I turned around and wrapped my arms around him, pressing my lips to his. Sweat trickled down his dirt-streaked face. He pulled away and laughed.

"We're a mess," he said.

"No doubt. I need to take a shower before I go to your grandmother's."

He took my hand in his, and we started toward the house.

"Hey, I have a question," he said.

"Sure, what's up?"

"Dad called last night. He has some papers I need to look at for school. He wants me to come home tonight, go out to dinner. You know, hang out for a while, maybe crash there."

"That's cool."

"You wanna go with me?" he asked like we were going to get ice cream.

"Uh, well, I... "

Would I have to talk to his supermodel mother? How strange would she act this time? Where would I sleep? Did this mean he wanted to take it to the next level? Oh, God... I wasn't sure if I was ready for all that.

"It only takes about an hour and half to get there," he said. "We can leave after you're done working. Come with me. Get away for the night. It'll be good for you."

"I'd like to, but I have to work at Smith's in the morning."

"We can get back in time. You said you didn't know me outside of the park. So... I'm here with you on your turf, now I want to show you mine."

"Won't it be weird that I'm with you?"

"No, it's all good. You know you want to."

"Yeah, I want to, but—"

"No 'buts.' This is my only chance this summer to take you home. It's an innocent twelve to fourteen hours of your life. We'll eat dinner, maybe go swimming. Just hang out."

The word "innocent" helped.

"Okay, I'll go. But only because you helped me."

"That's the only reason?" he asked as he leaned against the hood of his car.

"No. I want to go. I just don't want to lie to Mom anymore."

"So, don't. Tell her you're staying the night with a friend."

"That's kind of the truth." I chuckled. "Are you going back to your grandmother's?"

"I'll probably go for a run, but yeah, I'll be back before lunch." He narrowed his eyes. "Remember what I told you. Just ignore her, okay? She's all talk."

"You're right. I'll see you later," I said, turning to go to the house.

He caught my wrist and pulled me back to him. "You're not getting away that easy."

He wrapped his arms around me and kissed me goodbye.

Chapter

17

I walked into Mrs. Vaughn's kitchen at eight fifty-five, and headed straight to the utility closet behind the main staircase. Mom had given me a list of tasks to do on Wednesdays. Downstairs bathrooms first, then dusting, vacuuming, and finally the kitchen. I gathered my supplies and headed for the small bathroom by the mudroom.

As I wiped down the countertops, I heard someone walk into the kitchen.

"Claire?" Mrs. Vaughn's voice echoed off the walls. "Is that you?"

I peered around the corner. "No, Mrs. Vaughn. It's me, Elsie."

"Oh. I forgot about you," she said, without a smile.

"When does your mother return?"

"Monday morning, I think."

She gave me an annoyed glance and turned away.

Gritting my teeth, I returned to the sink and sprayed the mirror with cleaner. My arm shook as I rubbed the glass. Maybe she would leave. She was all talk. Her words couldn't hurt me if I didn't allow them to.

Ten minutes later, I collected the supplies, took a deep breath, and stepped into the kitchen. Mrs. Vaughn sat at the island, holding a coffee cup, drumming her long red claws on the side. She shot me a dismissive glance, then looked out the sunroom windows.

"Elizabeth," she said to the glass.

"Yeah?... Yes?" I stuttered, almost dropping the toilet cleaner.

"Those cleaners are too strong. Don't use so much."

"Yes, ma'am." I answered to the back of her head as I hurried out of the room.

Three hours later, I traded the bathroom supplies for dusting and polishing tools. I walked around the staircase and glanced over my shoulder. Tyler. He flashed me a smile from the kitchen. My insides fluttered. I grinned back and headed to the great room.

Starting at the French doors, I sprayed cleaner on the glass and began wiping it off. A few minutes later, I heard, or more so felt, someone walk in the room. I froze. Please don't be Tyler.

In the refection, I saw Mrs. Vaughn standing rigid in the middle of the room, staring me down. She cleared her throat. I slowly turned around, trying not to look terrified.

"These are priceless artifacts," she enunciated her words, pointing at various tables in the room. "I expect them to stay intact. In fact, why don't you skip dusting today and leave it for your mother next week?" She tilted her head. "You know the saying... you break it, you buy it. That goes for anything in the house, so be sure to mind yourself in the study, as well."

She pivoted and walked out. Speechless, I turned around.

"'Priceless artifacts,'" I mimicked as I returned to my task.

By twelve-thirty, I'd finished cleaning the glass and vacuuming, giving me an extra half hour to clean the kitchen. I headed to the utility room to swap out my supplies again. Lost in thought, I grabbed the broom off the hook on the wall and turned around.

I gasped. The broom handle fell to the floor with a loud smack.

Tyler. He pressed his finger to his smiling lips, shushing me.

I covered my mouth to resist the urge to talk. He stepped inside and shut the door with a quiet click. Then, he took one long stride and pressed his lips to mine. I held his solid arms, surrendering to his deep, passionate kiss. He slowly eased away, letting the current linger between us. Gently, he brushed his lips over mine again, grinned, and within seconds, the door clicked shut, and he was gone.

My heart raced, lips tingling. I could still feel his hands clutching my face. A hint of his cologne drifted off my chest. I pulled my shirt to my nose and took a deep breath.

Complete bliss.

After taking a few minutes to gather my composure, I headed into the foyer to finish my last job. Mrs. Vaughn's voice floated my way from the kitchen.

"How sad, yes, it is," she was saying. "That family will never survive without him—"

"Nana, enough." I heard Tyler's dry tone.

"Oh, Tyler, darling," she cooed. "You're always so sensitive. It's just how it is for some people. They'll never get ahead. It's a curse."

"Will you please stop?" he said. "No one's cursed. Give people a little more credit."

"Well, aren't *we* in a foul mood. You're so defensive about those... Yank—people. This is the second time you've snapped at me about them."

I closed my eyes, completely mortified that my family was the topic of conversation.

"Yes, ma'am," Tyler said. A chair moved. "I'm going for a swim."

"Tyler Jackson," she declared. "Come back here."

A door opened and clicked shut.

Blood rushed to my face, and my skin prickled like needles were poking me. I peeked around the corner. Mrs. Vaughn sat at the kitchen table in front of the large windows. Making a beeline to the sink, I realized I was squeezing the cleaners so tight, they were gouging my arms. I set them on the counter with an audible sigh that I didn't mean to share.

"Are you having a fine day?" Mrs. Vaughn asked.

"Yes, ma'am," I said, and then I turned on the water to rinse dishes.

"That's nice." Her words were simple, but her surly tone made my skin crawl. I fumbled the wet plate in my hands and it clanked in the metal sink. "So, you've met Tyler, hmm?"

"I, um... yes," I glanced at her, "I have."

"Awfully fine young man, isn't he?"

"Mm-hmm," I nodded, scrubbing the plate harder.

Why did she end every sentence with a question? *Just. Leave. Please.*

"I'm sure you've noticed how handsome he is. Who

wouldn't?" She smirked at her rhetorical question. "You know... we have high expectations for him, nothing second rate."

I clenched my jaw.

"Nothing but the best for our Tyler," she continued. Out of the corner of my eye, I saw her flick her red fingernails. "Are you aware that he started college at sixteen?"

I looked at her. Her expression said: You're a dumbass, Elsie. I see right through you.

"I had no idea," I said slower than I intended.

What the hell was she talking about? He'd never mentioned anything like that.

"Yes, yes. He scored a thirty-six on his ACT. High school just wasn't a challenge for him. He needed to move on, as he will again. We expect him to begin his Master's soon."

She may as well have kicked me in the gut. I wiped the counter, resisting the urge to scream, *"You're the fool, old woman. I'm his girl. Ha, ha, joke's on you!"*

Turning to the island, I wiped the granite top, then my adrenaline spiked and I saw dirt everywhere. I knew he was smart, but a thirty-six on his ACT, at 16? That's pure brilliance.

I polished the faucet, then sprinkled powder cleaner all over the sink. While scouring the stainless steel, I stole a glance at Mrs. Vaughn.

She was watching me like a union foreman.

A few moments later, she said, "You silly girl... I just realized you did the dishes by hand. That hunk of metal right next to the sink is a dishwasher. Don't you have one, child?"

I cringed. Her intentions were to antagonize me until I broke. I had no choice but to take it. I glanced at the clock. One thirty-one. Twenty-nine more minutes and I could leave.

"Claire usually polishes the refrigerator," she said. "And the oven, as well."

"Yes, ma'am."

I wiped the front of the oven with the stainless steel wipes, repeating the process on all of the other appliances. Every piece gleamed when I finished. I needed to sweep and mop, then I could get out of the temporary hell I was trapped in.

She sat with her elbow on the table, chin resting in her hand with one red fingernail between her teeth. *Crack!* The broom handle hit the cabinet. My nerves spiked. *Smack!* I did it again. Rolling my eyes, I took a deep breath and slowed down.

When I made my way near the table, she let out a long yawn like my presentation had started to bore her. She gracefully stood and stepped beside me. Cocking her head to the side, she looked me up and down.

"Elizabeth, you look like you've toned up this summer." She raised her eyebrows. "Have you been jogging?"

My whole body began to tremble.

"I sure do love Shiloh in the summer," she continued. "You must visit in the Spring, though. The true spirit of the battle is in the Spring. I'm sure you know all about the history by now. I had many ancestors who gave their lives out on those fields. Damn Yankees." She curled her Botoxed lip. "Oh, excuse me. No offense."

As she stepped around me, her overpriced shoes scattered the pile of dirt I'd swept. I let my head flop back and stared at the ceiling. For crying out loud. I couldn't even defend myself. I couldn't go off on her. I couldn't do anything but stand there and take it. How in the hell did she know Tyler and I had been jogging? She knew something, and she wasn't going to let it go. When Tyler asked me to be his girl, he'd said we couldn't let anyone around us matter. Our relationship was between us. That cruel old woman was exactly who he'd meant. He knew damn well she didn't think I was good enough for him, and she'd just delivered her first warning. I shivered at the thought.

I swept and mopped the kitchen in record time, hurried through the garage, and climbed into the truck before I could be seen again.

Chapter

18

Half an hour later, I paced from my living room to the kitchen, wringing my hands. Going to Memphis sounded like a really bad idea now. Mrs. Vaughn had just scared the hell out of me. What if the rest of his family treated me the same way?

I looked out of the dining room window and scanned the field. Mark was walking the rows near the pond. *Yes!* He was finally out there. I ran out the back door.

"Yay!" I squealed, as I hurried down a row.

"What's up?" he asked, as I wrapped my arms around his sweaty shoulders and gave him a hug. Tensing, he wiggled away. "Would you stop? I'm trying to work here."

"Thank you! I promise I'll help more later. I'm going to

Memphis for the night."

"No way. You're nuts."

"It's no big deal," I said. "Tyler wants to introduce me to his parents. Isn't that sweet?"

"Sweet," he mocked. "You won't even tell Mom about him."

"I'm going to when everything settles down." I pressed my hands together. "I promise."

"When do I get to meet this guy?"

"He's picking me up. I'll introduce you."

He shrugged. "As far as I'm concerned, you're with that Josie girl, as usual."

"It's Jenna," I stressed. "Just meet him. I'll bring him out when he gets here."

On my way back to the house, I got a text alert.

Tyler: I'll be there at 3:30

Me: Okay.

I hurried back inside, took a shower, and dressed in a gray T-shirt and dark jeans. As I brushed my hair, my phone dinged again. Another text. He shouldn't be texting and driving. I snatched the device off the dresser.

Mom: Sorry I can't call right now. The doctor just stepped out for a second. Hope your day was good. Dad's stable.

Me: I miss you guys.

Mom: Me too.

Me: When are you coming home?

Mom: Saturday. They're sending your dad home.

Me: Okay. Mark told me. Will we have someone to help?

Mom: Yes. Hospice. I'll call soon. I need to go. Love you.

Me: Love you too.

Hospice. I didn't want to think about it.

I heard a knock at the front door. Holding my breath, I

walked through the house. *Here we go.* I grabbed the knob and pulled. Tyler's radiant smile instantly melted my defenses.

"Hey, beautiful," he said. "Ready?"

I waved him inside. He stepped past me and stopped in the middle of the living room. Our eyes met. I was powerless against them, but I needed his reassurance before I could leave.

"Um, Tyler. I don't know if this is a good idea."

"Why?"

"I don't think." I sighed. "I'm not—"

"You're not what?" he asked in a gentle tone. "Just say it."

"Your grandmother. She's—"

"Crazy?" He smiled and wriggled his eyebrows.

I deflated in relief, and then we both started laughing.

"Come with me." He took my hand in his. "We can talk about it on the way. I really want you to go. Please."

I couldn't tell the guy no for anything.

"Okay," I said. "But come meet Mark. He's in the field."

By the time we walked out to the backyard, Mark was headed toward the house. I snickered. He couldn't resist. He'd been dying to know who drove the Mercedes.

"Um, you might not want to tell him you're a Vaughn," I whispered. "He'll freak out if he realizes Mom works for your grandmother."

"I got your back," Tyler said.

When Mark walked up, sweat was pouring down his red cheeks, and he looked in dire need of water. I sucked in a deep breath. *Please, don't be an asshole.*

"Mark, this is Tyler," I said.

Tyler held out his hand. "Nice to meet you, man."

"Same to you," Mark said, returning his handshake.

"You're from Memphis? What brings you to this god-forsaken place?"

Tyler chuckled. "My grandmother."

I tensed. Tyler casually took my hand, squeezing my fingers tight.

"So, you wanna take my sister home for the night?" Mark smirked, as he wiped his face.

"Mark... " I said like any annoyed sister.

"This is my only chance to introduce her to my parents," Tyler said. "Nothing to worry about. We'll be back first thing in the morning."

"I have to be at Smith's by nine," I said.

"I don't give a shit what you do," Mark said with his typical sarcasm. "Just don't throw me under the bus with Mom." He looked at Tyler. "I saw your Mercedes the other night. CL63, right?"

"Yeah." Tyler smiled. "Wanna check it out?"

"Hell, yes. Is it an AMG?"

Tyler nodded.

"I'm gonna grab my stuff," I said.

Tyler waved. "Okay."

Ten minutes later, we said goodbye to Mark and headed for Memphis. Tyler turned down the radio and gave me a quick glance.

"Talk to me," he said. "What happened at the house?"

My heart skipped. I'd almost forgotten about the evil woman.

"I'm pretty sure your grandmother knows about us."

Another glance. "Why?"

"She freaking cornered me. I thought I'd pee my pants."

Tears stung my eyes. Turning toward the window, I watched the passing trees until the burn subsided.

"Don't let her do this to you," he said.

"But what if your parents hate me like she does? She told me, 'Nothing but the best for our Tyler... nothing second rate.' She may as well have said, 'Elsie, you're a piece of shit, and I won't let you have anything to do with my grandson.' And then, then... she made fun of me for washing the dishes by hand." That one hurt to admit. Tears began to stream at an alarming rate. I wiped them as fast as I could, but I was outnumbered. "Worst of all, she like, cornered me as I swept the floors," I said. "She told me I looked like I'd been jogging, and then she talked about Shiloh. After her recommendation to visit the park in the Spring, she basically called me a damn Yankee. Oh. But she said, 'No offense,' so I guess that makes it okay. Tyler, she totally knows."

Mrs. Vaughn's comment about his ACT score nagged the back of my mind. I shook it off. There was no way he would keep something like that from me.

Tyler let out a long sigh. "I'm not sure how she figured it out. But I suspect it has something to do with the black Cadillac I see at the park every day."

I gasped. "You've seen it, too? Oh my gosh! I saw him Sunday, and Monday morning."

"You saw his face?"

"Yes. He took a picture of the truck. It creeped me out."

"I don't know who the hell he is," Tyler said, irritated. "I couldn't get a good look at him. His windows were too dark. It doesn't matter though, I'm not ashamed of us. And I promise I won't let her speak to you that way again. As for my parents, I've already told Dad."

"When?"

"Um, Monday." He chuckled. "I might've... overreacted when you were dodging me at the house. Anyway, Jonathan, the guy we ran into at the club? He called Dad like I said he would. He told him he saw me with a girl and that I'd volunteered to show Rachel around campus. Asshole. I'll buy and sell his ass someday, and I can't stand his daughter. Regardless, Dad already knew something was up. Honestly? I couldn't wait to tell him about you."

I looked down at my lap. "That's really nice of you to say."

Poor guy. The tentacles of his overbearing family hid around every corner.

"It's the truth. Elsie, I wish this was as simple as Nana just being a bitch, but it's not. She was diagnosed with early dementia two, three years ago." He held up his hand. "I'm not making excuses for her. However, this is what we're all dealing with. She's gone from naturally mean and hateful, to hateful and downright cruel."

"I'm sorry to hear that, but I'll only take so much."

"I understand. You certainly don't have to take abuse from anyone, and I'll be the first to stand in your defense. Now, as far as my parents are concerned, Dad had asked if I would bring you along. We're meeting him for dinner. Are you okay with that?"

"Of course," I said, relaxing in the seat. "What about your mom?"

"She knows you're coming. It'll be fine. I promise."

"Okay."

For the rest of the drive, we chatted and laughed, enjoying our private world alone.

An hour and a half later, we pulled up to a gate at Spring

Creek Ranch. The guard recognized Tyler and waved us through. The black gate parted, and he drove us into a paradise of golf courses with a sprawling brick clubhouse at the front of the grounds.

"This is beautiful," I said.

"Yeah, we hang out here a lot."

Tyler parked the car and led me inside, holding my hand tight in his. The dining room was full of people dressed in polos and khakis, eating and chatting. Everyone had a similar appearance with the exception of color choices (which ranged from shades of blue, red, and black). Tyler shook the hands of several men as we passed through, each one glancing my way with a smile. Then, Tyler casually led me toward a table tucked in the corner of the room. Greg was staring out the floor-length windows overlooking the golf course.

"Hey, Dad," Tyler said as we walked up.

"You made it." Greg stood up and gave Tyler a quick hug. "Nice to see you again, Elsie."

"Nice to see you, too."

"Where's Mom?" Tyler asked, as we all settled in our seats.

"Oh, she had a homeowner's ass meeting," Greg said with a chuckle.

"Dad hates the homeowner's association," Tyler murmured to me.

I shook my head. "I don't even know what that is."

"Well, you're better off!" Greg laughed. "Stupid people. All they want is to control what you do with your own house."

"Mom supposedly wants to monitor their tendencies, as she calls it, but she's as much of a control freak as any of them," Tyler said, then he took a sip of water. "So, what's the verdict?"

Greg glanced at me, then Tyler. "May I speak freely?"

"Of course," Tyler said. "Let's get this over with, I've been avoiding the subject."

Greg scrunched his brow at the comment. "Okay. You've received letters from seven places: Columbia, U of I, Stanford, UT, Northwestern, Brown, and Yale."

Columbia? Yale? Brown? What the hell?

"You have offers to go to all those schools?" I blurted. "So, she was serious?"

"Who?" They asked in unison.

"Your grandmother! She said you started college at sixteen, is that true?"

Greg flinched. "You haven't told her?"

Tyler timidly shook his head. "I started to one day, but we were interrupted."

"You're always so damn modest." Greg rested his elbows on the table and started talking like Tyler wasn't there. "He studied like crazy his freshman year of high school. Then, after he turned fifteen, he took his ACT to prove his mother wrong, as usual."

Tyler sighed.

"And he scored a thirty-six," Greg continued. "Every school in the country contacted him. He started at Vanderbilt the fall after he turned sixteen, and now he's almost done with his bachelor's. These are his choices for graduate school."

I sat there in disbelief. "You're almost done with your bachelor's?"

Tyler inclined his head without a word. An awkward silence settled around the table. Not sure how to react, I looked down at my lap, and then I heard Greg push back his chair.

"Why don't we get something to eat?" he said. "The chef's

serving a buffet tonight."

Greg stood up. Tyler and I didn't move. Greg took his cue and walked away. Tyler started spinning his water glass between his fingers, chewing on his bottom lip.

"Does that bother you?" he asked, staring at the glass.

"Um, no. But I don't understand why you haven't told me. If you want me to trust you, you have to be honest with me, too. You definitely haven't mentioned being a child prodigy."

"I'm not. I just test well," he said deadpan, and then he let out a burdened sigh. "I didn't mean to keep it from you. I just didn't want to scare you off."

"Tyler, you couldn't scare me off for being smart. It's pretty obvious you're not dumb. I thought you were on scholarship for cross country."

"I'm on scholarship, but cross country's only one aspect of it," he said. "I was offered that after I started. I was kind of young to compete at that level at first."

"Sounds like it."

He rested his arms on the table, looking me over with gentle eyes. Once again, I couldn't be mad when he looked at me that way. I quickly ran my options through my head. I could make a big deal of it, throw a fit and ruin the night, or I could just do as he had asked, and trust him.

Tyler leaned in and brushed his lips across my cheek.

"Let's get some food," he whispered in my ear. "We have all night to talk about this."

"Okay."

He stood up and held out his hand. I accepted and followed him to the buffet table. My mind raced as I filled my plate. *He's brilliant. Who scores a thirty-six on the ACT? A bachelor's degree before he turned twenty? That was insane.* Next thing

I knew, I had more food piled on my plate than I could ever dream of eating. *Chill, Elsie.*

Greg had waited for us to return before he started eating. "We all good?" he asked.

"Yep," Tyler said.

I smiled, and took a bite of scalloped potatoes.

"Okay, so where are you thinking?" Greg asked.

"Well, Stanford and Brown are great," Tyler said, "and the U of I has the best engineering program in the country, but I'm not sure that's what I want to do. You said Yale and Columbia, too?" He smirked behind his fork. "No way. Flattering, but no way."

"Really?" Greg said. "You don't want Yale?"

Tyler set down the utensil and wiped his mouth with his napkin. "No. I don't want to live out East. I like Stanford, always have. But I'm curious about Northwestern."

"Chicago, eh?" Greg grinned. "Your grandmother will have a fit." Chuckling, he picked up some food with his fork and held it midair. "Won't that make the holidays fun?"

"She's going to have to let it go, Dad. I'm already pissed at her."

"Yeah, get in line. I promised you could choose your graduate school. I'll deal with her."

Tyler nodded and dropped the subject. Greg made dinner pleasant for the rest of the evening, talking and laughing about the neighbors' bad habits.

After an hour or so, we said goodbye and headed for Tyler's house.

Chapter

19

In less than five minutes, Tyler turned on a concrete driveway, leading up a slight incline to a beige brick, two-story house.

"Nice," I said.

"Like it? We've lived here since I was six."

Within minutes, we were walking to the back of the house across a sandstone patio with a bean-shaped pool in the center. He led me through French doors into a warm living room done in muted shades of brown. One wall had a fireplace with an enormous TV hanging above the mantel. A long, russet leather couch faced it. Behind the couch, the space opened to an expansive kitchen. Rustic, oak cabinets and stainless steel appliances lined the walls in an L shape, cupping a woodblock center island.

"So beautiful," I said.

"Thanks. Mom's an interior designer. She's pretty good, too."

He tossed his keys on the kitchen counter, opened the refrigerator, and bent down to inspect the contents. He handed me a Pepsi and grabbed another one for himself.

"My room's upstairs," he said with a wave.

I followed him, scanning the photographs on the walls. Family portraits, years of baseball pictures, candid shots of him and his mom at a ski resort. He headed up the stairs. Frames lined the stairwell, displaying certificates of academic awards. I walked slowly to inspect each one. He stopped at the top landing and turned around.

"Don't mind all that," he said.

"Are you kidding? I'm going to learn as much as I can. You called me guarded... Jeez, look at all of this."

He blushed and waited. The last one I read was a certificate for the President's Award for Educational Excellence, signed by President Obama. *What in the world?* Tyler was smarter than my whole gene pool combined.

Trying to process all the new information, I followed him to the end of the hall. He turned around and wrapped his arms around me. Staring into my eyes, he leaned down and gave me a kiss.

"I've been waiting all night to do that," he said. "I loved taking my girl to the club. First time I've done that, thanks to you."

"You've received an award from the President, but never taken a girl to the club?"

"Yep."

He stepped aside and pushed the door open. I walked

into a blend of a bedroom and living room. A brown couch stretched down the wall with a wide-screen TV hanging on the opposite side. Framed prints hung all over. One was a picture of a long, winding road with *perseverance* printed at the bottom. Another framed poster in black with white text read: *Your body can stand almost anything. It's your mind that you have to convince.* At the far end of the room, a king-sized bed was covered in navy and white bedding. An oak desk piled with books, papers, and a laptop were nestled in the corner. Above the desk, two shelves were stacked with golf and baseball trophies, medals, and a rainbow of martial-arts belts.

He flopped on the couch and grabbed the remote. "Ah, it feels good to be home."

ESPN sportscasters filled the screen. I sat down at the other end of the couch, and nudged his leg with my foot. "Obviously, you haven't told me everything."

"Sorry about that," he said. "I'm a little... advanced."

I narrowed my eyes. "Like freaky smart."

"Yeah, like freaky smart." He laughed. "I'll be sure to use that on my résumé."

"Glad I can be of service." I bowed my head. "Where did you go to school?"

"I started out in private school, but I kind of got kicked out in junior high."

"What for?"

"Um, fighting," he said, tilting his head. "I have a bit of a temper if I'm pushed."

"You don't seem like the type to hurt anyone."

"I didn't, really. There was a no tolerance rule for fighting. The kid deserved it. I'd watched him pick on a sixth grader, Cillian, for weeks." He shrugged. "So, I beat the guy's ass. It didn't take much. Bullies are all talk."

"Where did you go after that?"

"I studied at home. I could go as fast as I wanted to and study whatever I chose. Mom was pretty cool. She helped me figure out what worked and made sure I had plenty of arts and culture, including languages," he said. "It worked because Tennessee looked at it as private schooling. She'd turn in my grades to the counselor at the high school, and I had access to all the extracurricular stuff. Hell, I played golf every afternoon at Spring Creek for two years."

I leaned forward to take his hand. He clutched my wrist and pulled me across the couch. Giggling, I snuggled beside him and laid my head on his chest.

"Why did you take the ACT so early?"

"Mom kept giving me work that I'd already studied or knew in general. She insisted I complete the curriculum. I had to prove it to her somehow."

His deep breath rippled underneath me.

A 36 ACT score...

"How did they react?" I asked.

"They freaked out," he said. "Within weeks, they had me enrolled at Vanderbilt, and I headed to Nashville that fall. What sucked was Mom did, too. Talk about helicopter parents. Since I was only sixteen, she didn't want me there alone. By second semester, I finally convinced her to go home."

The bedroom door flew open.

"Tyler!" his mom squealed.

She slowed down when she saw me. I sat up. Tyler didn't flinch. She looked from me to him, then stepped his way and held out her arms.

"Hi, Mom," he said, standing up to give her a hug.

"I'm so glad you're home," she said, patting his face with a loving look. She turned to me. "Elsie, right?"

"Yes. Nice to meet you again."

"Awfully nice of you to come along," she said with all sincerity.

"You have a beautiful home, Mrs. Vaughn."

"Oh, please, I'm Katherine," she said. "Y'all are staying the night, correct? It's too late to drive back now."

"I'd planned on it," Tyler said.

"Great. I'll make breakfast in the morning. You should take her to downtown Memphis tomorrow. It's a beautiful city, Elsie."

"She has to get back early," Tyler said. "But we can do breakfast if it's before seven."

"Will do." She looked around the room, and then she eyed Tyler. "Where do you plan on sleeping?"

"In here," Tyler replied like it was a stupid question.

She leaned toward me. "How old are you?"

"Seventeen," I said. "I'll be eighteen soon."

She cringed. "Tyler. I'm not exactly comfortable with that."

"All right," he said. "One of us will crash in the spare room." She pursed her lips. "I promise, Mom. It's all good. You know that."

"Okay, then. Your dad's on his way home. I'm beat, so I'll leave you two alone." She gave Tyler a kiss on the cheek. "Don't stay up too late."

"Goodnight, Mom."

I smiled and waved.

"See you in the morning," she said, as she closed the door.

He flopped back down on the couch. "Wanna go for a swim?"

"Yeah, but I didn't bring a swimsuit."

His eyes danced.

"What does that look mean? I can't figure you out some-times."

"You don't want to know what I'm thinking. Do you have a pair of shorts?"

"Yes."

He got up and started across the room. "I have a T-shirt."

"What you have is a lot of energy."

"Yes, I do," he said over his shoulder. "And I need to burn some, or it's going to be a painfully long night."

He opened the top drawer of his dresser. Digging through layers of shirts, he held up a white T-shirt and grinned.

I laughed. "I don't think so."

He put it back and grabbed a black one. "This is too small for me now. It should fit you."

He handed me the T-shirt and walked to a door beside the couch.

"Bathroom's in here," he said. "I'll go down the hall."

After he walked out, I stepped inside to change. The room was done in navy tile lined in bright white grout. I scanned the counter, curious as to what products he liked. Nothing in particular, with the exception of a bottle of *Sauvage* cologne by *Dior*. I popped the lid and inhaled his scent. *Nice.* Tyler in a bottle.

When I stepped out, he was sitting on the couch in long, black swimming trunks and a T-shirt. He hopped up and led me through the low-lit house into the humid night air. He headed to the pool house beside the patio, returning with two towels, tossed them on the patio chair and pulled off his T-shirt. I held my breath as he walked away. Michelangelo couldn't have created such beauty.

He stepped on the diving board, bounced in the air and dove in with hardly a splash. I decided to follow him. Walking across the board, I bounced, grabbed my knees, and did a cannon ball in the center of the deep end. I couldn't touch his grace, might as well cannon ball.

As I surfaced, I took a deep breath, wiping my face. He swam to me and pulled me close. I clutched his smooth shoulders as he gave me a long, wet kiss. After he pulled away, the wake of the water moved between us.

"You have no idea how much I dread going back to school," he said.

"Me, too."

"I wish we were ready to start our own lives," he said. "We can make an amazing life together, you know? But I have to finish school first. Please... wait for me."

"Tyler, I'll wait for you for the rest of my life if that's what it takes."

"Good," he said, and then he kissed me again.

After we let go, we swam a few laps together. He wasn't lying... he needed to burn some energy. I swam until I had to take a break, then made my way to the edge, and watched him swim ten laps at record speed. Meanwhile, a guy with curly brown hair came strutting across the patio. Lean, at least six feet tall and with olive skin, he wore plaid flannels and a green Teenage Mutant Ninja Turtle T-shirt.

"What the hell, Vaughn? I saw your car in the driveway. You're in town, and you don't call me?" He stopped short and crossed his arms when he saw me. "Oh, I see what's going on."

"I thought you were in France," Tyler said, swimming the backstroke.

"We got back Sunday. Who's your friend?" The guy kicked off his shoes, sat on the edge of the pool and shoved his feet in the water.

"Wouldn't you like to know," Tyler said, then he rolled in the water and winked at me.

The guy kicked his feet, splashing Tyler in the face. Tyler splashed him back.

"Come on, man, you're never with a girl." He waited. Tyler kept swimming. The guy waved. "Oh, forget you." He looked at me with a crooked smile. "Hi, I'm Zach."

"I'm Elsie."

"Nice to meet you," he said, and then he nodded at Tyler. "She's pretty damn hot, man."

My cheeks burned, and I looked away. Tyler swam to me and wrapped his arm around my waist. I clutched his neck.

"Don't even think about it," he said.

"It's not like I'm up for sale," I murmured.

"I know..." Tyler whispered back.

"Must be nice," Zach said. "I did meet a sexy French girl while we were in Paris. She might have been an anorexic, though."

Zach had big dimples and round cheeks, an adorable baby face that hadn't quite caught up with his muscular built. Tyler kissed my cheek and swam to the middle of the pool.

"Elsie's from Morris Chapel, it's not far from Savannah. Well, actually, she's a Yankee who migrated south."

I splashed him. He laughed and disappeared under the water.

"How did you two meet?" Zach asked me. "It's not easy to get the guy's attention."

"At his grandmother's house. My mom cleans there."

"What?" Zach burst out laughing.

My stomach sank. Why did I introduce myself that way? Tyler surfaced. "What's so funny?"

"Are you fucking nuts?" Zach said. "Her mom cleans for

your wicked grandmother?"

The word 'wicked' helped. He'd evidently met the woman.

"Who cares?" Tyler said with a long drawl. "She can kiss my ass. I think she's hired someone to follow me again."

"Seriously? I told you she's crazy." Zach looked at me. "She had us followed one summer... for what, a month?" His eyes darted to Tyler. Tyler nodded. "It was creepy, but once we figured it out, we had a blast messing with the guy." They both laughed. "Tyler walked in the triple-x shop up on First Street to see if it would get back to her. I thought I'd die laughing."

"I'd heard there was a back door the pervs used to sneak out," Tyler said. "I was freaking out, trying to get out of there. The place was nasty."

"Why is she having you followed all the time?" I asked.

"'Cause Tyler likes to beat people's asses at random."

"Whatever," Tyler said, with an annoyed glance. "She thought I was doing drugs or something. It made for a long summer. I finally told Dad, and the guy stopped coming around."

"Have you met her?" Zach asked me.

"Unfortunately."

He chuckled and shook his head. "I did last Christmas. She's nuts."

I giggled. Thank God he felt the same way.

"She was exceptionally crazy that day," Tyler said, bobbing in the middle of the pool. "She had her meds all screwed up."

I pushed across the water toward the shallow end. The boys went silent as I walked up the steps. My nerves spiked. I had to get out of the water, my skin was pruning. I quickly grabbed a towel and covered my soaked body.

"Your grandma's always crazy," Zach finally said. "She insists on calling me 'Zachary.'"

I spun around. "I know, right? She told me, she prefers 'Elizabeth.'"

"I can't stand it when people call me by my full name," Zach said, shaking his head.

I sat down in a chair next to him. "At least it isn't just me."

Tyler swam in circles, then he dove under the water, did a flip, and swam away.

"Is he always this energetic?" I asked.

"I don't think the guy sleeps, to be honest," Zach said. "I used to jog with him. We'd run over ten miles, but when we'd get back home, he'd just wave and keep going. He's a freak."

Tyler re-emerged from under the water and wiped his face. "You know how she found out about us?" he asked. I shook my head, no. "The guard who kicked us out the other night? He's worked there forever. He lives in Savannah. I bet he told her."

Tyler smirked at his epiphany, swam to the edge, and looked up at me. His eyes were breathtaking. They'd turned a burnt umber with flecks of emerald green outlining the iris. I shook my head and refocused on what he'd said.

"That's not the guy in the Cadillac," I said.

"I know. I'm just saying, he told Nana, and then she hired someone to go out there."

"I can draw him."

"What do you mean?" Zach asked.

"You'll see," Tyler said. "Run inside and grab some paper and a pencil, you know where everything's at."

Zach pulled his feet out of the water and stood up. "Where are your parents?"

"They're already in bed."

Zach waved and walked away.

"Tyler, this kind of freaks me out," I said. "Why would she have us followed?"

"She's nosy, that's all. The guard probably told her he saw me with a girl, and she's been snooping around ever since. Hell, she's probably read my journal, too." He shook his head. "I'm going to have to hide it."

"Leaving it on the nightstand makes it too tempting. Are you going to say something to her when we get back?"

"I'm not sure yet. I'll talk to Dad if I have to."

Zach returned and handed me a notepad and pencil. He sat on the edge of the pool and stuck his feet back in the water. I started sketching the square-faced man in the Cadillac.

"So, you're just going to draw the guy?" Zach asked me "No photo or nothing?"

"Yep," I said.

I worked on the man's beady eyes, then started on his overstated nose.

"Are you transferring come January?" Zach asked Tyler.

"Yeah, I have to choose something," he said.

"Man, it's going to suck when you leave. Are we getting our own place this semester? I can't do the dorm thing again."

"Allen said he's moving out. Thank God. So yes, you can have his room."

"Sweet. I hate the dorm. Way too many crazy people."

"This is roughly what he looks like."

I held up the paper. Tyler winced.

"What the hell? That's my uncle!"

"Wow, that's good," Zach said, then he laughed. "That's your uncle?"

"Yeah, my dad's older brother, Ron."

"He doesn't look like you guys," I said. "Not even close."

"He looks like one of Nana's brothers. Damn it. I'll have to go visit him when we get back. He lives in Crump, probably broke again."

"Who needs money in your family?" Zach asked.

"Uncle Ron. He's the only one of Nana's kids that didn't go to Vanderbilt. She can make him do anything for a buck."

"Well, it makes me feel better that you know him," I said. "It's still creepy, but at least you can do something about it."

"I guess. I don't really like the guy. He's a sleazy used-car salesman."

Zach raised his hand with big, round eyes like a little boy who needed to speak.

"Do me, do me!"

I laughed. "What?"

"Draw me," he said with a cheesy smile.

"Okay. Give me a minute."

Zach reminded me of the cartoon character Jimmy Neutron. Instead of an accurate sketch, I drew a caricature, exaggerating the size of his head and round cheeks, attaching him to a tiny body with little feet dangling in water. I made his eyes fill three-quarters of his face, added a round nose between them with puffy, overstated lips above a square chin.

Tyler pushed off the wall and started swimming in circles.

"Are you going to your graduation?" Zach asked.

"I'll have to go back in May if I want to. I'm not sure."

"Why wouldn't you? You'll be the youngest person there. You'll get all kinds of awards."

"I don't care about that," he said, swimming to the edge of the pool again. "My plans have kind of changed... as of late."

"What?" Zach's voice cracked. "Are you two that serious?"

"I am," Tyler said.

I glanced up and smiled.

"But I haven't given my approval yet," Zach protested. "Well, I guess I did say that you're hot. You passed the first part. But do you have substance? This guy needs substance. Obviously, you have talent. Let me see that." He reached out. I handed him the notepad. He burst out laughing. "Check this out, man!"

Tyler laughed. "Looks right to me."

"You're good," Zach said, setting the notepad aside. "So anyway, as I was saying... Do you know, he has no tolerance for anyone who whines, or most of all, anyone who interrupts?"

"No," I said. "I did not know that."

"She wouldn't," Tyler said. "She doesn't interrupt me like some people I know."

"What about whining?" Zach asked.

"She doesn't whine, either," Tyler said. "Unlike you."

"Not to you," I said. "Mom would totally disagree."

"Okay. So far so good. Do you come from money?"

Tyler sighed and pushed off the edge of the pool.

"My mom cleans at his grandmother's," I said, slowly to emphasize my point. "No. It seems to be an issue, though."

"Not for us," Zach said.

"Us?" Tyler countered, as he swam back to the edge.

"I said, I have to approve. How old are you? Are you going to have him arrested?"

"Zach, she has no reason to have me arrested. You and Luke are the only ones who date fifteen-year-olds posing as adults."

"That wasn't cool. Those girls did not look that young. Anyway, you're the only virgin I know, who can get laid at any given moment, and won't."

"Thanks, Zach," I said. "That's comforting."

"Shut the fuck up," Tyler said, pushing out of the pool.

He walked to the chair and grabbed a towel. Zach looked at me with an ornery grin.

"Your boy, here, doesn't chill. Ever. He's too busy being Mr. Athlete and Einstein."

"No one forced you to come to Vanderbilt, you know." Tyler pulled a chair beside me and sat down. "I won't apologize for making you look bad."

"Shit. When it comes to grades, you've always made me look bad. I thought I had you with the girls, but you've trumped me again."

"I have standards, that's all." Tyler nudged me. "He's found a few crazies over the years."

"Only one." Zach spun on the concrete, pulling his legs out of the water. Tyler threw his towel at him. He caught it and started drying his legs. "How can I tell if a girl's crazy or not? I have to take some chances. I'm sure you've seen a hint of crazy. No?" He eyeballed me.

"Elsie's solid," Tyler said, grabbing my hand. "No crazy here."

I smiled, lacing my fingers with his.

"What the hell, Tyler? Sorry, Elsie, just roll with this for a second." He looked at Tyler. "You're telling me you went to your Nana's, for a summer trip you hate every year, and now... look at you. You're never this happy." Zach squinted at me and pooched out his lips. "What have you done with my friend?"

Tyler slouched in the chair with a shy smile.

I shrugged. "All I know is this guy."

"Well, believe me," Zach said, "that isn't the normal Tyler."

We laughed Zach's interrogation off and talked a little more, then realized it was after midnight. Zach headed home, and we went back to Tyler's room. I shucked off my wet clothes, laying them over the edge of the bathtub, and slipped on my yoga pants and a T-shirt.

A few minutes later, I was snuggled next to Tyler on the couch. He wrapped his arms around me, and we watched *Sports Center*. After the baseball highlights, he changed the channel, and we chatted through several reruns of *Frazier*.

"I hope you know, you're lying in the arms of a total geek," he said. "I've just been able to hide it from you until now."

"You don't look like one. That helps immensely."

"Whatever," he said under his breath.

"Well, it's true. You're a star athlete, as well as extremely smart, and gorgeous. That disqualifies you from being a geek. You're more of a... smart jock."

He laughed.

"Your parents are great, and I really liked Zach. I'm sorry I was so freaked out when we left. It's been a very nice evening. Thank you."

"It's all good," he whispered. "I get it."

He rubbed my back with one hand, his other arm holding me tight. So warm and comfy, his embrace was the last thing I remembered before dozing off.

Chapter

20

I woke up on Tyler's bed, covered in a plush, navy blanket. Stretching out, I inhaled the scent of his pillow. Utopia. I looked around the room. Where was he? Readjusting my clothes, I saw the time. Six-eleven. I gasped! Mr. Smith's.

I grabbed my bag and rushed into the bathroom. When I flipped on the lights, I cringed at my reflection. I looked a hot mess, hair piled everywhere, mouth mucky and dry.

After my rituals, I repacked my bag, then followed the aroma of breakfast downstairs. Katherine was speaking to Tyler over the sound of sizzling bacon as I came down the hall.

"You told me you'd sleep in separate rooms," she said.

"We did," Tyler said. "I slept in the spare room."

"You two haven't gone that far, have you? She's only seventeen."

I stopped outside the doorway. *Oh, my gosh. Sex?* I can't walk in there, yet.

"Mom. That's exactly why we haven't gone that far."

"So... you would if she was older?"

He sighed. "Not necessarily. You know, I'm not like that."

"Sorry. I just worry about you. Don't risk your future over a girl."

"Elsie is my future, Mom."

Sizzling bacon filled the silence. I took a deep breath and stepped in sight.

"Good morning," Tyler said, relaxing back in his chair.

Katherine turned around with a bright smile.

"Good morning," she said. "Would you like some bacon and eggs?"

"Yes, I'd love some. Thank you."

Tyler sat at the head of the kitchen table with a stack of papers in front of him. I sat down next to him and glanced at the letterhead. Yale's acceptance letter was at the top of the pile.

"Did you sleep well?" he asked.

"Yes. I can't believe I crashed that fast," I whispered. "When did you move me?"

"Not long after you fell asleep. You barely noticed."

Katherine set a plate of bacon and scrambled eggs in front of me.

"Thank you," I said. "Looks delicious."

"Do you like coffee?" she asked. "I have orange juice, too."

"Coffee's great. Thanks. "

She returned to the counter.

"Well, Mom, there's no way I'm going East," He pushed the papers away. "I don't want to live out there for two years."

"You could still hear from Duke. It's east, but it's in the South."

"Okay, Nana."

"That's awfully rude." She grinned. "So, Elsie, Tyler tells me you're an artist."

I nodded, taking a bite of bacon. They must've had quite the conversation about me.

"I find that interesting," she said.

Tyler immediately asked, "Why?"

Ignoring him, she leaned against the counter.

"Tyler's extremely selective when it comes to art. Don't let him fool you, he'll try, but he's quite particular." She raised her eyebrows at him, and then she looked back at me. "That tells me you must have an amazing talent, or he wouldn't have mentioned it."

Tyler shifted in his seat. She walked to the table and sat down.

"Thank you," I said.

I glanced at Tyler. He drew his lower lip between his teeth, dark eyes assaulting my composure. I shyly smiled and refocused on Katherine.

"Where do you want to go to school?" she asked.

"I've thought about Memphis College of Art, but with Dad's condition, I don't know."

"Oh, no," she said. "You can't let that stop you. MCA is a great school."

"She's going," Tyler said. "She's too talented to blow it off."

"Tyler told me about the festival," she said. "That must've

been scary."

"It was. Thank God, he was there."

"Is your dad improving?" she asked.

"No. They're sending him home."

By her look, I could tell she understood the implications.

"I'm sorry to hear that," she said. "Your mom just told us last week."

"I know. She's very private about her life."

"I've never met her, but she has done a fantastic job at the house. If she hadn't, believe me, we'd hear about it."

"Mrs. Vaughn's not real thrilled I'm working for her this week."

Katherine waved her hand. "Oh, just ignore her."

"That's what I said," Tyler interjected.

I nodded and took a bite of the eggs.

"I let Greg deal with her, and try to keep my mouth shut when we're there." She gave Tyler a suspicious glance. "Does she know about you two?"

Tyler sighed. "I think she's having me followed again. So yes. I'm pretty sure."

"Again? Jeez, the woman's crazy. I'll talk to your dad."

"Thanks," Tyler said.

The verdict was unanimous about Mrs. Vaughn, but I had to warn Katherine about Mom.

"My mom doesn't know we're seeing each other, though."

"Oh, so this is a secret?" She smiled, looking back and forth between us. "Well, I feel special y'all let me in on it."

"She's going to tell Claire soon." Tyler looked at me. "Right?"

"Yes." I pulled in a nervous breath. "She's just under a lot of stress right now."

"Understandable," Katherine said, then she cringed. "I hope it doesn't affect her job."

My stomach flipped. "Exactly why I haven't told her, yet."

"Mildred's ridiculously controlling. Be careful." Katherine looked at Tyler. "Your father's already doing damage control because of your choice of graduate school. The woman won't let it go."

"Why does she care where I get my Master's?" Tyler asked. "It's stupid. She isn't even paying for it."

"That's why," Katherine said. "She hates it that she can't hold it over your head."

"She's definitely proud of how smart Tyler is," I said. "I'm still trying to wrap my brain around it."

"He wasn't always this driven."

"Mom... "

"Well, you weren't. I'm just glad it worked out. Elsie, I worried about him all the time. After his grandpa died, I'd never seen him so angry."

"He told me a little about it."

"Thank God he only had cuts and bruises."

"Mom. I'm sitting right here," he said in a dry tone.

"I know, honey, but that's why you lashed out like you did. It's bad enough you were in a car accident, but it's horrible to lose someone you were so close to. At least you dove into your studies." She looked at me. "When he started school on his own, I couldn't keep enough work in front of him. I knew he was smart, but I had no idea."

"Tell me about it," I said. "A thirty-six? I only scored a twenty-three."

"Would you two stop?" Tyler scoffed. "A twenty-three is acceptable at most major universities. Precisely why you need to apply."

Katherine leaned forward. "You know? He's never brought a girl home before—"

"Mom, enough."

"Okay." She held up her hands. "It's nice to talk with you, Elsie. As usual, Tyler has impeccable taste. He has an eye for beauty, and not just on the surface."

"Thank you, Katherine, and thanks for breakfast, too."

"My pleasure," she said.

Tyler pushed back his chair, grabbed our plates, and followed her to the sink. After he set down the dishes, he gave her a kiss on the cheek. She smiled and patted his face.

He walked across the room, reaching out to take my hand, and then he led me upstairs.

"We have to go," I said. "It's after seven."

"I know. Let me show you something first."

I followed him to a closed door in the hallway. He pushed it open and stepped inside. I stopped. The space was done in French-country decor, all of the furniture whitewashed, a blue-and-yellow quilt covering a king-sized bed that stretched the center of the wall. Sheer blue curtains over the floor-length windows blew in the breeze. He headed toward the right side of the room. No way. I didn't even go inside my own mom and dad's room unless I had permission. He turned around and waved.

"It's okay. Dad left for work at six. Mom won't care."

I reluctantly stepped inside and made my way to a dressing area that separated the bedroom and master bath. He stood in front of a knotty pine door.

"You asked how I know so much about shoes." He pulled the door open. "This is why."

I gasped. Katherine's walk-in closet was shelved with

rows and rows of red-bottomed shoes, *Prada, Jimmy Choo...* I bounced up and down, pretending to clap my hands.

"Beautiful! Oh, she wears my size, too."

Hundreds of styles, colors, and designs, all in one closet. I picked up a four-inch, glossy black, open-toe pump with a scarlet bottom. Pure art. Giggling, I put it back.

"I told you, her shopping sprees taught me a lot."

"You've had a unique education."

"Yeah. Tell me about it."

A few minutes later, I grabbed my bag and said goodbye to Katherine on our way out.

"I don't want to leave," I said after we settled in the car. "Can't we stay here?"

"Elsie, I've got all the time in the world. Are you willing to blow off your day?"

"I can't." I flopped back in the seat. "I had a great time, though. Thanks."

He smiled and took my hand. "The pleasure's been all mine."

We pulled in my driveway a little before nine. I only had five minutes to get to Savannah. Hopefully, Mr. Smith would still be at breakfast. Tyler gave me a kiss goodbye, then I hurried toward the house to get the keys. I stepped inside and promptly stopped. *What the hell?*

The aftermath of a party was spread throughout the house. Mark lay sprawled out on the couch, snoring. Bobby was lying on the recliner, snoring. Some random guy in a leather jacket was passed out face down on the floor, snoring. I walked by Mark's room and glanced inside. A naked couple was sleeping in his bed. The guy was on his belly, and the girl on her back, with sheets laced around their exposed skin. *Yuck.* I hurried to the kitchen. Empty beer cans cluttered the table, several of them overflowing with cigarette butts. The place smelled of stale smoke and musty bodies.

I stepped over a pile of pizza boxes, looking for the keys in between liquor bottles and half-empty plastic cups. Nothing. Maybe Mark left them on the coffee table. Scanning the room, I didn't see them anywhere. I looked him over. His right pocket bulged. I wasn't about to stick my hand in my brother's jeans. I pushed on his shoulder.

"Mark. Wake up. I need the keys." He moaned and rolled over. I shook him again. "Mark, come on, man." I smacked the back of his head. "I need to go to work."

"Don't," he snapped, swatting his hand at me.

"Get. Up. I need the keys to the truck."

"So? Get 'em yourself."

"They're in your pocket, dumbass."

He dug in his jeans and slammed his fist on the coffee table. Coins bounced, rolling across the wood, and then he rolled over again. I snagged the keys and walked out.

Chapter

21

I slipped in the back door at Smith's ten minutes after nine, and thankfully, he wasn't in the kitchen. I darted to the cabinet under the sink and filled my arms with cleaning supplies.

Footsteps. I froze in my tracks.

"It's me, Mr. Smith," I squeaked.

He didn't answer. I clutched the plastic bottles in my arms and stepped around the corner. He stood in the hallway, swaying back and forth. *Seriously, another drunk?*

He pointed his crooked finger, wiggling his whole body. "Y'all's late."

He staggered forward, and a chill ran up my spine.

"I'm sorry, sir. It's only a few minutes."

I held my breath. My skin tingled, signaling danger. I needed to run.

As he moved closer, I stepped backward.

"You's gonna give me a smooch for it." He squished his lips together.

He couldn't be serious.

"No, I'm not!"

He let out a terrifying cackle that made the hairs on my neck stand on end. I started backing up until my legs hit a pile of newspapers, stopping my progress. I was cornered.

"Mr. Smith, please... I just want to clean the bathroom."

"You's a cute Yankee." He stepped closer, breath like gasoline. "Come on over here."

Arching back, I faked to the right. He lunged to grab me. I darted to the left. He stumbled over the pile of newspapers, catching himself with the wall. I tossed the bottles on the floor and started to run toward the kitchen. But the collar of my shirt wrenched around my neck as he yanked me backward. I spun around and the fabric twisted tighter. Eyes full of rage, he snarled in my face. I swung my fist, but I only skimmed his cheek. I jabbed his Adam's apple instead.

"You 'lil bitch!" he coughed out.

Gasping for air, I grabbed at my neck. He swung his arm high in the air.

"No!" I cried.

Smack! The back of his hand smashed against my cheek.

Pain reverberated through my head and down my spine as the lights in the room faded.

This can't be happening... Oh, God, please help me!

Within seconds, he tossed me toward the kitchen like a ragdoll. Breathless, I tried to stop the momentum so I didn't hit the wall. *Crack!* My head whacked the edge of the doorframe. I collapsed to the floor. My head throbbed as the room spun.

Taking only a second to recoup, I knew I had to keep moving. *Run, Elsie, you gotta run!*

The old man was still coughing, and then I heard him moving toward me. Watery eyes clouding my vision, I managed to shuffle across the linoleum, and run out the screen door. I jumped past the steps, landing on my hands and knees, blades of grass brushing my cheek. Immediately, I pushed up and sprinted toward the truck. Scurrying inside, I slammed the keys in the ignition, and backed out of the driveway as fast as I could.

I grabbed for my phone. It wasn't in my pocket. Frantic, I patted my legs on both sides.

Nothing. Tears poured down my face. "No," I cried out. "I need my phone!"

My cheek was on fire. My heartbeat thumping around my eye. I rubbed the right side of my head, and winced. Already, a hard lump had grown under my hair.

I didn't know what to do. Call Mom. No, I didn't have my phone. Mark had a party strung all over the house, and I couldn't just knock on Tyler's door. I pulled over on the side of the street and threw the truck in park.

Why? Why would he attack me like that?

The horrifying ordeal flashed through my mind – his breath, his sweaty hands touching me, the snarl on his face. Shivering, I looked in the mirror again. My eye had already turned a deep blue and was starting to swell shut.

"No, no, no, no," I said, touching my skin like I could make it stop.

My stomach rolled over. At the same time, my jaw tingled as bile erupted in my throat. I opened the door and vomited on the pavement. Slumping back in the seat, I put the truck in drive and slowly headed toward Main Street. I had to find Tyler. I needed him. I needed his help.

Driving down Riverside Road, I scanned the yard for any signs of Mrs. Vaughn. The only person I saw was the gardener in the side yard, trimming the bushes. Continuing several hundred yards, I pulled over and hopped out.

"Hello," I said, way too cheerful for someone with a half swollen face.

"Hola," he nodded, and then he furrowed his brow, looking me over.

"Mrs. Vaughn... Is she home?"

"Señora Vaughn, *si*," he said.

"Uh, Señora, *casa?*" I raised my eyebrows, instantly flinching from the pain.

"*Si, si*," he nodded, and then he shook his head. "*No, Señora.*"

"She's not here." I shook my head no.

"*No, casa*," he squinted his eyes. "*¿Te duele?*"

I shrugged. "I don't understand."

"Hurt," he said, pointing to his cheek. "You, hurt."

I nodded. "Is Tyler here?"

His face lit up. "*Si*, Señor Tyler!" He pointed toward the road. "*Si, él corre.*"

I shook my head. *What did that mean?*

He smiled. "Run, run."

Tyler must've gone for a jog.

"Oh, okay," I said. "Thank you."

I drove around, searching the streets. After fifteen minutes, I pulled over and threw up again. After that, I couldn't take it anymore, and I headed home. As I drove down the curvy roads, all I wanted to do was close my eyes. I pushed through the waves of dizziness. The old man was a monster. Tears stung my pulsating eye. On top of everything else, that man had bash my face.

I pushed the front door open, staggering inside the house. Bobby was still asleep in the chair. Everyone else was gone. The smell of stale smoke made my stomach churn.

Bam, bam, bam! I pounded on Mark's door, then shoved it open. His face was pressed against the sheets where the naked people had been.

"Mark," I shouted. "Get up!"

"Not so loud," he mumbled.

"Screw you!" I slammed the door.

Bobby rustled in the chair.

I took two steps toward him, towering over the recliner, and screamed, "Get the hell out!"

His hands shot in the air. "Okay, okay. I'm going."

"There's the door."

I stood my ground, watching him scurry outside. I slammed the door to seal my point, and spun around way too fast. My stomach lurched, dizziness swirled through my head. Dashing toward the bathroom, I fell to my knees in front of the toilet. White light flashed in my eyes and sharp stabs racked my head as I emptied the rest of my stomach. My skin felt like it would burst from the pressure of each heave.

After an excruciating few minutes, I fell back on the cold floor and started gasping for breath.

The room spun. I closed eyes.

Someone was pushing on my shoulder. I opened my eyes, pain instantly pierced my head.

"Elsie! Wake up," Mark said, panicked.

"Ah," I moaned, trying to sit up.

"What happened to you?" he asked. "Did Tyler do this?"

"No. It wasn't Tyler." The awful morning flooded my mind. I whimpered. "Mr. Smith."

"Who? The guy you clean for?"

"He was drunk and cornered me. Then he smacked me."

"Did you call Mom?"

I sniffled. "No. I dropped my phone while I was trying to get away."

"I'm gonna kick the guy's ass."

"No." I grabbed Mark's arm. "Don't go over there, please. She'll get fired."

"Who gives a fuck?" he snapped. "She'd better not go back after this."

I buried my face in my hands.

"What about the crops?" I bawled. "I'd planned on working in the field today."

"Aw... Elsie. Don't worry about that. You need to lie down."

For the first time in years, my big brother hugged me and said nothing else. I didn't ask what time it was when he carried me to my room, but the house sat in the dark. Mark laid me in bed. I rolled on my side, then he covered me with a blanket and left me alone.

The next morning, I woke up, confused. The clock read eight-fifteen. I hurried out of bed, but the room spun around me. I steadied myself and touched the lump under my hair. Wincing with a hiss, I stepped in front of the mirror.

"No... " I breathed out.

A deep purple, swollen, shut eye reflected back. I touched the puffy skin. Then, I saw a thick, red line on my throat where Mr. Smith had strangled me with my shirt. I couldn't let Tyler see me like this.

I gasped. *Tyler.* I missed our run. *Oh no! He might think I stood him up!*

I felt for my phone but I couldn't find it... *Probably dropped it at Mr. Smith's!* I stood there trying to think, but for the life of me, I couldn't remember Tyler's number. Pushing back the urge to cry, I started to get ready for work.

By eight forty-five, I drove toward Savannah. Glancing in the rearview mirror, I looked like I'd fought Rocky Balboa and lost. Mrs. Vaughn would eat me alive if she saw me. Nothing could hide a purple eye.

I walked through the garage, heart pounding. Tyler's car was sitting in the first bay. He usually ran until after ten. I quietly opened the door to the kitchen, and was glad I didn't hear anyone. I slipped around the corner with my head bent, hurrying toward the foyer. Darting toward the utility room, I gathered supplies and tiptoed upstairs. A door clicked. I glanced over my shoulder and saw Tyler stepping out of his room. I hurried inside the bathroom and closed the door.

The bathroom was a safe place, right? Not only at my house. It should be a universal rule. I walked to the sink and set down the supplies.

Within seconds, Tyler stepped inside and closed the door.

"What are you doing?" I snapped, turning my back on him.

"What's wrong?" He walked across the room. I stayed hidden behind my hair. "Where were you this morning? I called you a hundred times. Elsie, look at me. Please."

I slowly turned around and lifted my face.

"What the fuck?" He stepped back. "Who did that to you?"

I flinched. He grabbed my shoulders.

"Elsie, what happened? Talk to me."

I jerked away. "Don't!"

He quickly stepped back, raising his hands in the air. "Please... let me help you."

I pressed my face in my palms and cried. I felt Tyler's gentle touch slide over my back, as he pulled me toward him. I hid my face in his embrace.

"I'm sorry I didn't make it to our run this morning," I said against his chest.

"It's okay. I've been worried about you. Did Mark do this?"

At any other time, both men accusing the other would've been funny.

"No. Mr. Smith. He was drunk and thought I was late."

"He hit you because you were late? You weren't late."

He started to step back. I wrapped my arms around him so he wouldn't. Taking my signal, he tightened his embrace.

"It was only a little after nine," I said. "He yelled at me, and then he said he wanted a kiss to make up for it. He... he backhanded me when I tried to get away."

Tyler's whole body tensed as I told him the story.

"Then he slammed me against the doorway, and I hit my head. I finally got away. I totally lost Mom's job."

Tyler leaned back to look into my eyes, pain written all over his face.

"I'm sorry, but your mother getting fired is the last thing you need to worry about. Damn it. Why didn't you call me?"

"I dropped my phone at his house." I pressed my forehead to his chest. "When I got home, I threw up and slept all night."

"You have a concussion." He kissed the top of my head. "Thank God you woke up."

He touched my chin. I looked up. His eyes narrowed as he inspected my wounds.

"I tried to find you," I said. "The gardener told me you were out running."

"What time were you here?"

"Around ten-thirty."

"Really?" He sighed. "I was here. He didn't know."

Tyler gently kissed my forehead, then he took my hand and led me out of the bathroom.

I shuffled my feet to keep up. "Where are we going?"

"To get your phone."

"Tyler, I have to clean. I'll get—"

"Don't worry about it," he said, hurrying down the stairs.

We walked through the house and into the garage. Tyler headed straight to his car. I stopped in front of Mrs. Vaughn's Jaguar. He opened his car door and turned to me.

"What is it?" he asked.

"We can't go there."

"Elsie, listen to me. I won't stand for some guy hitting you."

"You're angry."

"Yes, I am," he said, calmly. "But I promise I won't hurt him. I just want to get your phone. Will you get in, please?"

I watched him. He matched my stare, standing his ground. Giving in, I walked to the passenger's side and climbed in.

I gave him directions to Mr. Smith's as he backed out of the driveway, then told him the story in detail. Tyler chewed on his lip, focusing on the road. I'd seen him agitated, but not pissed off. The intensity in his eyes, his tight jaw, his cold demeanor. *Shit. He did have a temper.*

Five minutes later, he parked in front of the old man's house.

"Stay here," Tyler said. "The windows are limousine black. He can't see you."

Tyler climbed out, taking long strides toward the house. Within seconds, he stood tall, pounding his fist on the front door. Mr. Smith answered with a smile and offered out his hand. Tyler didn't accept. Smith's expression went blank, and then he disappeared inside. Tyler stepped through the door, closing it behind him.

I started fidgeting with my shirt, keeping my eye on the house. I shouldn't have agreed to this. The only thing I wanted was to forget the man's existence.

The car door opened and I looked up, relieved to see his face. Thank God.

Tyler slid in the seat and handed me the phone. "Here, it's all taken care of."

He turned on the ignition and did a U-turn.

"Thank you," I said. "What happened?"

"I told him that if he ever touches you again, I'll kill him."

I pushed back a smile. "You didn't have to do that for my phone."

"It isn't about your phone." He glanced at me. "I can buy you a new phone. This is about you. I won't stand for anyone hurting you. Jack knows my family. Hell, I guess everyone does. He acted more surprised that I came there for you. Who the hell does he think he is, smacking you like that?"

"Did he admit it?"

"He didn't deny it. He sat down on the couch and started blubbering like a baby. He's too drunk, that's his problem. He could hardly remember." Tyler took a deep breath. "I'm sorry you were late. I thought we got back in time."

"I really wasn't that late. It was only a few minutes. He's been freaking me out lately, and I told Mom about it. It's like he did it because he knows she's gone."

Tyler took my hand. "You can always press charges if you want."

"No," I said. Involving the police scared me. "I just want to forget about it."

"Okay, it's up to you. Do you feel like working?"

"I have to."

"No, you don't. I'll deal with Nana. You need to go home and ice your eye."

"Tyler, she'll tell. Plus, it's Friday, I get paid today. I have to get the check for Mom."

He pulled in the driveway and parked the car outside of the garage. He turned in his seat. "Elsie... " he pleaded.

"I have to get through it. It's only a few hours."

"You blow me away. You don't know how strong you are."

I lowered my head. "No, I'm not."

"Bullshit. Look at me."

I turned to him. He tilted his head as if he wanted to convince me with just a look. Then, he leaned across the seat and kissed me. I winced. I needed to feel his touch, but any pressure on my face felt like a burning match on my skin.

He smiled, gently touching my bruised cheekbone. "Sorry."

"Thank you for getting my phone."

"It was the least I could do. I have to go for a swim, but I won't leave. When you're done, text me. I'll either be at the pool or in my room."

"What if your grandmother sees my face? She's going to think I'm total trash."

"Just try to avoid her."

"I hope she isn't in the same mood as Smith," I scoffed. "I gotta get inside."

I followed him through the garage into the dimly lit mudroom. He turned around in the shadows and slid his hand through my hair, then gently gave me a kiss goodbye.

"I'll see you when you're done, okay?" he whispered.

"Okay."

"I'll come over tonight. We can spend the evening together."

I nodded, and then he gently kissed me again.

After we parted ways, I hid in the utility room for a few minutes, pacing the small space in an attempt to gain my composure. Tyler had taken care of Mr. Smith. All I had to do was get through the day. *You can do this, Elsie.* Just a few more hours and you'll be done cleaning for good.

For the next few hours, I vacuumed, dusted, scoured the bathroom and polished the glass on the upper level. Mom always cleaned when she was mad or frustrated. Now I understood why. As the day moved on, I started feeling better.

At one-thirty, I walked down the hallway toward Mrs. Vaughn's bedroom. The passage seemed to narrow as apprehension overwhelmed me. I slowed my steps. Why did I feel like sprinting out of the house? A doorknob clicked. The hair stood up on my arms. That's why.

Mrs. Vaughn's bedroom door slowly opened. I stopped. She stepped out and sized me up.

"You look awful," she stated. "What is wrong with your face, child?"

I ran my hand through my hair to cover my eye.

"It's no big deal," I said, nerves making my voice crack. "I just need to finish your room and I'll be done for the day."

"Why did I see you get out of Tyler's car? Where did you go with him?"

Blood pumped around my bruise. Mr. Smith's face flashed in my mind. *Oh, hell no.* I wasn't doing this again, especially with her.

Standing straighter, I said, "I apologize for leaving earlier, but I'd like to finish my work, now. Then, I'll be gone for good."

She stepped closer to me. Too close. "You're just a troublemaker."

I stepped backward to get away from her mothball breath.

"Are you seriously going to add insult to injury?" I said. "I've already had a really bad day."

"You have no business with Tyler," she said through clenched teeth. "I saw you kiss him in his car. You're nothing but a little whore!"

"Are you serious? You can clean your own fucking house!" I shouted and threw my dust rag at her overpriced heels. "My mom might put up with your bullshit, but I won't."

I spun around. Tyler stood at the top of the stairs, wearing only his black warm-ups and his hair wet from his swim. He walked barefooted toward us, staring down his grandmother.

"Elsie, why don't you go on ahead," he said, eyes still

locked on Mrs. Vaughn. "I'll catch up with you in a bit."

I hurried past him and started down the staircase. Half-way down, I heard her shrill voice.

"You deserve better than that!"

I ran.

Chapter

22

I ran inside my house, ripped off my work clothes, and pulled on a T-shirt and shorts. No hiding. I can jog, but I can't run. I grabbed my iPod and headed back to the front door.

Mark sat on the couch, watching TV. "Where are you going?"

"Running."

"You'd better mean for exercise. I'm not chasing you—"

I let the door slam. Pushing in my ear buds, I jogged to the road and stopped. The old house. I could hide there for hours. No one would find me. *Tyler. No. Don't do it.* I turned away and started running in the opposite direction toward the rolling hills.

LIFE HAPPENS ON THE STAIRS

I bombed it. I failed Mom. She would totally lose her job. Two jobs. I imagined the disappointment in her eyes. She had trusted me. But would she want to go back? What if she didn't stand up for me? What if she thought I'd instigated it? Oh God, that would kill me.

Enduring each hill as if I deserved the punishment, I could still hear Mrs. Vaughn's sharp words. *You deserve better than that... you're nothing but a little whore...*

I'm a freaking virgin!

Anger boiled inside of me as I fought the momentum pushing me down the hill. I'd show that woman. *Fuck her.* Nothing would keep me from Tyler. I'd take her abuse until she couldn't fight anymore. I pushed up the incline, calves burning along with my rage. She thought she could break me? Never.

I hit flat ground, adrenaline pushing me on for the next two miles. Thirty minutes later, I jogged around the curve toward home. The truck was gone. *Great, I'm stuck.* Mark had better be doing something productive.

I opened the front door. The place was empty, save for the beer bottles and trash. Maybe he'd taken a load of peppers to the processing plant. I looked out the dining room window. The tractor sat at the edge of the field with an empty scoop. I sighed in relief, turned around, and scanned the house. Trash everywhere. *Thanks, Mark.*

As I grabbed a bottle of water, my cell phone rang. *Oh crap.* I didn't check if I'd missed any calls. Hurrying to my room, I grabbed it out of my work pants.

"Hello?"

"Where have you been?" Mom shouted.

"I just got back from jogging."

"I've been trying to call you since yesterday. I'm worried

sick here."

"Sorry, I lost my phone. I just got it back."

"Where's Mark? I've been calling the house, too."

We'd planned to surprise her with the money from the harvest, so I didn't want to say.

"He left in the truck," I said, hoping she'd accept my vague answer.

I listened to her long sigh on the other end. Her tension gnawed my nerves.

"Your dad and I are coming home tomorrow. We should be there by four. I need you to do a few things for me."

I slumped on my bed. "Okay."

Could the day get any worse?

"Strip the sheets off my bed and clear anything blocking the way for the paramedics to bring him back to our room. Hospice should be there around noon to move out the old bed and bring in a hospital bed. You need to be there to let them in. Please, don't forget."

"Mm, hmm."

"How did work go today?"

She didn't hesitate from giving orders to wanting updates. I couldn't go there yet.

"Mm, okay."

"Are you all right?"

I took a deep breath. She asked...

"No. Not exactly," I said. "You chew me out for not being at your beck and call. Then you start barking orders to clean your room. You have no idea how crappy this week has been. You don't even ask unless it's about your jobs. I don't want Dad to come home like this. It sucks! Why are they sending him home to die? I wan—"

"Enough!" she said. "Watch your tone, little girl. Your

dad is coming home because it's where he belongs, and you're going to suck it up and do as I ask. This is our only option. You have no idea what I'm going through, and I don't ever want you to know how this feels."

Her voice quivered. *Oh no.* I'd just kicked a wounded woman. Of all people, Mom. Tears filled my eyes.

"He's dying, Elsie," she exhaled. "They can't do any more for him. The hospital's been fantastic, but we have no idea how long he'll live. He needs to be at home, where he belongs."

I wiped the tears off my cheek. "Oh, Mom... "

"I love you. I know this is hard, but it's the way it is right now." She took a deep breath. "This too shall pass, right?"

Her motto would have helped if "this too" wasn't my dad.

"Right," I said, gently. "I'll see you when you get here."

"Okay. Thank you for your help."

"Yeah. Love you," I said, then flipped the phone shut.

Being called a whore with a black eye was pleasurable compared to watching Dad die. I stared into space, paralyzed with fear. Everything would change when they came home. My time to accept it had run out.

The phone rang. I glanced at the screen. Tyler.

"Hello?"

"Hey, can I come over?"

"Please."

"Are you all right?"

"No. I just talked to Mom."

"I'm already on the road. I'll be there in a few."

"Okay."

Another surge of adrenaline hit me. I took a three-minute shower, dressed in cut-off shorts and a fresh T-shirt, then brushed my hair. Hurrying around, I gathered all the trash from the party. After hearing Tyler's voice, all I wanted was to fall into his embrace.

As I shoved the last blanket in the closet, I heard a knock at the door. Expecting his usual bright smile when I pulled it open, I instantly deflated. He hesitated like he didn't know if he should come in or not. I stepped aside. He looked angry. Would he really take her side?

Without a word, he walked to the center of the living room, then held out a folded check.

What the hell was that for? Oh. Payment.

"I wanted to make sure you got that," he said.

"Thank you." I took the piece of paper. "I'd forgotten all about it."

Tyler stepped back. I glanced down at the check. Mom needed the cash, but I felt like he'd come over to pay me off. Cold and reserved, I couldn't read him. He still looked pissed.

"I'm really sorry for throwing an F-bomb at her," I said.

Tyler crossed his arms. "Elsie, how much more can you take?"

I shrugged. "Hell if I know."

I flopped down on the couch, leaned forward, and set my head in my hands. His detachment. *Why?* I wanted to scream, *what the hell happened?*

"Tyler, what's going on?" I asked. "You're not telling me something."

He shifted his stance and ran his fingers through his hair.

"I don't know what she's gonna do when Claire gets back," he said. "I tried like hell to talk her out of anything irrational. But, she's pissed we're together."

His words wracked me with regret. I'd run my mouth, lost my cool, lied to Mom. A gnawing headache pulsed behind my eye. I rubbed my forehead, pushing out the tension.

"I've screwed everything up. She's gonna fire Mom."

He sat down next to me. Silence. He didn't reach out or console me. Hell, he wouldn't even look at me. I felt nauseous. *Did he come over to dump me?*

I cradled my head in my hand, trying to cover my ugly eye. "Can I ask you something?"

He gave me a nod, still staring forward.

"Did she change your mind?"

He looked at me like I'd gone crazy. "About what?"

"Us."

"No. I've known all along she'd freak out. It's not about who you are; it's about who she expects me to be with. That's why I took you to Memphis. I wanted you to see what my life's really like. I come to Savannah because it's expected of me, but I wouldn't change anything about the past month." His eyes softened with the gentleness I craved. "Except your black eye. Or sneaking around so your mom doesn't find out. And definitely what's happening to your dad."

He stood up and walked across the room like he'd been hit with a burst of energy.

"All of this is driving me crazy!" Tyler flipped his hands in the air in frustration. "I want to tell the world how I feel about you. That's the problem, not my grandmother. I told her to get over it. This is my life. She calls you a whore and expects me to kiss her ass? I heard what she said to you." He cocked his head to the side with a slight glare in his eyes. "But what about you? Where are you at? You seriously think I'm going to change how I feel because my grandmother doesn't like it? When Claire finds out, will you change your mind? Is it that simple?"

"Damn it, Tyler. What do you want from me?" I snapped.

"The woman's determined to convince you that I'm not good enough."

"No one will ever convince me of that."

I stood to my feet ready to duke this one out.

"I don't know how I'm going to tell Mom, but I promise, I'm not ashamed of how I feel about you. Everything's going to change tomorrow. And when you leave. And when Dad dies. It's inevitable. All I can do is brace myself for the blows. It's going to hurt like hell." I stopped to take a breath and calm down. Tyler didn't respond, letting me continue. "What I do know, is every time I'm with you, for just a little while... I feel safe. That's what I can't handle. Doing this without you. I need you, and I'm scared of my life after you leave."

His intense stare took my breath away. Holding... waiting... I broke eye contact and looked at the floor.

"You have no idea how much I needed to hear that."

Two steps and he was right beside me, running his hands into my hair as he pressed his lips hard against mine. I wrapped my arms around his neck and relief flooded my body. He lifted me off the floor, kissing me deeper.

"God, I want you so much," he said against my mouth.

I ran my hands through his hair, returning his deep kiss. He gently laid me down on the couch. Bodies pressed together, he pushed up to look in my eyes.

"I'm sorry I scared you when I got here," he said. "I'm mad at her. Not you."

He swept his lips over mine, kissing me so tenderly, so gently, a tear rolled down my cheek. He slowly pulled away, and then he wiped the tear with the back of his fingers.

"I am unconditionally in love with you, Elsie."

As he kissed me again, I replayed the moment in my mind. I wanted to say it, too. But his conviction didn't require my courtesy – just my acceptance. He pulled away and shifted beside me and I relaxed in his warm embrace.

"What did your mom say?" he asked.

"They're coming home tomorrow. It scares the shit out of me, and I keep pissing her off."

He laughed. "You're batting a thousand today."

His phone vibrated against the couch. He shifted and pulled it out of his back pocket. I saw "Nana" at the top of the screen. Ignoring the call, he set the phone on the coffee table. A twinge of guilt stabbed me.

"I'm sorry I said that to your grandmother. I'm so embarrassed."

"Stop," he said. "Nana deserved it. When will they be home?"

"Around four." Tears stung my eyes at the thought. "Will you stay with me tonight?"

"Would be my pleasure."

All worn out, we settled into each other's arms and slept for over an hour. We woke up starving and made our way to the kitchen, giggling and flirting as we fried two hamburgers on the stove. I made sweet tea, nuked two potatoes, and then we ate, enjoying our freedom together.

Afterward, we washed the dishes, then he started reciting facts about how many men died at Normandy. He concluded his point and sat down. Within seconds, he stood back up and started pacing. I watched him for a moment. He needed a run or he'd go nuts all night.

"Should we go for a jog?" I asked.

He smiled. "Hell, yes."

"You have a change of clothes?"

"No, I didn't think about it when I left."

"Well, you can't run in designer jeans," I said. "Let me see what I can find in Mark's room. What about your shoes?"

"I always have my wheels."

"For real?"

"Yeah, I keep them in the car."

I giggled. "Running in Italian leather loafers would suck."

"Tell me about it."

After I found a pair of Mark's basketball shorts, Tyler came out of the bathroom before I realized I needed to change, too.

"Do you want to go to Shiloh?" he asked from the living room.

"We can," I said, slipping on my jogging shorts. "I already ran here today."

"Oh, really? When did you do that?"

I grabbed my tennis shoes and walked out of my room. "After I left your house. I needed to jog, or you'd still be looking for me."

He reached out and pulled me close.

"You'd better not run and hide. I'll search the ends of the earth for you."

The evening air felt cool and refreshing as we jogged the paths at Shiloh. Tyler seemed relieved to burn his excessive energy, but it didn't take long for me to fizzle out after all the running I'd done. When the sun began to move behind the tree line, we turned around and walked back to his car. Instead of going to my house, he drove into Savannah.

He'd better not take me back to that awful house.

"Where are you going?" I asked.

He turned into the first fast-food restaurant on the strip. "I'm hungry."

"Again?"

He smiled as he slowed next to the intercom, and then he rolled down the window.

"Three double cheeseburger meals," he said. "Only two drinks. Thanks."

"That's insane, Tyler."

"I have to eat a lot. All I've had today is breakfast, then dinner at your house."

"How much food do you need?"

"I burn over fifteen hundred calories a day. So, I have to eat at least three thousand, or more." He chuckled. "That's a lot of food, if you think about it."

"Yeah, it is."

The cashier gave him his change, and then two bags of food, and two drinks.

He handed them to me. "Don't open them."

"Why?"

"No eating in the car," he said, as he pulled on the highway.

"Can't blame you, there. One of my greatest talents is spilling food on car seats."

He nodded. "Glad you understand."

When we settled in at my house, he reluctantly offered me one of his sandwiches. We ate, and then he wanted to take a quick shower. I rummaged Mark's room again and found a pair of sweats and a T-shirt for him. As I waited for him to finish, I watched TV, and then we swapped places. Relieved to wash the sweat off, I rejoined him within ten minutes.

A bit later, we went to my room, snuggled next to each other on top of the covers, and talked for hours. I told him how much I worried about my family, and how hard it would be to get the peppers harvested. Then we joked that I'd probably kill myself trying, and no one would find me for days. He totally got me, even down to my twisted views on life and death.

We'd just concluded that we both didn't like mayonnaise, when he grabbed my iPod.

"Elsie, look at this thing. It's ten years old."

I rolled on my side, propping on my elbow. "Who cares? It works."

"Yeah well, it holds like three songs."

I snatched it from him. "I have a hundred songs. See?"

He took it back and started scrolling through my playlist. "You like weird music. *4 Non Blondes*, seriously?"

"That's a great song."

We chatted while we listened to *What's Up?*

"It's not that bad," he said, after it stopped.

Heatbeat by *The Frey* started. I studied his face as he scrolled through the songs.

"Will you tell me about your accident?" I asked.

"Sure." He set down my iPod, then rolled on his side to face me. "I was fifteen and here for the end of the summer. Grandpa and I had gone to the country club for dinner. On the way home, he babbled on about some guy who thought he could rip off the stock market. A deer ran out in front of us. The impact snapped Grandpa's neck and he died instantly."

"It's crazy that it didn't hurt you, but it killed him."

"Weird, isn't it? I hit my head, and glass shattered all over me, but like Mom said, I walked away with only cuts and bruises." He lifted his sleeve. "See, I have scars, too."

He pointed to his shoulder. Then he rolled on his back, pulled up the bottom of his shirt, and showed me a few more scars on his chest and stomach. I ran my finger over a fine line hiding between his abdominal muscles.

"I do miss him, though," Tyler said with a heaviness in his voice that I rarely heard.

"You two were close, weren't you?"

He took my hand and pressed his lips to the back of it. I could feel his pain in his gentle touch. He'd been withholding this side of himself. He didn't have to hide it. I needed to know he wasn't a superhero.

"Yeah, we were. He taught me what it means to be a man. Old school, you know? A baby boomer. His integrity was beyond reproach. I don't know... " He sighed. "Everything was different when he was alive. Nana wasn't so bad back then. She's so damn controlling now."

"Ugh." I flopped on my back. "Don't tell me that's how Mom will be if Dad dies."

He laughed. "Maybe." He leaned down and kissed me. As he pulled away, he spotted my sketchpad between the bed and the wall.

He nodded with a grin. "May I?"

"Mm, I don't know... You might be surprised at what's inside."

"Oh, really?" He raised his eyebrows. "You owe me. My journal, remember?"

Blood rushed my cheeks. *Crap.*

I gave him a quick nod. He snatched the sketchpad, rolled over, and propped it on his legs. Opening the book, his eyes widened.

"Wow. When did you do this?" he asked. "You nailed me."

"I keep missing something, though. I can't figure it out." I turned to a drawing of him leaning against a spilt-rail fence.

"See, something's missing."

"Well, that's easy. It's you."

I smiled.

"I'm serious. Especially, standing next to *that* fence. You still don't get it, do you? You're the reason my eyes light up, and for the smile on my face. All the energy you think comes so naturally to me? It's because I'm with you. I'm just not the same guy unless you're standing right there." He tapped the page. "You belong next to me."

I laid my head on his chest. "I never would've thought of that. What a cool idea."

He kissed the top of my head, and then we looked through the drawings: the river, my brother, the collage of Dad's expressions, another portrait of Tyler.

"Remember the first day at Shiloh?" he asked.

I nodded. Shiloh would always have a place in my heart. We talked for another hour about all the days we'd met each morning.

After midnight, we put the sketchbook away and turned out the lights. He pulled me close, twisting our legs together, our clothed bodies pressed tight.

I rolled over and kissed him. Shrouded in darkness, he smelled like my vanilla body wash. I smiled on his lips, then pushed a little further with another long kiss. His hands moved through my hair, deepening our embrace. I found the bottom of his shirt and ran my fingertips over his smooth stomach. He pressed his body against mine, our mouths moving in perfect rhythm. After a few moments of pure bliss, he softly moaned and pulled away.

No... don't stop.

"You know what I've always wanted?" he whispered in the dark like he could read my mind. "To marry my girl, and that night, then and only then, will we finally know everything about each other. Can you imagine how incredible that will be?"

"Yes."

Please, let me be that girl.

Ever the gentleman, he gently kissed me again, then shifted behind me, and held me close through the night.

The next morning, I woke still wrapped in his arms. Afraid of him leaving, I snuggled deeper in his embrace and dozed back to sleep.

At eleven, he kissed me goodbye on the front step. I watched him drive away, then went inside and sat on the couch. Wedging in the corner, I curled in a ball and cried until hospice arrived at noon.

Chapter

23

At four that afternoon, I returned to the corner of the couch. Mark came out of his room and plopped down in the recliner. He stared out the window, looking like a mad rooster, hair sticking up, arms crossed. Dad coming home like this had us both fighting off demons.

Mark scowled. "Dude, your eye looks like shit. Mom's gonna freak when she sees you."

"Don't remind me."

My stomach churned. Mom would freak out. The color had faded to yellows and blues, but makeup still couldn't hide it. And then there was Mrs. Vaughn... Should I tell Mom, or just ride out the storm?

I heard a car door shut, so I walked to the picture window

and looked out. Mom was parking the car in the side yard, and a small ambulance was backing into the driveway. Within seconds, she walked inside and set her purse on the coffee table.

"How was the drive?" I asked.

"Easy and quiet." She pushed the coffee table up against the couch to make room. "How are you two?"

Mark grunted.

My heart pounded. She hadn't made eye contact yet. Letting out a sigh, she scanned the room, then smiled at me. Her face went blank.

"Elsie, your eye!" She rushed toward me. "What happened?"

Grabbing my chin, she moved my head back and forth.

"It's okay, Mom." I pulled away. "I'll tell you about it later."

She stared me down, then turned to Mark.

"Don't tell me you just woke up."

She had no idea how caustic she sounded. My heart broke for Mark.

Welcome home, Mom.

"Yeah, I was up late last night," his tone calmer than I expected.

She looked back and forth, sizing us up, then she scanned the house.

"Who had the party?" she asked. "One of you did."

Mark glared at me. I returned his scowl.

"Is that where she got the black eye?" Mom said to Mark.

Mark slammed his palms on the arms of the chair and stood up. At the same time, the paramedics stepped inside, lifting the gurney into the room.

Mark started toward the kitchen. "No, Mom. You own

that one."

She gave me a questioning look. "We'll talk in a few minutes."

"I'm glad you're home."

"Me too." She gave me a quick hug, then turned to lead the men to the bedroom.

Then the scene slowed to a crawl as they pushed Dad, unconscious, through the living room. Emaciated cheeks, dusty gray skin – he looked like a complete stranger. A metal hook extended above him, with a rubber bag swinging back and forth. I stepped aside as they turned the corner to go down the hall.

I rushed out the front door and sucked in a deep breath, fighting the urge to run.

"This is insane!"

"What's insane?" Mark stepped around the corner of the house.

I jumped. He smirked and took a long drag from a cigarette.

"Mark!" I recoiled. "You're smoking?"

He disappeared to where he had come from. I followed.

"Did you tell her I had a party?" he asked over his shoulder.

"No. Why would I do that?"

"I don't know. The place looks fine. It doesn't make any sense."

"She just wanted to see how we'd react."

I sat on the back step and stared at the field of peppers. Nothing would ever be the same.

"He's gone," I whispered.

"What do you mean?" Mark snapped back.

"Dad's never going to be the same."

He let out a sigh and sat down next to me. "No."

"Do you think he'll be like this long?"

He flicked his cigarette. "Well, he isn't going to get better."

"How long do you think?"

"I don't know... It could be any day, I guess." Resting his elbows on his legs, he ran his fingers into his hair. "Isn't it great Mom's home? I never know what I'm going to get from her."

"She's stressed."

"I know, but we aren't exactly on vacation. She acted like I'd let that happen to you."

"She doesn't know." Compassion for both of them tore me inside. "I have to tell her Mr. Smith did this, and—"

"And what? You'd better not rat me out."

"I'm not going to say anything about your party." I shook my head. "It isn't on my radar. Oh, and by the way, you're welcome for cleaning the house. I saved your ass."

"You just did that 'cause Tyler came over."

"Yeah, well," I started, and then it dawned on me. "You did know he was here."

"His car kinda gave him away." He rolled his eyes. "You're damn lucky you were both dressed when I looked in your room. I'd hate to beat the pretty boy's ass."

"Stop it." I nudged him with my shoulder. "Anyway, you're the one who had naked people in your bed. Yuck."

"Yeah, Misty and Trent. They have no shame."

"No kidding."

We sat in silence, staring across the yard. My fears must've paled in comparison to his. He'd screwed up his future, thrown away a scholarship, and had wandered in limbo ever since. Dad's death could affect him for the rest of his life.

Hell, it could affect all of us for life.

Mark dug in his shirt pocket and pulled out another cigarette.

"Did you take a load of peppers yesterday?" I asked. "I saw the scoop was empty."

"Yeah." He flicked the lighter and took a drag. "We made three hundred dollars."

"You're going to give it to Mom, right?"

He chuckled. "If she chills."

"Let it go, man."

"I'm joking." He waved his hand. "Of course, I'm going to give it to her. I'm hoping to get out there this evening and pick for a while. You up for it?"

"Sure. I'd like to see Tyler, but she would totally suspect something."

"Why don't you just tell her about him?"

"Um, I plead the Fifth."

He scrunched his forehead. I shrugged and stood up, then walked through the back door into my bedroom. The less Mark knew the better. I had to protect my private world. My time with Tyler was ticking away fast.

As I walked out of my room, the paramedics were pushing the gurney back through the house. Mom followed, thanking them for their help before she closed the door. I went in the kitchen and waited.

"Now what?" I asked.

She headed to the sink and turned on the water. "We do our best."

"Can he talk?"

"No. He wakes for a little while sometimes." She turned around. "Do you want to go see him? I need to show you everything."

I didn't know what to say. I wanted to see Dad, but not like that. Somehow, I had to accept that he was dying. I hated being told *no*, and I felt like that was the answer to my prayers. No. Sorry. Not answering this one.

She looked at me with her kind blue eyes. I'd missed her. I hated what we were going through, but I was beyond thankful for her strength.

"Elsie, it's going to be hard, but we'll be okay." She tilted her head with a loving look. "Will you please tell me how you got that awful-looking eye first?"

"You're not going to like it."

"I didn't figure I would." She leaned across the counter, reaching out to my face. "It looks terrible. Who would hurt you like that?"

"Um, well... I was a few minutes late to Mr. Smith's on Thursday—"

"I told you to get there early."

I took a deep breath. "He wanted a kiss to make up for it. It got ugly after that."

Gasping, she stood straight. "He tried to kiss you, and then he hit you?"

I gave her some time to absorb the words. She paced in a circle, hands pressing her forehead, and then she looked at me with wet eyes.

"Elizabeth, I'm so sorry. You tried to tell me."

Tears poured down her scarlet cheeks. She walked around the counter and pulled me into her arms. I buried my face in her shoulder and cried along with her. I wasn't sure who my tears were for: her, Dad, missing Tyler. But they weren't for Smith. Tyler had fixed that.

I told her the whole story with the exception of Tyler going back to get my phone. She stood there appalled, gasping every so often.

"That's why Mark said that," she whispered. "I would've never asked you to go there if I thought Smith would do something like this."

"It's okay." I gave her a weak smile. "Makes me stronger, right?"

"Right... " Her expression told me this wasn't how she expected me to grow stronger.

She excused herself and headed down the hallway. I needed to see Dad. As I passed the bathroom, I could hear her crying. I hesitated at the door, needing to give her some comfort. *No, let her be.*

I slowly stepped the last few feet to the bedroom and peered inside.

Dad lay perfectly still except for the rise and fall of his chest. My body trembled. It felt weird to go in their room without permission. Mark and I were only allowed to enter after Dad bellowed, *Come in.* How I wished he would wake up and say, "Elsie, go on now, get out of here. We'll be out in a minute."

Mom walked to the foot of the bed, beside me.

"They sedated him pretty heavily for the ride home," she said. "He might not open his eyes for a few hours."

"I'm sorry about Smith's."

"Elsie, you don't have to apologize for being assaulted. I'm the one who's sorry."

"It's okay. It's getting better."

"Really?" she said, deadpan. "I'm glad I didn't see it earlier then."

We smiled at each other, then stared at Dad like he was already in a coffin.

I pointed to a bag attached to the side of the bed. "What's

that?"

"For his catheter. It has to be changed several times a day."

His head was wrapped, covering the scar tissue, but he looked like a skeleton.

"He looks so different," I said.

"It's from the heavy doses of steroids. I'm supposed to give him all those pills somehow. Hopefully, the nurse will help."

"You look tired."

"Don't remind me." She sighed. "I know I look like crap."

"You don't look like crap. You look tired," I repeated and searched the room. "Where will you sleep?"

"I guess on the couch. I'd like to find another cheap recliner to put in here."

Mark stepped in the doorway. Mom turned to him.

"We need to talk." She walked out and led him down the hall. "I owe you an apology."

Alone in the room with Dad, I tried to say something, but the words stuck in my throat. I swallowed and tried again.

"Hey, Daddy," I whispered. "Welcome home."

By six-thirty, Mom had fallen asleep in the recliner. Mark and I headed out the back door to go to the field. We strapped on our sacks and started picking where he'd left off. Between his effort, plus Tyler's and mine, we'd managed to pick over ten of the forty-five rows.

We worked until sunset, filling the scoop almost full. One more pass and we'd have close to six hundred dollars for Mom. I headed back inside. Mark stayed in the barn to inspect the harvest.

When I went to the bathroom, I saw Mom sitting beside Dad's bed. I washed up and went to their room to say goodnight. Her face was buried in her hands as she cried. I tapped on the door. She snapped to attention, wiping her cheeks.

"You okay?" I asked. She nodded. "I'm off to bed. I'll see you in the morning."

"Goodnight. Sleep well."

"Love you."

"Love you, too."

At six-thirty in the morning, I climbed out of bed, dressed in my jogging clothes, and headed to the kitchen to grab some breakfast. Mom stood by the sink, sipping her coffee.

"Oh good, you're up," she said. "The nurse will be here soon. I want you to meet her."

I deflated. "Mom, I'm supposed to meet Jenna at seven."

"I'm sorry, but you'll have to go later."

"It'll be so hot by then," I said, walking back to my room.

After I stepped out the back door, I flipped open my phone and pressed Tyler's name.

"Hey," he answered. "I'm on my way."

"I have to stay here to meet the nurse. Sorry."

"Okay. That's important. Can we meet later? I really want to see you."

"Me, too. I'll try to get away this evening. How about six?"

"That works."

"Okay. I'll text you when I leave."

I sat on the step, letting my tears flow in private before I went inside. I needed to see him. Everything around me had changed, and I needed him to be my constant. He was the only one who would listen, the only one whose arms could comfort. I wiped my eyes, sucked in my emotions, and went back inside.

"We're going tonight at six," I said, returning to the kitchen. "I hope that works because I don't want to skip today."

"That should be fine," she said. "You really like jogging?"

"Yes."

"Well, it's good for you. I can't argue with that."

She smashed bananas and a powder packet, making a soupy mess in a bowl.

"What's that?"

"Breakfast for your dad."

I scrunched my nose. "Nasty."

At seven sharp, I heard a knock at the door. A petite, green-eyed girl with strawberry blonde hair pulled in a tight bun greeted me.

"Hi, y'all," she said in a high-pitched drawl. She wore light blue scrubs and clean white tennis shoes.

"Hi." I smiled, waving her inside. "Come on in."

Mom walked across the living room, greeting the girl with a handshake.

"I'm Claire, nice to meet you. This is my daughter, Elsie."

"I'm Megan." She shook Mom's hand, and then mine. "Wow, you gotta big shiner! I'd hate to see the other guy."

Mom and I glanced at each other.

"I'll be here every weekday and Saturdays until he's... " She paused. "Until... well, you understand." Her face turned red. "I'm sorry. I didn't mean to be awkward."

"It's okay," Mom said and waved for Megan to follow her. "I'll show you to our room. I'm hoping you can help me figure out the best way to feed him."

"They don't have him on a feeding tube?" Megan asked. "They told me there'd be one."

"No, I wish they had done that. I'm afraid he's not getting enough nutrients from the mush I keep pushing down his throat."

"Hold on!"

Mom and I flinched. Megan grabbed her phone, pressed a few numbers, and then she looked back and forth between us with big, green eyes.

"Megan here. Y'all told me my patient's on a feeding tube. Where is it? I need one stat."

I smiled. I loved the girl already.

"Mm. Uh, hmm, yes... okay." She looked at Mom and then me, nodding like she heard good news. "Very good... Thank you, we'll see y'all soon." She ended the call. "They'll be here in an hour. Man's gotta eat, right?" She winked at Mom.

"Thank you," Mom said with relief. "Come on in."

Megan looked over Dad's bed and all the tubes, and then she said, "Hello, Mr. Richardson. I'm Megan Prescott. I'll be taking care of you. Please feel free to talk to me if you can, and always let me know if you're uncomfortable or in need of something."

His eyes were open, but he didn't focus on her. I walked up and leaned on the railing.

"Hi, Daddy."

His eyes rolled toward me, and then he blinked. I smiled and rubbed his hand. Megan rearranged something under his sheets. I had no idea what and didn't want to know what he had going on under the covers, so I stared at his hand.

"It looks like the feeding tube attachment is still in place from the hospital," she said. "I can't believe they'd let y'all come home without explicit instructions on how to feed him."

She tucked in his sheets, checked his pulse, and listened to his breathing through a stethoscope. His eyes followed her, but he didn't move otherwise.

"Brandon, honey." Mom patted his leg, and then her face filled with worry. "Brandon?" she repeated, her voice pitching higher.

His eyes rolled back, then I heard the bed rattle as his body went rigid.

"Elsie, go!" Mom shouted.

"No, Claire," Megan said. "I think she needs to see this. We're all in this together."

Mom's terror-filled eyes darted from me to Megan, and then she nodded.

"Now, this is what we do." Megan took hold of Dad's arm. "Elsie, you hold his other arm. We don't want him hurtin' himself. Claire, grab the medicine bottles."

Trembling, I grabbed Dad's arm and held him down. Mom handed Megan the medicines, swapping places with her. Megan searched the bottles, finding the one she wanted, then quickly administered the pill by pushing it under his tongue.

"The pill will dissolve fast," Megan said. "We just need to wait and see if it does its job."

After a few chilling moments of watching Dad's body wrench with convulsions, his muscles started to relax, and the tremors stopped.

"There we go." Megan wiped his forehead with a washcloth. "All better."

I sighed. Thank God. My mind flashed back to the day at the festival. At least he was lying in bed this time, and there wasn't any blood. Feeling like I'd just run a marathon, I excused myself and went to my room to cry in private.

An hour later, the other hospital worker arrived. Everyone crowded in the bedroom to watch a demonstration about the feeding tube. Megan gave Dad a sedative so he could rest and be spared the humiliation of everyone staring at his abdomen. Luckily, most of the activity took place outside the covers, and only Mom would have to check the tube near his belly.

Overwhelmed by the responsibilities, I started to feel lightheaded. No one could drop the ball. We would have to live with any mistake we made for the rest of our lives. *What if I did something wrong?*

"Now this is how y'all clean the incision from the scar." Megan pulled back the bandages. "Just wipe it with alcohol. We have to keep it clean. "

The red scar looked like baseball stiches, starting from the top of his ear, wrapping all the way behind the back of his head. My head spun again. I coughed, then my jaw started to tingle as sweat beaded on my forehead. A cold chill surged through me.

"Elsie, are you—"

All went black.

When I opened my eyes, everyone was standing over me. *What the hell? Why was I on the floor?* Still tingling with numbness, I sat up. Mom clutched my arm but I pulled away.

"Oh, Elsie."

She held out her arms. Mortified, I pushed off the floor

and went to my bedroom.

The afternoon crawled as I waited for Mom to return from the store. The longer I sat there, the more I started to worry about her going to work the next day. What if the old woman fired her tomorrow? I had just a few days left with Tyler. I couldn't let anything get in the way.

At five-thirty, she finally returned. I helped her put away the groceries and made my escape to see Tyler. After I parked at the visitor's center, I texted him.

Me: I'm here

My phone vibrated in my hand.

Tyler: Be there soon.

Me: Ok

I opened the door, put on my running shoes, and started stretching my legs. Within minutes, he pulled up behind my car. The black-tinted window slid down.

He grinned. "Get in."

"Thought we were running."

"Take the day off."

I hesitated. He answered by leaning across the seat and pushing the passenger's side door open, and then he looked at me with pleading dark eyes, sending my heart into palpitations.

"You know, it's wrong to use your charm and good looks to get what you want." I sat in the bucket seat and shut the door. "It's not right... not at all."

He smiled and drove out of the parking lot, then turned south on Confederate Road.

"Where are we going?"

"Just wait. You'll love it."

Patina-colored cannons lined the side of the road, and trees flickered in the evening light. It was a beautiful drive, but I'd rather run. I wanted to jog off the anxiety eating at my nerves about Mrs. Vaughn. Mom had trusted me, and I'd blown it.

"Tyler, I'm really worried about tomorrow. Is Mom going to get fired?"

"Don't worry. Nana left for Chattanooga Saturday morning." He chuckled. "I timed that one well. When I got back from your house, my aunt had already picked her up."

I relaxed back in the seat. "That's a relief. At least, two of our five days are clear. Mom works at the Johnson's and a few other houses on Tuesdays."

"Maybe you should just tell her. Stop torturing yourself."

Torture summed it up. I'd had a persistent knot in my stomach for over a month.

"I just want to get through the week."

"I know. Me, too."

Tyler turned left toward the river. Moments later, he parked on the side of the road and shifted in the seat to give me his full attention.

"Let's forget about everything else, and enjoy the evening."

"After today, I could use a nice evening."

He leaned across the seat and gave me a kiss. "Come with me. You'll love this."

We climbed out of the car and he led me to a viewing deck overlooking the river. I leaned on the rail and took a deep breath of the earthy air. He stepped behind me and wrapped his arms around my waist. He knew I loved the river.

"Your eye looks a lot better." He kissed my cheek. "Sounds like you've had a rough day. How did it go with your dad?"

"Not great." I turned around. "I kind of passed out."

He tilted his head with a sympathetic smile. "Are you okay?"

"Yes." I pressed my forehead to his chest. "His scar freaked me out."

I told him about Mom and Dad, Megan, and how I went into overload. I tried to be funny instead of wallowing in pity. He laughed along, until I broke down and started crying.

"It'll get better." He touched my chin, persuading me to look up. "I have a birthday present for you."

I wiped my face and sniffled. "My birthday's in November."

"I know. The 2nd."

I smiled. "I forgot you have a photographic memory."

"That hasn't been confirmed yet." He reached in his back pocket and pulled out a long, narrow envelope. "You have to promise me, no matter what, and I mean, no matter what in the world is going on, you'll be here for this. Death is the only excuse, okay?"

"That kind of creeps me out. But, okay. I promise."

He let the envelope fall toward me. I took it, inspecting the outside, and then I opened the flap. Inside were two Bears vs. Saints tickets, December Fifteenth, Monday Night Football.

"Tyler! At Soldier Field? I can't believe it!"

I wrapped my arms around his neck and kissed him. He lifted me up and set me on the railing. Eye to eye, I couldn't control my smile.

A quick kiss, then he said, "I'm glad you like the idea."

"I love it. Thank you."

Chapter

24

Five days until Tyler had to leave.

We agreed to meet at six on Monday morning, stealing every hour possible. As we jogged past the Bloody Pond, a pickup truck passed us on the road. I remembered the black Cadillac. I hadn't seen it in days. After a few more yards, I slowed down to walk.

He glanced over his shoulder and started walking with me.

"You done?" he asked, barely winded.

"Yeah, for the moment," I said, breathless. "Hey, did you ever talk to your uncle?"

"Yeah, I took care of it."

"Was he weird?"

"No. Just broke, like I said."

"At least he isn't following you anymore."

"Nana got what she wanted. Leverage."

"That seems to be her mission."

He sighed. "Why do you think I want to get through school so fast?"

"Because you can."

"Sure, I can." He shrugged. "But I don't have to push this hard."

"Then don't. There's no hurry."

"Yeah, but if I get my Master's by twenty-two, I'm set. All I have to do is get the fuck away from everyone."

He rubbed his forehead, like he was fighting a headache. He worried me.

"Something happen?" I asked.

"Mm... " He glanced my way. "Nana called Dad."

Of course. I hadn't even thought about his parents.

"Everything okay?"

"Once he heard the whole story. Nana had failed to mention her comment about you being a whore. Convenient, huh?"

"Doesn't surprise me."

"If it wasn't for you, I would've left already."

I laughed. "If it wasn't for me, you wouldn't have this problem."

"You're not the problem. But if I can stay focused, no one will mess with me. I didn't need a high ACT to figure that out."

"It's helped you expedite your master plan."

"Yeah, it has." He smiled. "Speaking of, I need to talk to you about school."

"What about it?"

"Elsie, I'm taking sixteen semester hours and running cross country. If I get too busy, you'd have to understand that I'm not ignoring you." He stopped me in the middle of the road. "I'm a total recluse who does nothing but study and run. Zach wasn't lying."

"Have you chosen a school?"

"I like Stanford, but I don't want to go to California. That's beside the point. What I'm trying to say is, please don't worry."

"About what?"

"There may be days when you don't hear from me. Depending upon what's going on, maybe several. I'll try my best to stay in touch, but I won't always be able to."

"I understand."

He touched my face. I looked into his eyes.

"I feel the same way as you," he said. "We *will* be together again. You have to trust me when I say that."

"I do trust you."

"You do now. But when it's been over a week and I've barely had time to text you, please, don't think I've given up on us."

If only the next four months of my life would fast forward.

"When will I see you again?" I asked.

"I'll have some time around Thanksgiving. Until then, I don't know."

I stepped toward him. "I hate this."

"Me, too."

He wrapped his arms around me. I pressed against him. Visceral and raw. We were connected by something beyond our understanding. He cupped my face in his gentle touch, and we mended our pain with a long kiss.

LIFE HAPPENS ON THE STAIRS

We spent the morning walking around the park, talking. Around noon, he drove us to Savannah and bought lunch at Jack's drive-through. After we got back to the park, we went to the Shiloh church, and settled under an oak tree near the log cabin to eat our lunches.

"Are you busy tonight?" he asked.

"Not really."

"Meet me at the café, around six?"

"Sure."

As we sat in the shade talking, I told him about the first time I'd dreamt of being an artist.

"It was 2005, the February before I turned eight. We were watching that Sunday morning show, you know, the boring one that showed a bird chirping or a river flowing for three minutes between segments? Anyway, the next report was on Christo and Jeanne Claude, the couple who wrapped islands and bridges in fabric. You know who I'm talking about?" He nodded, yes. I continued. "Well, they'd been trying for years to set up an exhibit in Central Park called The Gates. The idea was for people to be a part of the project, to feel it, walk through it, merging the individual with art. They built orange steel posts that straddled the sidewalks with matching orange fabric cascading in the breeze. It was so beautiful. But it didn't impress me as much as the story of their determination. It had taken them years, over two decades, to get the city to agree. Mayor Giuliani refused, but within months of Mayor Bloomberg taking office, he gave the couple approval. I've wanted to walk through Central Park ever since. Anyway... " I shrugged. "As I got older, I started researching them. Jeanne Claude died in 2009, but Christo's still working. What an amazing couple. Their ideas weren't just the installations, it was the planning, the drafts they drew, the way they worked for years to achieve their vision. I thought, 'Hey they're old. If they can do it, so can I.' So, I started drawing. And studying – Frida Kahlo, Mary Cassatt and her shady relationship with Degas. All of the Impressionists, and the drama around them. Picasso and the Cubism period... I could go on for hours."

Tyler smiled. "I totally understand. The first time I saw Peter Rothermel's painting of *Patrick Henry before the Virginia House of Burgesses*, I had to look into the history behind it. Patrick Henry was one of the Founding Fathers. You know who he is. His most famous words were, 'Give me liberty—' "

"Or give me death," we said in unison.

I laughed. "I didn't remember his name, but who can forget that quote?"

"I know, right? In this particular painting, he was protesting the Stamp Act of 1765. All the men's faces were angry and suspicious-looking. Patrick Henry wore a bright red cloak with his arm raised high in the air. It gave me goosebumps." He laughed and waved his hand. "I was ten. It's kind of funny now."

We talked for another hour, then he dropped me off at my car and kissed me goodbye. I drove home and went straight to the field to pick.

At four o'clock, sweaty and tired, I plopped down in the recliner. Where was Mark? Within seconds, I saw him walking down the hall carrying a basket of towels. I snickered. Megan had him whooped already. For the next hour, she worked that boy like a tool. He washed the dishes, folded towels, took out the trash from Dad's room. All the while, she'd smile and thank him in her sweet Southern drawl.

When they went to the kitchen to start dinner, I headed to

Dad's room.

"Hi, Daddy. I hope you're feeling better."

He turned his head toward me. I smiled, thankful to see his beautiful blue eyes again.

"Things are going pretty good." I put my hand on his. He didn't move. "We're trying to get the crops out. Mark can take the second load tomorrow."

He blinked.

"We have almost two acres covered. We'll go back over it as the season moves on, just like you taught us."

He blinked again. I wanted to hear him say something. I missed his voice and his reassuring words. They'd been stolen from me, just like his strength had been stolen from him. The way the disease had destroyed him was cruel. I pushed back the pain and gave him the only thing I could.

"Mark and I will get it done, Dad. I promise."

The door swung open. Megan stepped inside. She glanced up.

"Oh, my gosh! I didn't think anyone was in here!"

I laughed. "It's okay."

"That scared the daylights out of me." She walked around the bed and set the towels on the nightstand. "It's good you're talking to him. He needs to hear your voice."

"He's been in the hospital for a long time. It's different having him home."

"This can be a long journey." She leaned against the wall. "How old are you?"

"Almost eighteen. You?"

"Twenty-one." Then, she whispered, "This is my first job. I just finished school."

"Well, you're doing great. You handled yesterday a lot better than I did."

"Oh, you're okay. I passed out in the cadaver lab the first time I saw a dead body." She giggled, waving her hand by her nose. "The place smelled so bad."

We chatted for a while, then I went to my room. My phone alerted me to a text.

Tyler: Do you have your portfolio on file somewhere?

Me: Yep. On a flash drive.

Tyler: Bring it.

Me: Okay. Why?

What was he up to? I let it go and headed to the bathroom to shower. By the time I'd finished dressing in my room, I heard Mom in the kitchen.

I stepped out of my bedroom. "Did you have a good day?"

"Not bad." She grabbed a pitcher of tea out of the refrigerator. "You did a nice job."

"Thanks. Was the wicked witch of the South home?"

She smiled. "No. I'm not sure where she's at."

Chattanooga.

"Oh." I cleared my throat. "You care if I go to town and get some stuff for school?"

"Go ahead." She set down the pitcher and grabbed her purse.

"Put that away. I have cash."

"You sure?"

I nodded.

"Don't be so late." She gave me a hard glance. "You were out past ten, last night."

"Sorry." My voice cracked. "We talked for a while."

"Who's 'we'?" she asked with an edge of sarcasm.

I twitched. "Jenna."

"I want to trust you, Elsie."

"You can." I glanced left. "It's all good."

She could see through me. Blood rushed to my cheeks. I scratched my forehead. She knew.

She narrowed her eyes, staring me down. "Are you hiding something?"

Focus. Don't fidget. I looked her straight in the eyes.

"Of course not." I squinted. "I might stop by the Worleybird and grab a burger, too. But I won't stay long."

"Okay. Where's Mark?"

"Outside, talking to Megan."

"Oh. She sure is a sweet girl."

"Yeah. She's cool." I grabbed the keys off the counter. "I'll be back soon."

At six o'clock, I parked in front of the café. Tyler sat at a corner table with his PowerMac. I sat down across from him. He smiled, then typed something.

"What are you looking at?" I asked.

"School of the Art Institute of Chicago's website. Check this out."

He leaned across the table and gave me a quick kiss, and then he turned the computer so I could see the screen.

"See, they'll help pay for everything federal aid won't with their scholarship program. You just have to apply," he emphasized his words.

"Chicago?" I cringed. "I'd planned on staying in Tennessee."

"I wouldn't rule anything out at this point."

So that's why he wanted my files, I thought, as I gave him my flash drive. He uploaded my portfolio on his hard drive. While we ate, we looked at several different schools: Memphis College of Art, University of Tennessee, School of the Art Institute of Chicago, as well as the Art Institute for Graphic Design.

"Let's fill out some of the applications," I said, suddenly excited.

"I was hoping you'd say that."

After applying to four schools, he kissed me goodnight in the parking lot, then I drove to the dollar store and bought some notebooks and pens.

When I walked in the house at nine, Mom seemed pleased to see me so early.

Chapter

25

Four days left.

Tyler and I met Tuesday morning at six. As we walked toward each other in the parking lot, I could see it in his eyes. The countdown to Friday haunted him, too. He pulled me into his arms and I closed my eyes and inhaled his scent. The cool morning breeze rushed over us. He squeezed tighter. Minutes passed. We didn't move. No kiss. No words. We just held each other.

Several minutes later, he stepped back with a shy smile.

"How am I ever going to leave you?"

"Don't," I said. "Just stay."

He shook his head, then he pressed his lips to mine. I trembled under his gentle touch.

Stay. Stay, for me.

When we pulled away, he took my hand, and we started toward the river.

I went home around noon still fighting my sour mood. As I headed to the refrigerator to grab a soda, Megan walked in the room.

"How's it going?" I asked.

"Good." She sat down at the counter. "I don't mean to intrude or nothin', but Mark left with a guy that looked higher than a kite. Thought I should tell his sister instead of his momma."

"Did you see what the car looked like?"

"Yep. An old, red pickup."

"Bobby."

Great. The last thing we needed was Mark running around with Bobby.

"Oh, girl. He's an excuse to turn away from all men. Heavens, he made my skin crawl when I answered the door. Why does your brother hang out with him?"

"That. I don't know. We've been trying to figure it out for years."

She wiped her face like she'd been crying. "Well, Mark's got too much going for him to be around that."

I grinned. "What exactly does Mark have?"

Megan blushed. "Oh, I shouldn't say." Then her bright eyes rose to mine. "He's really sweet. He helps me out all the time, and he's funny. Not to mention how cute he is."

"Well, I'll let you in on a little secret. He feels the same."

"Really?"

"You're adorable. Who wouldn't?"

"I shouldn't have said anything."

"Don't worry, I won't tell."

"I hope that Bobby guy doesn't do something stupid. I got a bad vibe."

A few minutes later, I went to Dad's room. Standing beside his bed, I rubbed his hand. He blinked and his lips moved into a faint smile.

"I love you," I said. "I really miss talking to you."

He blinked again. I kissed his forehead and sat down in the chair next to him. What could I tell him? Everything that happened last week would've upset him. I thought back. He'd love to hear about Tyler in the field.

"Remember Tyler?" I said. "You won't believe it. That city boy helped me in the field."

After I told him all about Tyler and me picking the first crops, I headed outside to continue where Mark and I'd left off. Around four-thirty, I went back inside to take a break.

When I walked through the door, the phone rang. I trotted through the house and snagged it off the wall. "Hello?"

"How y'all doing out there?" Ruby asked.

"Not bad. You?"

"Mighty fine. So. Roger called me. Mark's been raisin' hell up yonder."

"Where?"

"Between Milledgeville and Saltillo. He said, him and Bobby were drinking and driving."

"Crap," I huffed.

"That's one way to put it. When's your momma gonna get home?"

"Around five-thirty, six," I said. "Ruby, you don't have to deal with this. Let me call a friend. He'll help me find Mark."

"Your secret friend?"

"Yeah... "

"Well, y'all be careful. If they've been drinkin' all day, who knows what they're up to."

"Will do. Thanks for calling."

I hung up and grabbed my cell phone. Tyler answered by the second ring.

"Hey," he said. "I was just getting ready to call you."

"I've got a problem."

"What's up?"

"Mark."

"Okay. You want me to come over?"

"Please. I need to find him before Mom gets home. Ruby says he's out drinking."

"Give me a few minutes, and I'll head over."

"Thank you."

Twenty minutes later, he pulled into the driveway, and we headed north toward Milledgeville. After a quick drive through the ghost town, we cruised through Saltillo. Nothing. No Mark, no Bobby, no red truck.

Shit. Mom didn't need any more crap to deal with. As Tyler drove back toward the Hardin County line, I let out an irritated sigh and slumped back in the seat.

"This is ridiculous," I said. "Where the hell did they go?"

"Who is this Bobby guy, anyway?"

"Bobby Dale."

He rolled his eyes. "Great."

"What?"

He shook his head like he didn't want to talk about it. I wrinkled my nose. How did he know Bobby? Wrong side of the river for him to run with the likes of a Dale.

After driving for over two hours, the sun started to set. The sky shifted from a soft indigo to an eerie red-orange. A surreal neon haze illuminated the landscape, like we'd stepped inside a Maxfield Parrish painting.

Goosebumps rose on my arms. "It looks weird out."

"Yeah, it's like the heavens are warning us of something. Where should we go next?"

"Let's drive by Bobby's trailer."

He drove toward Morris Chapel, winding through the back hills.

When we passed by the dilapidated trailer, Bobby's truck wasn't there, either. The property looked like a junkyard. A path led through the overgrown lawn to a 1960s, rectangular, metal box. Four rusty cars rotted away in the weeds, and trash bags were piled around a burn barrel. The front door had a hole in the center with yellow insulation falling out, and aluminum foil concealed the inside of every window. The place wasn't fit for the shabby dog howling at us as we drove past.

"Lovely, isn't it?" I said.

"That's just wrong."

Tyler turned at the next road and headed toward Morris Chapel. As we drove over the hill in town, I spotted Bobby's truck at the pool hall.

"It's about time," I said.

Tyler pulled in and parked under a streetlight at the furthest side of the lot. He shut off the ignition and turned to me. "I'm going in."

"It's no big deal, Tyler. Once Mark sees me, he'll know he's busted."

He sighed and glanced at the bar. "You can look for him outside. I'll go inside."

"Okay."

Sweet Home Alabama, by *Lynyrd Skynyrd* blared from the beer garden as we walked across the parking lot. Tyler gave me a quick kiss and headed inside. I walked through the wooden gate. Heart pounding, I knew I had no business standing in a beer garden.

The courtyard spanned the back of the long pool hall, enclosed by an eight-foot privacy fence. Five guys at a picnic table turned and looked at me. Indifferent to my presence, they went back to what they were doing. The atmosphere was shrouded in a yellow haze from the florescent lights on power poles, and a cloud of cigarette smoke lingered in the air like smog. A few guys sat at a makeshift bar near the building. In front of it, four people were playing cards at a table.

Bobby. He towered over the card players, holding a beer, chatting with someone I didn't recognize. His head jutted back and forth, looking my way like he smelled fresh blood. Over six-foot-tall, he sauntered toward me, wearing grease-smeared jeans and a black AC/DC T-shirt.

"Where's Mark?" I shouted out over the music.

His arm was sleeved in tattoos up to his knuckles. Cupping his ear, he leaned closer.

"What's that you say?" he asked in a thick twang.

I arched away from his cigarette-laced, beer breath. "Where's my brother?"

"Who?"

Insufferable, sleazy jerk.

"Mark," I stressed. "My brother."

He took a swig of beer. "Oh. Y'all mean Mark."

I gave him a blank look.

"He just went inside to take a piss." Bobby pulled a pack of cigarettes out of his pocket and lit one. "You kicked me out the other day. Who the hell do you think you are?"

"You guys trashed the place."

His lips curled into a slimly-toothed grin. "Reckon we

did. Come on over here and wait for him. I's got somethin' to show you."

"I'm not supposed to be in here, Bobby. I'm only seventeen," I turned. "I have to find—"

He grabbed my shoulder and I was spun around. He stepped within inches of my face.

"You's gonna come ov'r here!"

"What the hell, man?" I smacked his hand off me. "Back off."

He grabbed my waist, pulling me toward him. "You sure is feisty."

I squirmed and shoved his shoulders. He let out an ear-piercing cackle. I stepped backward, balling up my right fist. *Just try it, asshole.*

Taking two long strides, he sneered, "Think you's better than me?"

I sucked in a breath and pulled back my fist.

Something flashed to my right. Air moved past my cheek and Bobby's head snapped back. Orange sparks exploded in his face as his cigarette burst in the air. I dropped my arm. He stumbled backward, slapping his hand to his jaw. Tyler stepped in front of me.

I exhaled. *Thank God.*

Bobby cringed as he wiped his mouth. "What the fuck, Vaughn?"

"Keep your fucking hands off her," Tyler shouted.

Reaching back, Tyler touched my hip. I took his cue and moved aside.

"Out slummin', TJ?" Bobby said. "You ain't got nothin' better to do than that?"

TJ? Why did he call him TJ?

Tyler crossed his arms. "Fuck off, Bobby."

"What'cha gonna do about it?" Bobby spit on the ground and wiped a bit of blood off his mouth. "You come back for more? One ass kicking ain't enough, huh? Pretty boy."

"You still kiss your sister with that mouth?" Tyler cocked his head to the side. "Hear she finally turned your nasty ass in. I figured you were somebody's bitch by now."

Bobby's face filled with rage. "You're the little bitch."

Gravel crunched. Bobby lunged.

"No!" I screamed.

Tyler grabbed his arms to stop him. Bobby's shoulder slipped through, ramming into Tyler's chest. They both slammed to the ground. Bobby nailed him with a right and then his left. Tyler jabbed Bobby's ribs. Bobby buckled, then his head snapped back.

I held my breath, trembling all over. A few people had gathered beside me to watch.

Tyler squirmed out from under Bobby, then kicked him square in the chest. Bobby flew backward, sliding across the rocks. Tyler dove on top of him and punched him in the face, then again, and again, and again. Blood burst from Bobby's nose and he swung at Tyler's ribs. Tyler absorbed the blow, pulled back his fist, then stopped mid-swing. Bobby moaned. Tyler lowered his arm and hopped to his feet.

I exhaled. It's over.

Tyler pulled his right leg back.

I gasped. No!

Like he was punting a football, he kicked Bobby square in the gut. He reared his leg back again, then he stopped, set down his foot and stood tall.

"Motherfucker. Don't you ever touch her again!" He wiped his mouth with the back of his hand and spit on Bobby's chest.

LIFE HAPPENS ON THE STAIRS

Mark ran across the courtyard, skidding to a stop in the gravel.

"Elsie! What the hell are you doing here?"

I rushed to Tyler's side. "Are you okay?"

Fist still clenched, lip busted and bloody, his eyes went cold when he looked at Mark.

"Yeah, I'm fine." He held out his hand. "Let's go."

"What are you two doing here?" Mark shouted.

"Ruby sent us to find you," I yelled back.

Tyler's started to lead me away. "Real nice, man—"

Out of nowhere, he lurched forward, his hand ripped from mine as Bobby tackled him from behind. Mark pulled me aside. I stumbled, bouncing off his chest. He grabbed my shoulders and held me steady.

Tyler and Bobby wrestled across the gravel, throwing punches. Tyler grabbed Bobby's shoulders and smashed him into the rocks, pinning his knee to Bobby's chest.

Then something shifted in Tyler, like he'd transformed into a boxer gone rogue in the ring. He reared back his right arm, and started hammering down on Bobby's face with a relentless fury.

I squeezed my eyes shut. *Please stop. Oh God, make them stop!*

"Tyler!" Mark yelled. "You're gonna kill him!"

I opened my eyes. Mark had Tyler under the arms, yanking him to his feet.

"Fuck you!" Tyler jerked free, spun, and threw his right fist.

Mark ducked. Tyler's arm shot through the air, but his left hand was already moving. Mark's head snapped back. He grabbed Tyler's shirt. Tyler clutched Mark's arms, and they both slammed to the ground.

Red lights flashed across the privacy fence. Blood rushed to my head, pressing on my ears like I was under water. A faint siren. My heart fell to my knees. Surreal as the evening sky, the whole scene slowed. Mark throwing a punch at Tyler's ribs. A cop running past. Muffled chatter. People scurrying. Bobby squirming in the gravel with his blood-soaked hands covering his face.

The cop pulled Tyler to his feet. Tyler spun, ready to swing again. Immediately, he deflated, lowered his fist and mouthed, "Fuck".

Another cop ran past and grabbed Mark. He rolled him on his belly and slapped cuffs on his wrists within seconds. The other officer grabbed Tyler's arms and pushed him against the fence. His hands were cuffed before my next breath. Both cops started reciting Miranda Rights.

I pressed my hands to my face, pushing back tears. The cop showed Mark to the parking lot, hands gripped on the cuffs. Tyler wrenched around, as the other officer moved him forward.

"Elsie, get out of here," he shouted. "Take my car."

Heart racing, I followed them out. The officer guided Tyler into the back of the patrol car and shut the door. The other officer did the same with Mark in a separate car.

Tyler's intense, dark eyes rose to mine. I took a sharp breath. His look said everything. We were screwed. I turned to run.

"Excuse me, Miss." A third officer in a blue uniform stepped beside me. "I'm going to have to get a statement from you. Can you tell me what just happened here?"

A swarm of butterflies filled my stomach.

"Um, yes. I can."

Chapter

26

I 'd been dying to drive Tyler's car, but not under these circumstances. I couldn't stop trembling as I glanced down at the neon-blue console.

Ninety-five? Oh crap.

I let my foot off the gas. Then a flash of Tyler bashing Bobby's face stole my breath. The way he kicked him in the gut. Bobby lying on the ground with his face covered in blood. Why did it escalate so far? How did they know each other? I hated Bobby, but Tyler's rage was terrifying. He had calmed down at one point, and he had walked away...

My phone vibrated in my pocket. I grabbed it. Ruby. I sighed, tossing it on the passenger's seat. I needed to collect my thoughts before I talked to anyone. The ringing stopped, then it started again. I glanced over. No... "Mom" lit up on the LED screen.

Bracing myself for the blow, I answered, "Hello?"

"Elsie, what the hell is going on?" she said in her low whisper-yell. "Where are you?"

"I'm on my way to Savannah."

"What happened? Ruby called and said she saw the police leave the pool hall."

I swallowed hard. I couldn't mention Tyler. His name had to be off limits.

"Mark got in a fight. I'm on my way to Savannah."

"Savannah?" She gasped. "Is he going to jail?"

"Yes, but I have enough to bail him out," I said as fast as I could. "We don't need you."

"For crying out loud! How do you have enough money for bail?"

"I'll explain that later."

"You'll explain now!"

"Mrs. Baltic's sister gave me a hundred dollars for sitting at the hospital," I said. "It's okay. Seriously, Mom, I've got this. We'll come straight home."

"Who did he get in a fight with?"

"Um... him and Bobby. They were drinking and a fight broke out."

"I don't even know what to say." She paused. "Get home!"

She slammed the phone in my ear.

We'd humiliated the poor woman while her husband, our Dad, was in his deathbed. Mark and I were terrible. She'd never forgive us. What if Ruby told her I was with Tyler? I shook my head. No. Mom would've mentioned it. *Please, don't come to the police station... Stay home, Mom, please.*

266

Ten minutes later, I rushed through the doors at the Hardin County Jail, determined that nothing would slow me down. A guard stepped forward and pointed at the metal detector. I let out a sigh and walked through the machine. *Buzz.* The plump guard gestured for me to turn around. I backtracked, took off my belt and tennis shoes, and stepped through the tunnel again. No jarring sound. The officer nodded. I gathered my stuff in my arms and hurried to the counter.

I over-dramatically, yet unintentionally, slammed my shoes on the counter, as I gasped for a breath and said, "Tyler Vaughn."

A middle-aged woman with puffy, brown hair looked over the edge of her glasses.

"Vaughn." She tapped the keyboard. "They're processing him. It's going to be a while. You can have a seat." She pointed behind me.

"Are they processing Mark Richardson, too?"

"Yes, ma'am."

"Okay. Thanks."

I scanned the room and walked to the furthest seat against the wall.

Two hours later, I went back to the window. The woman gave me a blank look.

"Tyler Vaughn?"

She tapped on the keyboard. "He's posted bond. Still in holding."

"Can I post bond for Mark Richardson?"

"I'll need a valid ID. You're eighteen, correct?"

Damn it!

"No. Seventeen."

"Well then, he'll need an adult to bail him out."

"Great."

I turned around and went back to my seat. How long could it take? Maybe if they let Tyler out first, he could help me get Mark out. I closed my eyes, inhaling slow, deep breaths.

Minutes later, the boom of a metal door slamming resonated through the room.

I opened my eyes. "Oh, shit."

Greg.

Standing by the door, he scanned the room and spotted me, but he didn't look happy.

I held my breath. Not another pissed-off man. Three was enough for one day.

He stepped in front of me. "Where's Tyler?"

"They haven't let him out yet." Then I blurted without thinking, "How did you find out?"

"That doesn't matter," he stated. "What the hell happened?"

"He was in a fight."

"I know that," Greg snapped back.

I flinched. He rubbed his forehead.

"Elsie, this isn't good. I've been on your side, and I've tried to help both of you, but this. You two just blew it."

His words were worse than Mr. Smith's backhand. Tears filled my eyes. Greg looked at me for a second like he might've felt bad for what he said, then he turned and went to the counter.

I slumped in the chair. How could this be happening? All we wanted was our last few days together.

The metal door boomed again.

Mom.

Another boom from the opposite side of the room.

Tyler.

Fear pierced every nerve in my body.

Mom saw Tyler first. Her eyes widened, then she whipped her head my way and glared. Clutching her purse strap, she moved across the room like she was ready to whip my ass.

I gripped the seat. I'm shot. Busted. Finished.

"Elizabeth, what the hell is Tyler doing here?" she barked.

"Mom." I put my hands up. "You have to hear me out."

"I don't have to hear anything!" No whisper, no restraint. She's had enough.

Greg turned around.

Tyler stopped. He and I made eye contact, then he looked at Greg, crossed his arms and stood his ground. I knew his stance was a dissent against his parents and grandmother. Greg took several long strides. Nose to nose with his son, he said something I couldn't hear.

"Elsie, I'm waiting." Mom stared me down. "Why is he here?"

"He was part of the fight, too."

"What?" She flinched. "Where's Mark?"

"They're still holding him." I pulled the hundred out of my pocket and held it up. "I'm not old enough to post bond."

"I know. He called me."

She stared at the cash. I looked over her shoulder. Greg had his arm around Tyler, as they walked toward the lobby. Mom stole my attention when she snatched the bill out of my fingers before proceeding to the clerk's window.

I flopped back in the seat, numb to all the lies and consequences. She had every right to be pissed. How could I blame her when she had one kid in jail and another who'd been lying to her for weeks, as she was about to lose the love of her life?

I cupped my head in my hands and stared at the floor. Nothing I could say or do would change what had happened. Tyler and I had definitely made our own circumstances. Our private world had just collided with reality.

A few moments later, a pair of dusty Nikes stepped in my small perspective. I raised my head. Tyler stared down at me, holding out his left hand. I accepted his warm touch and stood to my feet. He pulled me into his arms.

"I'm so sorry," he whispered against my ear.

I shook all over with tension, with fear, with love. "Me, too."

We held each other for a minute, and then he stepped back. His lip was swollen, and he had a small cut under his eye. I reached up and touched his cheek. He gave me a tired smile, leaned down, and kissed me.

"Come with me."

He took my hand and led me toward the lobby. Mom was leaning on the counter, squaring up the bill with the county.

When we stepped in the hallway, Greg was waiting for us with his arms crossed.

"I really wanted this for you two... "

"Dad, nothing's changed," Tyler said, tightening his hand around mine. "Just drop it."

"Tyler, I suggest you keep your mouth shut right now."

"Why?" Tyler snapped back. "I didn't go in there looking for a fight, and you know it. The Dales fucking hate us because of you."

Mom walked in and stepped beside Greg.

"I am so sorry," she said to him. "I had no idea."

Greg gave Tyler a questioning glance, and then he turned to Mom, placing his hand on her shoulder. He guided her toward the other side of the room.

"I think they need some space," Greg said.

Tyler sighed. "Elsie, I'm sorry I tore into Mark. I don't always play well with others."

He wrapped his left arm around me. I began to relax and squeezed him tight. He flinched.

I quickly let go. "Are you okay?"

"Yeah."

I saw the pain in his eyes. Gently lifting his right arm, I saw that his knuckles were bloody and swollen. I tried to extend his fingers, but stopped when he cringed.

"You need to see a doctor," I said.

"I'll deal with it tomorrow." He looked over at our parents, then tilted his head with a shrug. "Claire knows now."

"I'm just glad you're okay."

Was this it? Would I get to see him again? He wrapped his arms around me, covering me like a shield. If only for a few seconds, I felt safe.

"Elizabeth, it's time to go. Now," Mom said.

I turned to her. Tyler kept his arm around my shoulder. I started to step away, but he tightened his grip. I stopped. Greg pursed his lips, clearly annoyed.

"Elsie, did you hear me?" She eyed me like she didn't recognize me. Her hands flew in the air, and she took a step backward. "This is ridiculous. How long have you two been seeing each other?"

"Claire, I apologize," Tyler said. "I didn't want you to find out like this."

Mark walked in the lobby, cheek busted and bruised. Mom's cold stare shifted to him. She pointed at the door. "Get in the car."

"Real fucking nice, man," Mark said to Tyler. "Thanks."

"Where were you when Bobby had his hands all over your sister?" Tyler shot back. "Why do you hang out with that piece of shit anyway?"

"Fuck off, Tyler," Mark said.

"Enough! Get in the car, Mark. Elsie, let's go." Mom turned to Greg. "I sincerely apologize for all of this."

Greg nodded, and then she headed to the door.

I watched her walk away. We'd crushed her. I'd crushed her. She'd struggled with being broke, working her butt off, trying to raise two kids who insisted on finding trouble, caring for her husband... and what do we do? We were going to push her over the edge if she had to deal with one more thing by herself.

Tyler bent down and whispered in my ear.

"Meet me at the old house you told me about. After midnight."

He brushed his cheek against mine, then he slid his hand across my face, holding me with a loving gaze. I pressed deeper into his touch, wishing I could read his mind.

"I've got you, okay?" he said. "I won't let anything hurt us."

Just trust him... just trust him. I buried my face in his chest, tightening around him for a brief second, then I pushed away and ran out the door.

The car ride home amounted to a cold interrogation of the past few weeks. I confessed that Tyler was Jenna, and that I did know a Jenna, but we weren't really friends. I admitted that for almost six weeks, I'd spent every morning with him and sometimes more. Mark lay across the back seat, moaning every so often. I fiddled with my fingers, waiting for her eruption.

She didn't explode. Instead she stared forward, hands on ten and two. Her resounding silence was excruciating.

"Mom, I'm sorry. I never meant to lie about it. I just didn't want you to tell me no."

"I bet. That's usually why a person lies," she said. "I warned you about this, Elsie. I told you not to get involved with Tyler. What were you thinking?"

Mark sat up, and said, "You know him?"

"Yes, he's Mrs. Vaughn's grandson."

"You're shittin' me? Elsie, you dumbass."

"Mark, I'm not through with you," Mom said. "Shut your mouth."

"What do you mean you warned me about him?" I asked. "All you said was, well, basically... I'm not good enough."

"I did not say that." She looked at me wide-eyed. "I never said you weren't good enough. I said he was off limits because I don't want to get fired. It has nothing to do with your self-worth."

"I'm sorry, I lied. But he leaves in three days to go back to school. Please, just let me have three more days."

"I don't think you get it. Greg wants him home. You'd better brace yourself because this summer fling is over."

Tears stung my eyes. "You don't know what you're saying."

"What in the hell were you doing at the pool hall, anyway?"

"Ask your son."

She sighed and looked in the rearview mirror. "Why were you and Tyler fighting?"

"He was beating the crap out of Bobby, Mom. I mean bad. Someone had to pull him off, or he was gonna kill the guy."

She turned onto Coffee Landing Road, heading east through Morris Chapel, and looked at me. "Why did Tyler go at Bobby?" Under the glint of the streetlight, she pushed back a smile. At least Tyler scored points in that aspect. Mom hated Bobby.

For the rest of the drive home, I told her the whole truth about the evening. When she pulled into the driveway, she shut off the ignition and turned in her seat.

"You two. I'm trying so hard to trust you, but I'm beyond disappointed. Mark, you're twenty years old. Grow up. If you want to run around with the likes of Bobby, then find your own place to live. You're not doing it under my roof." She looked at me. "Elizabeth, I don't even know what to say to you. I don't understand why you had to lie to me. I thought we were closer than that." Mom's eyes filled with tears.

"Mom, you were pretty busy." I looked down. "I'm sorry, but I won't give up on Tyler. He hasn't been hiding this, I have. He's been trying to get me to tell you for weeks."

"You're not helping yourself."

"You need to know he never wanted me to lie. He's a good guy, and it doesn't matter what you think or what anyone else thinks. This isn't a fling."

"Elsie, please. Don't get your heart broken on top of everything else." She pushed open the car door. "I have to go to bed."

She headed inside the house. Mark slammed the car door and followed her inside.

I stayed.

LIFE HAPPENS ON THE STAIRS

She was going to take Tyler away from me. She'd freak out when Mrs. Vaughn fired her, and I'd never be able to see him again. I had one night. One last night.

Chapter

27

When I went inside, Mom and Mark were already settled in their rooms. I headed to the bathroom and took a shower. By eleven-fifty, silence filled the house. I sat on the edge of my bed, wiping my sweaty palms on the comforter. What if Greg didn't let him leave? I'd die if I didn't see him one more time.

At five after twelve, I quietly slipped out the back door. A brisk breeze blew through the air. I stopped on the back steps listening for any warning signs. The night was shrouded in black. I squinted. Nothing, but leaves blowing in the wind. Taking a deep breath, I started across the backyard. The walk to the house felt like a mile. Normally, I ran there and never in the dark.

LIFE HAPPENS ON THE STAIRS

Something rustled in the weeds. I crossed the pavement, quickening my steps. Moments later, I rounded the curve through the overgrowth to the two-story house, opened the back door and went inside.

The smell of the musty room tingled my nose. Pitch-black, I couldn't see a thing. I grabbed my phone out of my pocket and flipped it open to light the way. A dank hallway led me into the kitchen. I took a left into the living room and headed straight to the old Victorian couch.

After I settled in, I held up my phone to check out the room. Two green, wingback chairs sat opposite the couch with a filthy, oval coffee table separating the space. A cobweb-laced, stone fireplace filled the center of the wall to my left. Windows at the far end of the room were covered in decaying sheer curtains.

With all vantage points in sight, I relaxed and glanced at my phone. Twelve-sixteen. Give him time. Who knew what he was going through? Flipping the phone shut, I wedged in the corner of the couch and dozed off.

What felt like minutes later, I woke with a start. Footsteps. Light filled the doorway.

Tyler stepped into the room, holding his iPhone toward the floor. Relief filled me as he walked inside and sat down on the coffee table. His clean scent cut through the smell of red dirt and mildew. He'd changed his clothes, but his hair was still damp from showering.

He set his phone on the table, its light illuminating the ceiling. "Are you okay?"

"I am now. What time is it?"

"Almost one-thirty." He stood up, motioned me to move forward, then slid behind me. "Sorry. Nana wasn't exactly pleasant. It took a minute to convince Dad to go home."

Tyler wrapped his arms around me, then we laced our legs together. I settled back on his chest. He cringed with a flinch.

I sat up. "Tyler. Your ribs."

"I don't care." He pulled me back. "I need you right here."

I gently laid my head on his chest. He squeezed me tight, burying his face in my hair.

"They want me to come home," he said. "Tomorrow."

Tears filled my eyes. I only had hours, minutes, seconds left with him.

"Tomorrow?"

He stroked my hair. "I have to spend some time with them before I head to Nashville."

His gentleness and tender touch contradicted everything I'd witnessed earlier. My tears soaked his T-shirt as he took a deep breath of my hair.

"You know what pisses me off almost as much as Bobby coming at you?" His tone was low and calm. "My dad. I had it under control. I'd bailed myself out and called our lawyer. But the fucking sheriff knows Nana and called her. She insisted they hold me until Dad got there, which took what, over two hours? Nana's totally freaking out."

"They must hate me."

"No, they hate that I got into a fight, but I don't regret it. Bobby got what he deserved. I'm not playing when it comes to you." He grunted. "Or getting my ass kicked."

This was the third time he'd defended me. He certainly wasn't playing.

"You scared me," I whispered.

"I'm sorry. My therapist and I've had long conversations about how I should handle something like this. I'm supposed to walk away. Fuck that. This was different."

Therapist? He hadn't mentioned that. "You have a therapist?"

"For a while, I had one. Dr. Allen. I started seeing him after Grandpa died."

"Oh. Why did Bobby call you TJ?"

Tyler's heart pounded a few beats faster in my ear. "You caught that?"

"Well, yeah. You obviously know each other."

"My middle name's Jackson, so everyone used to call me TJ."

"I heard your grandmother say Tyler Jackson the other day. I like it."

"I can deal with that, but Grandpa used to call me TJ. I put a stop to it after he died. It reminded me too much of him."

I had so many questions, so many things I wanted to know before he left.

"So, how do you know Bobby?"

"When we owned the paper mill, Bobby's dad had worked there. He was welding on a piece of machinery one day – that was supposed to be shut down. Long story short, it wasn't."

"That's awful."

"If Grandpa and Dad would've compensated the family better, Bobby probably wouldn't care who I am." He sighed. "I suppose you wanna know when I got my ass beat, too?"

"Yes. Everything."

"Even the shitty stuff?"

I laughed. "Even the shitty stuff."

"Fair enough. I was fifteen, and here for the summer, of course. My buddy Josh and I'd walked up to the restaurant one night. When we left, Bobby and a couple of his friends were waiting for us in the parking lot. Josh freaked out and ran. He's always been a puss. I'd already been kicked out of school, and I thought I was untouchable. But three on one sucks."

"I bet."

"That's why I snapped on Mark. After that night, if someone grabs me from behind, I'm coming up swinging. I almost nailed that cop, too." He laughed. "That would've been stupid."

"No doubt," I said. "Mark's fine. I just wonder if Bobby is. You tore him up."

"I didn't mean to lose it like that. But how many times did he want to go around? I've waited a long time to get back at that sonofabitch. "

"Really?"

I didn't know what to think of this side of him. I'd been frightened during the fight, but now all my fears were gone. I loved his strength, despite his weaknesses.

"No. Well, kind of," he said. "I shouldn't have let you go in there alone. I couldn't believe it when you told me your brother was with Bobby Dale."

"I told you about Bobby. Mark and I were with him the night of my accident."

"One out of four guys around here are named Bobby. I never put the two together."

I giggled. "And you're the one that's freaky smart."

"I told you... I just test well."

He leaned down and kissed my cheek. The amber glow from his cell phone cast a halo across the ceiling. I closed my eyes and soaked in his warm embrace.

"I think Mom's proud of you," I said. "I caught her smiling when I told her about the fight. She hates Bobby."

He relaxed underneath me, as if he was relieved. He wanted Mom to accept him.

"How did she take everything?"

"She's hurt that I lied." I remembered Mom's words. "She thinks we're a summer fling."

"We're not," he whispered.

"No. We aren't."

We held each other all night, talking and recounting the past month. He eventually shifted so he lay next to me face to face. I rested my head on his firm bicep as he brushed the back of his fingers over my cheek.

"The next few months are going to feel like forever," he said. "I'll try my best to balance everything, but please... just wait for me."

"Of course, I will." A tear rolled down my cheek. "This just sucks."

He pulled me close to his chest, holding me tight. "I know."

We stayed there until the sunlight broke through the window. I never fell asleep. Instead, I spent my time feeling every inch of his exposed skin, etching him into my memory.

He continued to stroke my hair and kissed me every so often.

"Remember how much I love you," he whispered.

"I love you too, Tyler. So much."

Finally. I said it.

We went outside around six. The hot southern sun was already heating the humid air. We awkwardly stood there, neither of us willing to say goodbye first. After a few moments, he ran his fingers through his hair, then stepped forward and took both of my hands in his.

"This is it." He tilted his head with soft eyes. "It's not forever. Just for a little while."

He leaned down and brushed his lips across mine... tenderly... taking his time. My heart raced as I shivered under his touch. *Please don't leave, not yet.* Pressing against me again, he let out a low hum, kissing me deeper with every breath.

I clutched his neck. His hands slid down my sides, then with one smooth motion, he lifted me off my feet, cradling me in his arms. I wrapped my legs around his waist. He started walking forward, lips still locked to mine, and pushed the screen door open.

Moments later, we both went down on the couch. I held him tight, returning his passion. He pushed my shirt up my belly and over my chest. I raised my arms. He swiftly slipped off my top, then met my lips with his again.

I slid my hands under his shirt, up his smooth back, then down to his muscular chest, slipping too far past the button of his jeans, over his hipbones, and back up his rippled abs.

He swept his lips across my jaw and down my neck. Stopping at the hollow of my throat, he paused to breathe me in, then he moved to my collarbone, and brushed over my scar.

Squeezing my eyes shut, all my imperfections rushed my mind. I had so many scars...

"You are so beautiful," he whispered on my skin, as if he could feel my doubts.

Skimming his tender touch over my chest, he made his way full circle and kissed me again. Our warm bodies still pressed tight, he pulled away just enough that I could still feel his lips on mine.

"I love you, Elizabeth."

I inhaled his breath as he kissed me again. Elizabeth. I loved the way he said my name.

We made the most of the last minutes we had together,

but used infinite restraint and forced ourselves to stop before we went too far.

We returned outside a quarter to seven. The truth was inevitable... he had to go. He asked me to wait as he went to his car. Moments later, he came back with something in his hand. He stepped in front of me, his right hand in his pocket. In the left, he held up his brown, leather journal.

"This is so you don't forget what I've told you."

I hesitated before I accepted the book. "Tyler, this is too much."

"Not at all. I wanted to have something more for you," he said, looking thoroughly disappointed. "I thought I had more time."

He took a step toward me and wrapped his arm around my waist, pressing our bodies tight. Brushing my hair from my eyes, he looked me over like he was imprinting me in his mind. Then he kissed me one last time with so much love, I began to understand what it felt like to be one with another person.

As he pulled away, he took a sharp breath, as if the pain was too much to bear.

"I love you," he said.

"I love you, too."

He stepped back, lowered his head with that look in his eyes that I loved so much, and then he turned and walked away. I hugged his journal against my aching heart. As he disappeared behind the black-tinted windows of his car, I inhaled the edges of the book.

It smelled like leather and Tyler.

Chapter

28

Megan walked through the front door as I came in the back. I headed straight for my room, shucked off my shoes and crawled under the covers. Tyler's touch lingered in my memory, still resonating on my skin. I curled in a ball, hugging his journal to my chest, and replayed the last six hours until I fell asleep.

Bam! The door smacked the wall. I gasped, sitting straight in bed.

"Elizabeth!" Mom shouted. "Get up! Now!"

Nausea made my head spin as I tried to process why she was screaming at me. Then I looked at the clock. Four minutes after ten.

Oh crap. She was home way too early.

LIFE HAPPENS ON THE STAIRS

Worse than a bad dream, I remembered Tyler walking away, then his kiss, his "I love you," his touch, his lips. My heart started pounding as if I'd been given a shot of adrenaline, then suddenly the surge fled, leaving my body weary.

Mom headed toward the kitchen. I jumped out of bed and followed her.

Her wrath couldn't hurt any worse than what I already felt.

She sat down behind the counter and I leaned against the small island, creating a buffer between us.

"Do you know why I'm home already?" she asked. "Maybe, Mrs. Vaughn?"

"What did she say to you?"

Mom sized me up. The clock clicked on the wall. *Tick, tock. Tick, tock. Tick.* I wanted to scream, get it over with!

"Let me see... how did she put it?" Her contemptuous stare said it before she could. "'That whore of a daughter of yours told me to clean my own fucking house.' Then, she also informed me that she saw you and Tyler kissing." She raised her palms in the air. "But the best one was when she said Tyler had gotten into a fight because of my white-trash children."

I couldn't believe my ears. The old woman was pure evil.

"Mom, she called me a whore when she saw my black eye after Mr. Smith smacked me." I spoke slowly. "I had to go to the Vaughn's the next day. When she called me a whore, I couldn't take anymore. I did tell her that. I told her to clean her own f'ing house. I'd dropped my phone when I tried to get away from Smith, and Tyler had insisted we go get it. After we came back, he gave me a kiss. We were in his car—"

"He went to Smith's?" she said, horrified.

"Tyler was mad when he saw my face. All he did was get

285

my phone back."

"You know," she sighed, "a little warning would've been nice. Like maybe when we were talking last night?"

"I'm sorry," I said in my sincerest tone. "I didn't mean for all of this to happen, but I didn't want to add to your burdens. That woman hates me because of Tyler. I heard her yell at him that he deserved better than that." My voice cracked as tears filled my eyes. "She called me, *that*."

Mom softened her hard expression. "Elsie, she's mean and heartless. You aren't below anyone. Even Tyler."

I gave her a weak smile.

"He left for Memphis this morning, you know," she said. A tear rolled down my cheek and fell to the floor, confirming I already knew. "He sure is taken with you. You should've heard him. He told her he'd never step foot in her house again if he heard her say another bad word about you." She chuckled. "The old woman was terrified. She stammered around as Tyler grabbed his bags and walked out. I left, too. I'd had enough."

"So, there's no way you can get your job back?"

"Do you really think I'd work for a woman who has the nerve to call my daughter a whore? Or my children white trash? Never again, sweetie." She grinned. "She can clean her own fucking house."

We burst out laughing. Those words meant everything to me. I walked around the counter and wrapped my arms around her. She squeezed me tight.

"I'm so sorry, Mom. I never meant to lie to you. I never meant to get you fired. I screwed everything up."

"Shh... no you didn't. You've been through a lot. I'm proud of you, and I'm sorry. I wanted to protect you, not send you out to get hurt."

LIFE HAPPENS ON THE STAIRS

I pulled away and looked her in the eyes. "I had no intentions of seeing Tyler. He asked me to go jogging and... " I gasped, tears streaming down my cheeks. "I can't explain it. We couldn't stay away from each other. I am totally in love with him."

"I believe the feeling is mutual. He apologized to me for the fight, but before he left, he confronted his grandmother, told her he loved you, and if she didn't like it, then she didn't need to be in his life." She smiled. "He really cares about you."

She pulled me back into her arms, and I sobbed on her shoulder like a little girl.

For the next two days, I came out of my bedroom only to go the bathroom. Tyler didn't call or text. He'd disappeared like he'd warned me he would. I held my phone in one hand and his journal in the other, sleeping the days away.

Saturday afternoon, Mom knocked on my door, pushing it open even though I'd ignored her. She sat down on the edge of the bed.

"Elsie, you have to get up and do something. Emma's been calling you for days. You should talk to her, or at the least, take a shower. Remember, school starts tomorrow."

I groaned and rolled away from her.

She rubbed my back for a few seconds, then left me alone. I clutched Tyler's journal to my chest, nose pressed against the edges, and went back to sleep.

Sunday night, he finally called.

"Thank God," he said after I answered. "It is so good to

hear your voice."

"Same to you. Is everything okay?"

"Yeah. When I got home, Dad and I had argued and I dropped my phone. It shattered, and then I crashed out. I slept for like fourteen hours. I just got it replaced."

The sound of his voice produced a whole new pain I'd never experienced. It curled itself inside my belly and squirmed.

"All I've done is sleep, too," I said.

"I'm so glad to be out of Satan's sister's house." We both laughed. "You've been down in the basement. Didn't it smell like brimstone and fire?"

Our laughter numbed my wounds, and we talked for the next two hours.

Monday morning, I showered, gathered my stuff, and left for my senior year. After talking to Tyler, I felt a thousand times better. I needed to regroup and get my head straight. Dwelling on his absence was only making it worse.

Emma caught me at my locker before the first bell rang.

"Why didn't you call me back this weekend?" she asked.

I twisted the combination and pulled the metal door. "I'm sorry. It's been a bad couple of days."

"Is it your dad?"

"No, not entirely, but he's not doing that great either."

"So, what's up then?" She leaned against the locker next to mine and crossed her arms. "Your mom wouldn't tell me. She said I had to talk to you."

Just like Mom. She'd take a secret to the grave.

"Um... Do you remember the guy that helped me at the festival?"

She looked at me with her big, coal-black eyes. "Of course."

My cheeks burned.

Emma's face went paler than usual. She pushed off the wall, looking proud. "You owe me fifty bucks."

"I guess I do," I said. "He's amazing."

She squealed, jumping up and down. "Tell me about him!"

Her excitement triggered a high alert defense in me. I didn't want to share Tyler. He was my secret, and I missed my private world.

Run. Run, now!

"Uh... I gotta go. I'm sorry. I don't want to be late." I pivoted and hurried down the hallway.

Emma called out, "What the hell, Elsie?"

I sprinted out the main doors and across the front lawn of the school. Gasping for air, I stopped on the sidewalk. Tears stung my eyes as my heart pounded on my chest.

I'd been robbed. Robbed of my dad and now Tyler. I bent over and put my hands on my knees, sucking in deep breaths.

Get it together, I told myself. You gotta push through it. Just like cleaning houses, you just have to get through it.

As I stood alone in the blazing heat of September, the first bell rang in the distance. *Crap.* Tardy the first day of school. *Great job, Elsie.*

I walked back toward the building. Hopefully, Mrs. Kline was in a good mood.

When I came home that afternoon, I stopped by Dad's room

to see how his day had gone. He was asleep, and Megan was sitting in the recliner reading a gossip magazine. I chatted with her for a few minutes, then I went to my room and changed clothes to go pick in the field.

Tyler's journal peeked out from under the covers. I had to resist. I'd never get a pepper off a plant if I opened it. I slipped my phone in my back pocket and headed outside.

After an hour of picking the far corner of the field, I heard something rustling behind me. I spun around. A few rows away, the leaves of the pepper plants rustled. Please, don't be a snake. I stood still, like Dad taught me just in case it was a rattler. The plants stirred again, and then I heard a snorting sound. A black snout popped up between the rows. I stepped closer, and a brown basset hound moseyed toward me, sniffing my trail.

I winced when he approached. *Yuck.* He smelled like a yeasty foot.

Still sniffing the ground around my feet, he didn't acknowledge me. He was brown and black with long, floppy ears, and patchy fur covered in dust. I clicked my tongue to get his attention. The old dog looked up at me like I'd just appeared, and then he started howling a hound dog bellow. *Ba-woo, ba-woo, ba-woo!* His bay echoed like a warning signal from a barge.

I put out my hands. "Shh. Shush. It's okay... "

He bellowed on. I stepped closer, holding out the back of my hand. He paused his howl and sniffed me over. The quiet afternoon returned, as he decided if I was an acceptable human or not. His long, wet tongue licked the back of my hand, and then he looked up at me with pathetic, sad eyes. I knelt down and rubbed the top of his head.

"Oh... you poor thing, who do you belong to?"

He panted and tried to lick my face.

Giggling, I dodged his sloppy kiss, and rubbed his ears. He leaned against me, enjoying the affection. His pungent scent was almost unbearable, so I started back toward the house. He followed on my heels as if he'd found the person he'd been looking for. I went inside and filled a bowl of water for him. When I returned, he was sitting under the tree, panting in the humid air. His presence comforted me. He looked as sad as I felt. The broken-down old dog just needed some love. I set down the bowl and he instantly lapped up the water.

"You'll be 'Old Dog' until I'm told otherwise. That okay with you?"

He looked up at me like he understood the question as water ran out of his flabby jowls down his neck. I smiled and rubbed his stinky head.

Later that night, Mom and I sat at the table eating cheeseburgers. Her quiet manner matched mine, both of us burdened with feelings we didn't want to talk about.

"Has Mark given you the money for our first two loads?" I finally spoke up.

"Yes, he did this afternoon. I meant to say thank you hours ago."

I shrugged. "It's no biggie."

"Yes, it is, Elsie. It helps a lot." She held her burger midair. "I really appreciate what you and Mark are doing. It's awful work."

"It's easy... it just sucks, that's all," I said. She chuckled in agreement. "Do we owe Mr. McAllister for using the acreage?"

"I wanted to pay him, but he called me when I was in Nashville and told me not to worry about it," she said with an irritated edge. She hated handouts, but something else fed her tension. "I need to tell you. He's put the house on the market. Since we're living here, he isn't going to put a sign in the yard, mostly out of respect for your dad and me, but it is officially for sale."

"Will he give us time to find something else?"

"Of course. Kenny's a good man, he wouldn't put us out on the streets. Maybe we'll go back to Illinois. I don't know... It wouldn't hurt to be around our family."

Hearing the word "Illinois" made me want to run. I'd promised not to be that person anymore. But after the weight of the lie was lifted, the urge to run when my emotions went haywire had come back stronger than ever. I had to think about something else. Old Dog. I took a bite of my sandwich, and then I told Mom about finding him in the field.

I made up with Emma the next day. We ate lunch together by a fence covered in wild honeysuckle. I confessed my summer, even down to the night we spent in the abandoned house. She loved my stories about jogging, Mrs. Vaughn, the fight with Mr. Smith (a man she'd encountered when working as a waitress at the restaurant; apparently, he was an equal-opportunity jerk), my F-bomb that blew my cover, and when I told her about the fight at the pool hall, she went crazy as she listened to the details of how Tyler beat Bobby's ass. No one

LIFE HAPPENS ON THE STAIRS

liked Bobby.

On my way home, I picked up a bag of dog food. For the rest of the week, Old Dog met me at the field after school, and we walked the rows, gathering peppers. If I walked forward, he walked forward. If I took two steps backward, he'd take two steps back. No matter where I went, he was right on my heels. After two days, Mark joined me when he got off work at his new job at the machine shop. Once he met Old Dog, he seemed more motivated to do the tedious work, as well. We made the best of the time under the sun, even though I still wasn't ready to laugh and chat. Mark didn't push. He let me have my sour mood with more understanding than I'd ever expected. But for the first time in over a week, I wanted to say something. I stopped in the middle of my row. He was bent over, picking a few yards ahead.

"Mark," I called out.

He snapped to attention and spun around, holding three red peppers in his hands.

"What's wrong?" he asked.

"I'm sorry about the night of the fight. Tyler didn't mean to do that to you, he just has a thing about people grabbing him from behind. Anyway, I'm sorry you were arrested. That definitely wasn't the plan when we went there."

"Me, too. Sorry Bobby went at you like that. Several people told me about it. Elsie, you've dealt with enough shit, you know I'd never let him do that to you."

"I know. It's okay."

We stood there in an awkward silence for a second, then he started picking again. Relief settled my nervous stomach. Thank God, he understood.

Each night, I'd help Mom with dinner, and we'd eat in the bedroom with Dad. Afterward, I'd crawl in bed and stare at the cover of Tyler's journal. Thumbing the pages, I'd glance at his clean print written in blue, catching words like, *beautiful, flawless, outstanding,* or even simpler words: *her, she, mine.* Then there were phrases that piqued my curiosity: *absolutely tortured, freaking out, confuses the hell out of me...* I wasn't sure what held me back from reading it, other than I was afraid I'd think about him even more. He haunted my dreams, my thoughts. Then, my mind would play tricks on me. I'd hear his voice in a crowd, or I'd spot the back of his head as I walked down the hallway at school. His absence, or maybe it was our memories... was pure torment.

I'd lie in bed with his journal beside me, releasing into my sketchbook my memories of his face. Most nights, I'd receive a text that helped me not feel as alone in my heartache.

Tyler: I am completely lost without you. I can't even focus on basic math!

Me: Who can ever focus on math?!? LMAO

Tyler: Just keep the charcoal in your hand and you'll be fine. I desperately miss you.

Me: I desperately miss you, too.

After two weeks of adjusting to my new routine of school, picking peppers, and helping take care of Dad, I was sitting on my bed one afternoon, sketching a picture of Old Dog, when someone knocked at my door.

"Yeah," I answered.

Megan poked her head inside. "Hey, how y'all doin'?"

She stepped inside, walked to my dresser, and leaned against it.

"I'm good."

"So... I heard about your boy leavin'. What's his name, again?"

I stared at her for a second. Mark must've said something. "Tyler."

She strolled across the room and sat down on the edge of the bed.

"Heard he had to go back to school."

"Yeah. It's gonna be a long four months."

"It'll get better. Mark said you're pretty sad. Is there anything I can do?"

"Take me to Nashville," I said with a weak smile.

"I wish!" She laughed. "Love Nashville. I'd be in hog heaven if I could live there."

That comment made me laugh, but I still wasn't ready to be cheerful. Megan picked up Tyler's journal off my nightstand. Panic surged through me and I reached out to take it back, but stopped. *Calm down. She isn't going to steal it.*

"It's so pretty." She flipped the pages with her thumb. "Ooh, I love the way it smells."

"He gave it to me."

"Oh, wow, it's full." She looked at me. "This is Tyler's?"

"Yeah, I haven't read it, yet."

She opened to a random page, read for a second, and then she slapped it shut.

"Why aren't you reading this?"

"I don't know... I guess I'm afraid of what it says."

"This will make you feel better." She held the book mid-air. "Girl, I only read like two sentences. Do yourself a favor."

She laid it on my lap. I ran my fingers over the front and opened the cover. Inside, a piece of cream-colored stationery was wedged between the flap and first page.

Elsie,

Since you're so curious about my journal, I thought you might like to read it after I leave.

It's about you, for you, and anytime you forget how much I love you — Please, reread.

Love — Tyler

I glanced up. Megan had gone. She was like a little angel floating around the house, reminding us that joy was no further than our fingertips. I held the small piece of notepaper, reading it over and over, then slipped it inside and closed the cover.

I remembered his words about me haunting him. That was exactly how I felt, haunted by an enigma. The clock ticked in the background, reminding me of my solitude. Could a journal full of words really fill the void? I opened the cover to the first page.

Chapter

29

J uly 1 - FUCK! I leave for Nana's in two days. I hate this. Always have. After all these years, you'd think they'd get that I don't want to go back, but no. What I want doesn't matter. Grandpa. All I can think of is Grandpa when I'm there. Nana is one thing. An entirely different thing. But every night, I see Grandpa in my dreams, in my nightmares. It's constant. And then Dad wants me to go back. I can still smell his pipe tobacco in the study. I can still smell his cologne in the bathroom down the hall. I hear him calling out "TJ" sometimes when I'm swimming. Shiloh's the only place I can go. The one place I can get away. Six weeks. Fuck.

July 4 - Kismet. Maybe it's kismet. I swear, I'm crazy. A man drops with a seizure and all I can think about is his daughter? What's wrong with me? I need to go see Dr. Allen again. I haven't been there in over a year. My brain's all twisted. The whole scene freaked me out. But she's gorgeous. She's talented. And then she's crying in front of me, desperate, helpless, terrified. God. I'll never forget the look in her crystal blue eyes. Crystal doesn't even begin to describe them. They're more like a crisp winter sky. No. The clear blue water at St. Thomas. I asked her out. She's the first girl I've asked out in over a year. And that idea turned out to be a disaster. Hopefully, meeting Elsie won't be. Zach thinks I'm crazy for ignoring all the girls at school. I know I can get laid. God knows, I wouldn't mind. But I'm not that guy. I just want to get to know her. Maybe the next six weeks won't be a drag after all.

July 14 - I'm done. Tanked. Sank. Totally and completely in love with her. Ten days? I feel like I've known her my whole life. Or maybe it's like everything in my life has been leading up to this. She's amazing. She meets me every morning and we laugh and joke like we're teenagers. Oh. I guess, technically we are, but I didn't do things like this a few years ago. I stayed at home and ignored all human existence. Zach filled me in enough to keep me from being a complete hermit. He understands me. He loves his grandpa as much as I do, did... whatever. I asked Elsie to go to dinner. I need to take her out. I need to know she feels the same way I do. I'm so fucking needy all of a sudden. Why? It's like a monster's inside of me. After kissing her, I know exactly what I want in this life. Elsie.

LIFE HAPPENS ON THE STAIRS

Every day after school, I came home and picked in the field until supper. Mom would either call me in from the back door, or I'd make my way inside around six or seven and start cooking, if she hadn't already. Over the next four weeks, we kept our routine, eating dinner in the bedroom with Dad, and then I'd go to my room and read. Tyler's journal meant the world to me. If I couldn't talk to him or text him, at least I had his words. He'd written every detail about meeting me at Shiloh, and how he feared his grandmother's reaction to us dating. What I loved most was that he didn't care what the old woman thought. He wanted me more because I wasn't from privilege. From money. That part was the most amusing. He had no idea how much money my family had. The farmland that my grandparents owned paled in comparison to the Vaughn's wealth, but that was because nothing had been liquidated. Grandma and Grandpa Diefenbach were loaded. I resented their money because of the way they'd treated Dad, but the truth was, Mark and I were the only grandchildren in the lineage. My uncle didn't have any kids, and we were the last of the Diefenbach line through my grandfather.

Regardless, Tyler had poured out his feelings on the pages—unabashed. I had to assume he never thought he'd let anyone read them. As I read the passage I caught a glimpse of when I'd snooped while cleaning, I found more:

July 30 - I don't want to be at Shiloh without her. I don't want to be anywhere without her. After weeks of seeing her every day, I need to wake up beside her every morning, for the rest of my life. Can someone seriously fall in love this fast? I'm crazy. I told Dr. Allen, the odds were against me. If I had a brain that absorbed information like a sponge in water, I was bound to lose my mind one day. He laughed and said, "Tyler. You just need to get laid. You're eighteen."

SERIOUSLY? Is that all anyone in this world thinks about? I never went back there again. I still wonder about that guy.

August 3 - I can't sleep. Nightmares again. Long, vivid nightmares. It's easier to stay awake than go through the nightmares. Dr. Allen told me to write it out, like it was a fictional story so I could detach myself from it. I'll try it again. Maybe it'll work this time.

15 years old. 9:30 p.m. The Country Club.

"So, TJ. What you think of them Saints?" Grandpa asked. "Gonna be a good year."

"I'd like to see Brees get a ring."

"Me, too." He tossed back a swig of bourbon. "Your grandmother thinks the Saints are cowards," he slurred. "Crazy woman. She's going nuts. I swear, TJ, she'll be the death of me."

His forehead furrowed with irritation. Nana had lost it before we left for dinner. She'd wailed that Grandpa was a greedy old bastard, and how much she hated him. I walked out of the kitchen when she said it. Spending the summer there was bad enough. I didn't want to listen to her bitch him out in the process.

"Let's go home. I'm tired, Grandpa."

"Sure, son." He picked up his glass and smiled. "You can drive. Got your permit on you, right?" he asked, then knocked off the rest of the drink.

"Of course. I always have it."

"Come on, then," he said. "I'm ready."

I sat behind the wheel of his mint '68 Shelby Mustang. I'd been waiting my whole life to drive it. Black leather, bucket seat, 5-speed on the floor, painted white with a Ford blue racing stripe down the center. My dream car.

Driving the winding hills with utmost care, I listened to Grandpa rattle on.

"Sonofabitch thought he'd pull one over on the stock market," he said. "Here this guy has all this capital in a failing corporation, and then he gains more overhead by acquiring another."

A quick glance at him.

His hands shot in the air. "Oh, shit!"

I looked back at the road. A flash of brown. A deer? I nailed the breaks. BANG!

My head bounced off the steering wheel. Glass crackled, shattering all over the dash. Tires skidded across the highway. The car spun in a wide circle. Pop! The side of my head smacked the window. I jerked the wheel to the right and the car caught the shoulder.

Action. Reaction. That's all it was. The car tilted one way, and then it rocked, flipping over the side of the hill. We were airborne. My stomach bottomed out like I was falling in a bad dream. Bam! We slammed the hill. The car flipped. Bam! The noise pierced my ears. My head snapped back against the seat. I held up my arms to shield my face. Glass flew around like thousands of razorblades, cutting my skin. We rolled, then rolled again.

Bam! The car landed on its hood and stopped.

A pop and a fizz as steam spewed from under the hood. I scrambled to unbuckle my seatbelt, falling face first into the steering wheel. Grandpa hung in the air, limp and lifeless. I twisted around and grabbed him.

"Grandpa! Are you okay?" I choked. "Grandpa?"

My knees were on the ceiling of the car. Grandpa hung from his seatbelt like a ragdoll.

"Grandpa! You gotta wake up!"

Nothing.

I let him go and pressed my blood-soaked hands over my face. I'd killed him, I sobbed. I fucking killed him!

Okay, that's enough of that shit. My therapist is crazy. I shouldn't have done that.

Fuck it. I'm going for a jog.

Oh my gosh. Tyler was driving that night. I had no idea. My chest wrenched with compassion. Empathy. After reading his words, I felt like I'd witnessed the wreck, like I'd been standing on the side of the road as the car flipped through the air. His words. He had to write it down to tell me. It must've been too painful to relate the story out loud.

After I turned off the lights to go to sleep, I replayed the story over and over in my mind. No wonder his grandpa's death had messed him up so much. The guilt he lived with was eating him alive, yet it explained so much – all the miles he ran every day, the overachieving, his need to be trusted. It all led back to that night.

Chapter

30

The middle of September brought on a do-or-die period for the crops. Mark and I had worked every day, managing to cover almost three acres, but we needed to re-walk what had already been picked. Impossible at best.

My alarm went off early on a Saturday morning. I crawled out of bed and headed to Mark's room. *Bam, bam, bam.* The door swung open.

Already gone. I huffed and went back to my room to get dressed.

When I walked in the barn, Old Dog was lying on the floor with his ears curled by his paws. Pathetic eyes glanced up at me. He scrambled to stand.

"Ba-woo, ba-woo!"

I patted his head. "Good morning, you old thing."

As I headed outside, he followed right behind me. The morning felt pleasant and cool, inviting in the autumn air. After a few minutes, I stopped and listened to a mockingbird singing high in the trees. I imagined how proud the bird was of himself for mimicking everything from a doorbell to a cricket. I returned to picking, satisfied with my solitude. Mark could stay gone as long as he wanted.

About an hour later, I heard a car in the distance. I looked up at the house from the far end of the field. *Mark.* About time.

I turned around and grabbed a red pepper. Another distant rumble. I squinted, unable to place the sound. Old man Cramer must've been chopping wood.

I loaded my hands with red peppers and stuffed them inside my sack. Repeating the process, I topped off my bag and scanned the rows for any misses. *Damn.* I'd missed a lot. At least my sack was full. It didn't matter as long as I had a full sack.

Voices in the distance floated in the breeze. I looked at the backyard and gasped.

Mark, Ruby, Mr. and Mrs. McAllister, Emma, Pastor Larry and his wife Sue – they were all headed my way with a crowd of faces behind them that I didn't recognize. All of them were walking toward the field, carrying various kinds of bags, like they were here on a mission.

I wanted to shout and jump as I ran down the row to meet everyone. Then, I saw Woodrow at the back of the pack, limping along. Oh my gosh... even Woodrow?

I ran to Mark and wrapped my arms around his neck.

"Thank you," I said in his ear.

He quickly returned my embrace and let go.

"All right, all right," he huffed, pushing me away. "It's no big deal."

"Are you kidding? We're killing ourselves here. This is amazing!"

I gave Ruby a hug and then Emma.

"I can't believe you're here," I said to Emma.

"Girl, you know I'd never miss helpin' y'all."

"Now, we got all the people we could gather," Ruby said. "Let's get this harvest finished. You've done a fine job, but it's time for some help."

"Thank you!" I turned to Mark. "You lead 'em."

"Let's do this!" He clapped his hands like we were hitting the football field.

Mark separated people to cover three rows on either side of them. Emma and I went to our designated areas with Old Dog close behind. A dark-haired guy named Steve and another lanky man named Josh, parked two full-sized pickups by the field for us to empty our sacks into. Mark pulled our truck up behind theirs, giving us three means of transportation for hauling to the processing plant. Everyone fell into place with Mark's instructions, surrendering their Saturday afternoon to help my family.

As the morning moved on, people rotated back and forth from the field to the trucks, filling and dumping their sacks. I was bent down, picking an armful, when I heard someone walk up behind me.

"How's it going?" Mom asked.

I beamed a smile over my shoulder. "Look at how much we've gotten done. That guy over there," I pointed, "he's going to take a load to the plant soon, and we still have all day. Can you believe all these people are doing this for us? I don't know half of them."

"Your dad does," she said. "Mark went to Ruby's and

told her what was going on. Between the two of them, they rounded up half of Morris Chapel, a few from Saltillo and Savannah. I believe that couple over there live in Adamsville." She shook her head. "People never cease to amaze me."

"I can't imagine what Dad would have thought. Look at how they love him."

"He would be very humbled to see this."

I wrapped my arms around her. She clutched me tight.

"Mom, it's going to happen," I said. "We're going to get these crops out."

"Thank you, Elsie. Thank you for everything."

Her gratitude meant the world to me. She let me go, and then she grabbed my empty sack, pulling it over her shoulder.

"Have you told Dad about this yet?" I asked.

"No, he's been sleeping most of the morning."

"Can I? I can't wait to tell him what Mark did."

"Of course." She gave me a loving smile. "You've done this, too."

Tears filled my eyes. We'd fulfilled our promise. That was all that mattered.

After lunch a few people had to leave, but we still had twelve helpers to keep us going until six that night. Each truck made five trips, giving Mom fifteen loads. On top of it, Mark had another load he could deliver on Monday, and if the weather held, we could still harvest some more. Kind souls from three counties. Maybe they did have a soft heart for outsiders... The strange Northerners who'd gotten lost. But they'd found a good ole Yankee in Dad, falling in love with him despite of where he came from.

After the last car pulled away, I ran inside to tell him.

Pulling a chair next to his bed, I grasped his hand and re-played every detail. From Old Dog finding me, to the towns-people rallying to support him, to the amount of money we earned.

As I recounted everyone's generosity, he struggled to keep his eyes open, but when I said, "Everyone loves you, Dad. You're such a good man." He undeniably squeezed my fingers.

After his unexpected response, I let my tears flow. He was proud. But I wanted him to see what we'd done. I wanted him to feel it like I did. I wanted him to get out of bed and walk the field with me. Bittersweet victory.

"I love you so much," I whispered.

I sat there a bit longer, and then Mom came in after she'd taken a shower. I was ready to clean up, too, so we switched, and I headed to the bathroom.

After I crawled in bed, I opened up Tyler's journal.

August 14 - How am I ever going to leave her? I can't. I'm irrational. I want to skip next semester. I want to say fuck it, and not go. Wouldn't that be stupid? I'll just throw away eve-rything to stay in a town I can't stand. Nana's crazy. The de-mentia is worse than Mom and Dad want to admit. The other night, she forgot about the chicken breasts on the stove, and the pan scorched. I cleaned it up. She didn't even seem to care that dinner was ruined. Oh well. I'll tell Dad again, but he seems to be oblivious. I hope it isn't because of Alexis. When I took Elsie to my house, I noticed he didn't go back to Mem-phis when we left the Country Club. He turned down the side street toward Alexis' house. Mom asked me about it. I couldn't tell her. I'll talk to Dad later, but seriously, if he's fucking around, I'm gonna be pissed. I get that he's 43, and probably bored to death, but cheating isn't cool. Hell, he's the one who taught me that! Ugh. Just another thing I need to deal with. Nana having me followed is enough. I still have to go talk to my uncle. There goes my checking account.

August 16 - The shower's running and I need to get in. I've never fucked up so bad. Elsie and I had three days... Three days that I couldn't wait to spend with her. They're shot. I blew it. How can I ever tell her how much I love her? She doesn't know the half of how fucked up I am. I couldn't tell her. I tried... I tried to tell her about Grandpa, but the words... I couldn't say them without breaking down. Crying in front of her? That's worse torture than my nightmares. I would've been a blubbering mess. She has to understand I'm not violent. I only beat Bobby's ass because he had his hands on her. I tried to walk away. I'd grabbed her hand, her warm and comforting hand, and then the next thing I knew, I was rolling across the gravel again. All I wanted was to get her out of there. To leave. Fuckin' scumbag. I hate Bobby Dale.

I gotta get out of here. I have less than seven hours. Fuck! What can I give her? My cologne. No. That's stupid. A photo. Wow, that's even dumber. She can draw me from memory. I'll write her a letter... I don't have time for that. But. Wait. I could give her this. It's everything I tried to say, but couldn't.

His last words were scribbled across the page in black ink.

Elsie,

We're all at the mercy of circumstance.
I love what we've made of ours.

LIFE HAPPENS ON THE STAIRS

Please, don't give up, hold on to what I've said,
And please, wait for me.
I love you.

Tyler

I closed the journal and texted him.
Me: I finished reading :) Thank you.
Several minutes later...
Tyler: All good?
Me: More than I can say. I miss you.
Tyler: That's a relief. I miss you, too. Love you.
Me: I love you, too.

Chapter

31

Early October had brought in cooler air and rusty hues lacing the forests. Mark and I started watching football together again. As we shouted at the TV, it felt like old times before the accident. Mom hated football, so she left us alone to our Sunday afternoons and sat with Dad.

Tyler texted one Sunday night.

Tyler: Headed to Tallahassee this weekend for Regionals. 4 days. Be back by Monday.

Me: Good luck. Love you

Tyler: Love you

I stared at the phone. I hadn't talked to him for almost two weeks. Should I call? I never called him first. Dying to hear his voice, I pressed his name.

"What's up?" he answered in almost a whisper.

"Just miss ya. Wha'cha doing?"

"Oh... hold on."

Noise filled the background like he'd just stepped into another world; people chattering, clanking sounds like silverware and plates. A girl's voice. "We're ready for you, Tyler."

My stomach rolled over. *What the hell was he doing?*

"Elsie, I'll call you back. I'm at a fundraiser, and they're waiting for me. I'm sorry."

"Okay."

He didn't call or text for the rest of the week.

By Friday, I had a permanent knot in my throat. I went to Mom and Dad's room to say goodnight. Dad looked right at me when I came in. I placed my hand on his and smiled.

Mom's eyes brightened. "He's doing really well."

"Looks like it."

"Will Tyler be back for Thanksgiving?" she asked.

I shrugged. The knot wouldn't let me talk about Tyler.

"Are you okay?" Her face full of concern. "Did something happen between you two?"

"I'm fine." I gave Dad a kiss on the cheek. "Love you, Daddy. I'm so glad to see you're feeling good. I'll come in before I go to school tomorrow."

He blinked, and it almost looked like he smiled. An unfamiliar hope rose inside of me. Could he really get better? I gave Mom a hug and left them alone.

As I walked down the hall, Mark was headed to his room.

"Hey, I never told you," he said. "When Bobby got out of

the hospital, he left town."

That was a relief. "Good. Have they dropped the charges on Tyler and you?"

"Yeah. They dismissed the case when Bobby didn't show up for court." He opened his bedroom door and turned back. "And guess what? I asked Megan out."

"That's cool."

"She's adorable. I can't imagine how hard it would've been to take care of Dad without her." He flashed a cocky grin. "A nurse would make a damn good wife."

"She probably will." I started toward my room. "Goodnight, Mark."

"You okay?"

"I'll be fine."

"Goodnight, sis."

An hour later, I sat on the bed, finishing the sketch of Old Dog when my phone buzzed. Heart pounding, I hadn't heard the sound since Sunday.

Tyler: You must think I'm a real jackass.

Me: I don't know what to think right now.

Tyler: Can I call you?

Me: Do you have to ask?

My phone rang seconds later.

"Hi," I answered.

"Hey," he said in a gentle tone. "How are you?"

"Confused."

"I'm sorry I didn't return your call. I was at a black-tie fundraiser for my department and had to give a speech. This week's been crazy."

I imagined him in a black tuxedo and the thought made

me ache inside. "Okay."

"What are you confused about?"

I rolled my eyes. Was it just a guy thing to be so thick-headed?

"I'm... You're so... I have no idea where we stand right now," I blurted out. "Tyler, you haven't called or texted. I've felt like an idiot all week. You say you're a recluse, but that's bullshit. You're always doing something."

"Whoa... calm down. This is what I've been talking about—"

"Don't tell me I have to trust you. I'm trying really hard, but you just drop off the face of the earth without warning."

Dead silence.

I'd just whined like a little girl. I remembered Zach warning me that wasn't the way to Tyler's heart. An audible breath came from the other end of the line. I felt his irritation as if he stood in the room. *Shit.*

"It may be hard for you to believe," his tone low and methodical, "but I do think about you. Incessantly. I get that you trust me, but you have to trust that nothing's changed, even if we can't talk. I got stuck at that gala event. Class sucked all week. Plus, cross country. I've been running ten to twenty miles a day since school started. I'm exhausted." He sighed. "I just landed in Florida, and I'm finally settled in the hotel. Regionals are tomorrow. Please, tell me we're all good. You have no idea how much I need to hear that right now."

"We're all good," I said. "I'm sorry. I just miss you."

He let out another heavy sigh. "I miss you, too. Like more than I can even say. Seriously. I'd kill to just drive to you and never go back. I'm burned out."

How could I be so self-centered? He'd been working his ass off for months, and all I did was pine over his absence.

"You sound really tired."

"I'm fucking bombing one of my classes. I've never had this problem." He chuckled. "See? That's how much I think about you. It's killing my grades."

"Don't feel bad. I'm failing Trig."

"Trig? I can help you. Email me what you're working on."

"Like you need something else to do."

"It's fine. Now tell me, how did harvest go?"

I smiled. "You won't believe what happened."

We talked for over an hour, daydreaming and plotting how I could get to Nashville. After we discussed what we'd do if I made it, we decided it was probably better that I stayed home.

By midnight, I curled up in bed, satisfied that I'd finally heard his voice, and fell asleep.

Bam! My bedroom door smacked the wall as light from the kitchen flooded the darkness. I gasped and sat up, then glanced at the clock. Four thirty-two.

"Elsie!" Mark yelled.

"What?"

"Call 911! It's Dad. I gotta help Mom." He turned and ran.

I grabbed my cell phone. *No, no, no... God, please. No.* Fumbling, my fingers trembled as I pressed the numbers.

"911, what's your emergency?" a woman answered.

"We need an ambulance." My voice cracked. "It's my dad."

"Okay. What's your address?"

"1708 West McAllister Road. Morris Chapel."

LIFE HAPPENS ON THE STAIRS

I hurried out of my room, the phone still to my ear. All the lights in the house were on. Mark's and Mom's voices echoed down the hallway.

"Grab his arm!"

"The medication isn't working," Mark shouted.

The dispatch lady repeated our address.

I jogged to the doorway of my parents' room and froze. It looked like Dad's body was trying to eject his soul. The convulsions ripped through him, superhuman strength, fighting against Mark's grasp.

"Please, hurry." Tears clouded my eyes. "He's having a seizure."

"Stay calm, miss. We're on our way. Can you tell me what exactly is going on?"

"He's dying from a brain tumor. This is a really bad seizure."

"Okay. They're about ten miles away. Just a few more minutes."

"Thank you." I sniffled and ended the call.

Mom held Dad's shoulder and arm, his resistance reverberating through her.

She looked up, tear-streaked and red-faced. "Are they coming?"

"Yes. What can I do?"

"Go wait for them." Then she cried out in terror, "Brandon, stay with us!"

The hairs on my arms stood on end. I ran to the front door and shot outside into the cool morning air – sprinting toward the road. It was always darkest before dawn. I paced as I waited, shivering as warm tears turned cold on my cheeks. A faint siren. I held my breath. *Don't take him today. Don't let this be it. One more day. Please.*

Flashing red lights flickered through the ravines. Headlights appeared over the hill. I jumped up and down, waving my arms.

Moments later, they pulled into the driveway. A male paramedic jogged my way.

I shook all over. "He's in the back bedroom."

"Okay." He hurried inside.

Two more paramedics ran past, carrying a gurney. I followed on their heels but stopped at the end of the hall as everyone crammed in the small bedroom. Mark backed out, one slow step at a time.

I ran to my room and quickly changed clothes, then dashed back to the living room. Listening to the commotion, I pulled on my socks. Mark came in and flopped on the recliner.

"There's nothing they can do." Tears streaming, he stared into space. "Nothing."

What did he mean? Of course, they could do something. That was their job.

"What did you say?" I asked, irritated that he wouldn't look at me.

"What?"

"Mark, what's going on?"

"He's dying, Elsie. This is it."

I jumped up and darted toward the hallway.

"I need to say goodbye," I cried. "I won't ever see him again."

"No! Elsie, don't!" He shot out of the recliner and intercepted me before I made it to the hall, gently walking me backward to the living room. "Don't go back there."

I fell into his arms.

"We'll get through this." He held me tight. "We will.

We'll get through it." He repeated the words over and over, like he was trying to convince himself, too.

Moments later, another warm touch ran over my back.

Mom pressed her head to both of ours. "It's over. He's gone."

All three of us embraced, sharing our tears as one. The moment imprinted on my soul. The love for my family was overwhelming, but without Dad, we'd never be whole again. Our security. Our cover. The reason we were all together.

He was gone.

The next two hours were a complete blur, as if everything around me moved in fast forward, and I stood frozen in time. Paramedics. Coroner. The local sheriff. All of them in and out, following basic protocol. A police officer wanted a statement from me.

"Um, my dad died," I said, numb and tired. "He has... or had a brain tumor."

He tipped the wide brim of his navy-blue hat. "Sorry for your loss, miss."

I nodded. He left me sitting on the couch, hugging my knees.

By eight a.m., they were all gone. Including Dad.

The silence. There was nothing else to say, so we all returned to our rooms. I grabbed my phone and pressed Tyler's name, letting it ring twice. *Shit.* I hurried to press END. He was about to run at the NCAA Regionals. I couldn't tell him Dad died before he competed.

Another blow of disappointment hit me. Tyler was the

only person I wanted to talk to. I dropped the phone on my bed, snatched my iPod, and ran out the back door.

Sprinting as hard as I could, I had to get the hell away from the house. Away from the infestation of broken hearts and death. I couldn't take anymore. I ran toward the rolling hills, cold morning air stinging my lungs. The pain felt like punishment, so I pushed harder.

Fuck! I wanted to hit something. I wanted to scream, throw a fit, curse the sky. I sprinted faster. Gravity pulled me toward the dip in the hill. Straining all my muscles, the burn fueled my anger. Flames shot up my shins, stinging to my knees. I needed to feel the pain somewhere other than inside.

When I made it to the top of the hill, flashes of Dad's body rejecting him tortured my thoughts. The slamming sounds, Mom's cries, the sirens, flashing red and blue lights. Mark's affirmations as he desperately held me tight. The way he trembled in my arms.

"Why?" I cried out, face drenched in tears. "Why is this happening?"

I knew Dad would die. But why did he have to go like that? Why couldn't he just go to sleep and never wake up? Of course, he wouldn't go without a fight. Nothing ever came easy for him. He'd fought through the tragic death of his parents. Through the nightmare of dealing with Mom's family. The struggle of supporting all of us. He'd fought his whole life. And this was his reward? *Fuck!*

The faster I ran, the less I felt. Limbs numb, the pavement evaporated under my feet, like I floated over the road.

Adrenaline clouding my judgment, I abruptly stopped and bent over, gasping for air.

Tyler. He would've turned around and started coaching.

"Don't stop, not after pushing like that." I thought of his

voice. *"You have to keep moving. Tell your body what you want. Don't let it tell you. Don't quit."*

I wanted to quit. I wanted to collapse and not get up. Still winded, I slowly started to jog. Little by little, I picked up the pace. Outrun the pain. Just keep running. But no matter how fast or how hard I ran, the wound lived inside. Fear that it would never leave pushed me on for another two miles.

An hour later, I walked in the front door. Mom sat at the kitchen table, talking on the phone. Without saying a word, her look screamed, "Where have you been?"

I pointed at the sweat pouring down my face.

She shook her head and looked at the notepad on the table. I glanced at it. Names and numbers lined the page. She cupped her head in her hand.

"I know, it seems sudden," she said, like she had to justify Dad's audacity to die. "But he's been fighting this for close to five years."

It would take her hours to get all those phone calls made. I sat down at the table and waited for her to finish the call. She let out a long sigh as she hung up the phone.

"Do you want some help?" I asked. "I can make calls, too."

She looked over the list, weary and tired. "Actually, yes. Here, call these people. They won't be offended that I didn't tell them personally."

For the next two hours, Mom and I called all the various relatives in Illinois. I hadn't seen most of them since I was twelve. Awkward. I dreaded the next few days. Random hugs, random faces. I just had to get through it.

One was a painfully long conversation with Dad's Aunt

Sue, who wouldn't be able to make it, yet felt the need to tell me all about her china collection (which belonged to Dad's first cousin). I managed to cut her off before a story about the crystal goblets. I made a beeline to the shower.

Meanwhile, Ruby and Woodrow showed up with a casserole and hot biscuits. When I'd finished getting ready, she smothered me in hugs and kisses.

"Such a good man," she repeated over and over.

Woodrow sat at the table with a glass of tea. Forehead scrunched, he stared at the glass without a word to say. For such an old man, he reminded me of a brokenhearted, little boy.

Ruby insisted I eat. I tried. Her casserole tasted good, but I didn't have any appetite.

Around two, Mark still hadn't come out of his room. Mom left with Ruby and Woodrow to go make the funeral arrangements. She told me I was better off staying home.

Grateful, I grabbed Tyler's journal, crawled under the covers, and pulled out the piece of stationery. At least I could read his words. Within minutes, my eyes grew heavy and I dozed off.

I woke to the bed sinking under someone's weight. Mom.

I sat up and rubbed my face.

"How are you doing?" she asked.

"I'm so tired."

"It was a long night... All the arrangements are done. Ruby and Woodrow have gone home. Have you talked to Tyler, yet?"

"No."

"He'd want to know."

"He's in Florida at an NCAA meet." I stared down at my blanket, tears started pouring down my face. "Mom, I don't know how you'll get through this... it hurts so much."

"Oh, sweetie." She wrapped her arms around me. "We'll be okay." Voice cracking, she let go of her resolve and cried with me.

Moments later, she let me go, and we grinned as we wiped our tear-soaked cheeks. The little bit of laughter briefly scared the pain away.

She took a deep breath, returning to Mom mode.

"Elsie. You need to tell Tyler." She gave me a long, hard stare. "He cares about you."

"I hope so. I've never felt like this about anyone." I took a sharp breath. "I can't even believe he wants to be with me."

She winced. "Why?"

"I'm not." I shrugged. "Well, I'm just... me. Nothing special."

"And why is he so special?" She smirked. "Because of his money?"

"Because he's freaking gorgeous," I blurted.

"Okay. I'll give you that. He's very handsome."

"Handsome?" I repeated. "He's painful to look at. Seriously, he's God's masterpiece."

She shook her head. "Come on, now. That's a bit far."

"It's not only that," I said. "He's a total gentleman. Hands down the smartest person I've ever met. He's strong, and he's shown me a whole different world. Plus, he's undeniably old school. And believe me, he sticks to it."

She blushed. "Elsie... "

"What?" I giggled. "You should be happy I told you that."

"I suppose." She narrowed her blue eyes. "You aren't exactly easy to look at either, to quote you. Maybe I haven't told you enough, but you are so beautiful. You have no idea how you affect people when you walk in a room. And when you're willing to let them see it, you have a light that shines brighter than any I've ever seen. You have so much to offer him. You've been given great talents. Don't waste them by thinking you're not good enough." She patted my leg. Her words were like manna. She shook her head and continued, "I've never seen Tyler as happy as he was this summer. He had this energy about him. There was just something different about the guy. Come to find out, it was you."

Maybe Tyler's confidence had flourished after he met me. I thought of his journal. Maybe I *had* helped him be the guy he wanted to be.

"Mom. You don't know how much that means to me." I leaned forward and hugged her. "Thank you for understanding."

"Okay, now." She readjusted herself on the bed. "You need to know the arrangements we've made. We won't be having a visitation, just the funeral. Monday at four. Then, he'll be buried in Morris Chapel afterward."

"Who's coming?"

"Well, Mom and Dad are already on their way. Your Uncle Travis, and of course, Aunt Gail. That's about it, besides the locals."

"Is your brother coming?"

"No. They're still harvesting." She furrowed her forehead. "Please be prepared. Mom and Dad are going to be all over us about moving, especially your grandmother."

"Is that what you want?"

"Um, well... I don't know how to answer that right now." She stood up. "Let's get through the next few days, okay?"

She walked out. Moving to Illinois would only add salt to

my wounds. I didn't want to leave Tennessee, and she knew it. That's why she skated out as soon as I asked. My mind bounced between her comment, and when to call Tyler... until I fell back asleep.

The next morning, I woke to my phone buzzing.

"Hello," I mumbled.

"Hey," Tyler said, bright and cheerful. "You won't believe it. I finished first for individual time. Isn't that crazy? I'm going to Nationals."

It took me a second to register his comment. "Wow, that's great. I'm so proud of you. Will it change how long you're in Florida?"

"No. I'll fly back to Nashville tomorrow morning. I have a test at three. I don't mean to cut this short, but I have to go. I just couldn't wait to tell you. I'll call soon, okay?"

"Yep."

"I thought about you the whole race. I love you. I wish you could've been here."

"Me, too." I took a quivering breath. "I'm really happy for you. I love you, too."

"Are you okay?"

"Yeah, of course." I resisted the urge to squash his joy. "Just woke up, that's all."

"Okay. I'll talk to you later."

"Okay, bye."

I pressed END. The guy was phenomenal. Everything he touched turned to gold.

No way I could crush news like that. High on victory, his spirit soaring. Talk about a joy killer. I'd tell him about Dad when he called back. That wasn't the right time.

Chapter

32

I went to the living room around noon. My Bears vs. Mark's Packers. Mark sat in the recliner, eating a sandwich. Pre-game commentators babbled on the TV.

I sat down on the couch. "Tell me Rogers fell and broke his arm," I said, referring to the Packer's star quarterback.

"You wish." He took a bite of his enormous sandwich. "You're... " he said with a mouthful, bouncing his hoagie in the air, "getting your ass kicked today." A chunk of lettuce flopped on his lap. He picked it up and ate it.

"We'll see, big brother." I hurried to the kitchen to get a soda.

Walking back toward the living room, I glanced down the hall. Mom was rearranging the bed, moving out all of the hospital stuff in her room. I changed routes and headed to see if she needed help. A sniffle. A loud, wet sniffle. She needed space. *Don't hover.* I pivoted and went back to the couch.

Mark and I watched the game with a little less enthusiasm. He never said anything about Dad, and he avoided looking at Mom when she'd walk by. He seemed content with me, so I just let him be himself. Two and a half hours later, Green Bay scored the winning touchdown. Mark shot out of the chair, whooping and hollering at the TV.

I sat on the couch with my arms crossed. "Whatever."

I honestly didn't care. Mark needed the win more than me. They cut to Green Bay's quarterback. I'd had enough football for the week, so I went to Mom's room.

I pushed her door open. "You all right?"

"Yeah. Getting everything rearranged. It's filthy in here."

She sat on the floor sorting papers. Cleaning therapy. She always cleaned when stressed. She'd made a pile of items to return to Home Care, disassembled the hospital bed, and stacked the linens. The room smelled of pine, instead of medicine.

I leaned against the wall. "I bet you'd like to sleep in your own bed."

"Yes. Will you and Mark help me get it swapped out? The mattress is in the carport."

"Sure."

I felt numb and tingly, like my skin was literally absorbing reality. Emptiness filled my chest. A void. I couldn't describe it. Relief? What a horrible thought. Terrible. Why had the word "relief" popped in my mind? That wasn't what I felt. Sorrow. Anger. Not relief.

"Is Mark okay?" Mom asked.

I snapped out of my internal tirade. "Seems fine. But he is

M-A-L-E."

"I guess. It worries me when he shuts down. You're both so... guarded."

Glancing away, I mumbled, "I've heard that before."

She stopped sorting. "Have you talked to Tyler?"

Tyler. Like she knew he'd called me out once for being guarded.

"This morning." I took a deep breath and attempted to sound cheerful. "He won yesterday in individual time. Isn't that great? He'll go on to the NCAA Nationals." I looked up at the ceiling, swallowing hard. "I couldn't tell him, not today. It's like his greatest day ever. I didn't want to tell him about my worst."

We made eye contact. Her expression softened.

"You have a kind heart. But I hope it doesn't backfire on you. This isn't something you keep from someone."

"I'll tell him when he calls back." A pain pierced my stomach. "I'm gonna have to get through it without him."

"Is that what you want?"

"No. I just... I'm not going to do that to him." I started toward the door. "I'll get Mark. We'll get your room set up before everyone gets here."

"You know," she said. "Life doesn't always work that way."

I turned around. What did she want from me? I thought I'd used wisdom for once.

"We can't always protect the ones we love. Believe me, I try every day." Her tone was poignant. "Sometimes, disappointment comes in the midst of victory. Your father's death isn't going to ruin the fact that Tyler won. But being gracious can cross into selfishness if you wait too long." She shrugged. "Just sayin'."

I held back a smile. She never borrowed teenage phrases. "He's busy."

"I get that, but don't wait until after the funeral. That's not fair to him."

She was right, but I didn't have a choice. I had to wait until he called. Resigned to the facts, I headed down the hall and asked Mark to help me in the carport.

Around five p.m., my grandparents arrived. Grandpa came inside and gave me a hug. He smelled of pipe tobacco and Stetson. Mom had inherited his soft blue eyes, but his weathered skin had lines like the rows of crops he'd nurtured for years. He let me go without a word. Rarely did he take an interest in me. Mark was the chosen one.

Grandma stepped inside with pursed lips, casing the house with skeptical glances. She made little "humph" noises as she moved my way. A football helmet of light brown hair was set around her face. Soft wrinkles layered in milky white skin that hadn't been in the sun for years.

Something about her. She scanned me from my feet all the way to my eyes.

"Hello, Elizabeth." She pushed out red, pouty lips. "How are yoouu?"

I winced. So fake. "Okay."

She put her arm around me, squeezing me close. She smelled like Chanel No. 5. The same perfume Mrs. Vaughn wore. I pulled away.

"You'll be all right," she sounded like she was poohpoohing me. "Give it time."

I held my tongue and walked with her to the kitchen.

Mom turned around from the stove and forced a smile. "Hello, Mother."

Grandma waited for Mom to approach, held out her arms, and gave Mom a quick, cold hug. No tears. No "I'm sorry." Not an ounce of love in her embrace. Just a frigid air of "Let's get this the hell over with."

Mrs. Vaughn. Goosebumps rose on my arms.

She and Grandma were carbon copies of each other. Long and slender, dressed in brand name clothing, not a light brown hair out of place even after travelling for seven hours. Plus, she'd insisted on calling me "Elizabeth" my entire life.

No wonder Mom knew how to ignore the old southern woman.

Mom gave Grandpa a hug, then all of us sat down at the table. Grandma chatted about the drive and the weather. I chewed on my lip and fiddled with my fingers. She didn't ask about the services. I suppose she already knew the details. She didn't ask what happened the night he died. I had to assume she'd been filled in there, too. To her, it seemed like nothing important had happened, with the exception of her generosity for sitting in the car for seven hours. Tiring as that was, she made a request to keep the evening moving and go to Savannah for dinner.

Grateful for an excuse to cruise, I excused myself to take a shower.

Twenty minutes later, I passed through the dining room wrapped in my robe, feeling completely exposed.

"How can you stand having one bathroom?" Grandma glanced my way.

LIFE HAPPENS ON THE STAIRS

"We just remodeled the master bath," Grandpa said. "You'd love it, Claire."

I hot-stepped it to my room and locked the door. Bathrooms? I pulled on a pair of jeans and grabbed my T-shirt. That's what they wanted to talk about? Their daughter just lost her husband, and Grandpa wanted to share the joy of a remodeled bathroom. *Jeez.* Two whole days with those people. Could it get any worse? At least Uncle Travis and Aunt Gail were coming. They always helped balance the Germans.

I sat down on the bed and stared at the phone. I couldn't wait another second. I had to talk to him. Snatching it up, I pressed "Tyler" in neon green. His voicemail answered after the fourth ring. The sound of his voice ripped another hole inside of me. I pressed END, tossed it down, and returned to the dining room.

Ten minutes later, we piled into two cars and headed to Savannah. We waited for them to check in to the hotel, and then they followed us to a Buck's restaurant.

Everyone settled in at a long table in the center of room. Taxidermy all over the walls. Moose, deer, and elk, rabbits and fish – all looking down with glossy, angry eyes. Oak wainscoting covered the lower half – white wallpaper with pink and blue flowers – too soft and feminine to be the background for the kill zone of trophies.

I focused on the menu and tried to forget the animals' resentful glances. Grandpa waved his hand in the air to get the waitress's attention. He was thirsty. She took all our drink orders, but he asked her to get his pronto. Within a minute, she had brought him a sweaty Coors Light in a can.

"So, Mark, how's it going?" he barked across the table,

then took a long drink.

"Pretty good. Well, until yesterday."

Grandma wiped the table with her napkin. "Have you found work, dear?"

"I've been helping this guy at his shop." He cleared his throat. "I don't want to get locked in to anything, though."

"Good," Grandma said.

I gaped at her. *Whatever.* Sure, Mark shouldn't work.

"There's so much more out there than this." She glanced around the room. "You'll love it when you come home. There are plenty of jobs in Illinois."

No, there weren't. I'd just read in history class that people were fleeing Illinois at unprecedented rates, heading for Florida and Texas, even Indiana.

Mom excused herself from the table. Where was she going? She couldn't leave me alone. She was my buffer around these people. Fawning all over Mark kept them occupied, but I needed Mom to cope. After several minutes, I excused myself, avoiding eye contact with my grandparents, and casually walked across the restaurant. Quickening my step, I hurried around the corner to the bathroom.

When I walked in, Mom's voice echoed off the walls. She stood in front of the sink, talking on the phone. "Yes, that would be fantastic." She made eye contact through the mirror. "Okay, I have to go now. Elsie's here. Thank you so much. Have a good fli—night."

She put her phone in her pocket and started washing her hands.

"Who was—"

"So, what do you think of your grandmother?" she interrupted.

"That's why I came in here," I said. "She's Mrs. Vaughn,

all day long."

Mom gave me an amused smile. "Yeah. I can see that." She chuckled and turned on the hand dryer. "It's only for a few days, right?"

"Right."

I felt terrible for her. I could dodge them. She had to accept they were her parents.

After we returned to the table, everyone ordered as Grandpa finish his third beer. Tired and starving, I regretted leaving my phone at home. How could I have forgotten it? I wanted to asked Mom for hers, but I still hadn't memorized his number. Stupid phone. It made me lazy.

Grandpa took another long swig of beer.

"George, take it easy," Grandma snapped, then she turned to Mom. "So, the Donnelly house is up for rent. You know, the one two miles south of us on 400 North? You'd be close. And since Elsie will graduate early, it won't matter what district you settle in." She looked at Mark, then me. "Your babies are all grown up now."

"Yes, they are." Mom pressed her lips in a tense smile.

Mark elbowed me. I elbowed back.

Grandma frowned. "Well, I can look into it when I get back," she said.

"We'll see." Mom took a sip of water. "This isn't the time to talk about moving."

Our server arrived with our dinners, interrupting the purposed topic.

Thank God. It would've been a shame to ruin dinner by screaming, "I don't want to go to Illinois!"

"The university is hiring," Grandma said.

"Olivia," Grandpa snapped. "Cut it out. We're trying to eat here."

He went back to salting his vegetables, and then he shoved a big forkful in his mouth. Mark and I snickered. Grandma huffed and tossed her napkin on the table. Mom's foot cracked my shin. I winced, and sat up straighter.

After we finished eating, Grandpa's fourth beer had pushed him down memory lane. He babbled on for the next two hours. Story after story about relatives and Mom as a young girl. The more he talked, the more I could feel Mom's tension. She was going to blow.

I'd been up since four in the morning and could hardly keep my eyes open. Then Grandpa started in about a guy named Bob.

Bam! Mom smacked the table with her palm. Everyone flinched.

"It's late, Daddy," she stated. "Tomorrow's going to be a long day."

By eleven-thirty, we finally walked into our quiet house.

I went straight to my room and collapsed on top of the covers.

What felt like minutes later, I woke up and shot out of bed. Daylight filled the window, offering a gray clouded sky. I grabbed my phone. Five missed calls, and one text at 10:17 p.m.

My heart sank. I'd totally crashed out. Why hadn't I looked at my phone?

I opened the text message.

Tyler: I really wish I could talk to you.

I pressed his name. Voicemail.

"I'm sorry I missed your call." I said to the recording. "I really need to talk to you, too."

END.

I slumped on the bed. My face felt tight and swollen from the constant tears. I'd screwed up. There was no way he could get here by four. I dreaded going to the church to look at Dad inside a coffin, then lowering him in the ground without Tyler next to me.

I heard a knock on the door. Mom stepped inside and sat beside me on the bed. She didn't say a word, like a radar had alerted that her kid was in need, she arrived just so I could cry on her shoulder. After a few minutes, she spotted my sketchpad lying on the floor. Dad's eighteen-year-old face stared up at us.

"That's the picture of your dad right after we met. May I look?"

"Sure. I've been drawing his portrait from different ages."

She sat down on the floor and started turning the pages. Each picture showed Dad progressively growing older. I sat next to her.

"I hope it's okay that I borrowed all the photos," I said.

"Of course." She looked at me with tears in her eyes. "Elsie, these are amazing. Is there any way you can bring them to the church?"

"Sure. I have some matte board I can attach them to."

"Please. I want everyone to see him through your eyes. You've captured him in a way that's almost painful. Did you ever send your application for school?"

"I applied to the Memphis College of Art before Tyler left. He helped me do it online."

"He really is a good kid. Is that the only place?"

"We looked at some other schools – a couple in Chicago. I don't know... I've been waiting to see what happened with Dad."

She looked at the next drawing with a pained expression. "I'm sorry I haven't helped you look for schools." She broke down and cried. "I've been so oblivious."

"Mom, it's okay. You've been great. You're the strongest person I know."

"I don't feel very strong." She sniffled and wiped her cheeks. "Travis and Gail will be here soon."

She stood up and walked out. I didn't know how to help her. Guilt assaulted her everywhere she turned, and she blamed herself for everything. Without Dad, she wasn't the same.

I pulled the pages out of the binding and started attaching them to matte boards. The task helped distract my thoughts from Tyler. I worked for a few hours, putting everything together, and then I heard voices outside my room. I set the pictures aside and changed out of my sweats, feeling indifferent to the rest of the day. I just wanted it to be over. All romantic notions of death had been wiped from my mind. My one comfort was that Dad wasn't suffering anymore.

When I walked into the kitchen, Uncle Travis met me with a big hug, lifting me off the floor. I hadn't seen him in two years, but he still smelled like his black leather jacket and Marlboros. His chin was covered in a salt-and-pepper goatee, and leathered skin accompanied his rough, cigarette-scarred voice. Every other word out of his mouth was a cuss word, but he had a genuine heart, something a person could see only if they were willing to look past his rough exterior. He reminded me of Dad when I met his gaze. They had the same blue eyes, but Travis had long hair pulled into a low ponytail. And if I knew my uncle, he had a flask in his back pocket. What I loved most was how easy it was to be around him. Nothing about Uncle Travis was fake.

LIFE HAPPENS ON THE STAIRS

His girlfriend, Jenny, stood in the background, looking annoyed, her head cocked to the side, pushing all her weight on one leg.

Maybe it wasn't Jenny.

She looked a lot like the girl I'd met a few years ago, but she hadn't aged a day if so. She chomped on her gum and rolled her eyes when he set me down.

"Girl, look at you. You're all grown up. Damn, I'm getting old." He laughed, and then he reached out and pulled the blonde girl close to him. "This is Krissie." He laid a kiss on her cheek. She jerked away.

Pure white trash, wearing skintight jeans and a low-cut Harley Davidson T-shirt with a faded blob of an unidentifiable tattoo on her breast. Anorexic, sunken cheeks with stringy, bleached-blonde hair that needed a haircut. She was way too young for my uncle. *Gross.*

Aunt Gail stepped around her brother. Quiet as a mouse, she reached out to give me a gentle hug. I hadn't even noticed her.

She stroked my hair. "Elsie, you're so beautiful."

Gail suffered from old hippie syndrome. Too young to be a true "Summer of Love" child, however, her bohemian style and love for Jerry Garcia reinforced the fact that she should've been born a generation earlier. She always looked tired, lean and slender, toned like she did yoga every day. Certainly, she didn't look like she was nearing fifty. Not with her sandy blonde hair and big, blue eyes. She and Travis sounded like Dad when they spoke, but Gail was soft and gentle, compared to the manly brothers whom she helped raise.

The worst part was, I'd never been around them without Dad. I resisted the urge to look for him. He should've been standing there with us.

When Mark joined us, the volume in the room cranked another octave. I slipped into the background. Travis joked about his midlife crisis. I couldn't help but chuckle at them. I was different than Dad's family. I couldn't jump in and demand to be heard. Mom and I were more alike, but after twenty years, she'd conditioned herself to know her people. Uncle Travis shifted into a high tale about meeting Krissie. The girl ignored him, chomping her gum like a horse.

Uncle Travis started the next story with, "Remember when... "

That was my cue. Time to get out of storyland. I headed to my room to change clothes.

I grabbed my phone off the nightstand. No calls. I set it down and went to my closet to grab my black sweater dress. Picking up my red-bottomed heels, I considered wearing them for a second. I put them back. Don't taint them. I'd never wear the sweater dress again. Don't ruin the shoes, too.

Brushing my hair, I gazed out the window at the looming, hazy gray clouds. Cold and wet, the air would reek of sulfur and burnt broccoli when we went to the cemetery. *Damn paper mill. Damn autumn.* The shifting colors of fall would forever remind me of death from now on. Dead trees, dead flowers, dead fathers.

At two-thirty, I rejoined the crowd. Grandma and Grandpa had returned. They hated Travis and Gail. Judgmental of anything that came from Dad's gene pool, Mark was the one exception. He and Grandpa sat on the couch, looking at a sports magazine together. Grandma waited in the recliner, staring out the window. Travis and Gail were at the kitchen table, drinking coffee, ignoring my arrogant grandparents. The only one I couldn't find was Mom.

I headed down the hallway and knocked on her door. Pushing it open before she could answer, I found her sitting on the edge of her bed.

"Hey," I said.

She looked at me with red, swollen eyes. "Hi."

"Are you okay?"

"Sure." She shrugged. "No. I don't want to go back out there. I don't want to say goodbye to your dad. Most of all, after today, my husband's not only dead, he's buried."

Tears fell down her face. Lost for words, I sat beside her and gave her a hug.

She only held on for a second, unable to accept the affection for too long. Taking a deep breath, she composed herself and wiped her face.

"We have to be at the church in twenty minutes." She smacked her legs with both hands. "Let's get going."

Chapter

33

Twenty minutes later, Mark drove Mom and me through Savannah while the rest of the family followed in separate cars. The closer we came to the white church with its tall, pointy steeple, tucked in the woodland near the river, the tighter my throat closed. I took a deep breath. My stomach flipped.

Mom pointed at the front door and quietly said, "Drop us off, please."

Pastor Larry waited at the top of the steps. I watched Mom move up the first two before I opened the car door. Mark huffed like, *Get the hell out already*. I grabbed the drawings and started up the stairs leading to my dead Dad. Walking slowly, I climbed the steps covered in worn Astroturf, wet and mossy-looking. Juniper pine added just enough cat-piss sting in the air to burn at my nose, competing against the stinky smell of the paper mill. My heel scraped the spongy carpet. One more step closer.

"It's like we're on a staircase... " I remembered Tyler's words from the first day at Shiloh. *"... we have to accept what we've been given and embrace our circumstances, even if we don't like them. You know? Reinvent."*

Reinvent. Another moist step under my foot. Life happens on the stairs. I had to consent to my circumstances and keep climbing. I thought of my response that day, *"My staircase has wood rot."* I imagined my foot breaking through the wood, twisting my ankle, wrenching my knee, splinters gouging my skin. The tread had given way, but no matter the wounds, I couldn't let myself get stuck.

Last step. I stood shoulder to shoulder with Mom. She gave the pastor a weary smile as he took her hand. The pastor was a tall man with jet-black hair speckled in gray. Dad always said he was the godliest man he'd ever met. Looking into his tear-filled eyes, I felt like Dad was standing beside him, for some reason. They had been good friends outside of church, and just like Uncle Travis, if I was around either of them, Dad had always been there, too.

"How you holding up?" he asked Mom in his soothing Southern drawl.

"I'm okay."

"I'll help best I can." Mom accepted his offer with a nod, then turned and walked inside. As I moved past him, he set his warm palm on my shoulder. "I've been praying for y'all. Your momma told me you have some beautiful portraits of your daddy. Can't wait to see them."

"Thanks, Pastor."

As I stepped into the elongated foyer, cold air blasted my skin. Red carpet, dark paneled walls, the church felt foreign on a Monday afternoon in late October. I wanted to feel warm and comforted, like I did at candlelight service on Christmas Eve. I shivered. Not warm. I glanced through the sanctuary doors. Silver casket, lid open. Not comforted.

Pastor Larry gestured to the right side of the room where he'd set up five easels for my drawings, before he turned to Mom. I scanned the silver box again. Look forward. Don't think about it. Five long strides and I was standing in front of an empty metal easel, just as Grandpa, Mark, and Grandma funneled through the front door. I placed the first board on its temporary home and looked into my father's eyes. Twenty-five, young and strong. He reminded me of that actor, the one on the salad dressing jars. What was his name? I bobbed my head like someone stood next to me listening to me banter aloud, until I remembered. Paul Newman—yes. I laughed a bit too loud. A quick glance over my shoulder. No one noticed. I looked back at the drawing and smiled. This was the man I wanted to remember.

When I finished setting out the other four drawings, all of the family had filled the lobby. Woodrow stepped through the doorway, rocking side to side, bum leg curving out like an archer pulling a bow. He wore a gray suit that I figured got resurrected only for such occasions. Ruby followed in a black cotton dress with a thin, red belt around the waist. *Thank God.* Someone who had hugs to give. I moved straight to her and wrapped my arms around her. She clutched my shoulder and kissed the top of my head. I spotted Grandma. Her forehead furrowed as she sized Ruby up. That's right, Grandma... Ruby loves me, for me.

Pastor Larry signaled for our attention and instructed us

to go ahead and have a private viewing. Mom wanted a closed casket during the service, but we were getting the pleasure of viewing the silver box half open. I glanced at his portraits. That was Dad. Not the box.

A few moments later, we were walking single file down the center aisle. I barely wanted to breathe for fear of looking too alive. Fall colors: deep orange, shades of yellow, and burnt red flowers eased the jarring finality of the silver box. Rows of mahogany pews sat empty on either side, tall wood-plank ceilings met at a sharp peak, blood-red plush carpeting under our feet. We stepped slow like we used to in the Catholic church, palms out, begging for the priest to give communion. Dad wouldn't have liked it. I could hear him grumbling, *Skip the rituals, just prop me by the juke box. Celebrate like the Irish do. I'm part Irish. Good enough.*

Mark stopped. I slammed into his back, pushing him forward, chin cracking his spine. I imagined all of us going down like dominoes. He slapped the back of his head. I caught my balance and rubbed my burning jaw.

"Chill," he whispered over his shoulder.

I stepped back and readjusted. Can't even walk without slamming something.

Mom stepped to the casket and started to cry. Tears filled my eyes. The circuit that connected us wasn't shrouded in lies anymore. Her shoulders sagged forward and she clutched her face with her right hand. I blubbered. Audible and squeaky. Snot clogging my nose. A loud sniffle. Mom's bouncing shoulders. I sucked in another breath. She reached out and touched him one last time, then walked away... crying into her tissue.

Mark moved forward. Standing there for less than a minute, his shoulders sagging in the same manner as Mom, my insides twisted as my big brother wiped his eyes, and moved on.

My turn. Holding my breath, I took three steps and looked at my father for the last time.

I winced. *What the hell?*

His skin reminded me of plastic, caked with foundation makeup, sunken cheeks powdered with too much blush. They'd attempted to cover the scar on his head with fake hair, but it was two shades too dark. Violet lips, lifeless, bloodless, a stitch peeking out in the center. *Who in the hell did this?* I'd kick the mortician's ass if I was Mom. The whole scene pissed me off. Pointless. He didn't look like himself at all. Maybe he was an impostor or a mannequin they'd dug out of their creepy mortuary. That wasn't my dad. I made a "humph" sound and walked away. That sucked. The last time I'd ever see him – all plastic and rubbery. *Fuck.*

Stepping in the lobby, I made my way toward Mom and Mark.

"Are you okay?" Mom asked.

All I could do was glance at her. No words. If I had said what was running through my mind, she would've slapped me.

The front doors opened. We turned to see who would come so early.

Megan stepped inside, wearing a black dress with tiny white flowers. Cheeks flushed, she glided toward us quiet as a cat, her soft green eyes downcast.

"Hi, y'all," she whispered.

She reached out and gave Mom a hug. A quick hug for me, then she stepped to Mark and wrapped her arms around his neck. Mark held her tight, burying his face in her hair, practically lifting her off her feet.

Mom looked at me and smiled. I grinned back. Mark exhibiting blatant affection was completely alien to us. As he released Megan, they stared into each other's eyes for a moment, and then she turned to Mom.

"I'm so sorry, Claire. I wish I could have been there to help y'all."

Mom reached out and took her hand. "You've done so much already. If you want to see him, please feel free to go on inside."

Mark took her hand. "I'll go with you." Together, they walked back down the long aisle.

At the same time, the rest of the family started filling the lobby. Uncle Travis came out sniffling. It had finally hit him that his brother was gone. He grasped Mom, arms visibly vibrating around her. Gail stepped in, staring into space like she saw something profound that the rest of us couldn't see. No tears. Just shock.

Grandpa walked in next. Mom was letting Travis go when Grandpa cut in and wrapped his arms around her. She started crying on her dad's sleeve. Finally, someone in her family bothered to show her love. He cried with her, almost as if he regretted being such a jerk over the years. Grandma ignored them with the usual snide tilt to her head as if she'd been inconvenienced. Glancing around the room, she moved toward my drawings. I turned away. I didn't want to watch her scoff at them.

Then there was Krissie. I couldn't understand why she'd even tagged along. She wore a low-cut, too-short-for-church dress, avoiding eye contact with everyone. No one paid any attention to her, including Travis. I stood back, feeling lost and alone.

Mom chatted with everyone, gracious and kind. After fifteen minutes, people started to arrive, so she asked everyone to go into the sanctuary. We lined up in the front pew, sitting like little soldiers, staring forward as people began to fill the room.

Don't look back, only forward. No looking back.

At four o'clock, Pastor Larry stepped behind the pulpit. He cleared his throat and looked over the rows full of people. I peeked to my left. The pews were full.

"Several years ago, Brandon and I were at lunch one afternoon," Pastor started, jolting me to listen, "and I asked him when he'd met Claire. He chuckled as he took a bite of mashed potatoes." Pastor smiled, remembering the moment. "Brandon went on to tell me they'd been at a wedding of mutual friends when his buddy introduced them. Brandon, a self-proclaimed adrenaline junkie, had no use for settling down with anyone. But then he met Claire. He said, *'Her hair looked like gold and her eyes were sapphires.'* He told me that when she talked, he felt like heaven had opened in the sky, and he heard angels singing." Pastor held up his right palm with an amused smile. "I'm serious. This is what a forty-year-old man said about his wife of almost twenty years. I'd never heard such a good ol' boy, Yankee or not, talk that way. I laughed at him. I said, 'Brandon... I love my wife, but hold your horses.' He just smiled and took a sip of coffee. *'She saved my life, Larry,'* is what he told me. *'I was a ruined man with a death wish. But then, I met Claire.'*

Mom's cheeks were flushed, face turned down with a shy smile.

"Those were his words." Pastor Larry raised his eyebrow like he had to convince us. "Then, he told me how she'd snuck out to see him. And how they'd spent hours just talking. His love for Claire was only second to one other, and Claire had told me how she had shared the honor with joy.

"*You will seek Me and find Me, when you seek Me with all your heart.* Jeremiah 29:13," the pastor's voice echoed off the rafters. "Brandon asked me to read this scripture in this event. His love for God presided above all else in his life. Brandon sought the Lord with all his heart, and I'm confident that he will be received with open arms." His eyes swept the congregation, where only soft sniffles could be heard. "I'm going to step aside now. There's someone here who would like to say a few words."

I hid behind my hair, wiping tears falling faster than rain. Mom offered a white tissue. I snatched it up with a grateful nod and wiped my slick nose. Pastor Larry's eloquence was impossible to follow. Who would even try? Footsteps. I closed my eyes, warming my cold nose with the soft cotton cloth.

"Who's that?" Grandma whispered.

"I don't know," Grandpa mumbled. "Probably someone from town."

I let out a sigh, chest wrenched, tense, constricting. I envisioned running toward the side aisle and sprinting out the front doors. Bursting into the air, tainted with rotten sulfur and cat-piss shrubs, I'd fill my lungs and run all the way to Shiloh. I could hide in the park forever. Live off the berries. Sleep in one of the old cabins. There had to be a way to get in. They'd never know I was there.

"Hello, I'm Tyler Vaughn." His low drawl filled the sanctuary.

I gasped and looked up. Standing behind the pulpit in a tailored black suit, his dark eyes met mine. *Oh. My. Gosh.*

Heart racing, I wanted to jump up out of the pew. Tyler tipped his head with the tender look he reserved just for me, and then he turned to the congregation.

Mom. I made eye contact with her. "Thank you," I mouthed.

She patted my leg and pretended to be attentive, even though she looked thoroughly proud of herself. The tightness in my chest faded, as I relaxed against the hard-back pew. *What was he going to say about Dad?* Squirming on my tailbone, it took everything in me not to run up there and make an ass of myself.

"Several months ago, I had the pleasure of meeting Brandon." Tyler's mellifluous tone was relaxed and gracious, as if he were talking to a room full of old friends. "The introduction was brief. Within seconds, we were calling an ambulance. An unfortunate meeting. I'll never forget the fear in Elsie's eyes as Brandon collapsed with a seizure.

"After Elsie and I became friends, she took me to the hospital to see him at my request. We were under the impression he was in an induced coma. Despite his condition, I needed to reintroduce myself to the father of the girl I was falling in love with." He smiled and shook his head. "I honestly didn't think he'd hear a word I said. Then out of nowhere, he said, '*Elizabeth, does your Mother know about this?*'" Tyler laughed. "He scared us half to death."

The congregation laughed along. If they knew Dad, then they knew he loved to give Mark and me a good scare every so often.

"We were able to talk for a while until he needed to rest. Yet another unforgettable moment with Brandon. I wouldn't trade it for anything in the world. Well, except Elsie." Tyler shrugged. "But to know he gave me his approval to be with her was priceless.

"We have a way of putting a price on everything, like if we lose a job, or can't make the mortgage. If only we could hit the lottery, then we'd never have to worry about money again. When I met Elsie, she and Claire were working like crazy to keep their lives on track. I watched them loyally perform their jobs, work hard in the field, and take care of Brandon all at the same time. I admire these two women over anyone I've ever met. And so did Brandon.

"This is a little embarrassing to admit, but considering the circumstances," he gave me a quick glance, "I think it's appropriate. I went back to the hospital the next day and sat with Brandon, while Elsie was at work. He was having a good day, and we were able to chat for well over an hour about his beautiful family." He looked across the pew. "He loved y'all so much. His biggest fear was leaving, and he didn't hesitate to tell me." He returned to addressing the congregation. "I never told Elsie that I had gone back to see him. I don't know why. She certainly knows now. But for whatever reason, I had to ask him something because I wasn't sure if I'd ever get another chance. And I wouldn't, so I'm even more grateful for his answer. Even if it took years, at least I know how he'd felt about it." He took a deep breath, exhaling slowly as if he needed to gain his nerves. "I asked him if I could have his permission to marry his daughter someday."

My heart skipped. Permission? Marry his daughter?

"I have to say, he didn't respond right away. He made me sweat it out for minutes as he stared me down. But I'll always remember his answer. He said, '*Tyler, if Elsie loves you and you love her, that's all that ever matters in this life. Not your money, not your job, but the love you two share.*'" Tyler's eyes softened as he looked at Mom. "He told me that you, Claire, are the reason he got up every morning. Your love made him fight. Because of you, he became the man he had always wanted to be." She smiled, tears rolling down her cheeks. Tyler returned a sincere regard, and then he spoke to everyone. "He also said if that's how I felt when I woke up every day, and if that was what Elsie wanted, then yes, he would be proud that we marry. My point is how priceless love is. We can't waste a second. We have limited time to be with the ones we love, and when they're gone, even when it's temporary, it can be some of the worst pain ever felt." He took a deep breath and looked over our pew, making eye contact with each of us. "Brandon will be deeply missed. I'm thankful I had the honor to meet him."

He paused for a few seconds, then stepped away from the pulpit.

I stood up and headed toward the side aisle, pushing past legs and knees. He walked down the steps of the altar in the same direction and met me with open arms.

I fell into his embrace. "I can't believe you're here."

He held me tight, burying his face in my hair. I felt him breathe me in, and then he slowly pulled away. Gazing in my eyes, he brushed my cheek with the back of his fingers.

"We have a lot to talk about."

"I know," I said, torn with regret that I didn't tell him myself.

As always, he kept his cool in front of the crowd, took my hand, and led me to a pew. I snuggled next to him, inhaling his cedar-laced scent. He wrapped his arm around me, holding me close. So tender. So loving. He needed to be here for me, as much as I needed him.

The piano lady played *Amazing Grace* as six men stepped forward to carry the casket outside. Woodrow took the lead, red eyes, swollen face. Wally on the other side, along with Uncle Travis, Mark, Mr. McAllister, and Steve, the man who helped at harvest.

LIFE HAPPENS ON THE STAIRS

The certainty that Dad would never come home engulfed me like an ocean wave. Grown men unable to arrest their tears, standing tall with their heads high. I couldn't take it.

I bent forward, buried my face in my hands, and bawled.

Tyler's warm touch rubbed over my back. His arrival had torn down my fortification. All the guilt for not telling him was like static, black and white fuzz, clouding my true grief.

These tears were exclusive. The big ones that soak your shirt and show all your ugly, kind of tears. They were for Dad. And Dad alone. For months, my emotions had been all jumbled up. I never knew who or what I was crying for. This time, I knew exactly what they meant.

I let all the pain flow, releasing my flood right in front of the man I loved.

After the music stopped, I took a deep breath and glanced up. A brilliant white handkerchief floated in front of my face. I smiled and accepted the soft linen.

Looking over my shoulder, I chuckled. "Who carries a handkerchief?"

He flashed a cocky grin. "It goes with the suit."

"Only you, Mr. Vaughn. You look like a million bucks."

"Come on, now. Stop that. You need to be with your family."

People were filing down the center aisle toward Mom and Mark. Mom's graciousness floored me. No more uptight, stressed out, what's everyone going to think woman. She didn't interfere with Tyler and me, nor did I get a nasty look when we walked in the foyer. Mrs. McAllister held her in a tight embrace. They let each other go, and then the next person in line stepped forward and shook Mom's hand. We settled in next to Mark at the end of the line. Tyler stood close behind me, humbly accepting compliments for his eulogy.

"Where's the ring?" said a plump lady with frizzy red hair, snatching up my fingers.

My faced burned. "Not yet."

Marrying at seventeen didn't seem to bother the locals.

"All in good time," Tyler said to her, rubbing my shoulders. After the third person asked, he took my hand in his and mumbled, "Sorry."

I smiled up at him. For once, I wasn't embarrassed by the attention.

A few minutes later, Ruby made her way through the line, giving out big hugs. I sensed her rushing the formalities, and then she skipped past me and went straight to Tyler.

"You, young man, are something else." She lightly patted his face. "That was the most beautiful eulogy ever. You take care of her, you hear?"

"Of course."

She eyed him. "We'll be watching. Don't you worry." She started to walk away, and then she turned around. "By the way, you kicked that Bobby's ass right out of town." She winked. "You done good, son."

Tyler's face reddened at the compliment.

Within minutes of everyone exiting, we headed outside to go to the cemetery. The paper mill stench filled the air. Sprinkles bounced off the pavement as I darted to Tyler's car and slid into the warm leather seat. We had ten minutes alone. Ten whole minutes. Butterflies swarmed in my stomach, anxious to have him all to myself.

He climbed in and shut the door. "You okay?"

"Better now that you're here."

"Those eyes... I have missed you so much."

Leaning toward me, he slid his hand over my cheek and kissed me. The world disappeared as we reconnected. My insides warmed from the feel of his gentle touch. The wait. Finally, it was over.

"It's been way too long since we've seen each other," he said as he pulled away.

Then he turned on the ignition, and I relaxed for the first time in hours. The stereo played a low, soothing classical piece that I didn't recognize. A few cars passed, then someone stopped to let us join the procession.

"When did you decide to do this?" I asked.

"Claire called me last night to tell me... since you didn't." He frowned, glancing at me out of the corner of his eye. "I told her about seeing Brandon in the hospital, and she asked if I would share the story. Not sure where she was, but she said you'd walked in before we hung up."

"She was hiding in the bathroom when we went out to dinner. She didn't tell me."

"What do you expect?" His voice cracked. "Luckily, I had enough time to change my flight. Why in the hell didn't you tell me your dad died?"

"Don't be mad," I said softly like a hurt child. "I'm sorry. When you called, you were on top of the world. I wanted to let you have your day. Anyway, I did try to call you. Several times in fact. This morning at six was my last hope."

"I was on an airplane." he said in a monotone.

Suddenly, I felt defensive. "I didn't know."

"Brandon diiieed," he said, emphasizing the word. "It wasn't like you'd gotten a new haircut. For cryin' out loud, I've been with you for months. You have to know I care by now."

I turned inward. Knowing I hurt him didn't help how shitty I already felt.

"What can I say? I can't fix it. I'm just glad Mom called

you." I shifted to a slightly smart-assed tone. "Not so happy 'bout all the secrets, but I can move past that."

He smiled. "She just wanted to surprise you. She explained everything to me when she called. Elsie, I don't want to make you feel worse, but... you obviously still don't trust me."

He watched the road, eyes fixed on driving steady.

Trust. What exactly did that mean? I thought I was protecting him. "Tyler. I trust you. This wasn't about trust, it was timing. And my timing sucked."

"Your timing did suck." He chuckled. "I knew something was up last Saturday. But you're so damn convincing. *'Just woke up, that's all.'* You could've told me right then, and I'd have dropped everything to get here."

I flipped my hands in the air. "That's my point! You've worked, how hard? Months and months? I didn't want you to drop everything. You deserved to have your moment."

He shifted in the seat like he wrestled with the idea of his own glory, glanced at me, and sighed. "I appreciate that, I really do. But you don't have to protect me. Even though we're together, we have to give each other the freedom to make our own decisions. Especially in a case like this. You'll always be my first concern."

He refused to accept that I felt exactly the same way. I didn't know how to get my point across. What did he need to hear?

"Tyler. I love you. I love you more than charcoal swirls and pastel blends. I love you more than cold water after walking the fields in the hot Tennessee sun. I love you more than the Bears. I love you more than red-bottomed shoes and Mercedes Benz. I don't know how else to say that this was merely a series of mistakes that have done nothing but come back and bite me in the ass. I. Love. You."

A smile plastered his face. "Elizabeth, what the hell can I say to that? I love you, too."

"Good. Can we forget about it now?"

He agreed by taking my hand in his, driving with his left arm swung over the black steering wheel. He'd driven hours to get to me, dressed to the nines, and was still willing to hold my hand. His words from the funeral rang in my head: *"I asked him if I could marry his daughter someday."*

"I can't believe you went back to talk to Dad. You didn't write about it in your journal."

"I tore out the page."

"Not cool." I laughed. "Why?"

"I didn't plan on telling you. Maybe after I asked... I shouldn't have mentioned it. I didn't mean to embarrass you."

"You didn't embarrass me at all. A little taken off guard, but not embarrassed."

"That wasn't the reason I went to see him. But after a while, this sense of urgency nagged at me, like something kept nudging me to ask. I'm not rushing you, it just fit with my point."

His cheeks the color of strawberry lemonade, the honesty wasn't easy for him. It wasn't easy for me, either. Dad said he approved of us, something I never would've known other-wise. Tyler had no idea how precious those words were.

"I really am sorry I didn't tell you about Dad," I said, squeezing his fingers.

"It's all good. It worked out. I just hope you get it. You're more important than a race, or a win, or anything else going on in my life. Got it?"

We smiled at each other to seal the understanding. He followed the procession down Coffee Landing Road into the ghost town with a pool hall and a post office. After a few blocks, he turned left into the cemetery. Rolling hills of variously shaped marble and granite headstones set the tone. He parked on the side of the gravel drive as a light rain misted the windshield. People walked toward a blue tent silhouetted against the horizon as dusk cast an orange and yellow glow across the sky. Halloween was a week away but goosebumps rose on my arms. We should've done this earlier in the day. Freakin' creepy.

Tyler reached in the back seat. "You need a coat." He handed me his black NorthFace jacket.

"Thank you." I slipped it on and buried my face in the warmth. "I don't want to go out there." I looked up with my most pathetic-looking eyes, a shit grin to confirm the joke. "Can't we just go home?"

"Come on now." He leaned over and gave me a kiss. "It's only for a little while."

Moments later, he held my hand as we walked toward the tent at the top of the first hill. An odd bunch of color moved in the air. Squinting through the raindrops, I didn't understand what it was. A balloon bouquet? It looked strange juxtaposed against the scene. A rainbow of primary colors blew in the wind, next to a casket and grave. *What the hell?* This wasn't a birthday party. I slowed. Tyler felt the tug on his hand and turned around.

"What's wrong?" he asked.

I nodded at the balloons. "What are those for?"

"You'll see." He looked back at the gravesite.

I stood my ground. "You know about that, too?"

"No. But you won't either if you don't go. Right?"

"Right," I said, apprehensively.

LIFE HAPPENS ON THE STAIRS

He didn't understand. Balloons didn't belong. I could only take "celebration of life" so far. I didn't feel like rejoicing. I was kind of pissed at how Life liked to fuck me.

Tightly holding his hand, we walked the final stretch to say goodbye to Dad. As we sat in the front row next to Mom, the primary balloons bounced off each other, muted thumps rubbing like a dry erase marker squeaking across a white board.

I leaned toward Mom. "What's with the balloons?"

Tired-eyed, she gave me a weary smile. "You'll see."

Grandma sat behind us, rattling on in a not-so-quiet whisper. "What the hell is that for? Damn rain, it's miserable out here. What in the hell is that smell in the air? Who chose those colors? George, what are those balloons for?"

Tyler laced our fingers together and whispered in my ear, "Your grandmother is Nana's long-lost sister."

I snickered. "I know, right?"

Pastor Larry stood in front of us and led us in prayer. After we said, "Amen," he recited Psalm 23. The sound of raindrops replaced his voice. He wiped his eyes, then broke down and cried. He'd lost a dear friend. A brother. A lump welled in my throat, as tears stung my eyes. He loved Dad. All humility set aside, his tender heart melted in front of us.

A few moments later, he took a deep breath and rubbed the pain off his face. "Here are forty-one balloons. Each one represents a year of Brandon's life. I want to challenge each of you to look back at the years you've spent with him, and be grateful for the time that he was here, instead of mourning the years that he's not." His eyes swept the front row. "I'd like to ask the family to make gratitude your mantra. Be grateful for the memories, and don't dwell on the what-if's. Celebrate the great life he lived by releasing color into this gray sky to honor his vibrant spirit."

He offered Mom his hand, helping her out of her seat. She turned to Mark and me, and we followed her out of the tent. Pastor Larry untied the strings, then handed them to Mom. She divided them between us. The three of us stepped between two white marbled headstones, raised our arms, and as a family, we let them go. They rose into the sky, colors separating, spreading in every direction. Blue, green, red, yellow – rising higher and higher, free like Dad. I watched them ascend, slowly growing smaller in the sky, as raindrops washed the tears from my cheeks.

Chapter

34

Everyone was welcome to come back to the church for dinner. Ruby and her army of Southern-cookin' women had a spread waiting in the warm fellowship hall that made the Golden Corral look like a soup line. Tyler and I filled our plates and settled in next to Mom and Gail. Travis and Krissie were on the opposite side of us. Grandpa and Grandma sat at the far end, talking to Mark and Megan. Ravenous, I tried not to eat fast. Tyler's plate overflowed with food.

"Got enough?" I joked.

"I'm starving." He affirmed with a bite of broccoli salad.

Travis chuckled to himself after he took a drink of tea. "Claire, you remember that night Brandon convinced you to sneak out and go to the Pay Lake after hours?"

Her cheeks reddened. "I got into so much trouble."

"Shit! You?" Travis's voice reverberated off the walls, drowning out the rest of the chatter. Mom cringed, holding up her hand to shush him. "Brandon and I sat in jail for the rest of the weekend."

She shyly covered the left side of her face with her hair. "Travis... the kids are here."

"Stop it, Mom," I said, and then I looked at Uncle Travis. "What happened?"

"Your dad. Crazy fucker. We were all in the pond skinny-dippin'—"

"Travis," Mom huffed. "Details are not necessary."

"Oh, come on. Stacy was with us, too." He looked at Tyler and me. "Stacy was *hot*. Black hair, black eyes. Crazy bitch, though."

Krissie curled her lip. "Seriously?" Her voice was high pitched like a 1980s Valley Girl.

Travis ignored her and continued. "Claire, you remember her?"

"Of course," Mom said in a dry tone. "Who could forget Stacy?"

"She's an accountant now," he said. "Anyway. Evidently, one of us was too loud."

"I wonder who that was?" Mom shifted to sarcastic mode.

"The owner of the pond called the police. We saw flash-lights beams bouncing off the trees," Travis said to Tyler and me. "Of course, we were naked, fuckin' ducks sitting in the water. Then, two cops stepped to the edge of the pond."

Tyler and I started laughing. Mom smiled one of those bittersweet memory smiles.

"I was scared to death!" Travis laughed. "Brandon

tromped up the shore, all his glory hangin' in the wind, and shook both cops' hands like he was wearing a business suit. Then, he convinced them to let the girls go in exchange for us. When we walked in the jail – and yes, they made us get dressed first – Brandon stood two inches taller, chest out, looking every man in the eyes. By the time Gail was finally able to bail us out, he'd made friends with practically the whole cellblock. I swear he didn't know a stranger. The guy could charm a snake."

"He stayed in touch with one of those guys," Mom said, sitting straighter. "Oh, what's his name? Scott. Scott Pierce. Nice guy, actually."

"I remember him," Travis said. "He was pretty cool."

For the next two hours, we listened to tales about Dad and Travis, Mom and Dad, Gail and Travis, Travis and various women. With each story, the tension in Krissie's face tightened. Tyler and I laughed along, listening to tall-stories of Dad riding motocross, meeting Mom, and trying to grow up in general.

When the clock hit nine, I laid my head on Tyler's shoulder. Too many emotions in one day. I had to go home.

"Do you care if we go?" I asked Mom. "It's nine."

"Sure. I won't be far behind you."

"Thank you."

Tyler and I told everyone goodbye, passing out hugs to Gail, Travis, Grandpa, and Grandma. We found Ruby in the kitchen and thanked her for all her hard work. Hugs all around, we were finally able to escape back into Tyler's car.

On the way home, he turned down the radio. "Why aren't your dad's parents here?"

"They died in 1993."

"Both of them? Why?"

"They went on a trip for their twenty-fifth anniversary, and the charter bus they took to Florida hit bad weather on the way home. A horrible pile up on the interstate killed half the people on the bus. Dad was my age then, and Travis was sixteen. Gail pretty much raised them after that."

"That's awful. I can't imagine losing both my parents at the same time."

"Me either. Not after all of this. Can you imagine what Dad went through?"

"No."

"I had nightmares for years that Mom could die, too." I hated those nights when my brain decided to torture me with all my fears and anxieties. "I don't know what I'd do."

He reached across the console and took my hand.

Ten minutes later, I stood alone in my bedroom, looking in the mirror. I felt raw and numb, like I'd just gotten over the flu. I brushed out my hair, then started changing clothes. This was it. All the uncertainty, all the worries, they were gone. Just like Dad. It still didn't feel real. When I stepped into the kitchen, Tyler was hanging up his suit.

He turned around and spotted my Bears sweatshirt. "You need some black and gold with a fleur-de-lis."

"You know you love the Bears."

He grinned. "You wish."

A few minutes later, we settled on the couch next to each other. Being with him was all I wanted after my second worst-day ever. The night of the accident had been downgraded to third in light of the past few days. We watched TV for a while wrapped in each other's arms.

"What happened the night your dad died?" Tyler asked.

"Mm... " I rolled over, using his arm as a pillow.

"I understand if you don't want to talk about it."

"It's not that, I just haven't said it out loud, yet." I took a deep breath, and then I told him what happened from the moment Mark woke me to the second the last EMT left the house.

"You didn't run," he said gently, yet matter-of-fact.

"You know, it didn't even cross my mind."

"See. You've grown past it."

"Maybe I have."

"You're stronger than you give yourself credit for."

"Mm... "

He twisted a lock of my hair around his fingers. "I think you are."

I rolled closer to him and cried in his arms. He held me close, stroking my hair without a word, like he knew his embrace was the only way to ease my pain. I just needed to be held. Would I ever feel like myself again? How would I ever move on? I hated all the tears, all the sadness. When would it stop? Or would it haunt me for life?

"You all right?" he asked. I answered with a nod and a sniffle. He brushed my hair from my eyes, giving me time to regroup. "I have a question for you. I need to leave tomorrow by eleven. I have a test I have to take at three. But, will you come to breakfast with me before I go?"

"Of course."

He raised his eyebrows. "Do you trust me?"

"Would you cut that shit out?"

He giggled like he'd said that just to irritate me. "All right then, give it some thought before you say no. Nana's going to be there."

A chill ran over me. "Does she know I'm coming?"

"Yes. We talked this morning for the first time since I left. She wants to see you."

"Mm... " Sounded like a trap.

"Would you stop humming at me?" He laughed. "Maybe we can get this all worked out."

I closed my eyes for a moment, letting the idea sink in. I deeply missed our private world that no one used to interrupt. "Yes, I'll go. I can survive a meal with the woman."

"Promise no F-bombs?"

"I cannot promise that." We both burst out laughing. I held up my hands. "I *will* promise to be on my best behavior."

"Thank you." He leaned down and pressed his lips to mine.

At the same time, we heard car doors closing outside. We changed our position and sat up on the couch. Mom stepped in, her face pale and drained, eyes no wider than slits.

"How are you?" I asked.

"Exhausted. I'm going to bed. Don't move from that couch, and you can stay, Tyler."

"Thank you," he said.

"Goodnight, Mom." I hopped up and gave her a hug. "Love you."

"Love you, too."

Mark came inside and sat down in the recliner with a thump.

"Are you okay?" I asked as I settled in beside Tyler.

"Sure."

"When are Grandma and Grandpa leaving?"

"In the morning."

Thank God. Spending more time with my aunt and uncle would've been nice, but I was grateful to hear Grandma and

Grandpa were headed out.

"I'm going to bed." Mark rubbed his forehead. "What a long-ass day."

We all said goodnight, and Mark went into his room. I grabbed the afghan and spread it over Tyler and me, snuggling down for the night.

"I've missed you so much," he said. "Thanks for going tomorrow."

"It's the least I can do after all you've done for me."

He gave me a soft kiss, and then we talked until we fell asleep in each other's arms.

Chapter

35

The next morning, I woke up to Mom shaking my shoulder.

"Elsie," she said in a harsh whisper.

"Is it Dad?" She took a step back. Then I realized what I'd said. "Oh, Mom, I'm sorry."

"It's okay. Your grandparents are on their way. It won't help me at all if they find you sleeping on the couch with your boyfriend. Can you two get up?"

Tyler stretched, then glanced at his watch. "Shoot. I can't believe I slept this late."

He spread the blanket over me, and went to the bathroom. I flopped back on the couch, irritated by how the morning began.

Five minutes later, I was folding the afghan when Grandpa walked through the door.

"Hey, kid," he said. "How you holding up?"

"Fine, thanks. Where's Grandma?"

"She's putting her bags in the Crown Vic. She's going to drive it home, and I'll follow her in the truck. Is Mark up?"

"I haven't seen him."

Grandpa walked across the room and knocked on his door. Grandma stepped inside at the same time.

"Hi, Grandma." The sneer on her face sent a shiver down my spine.

"Elizabeth," she stated. "Where's your mother?"

She was colder than an Illinois blizzard. "In the kitchen."

She strutted across the room like she was on a mission. I followed, sat down next to Tyler at the kitchen counter, and watched the saga unfold.

"How are you this morning, Claire?" Grandma's tone was curt.

"Okay." Mom leaned against the counter on the opposite side of the kitchen. "Did you sleep well?"

"I suppose." She cleared her throat. "Now that all the formalities are over, are you going to consider moving home?"

Mom's eyes narrowed from behind her coffee cup. "I don't know. The *formalities* may be over for you, but I'm not in the position to make such a hasty decision."

"Dear, there's nothing here for you now," Grandma said. "There was never anything here for you to begin with. Brandon was obviously irrational when he made this decision."

"Mom. Don't."

"What? He was diagnosed weeks after you arrived. The tumor didn't grow overnight. What made him want to come down here in the first place, I'll never understand."

"He saw an opportunity and took it," Mom snapped. "When we started farming, there was a contract, and he had been guaranteed a steady income as long as he could get the crops in. Everything was fine until earlier this year. How would you know, anyway? You've treated him like shit since you met him."

"Claire. Why can't you accept the truth? Brandon did nothing but bring you down."

I'd heard enough. "Please stop talking about my dad that way."

Grandma whipped her head toward me so fast I thought it spun a 360. Tyler slid his arm around my shoulder as she stared me down. Grandpa stepped out of Mark's room and looked around the kitchen. "What's going on?"

"Your granddaughter thinks it's okay to sass me," Grandma said. "I think it's time to go."

"Elsie isn't sassing you," Mom said. "You really need to keep your opinions to yourself."

"Well, I never—" Grandma pivoted and headed toward the front door.

"She's just pissy because she has to drive," Grandpa said. "Ignore her."

Mark stepped out of his room. "What's going on?" He sounded just like Grandpa.

"I'm gonna change clothes," I whispered to Tyler.

He gave me a sympathetic smile. "Me, too."

By seven-thirty, my grandparents pulled out of the drive. Everyone let out a sigh of relief and relaxed. I gave Mom a hug. She pushed back tears as she clung to me and then she went to her room. Tyler and I headed to the car to go meet my grandmother's long-lost twin.

"I'm sorry you had to listen to all of that," Tyler said on

the way to Savannah.

"I should be apologizing to you. I don't understand at all. Who says those things to their daughter the day after she buries her husband?"

"Maybe Illinois wouldn't be so bad."

I leaned away from him. "Are you crazy?"

"What? I'm considering the Northwestern."

"That's Chicago. Not Illinois." I smirked. "They may as well be separate states." He chuckled in agreement. "Seriously, Tyler, I'm gonna be pissed if she makes a quick decision."

"What if your house sells? She might not have a choice."

"I don't know." The whole idea irritated me. I didn't want to move and then move back to Memphis for college. It didn't make any sense. Plus, it could screw up my tuition and fees. "She knows how I feel. All I've wanted for years was to go to MCA."

"I'm sure it'll all work out." He cringed just enough to make me do a double take. "The only thing is... I can't go to college in Memphis. Maybe that doesn't matter to you, but it does to me. The closest I could get would be Washington University in St. Louis."

"It's a good school."

"Sure, it is. But I haven't even applied there. It could set me back months."

"Oh." My stomach dropped. That did matter to me, more than anything. Long stints without being able to see him were killing me. Chicago. It'd be better than cornfields.

A few minutes later, we arrived at Buck's restaurant, followed the server to a table near the back, and settled in with a cup of coffee. A glossy-eyed, stuffed deer head mounted on the wall stared at me from across the room. Its head tilted just enough to watch me the entire meal.

Tyler stretched out his long legs, slouching in the chair, relaxed and comfortable. A cold chill ran down my spine, and my palms were clammy and sweaty.

"You okay?" he asked.

"Sure." I curled my shoulders and rubbed my hands. So damn cold. "You seem content."

"Don't worry about it." He laced his fingers behind his head and inclined the chair back on two legs. "She's all show. Have I told you how gorgeous you are?"

"You just did." I smiled, then tilted my head, scrutinizing his demeanor. "If I learned anything from your journal, you aren't half as relaxed as you seem. You should be an actor."

He set the chair down and grinned. "You think you have me all figured out now, huh?"

"Maybe." I looked over his shoulder. My heart skipped. "She's here," I muttered.

Mrs. Vaughn appeared at the other end of the dining room, dressed in a burnt-red blouse and a navy pencil skirt. She moved between tables, shoulders back, chin high, her youthful vitality masking her age. She approached the table and waited for Tyler to stand. He kissed her on the cheek, then pulled out his chair for her, and sat down next to me. She settled in across from him without acknowledging my presence. Tyler snagged his coffee cup and took a sip.

"Well, dear, how have you been?" she asked in her haughty tone.

"Mighty fine," he said, glancing at me.

"Yes." She slowly moved her eyes from his to mine. "Hello, Elizabeth."

"Good morning, Mrs. Vaughn." I used the softest, sweetest tone I could conjure up.

Blank-faced, she gave me a slight nod in response, then her icy eyes moved back to Tyler's. I fidgeted in my seat. He placed his hand on my leg with a gentle squeeze.

"Have you been studying?" she asked him.

"Of course. I qualified for Nationals."

"Fantastic." Her face brightened. "Where will you compete?"

A thin, brunette server with sunken, dark eyes and bright pink lipstick approached the table. Mrs. Vaughn flinched at the interruption.

"Can I get y'all something to drink?" she asked Mrs. Vaughn.

"Coffee, black," she said without eye contact.

The girl glanced at me, cringed and walked away.

Tyler stared at his grandmother, unamused.

Mrs. Vaughn motioned to him with her manicured nails. "Well? Go on."

"Terre Haute, Indiana. The weekend before Thanksgiving."

"Will you take a flight?"

"Probably."

"Well, you must. That's too long of a drive to run the next morning."

"I'll take the bus if I can't fly."

"Nonsense. I'll make sure you're flying. I'll call your coach."

"Nana, no." He scratched the side of his head, fully irritated. The way his family hovered made him crazy. This time I rubbed his leg. He placed his warm hand on mine and squeezed. Letting out a calm sigh, he asked her, "What would you like for breakfast?"

"I'll have grits and toast," she said. "I trust they can't screw that up."

The server returned with black coffee, took our orders, and refilled our cups. The caffeine wasn't helping my anxiety.

"You wanted to meet us, so here we are," Tyler said. "What's on your mind?"

Her eyes turned up to the left, then darted at Tyler's, and back again at the ceiling. He stared her down expectantly, like a cop waiting for a confession.

"I suppose I owe Elizabeth an apology," she said.

"It's Elsie, Nana," he said in a low tone. "Cut the 'Elizabeth' crap."

"Elsie." She let the word fall out of her mouth like my name tasted bitter. "I'm sorry I said such a horrible thing to you. It's obvious Tyler is taken with you. I will try to respect that."

Her apology sent a shiver down my spine.

"Thank you. I apologize for what I said, as well."

"Well, I hope so," she balked. "No one has ever—"

"That's good." Tyler held up his hand. "Nana, you did great."

She fluttered her lashes.

"I truly am sorry," I repeated. "I don't usually talk like that. I was... well, under a lot of stress at the time."

"Yes. Tyler told me about your father. I'm sorry to hear that." She bowed her head almost like her grandson did, but she had a gleam in her eye that caught me off guard.

The server returned with our food. As we ate, Mrs. Vaughn talked to Tyler like I wasn't there. She complained about her thick grits and undercooked toast, and sent them back to the kitchen. When the girl came back with a different set, Mrs. Vaughn didn't hesitate.

"Excuse me," she said to the server. "You think this is better than the one I sent away?"

"Um, ma'am, that's as good as it gets 'round here."

She pushed her plate aside. "Take it then."

The girl started to pick up the dish.

"I'll eat it," Tyler reached out.

She handed him the plate. He shot his grandmother a look, and then he smiled at the girl, who blushed before scurrying off. An awkward silence filled the table. Minutes passed while we ate with only the sound of the chatter and clanking dishes in the background. I sensed Mrs. Vaughn's irritation that Tyler was simply enjoying his breakfast. Setting down my fork, I was about to go to the bathroom, but Tyler pushed his chair out and stood up before I could.

"Excuse me, I'll be right back," he said.

I pleaded for him to stay with the look I gave him. He shrugged like he was sorry, and then he headed to the bathroom. Butterflies swarmed my stomach. An even thicker tension filled the air. I scooted my chair forward, fidgeted with my napkin, and then I grabbed my glass of water. Taking a sip, I peered over the rim. We made eye contact.

"Elizabeth, now that we have a moment alone," Mrs. Vaughn said, "I want to make sure we don't have any misunderstandings. Please don't get the impression that I'll ever support this ridiculous affair Tyler thinks he has with you. He required me to apologize if I want to see him."

"Affair?" I set down the glass. "Why am I not surprised you'd see it that way?"

"So, I've done as he asked, and now here we are." She picked up her napkin, tapping each corner of her mouth. "This has been quite uncomfortable, hasn't it? Oh well, no matter. Come January, he'll be in California. You needn't worry about this lasting much longer. It just occurred to me, since your daddy's dead, won't you be leaving, too? I'm sure that adorable house your family rents will sell quickly."

I stared her down, tapping my fingers on the side of the glass. Ignoring the urge to run, I sat straighter. "I'm going to pretend you didn't say that, for Tyler's sake. You don't scare me. I love him, and you need to get over it because he loves me, too."

Our eyes locked for several seconds. She was about to speak, but then she spotted something over my shoulder. A fake smile filled her face. Tyler pulled out his chair and sat down. I leaned back, waiting for her next move.

"What?" Tyler smirked at her, and then he looked at me. "All good?"

"Yes, everything's fine," I said.

"Good. We need to get going. I have to get on the road. My test is at three."

He picked up the bill and grabbed his wallet out of his back pocket.

"Awful shame, you can't stay longer," Mrs. Vaughn said. "Will you be back for Thanksgiving?"

He tossed a fifty on the table. "I'm not sure yet."

"It was grits and eggs, Tyler," she huffed. "That's ridiculous."

"She'd earned it. You're impossible sometimes, Nana. I swear, you're lucky you don't get food poisoning the way you piss people off."

Mrs. Vaughn didn't react, like she had no idea his comment was an insult. Tyler stood up and offered his hand to me. I accepted, feeling Mrs. Vaughn's hateful glare as I stood. He stepped around the table, not forgetting about her, offered a hand, and gave her a hug before we left. As we walked outside, she wouldn't look at me, let alone say goodbye.

I flashed a fake smile and waved. *Bitch.* I wanted to flip her off, but that would've blown my charade. Minutes later, we climbed in the car and headed toward my house.

"Not so bad?" Tyler asked.

"Um, yeah, interesting."

He glanced at me with a worried look. "Did she say something to you?"

"It's fine. You do know she's never going to accept me, right?"

He swayed his shoulders back and forth in reluctant agreement. "I'm hoping to fix that."

"Good luck. I'll say, you don't beat around the bush with her, do you?"

"She's a snob. You saw how she treated the waitress. It's ridiculous."

We joked about our grandmothers being so much alike for the rest of the drive home.

When I stepped inside the house, Mom was curled in the corner of the couch, crying.

"Oh, hi," she said, immediately sitting up.

I sat down next to her. "Aw, Mom. Are you okay?"

"Excuse me," Tyler said and headed to the kitchen.

"Sure," she said. "I guess it's going to be like this for a while."

"I'm sorry I left this morning. Tyler wanted to take me to breakfast."

"No worries. You don't have to sit around being sad." She patted my knee. "I'm glad he's here. You're so happy when he's around."

I gave her a hug. "I can't thank you enough for calling him."

At eleven sharp, Tyler tossed his bag in the back seat of his car, hung up his suit, and then he leaned against the door. Grabbing my waist, he pulled me against him and laid a playful kiss on my lips. We both laughed. He searched my eyes, then softly touched my cheek, and kissed me again. One hand moved down my back and over my hip, the other held me steady as he pressed our bodies tighter. Running my hands through his hair, I felt down his chest and over his tight stomach as our mouths moved in tempo. A low growl vibrated on my lips. He pulled back and looked me in the eyes.

"I'll see you soon, okay?" He lightly cupped my face. I nodded between his hands. He pressed his lips to mine with another soft kiss. "Call you tonight?"

I wrapped my arms him and buried my face in his neck. "I'll be here."

He squeezed me tight, lifting me off the ground.

"Don't go," I said in his ear.

"I wish." He kissed me again, and then set me on my feet. "Only a few more weeks."

"I love you."

He let me go and opened the car door. "I love you."

He slid inside, and within seconds he drove away. My chest clenched. Alone again.

Chapter

36

After the funeral, I fell back into my routine: school, home again, dinner, homework, talk to Tyler. Except this time, the heavy weight on my chest was because all of the chaos and uncertainty was gone. *Poof.* I'd heard of survivor's remorse – more so when a person's life had been threatened rather than when another life was lost. I resented the sun for rising and setting, the alarm for reminding me I had to put my feet on the ground, and smiling faces in the hallways who complained about their fathers.

Thankfully, Tyler called every night. He'd talk me down when I thought I would burst from the grief. He soothed me with his dulcet accent, loving words reassuring me that my guilt was unfounded. Once again, he was my refuge.

On November second, he texted first thing in the morning.

Tyler: Happy birthday!!!! Love you! Hope you have a great day.

Me: Thank you! I love you, too!

Emma brought cupcakes to school for me. Chocolate with white icing. I tuned out the chatter in the lunchroom, sinking my teeth in the buttery frosting and moist cake.

Holding up a finger, I finished chewing. "Thanks, girl."

She licked icing off her thumb, and asked, "Is your mom doing anything for you?"

"We'll go out for dinner tonight." I shrugged, nipping another small bite. "No one's in the mood to celebrate. It's cool, though."

"Bullshit, it's not cool. I'll come along. You know I'll spice it up for y'all."

She would help us laugh. "I'd love that."

"Have you heard from MCA?"

I shook my head, then countered, "Did you finally make a decision?"

"Yep! I'm goin' to the beach—Florida State. Well, pretty close to the beach." Her bright smile slowly deflated. "Mom's pissed. She thinks I'm choosing Dad over her."

"You love Florida," I said, indulging her. She knew Emma wanted to get away from her mother more than her pursuit of a physics degree. "You're going to college, not moving in with him."

"I know, right?" She took another bite of cupcake. With a full mouth, she said, "Oh well, she'll get over it."

After school, I drove home with the windows down and the

heater blasting. Summer without the humidity. Turning out of Morris Chapel, I followed the winding road toward home. Within minutes, I stepped inside the house to savor the silence. Mark was at work. Mom was gone – hopefully, she'd gone to work or was at Ruby's. I worried about her.

The past two weeks had been rough, and even though she said she was looking forward to cleaning houses again, the flat tone she used wasn't convincing. She'd never aspired to clean homes, but the job was lucrative, as long as she could withstand the work. Regardless, she'd always wanted to go back to school. Criminal justice, law and order, subjects like that made her tick. Maybe she could start at the community college in Savannah. She needed to find a passion, something she could focus on. I sorted through the mail on the counter. An advertisement for the local college was hidden under the power bill. I set the flyer on top of the stack. A knock at the front door echoed through the house.

I hurried to the living room, opened the door, and a stout, bald-headed man stood outside.

"Hi." I waved my hand, brightening out of my dull mood.

"Miss Richardson?" the man asked in a surprisingly high-pitched tone.

"Yes."

"These are for you." He held out a cobalt blue vase, bursting with long-stemmed, red roses. The magnificent bouquet was so large I lost sight of his face.

I pressed my nose against the firm petals, stealing a moment to inhale the antique scent of sweet roses. Setting them on the coffee table, I returned to the door. He handed me a small rectangular box wrapped in plain brown paper.

"Thank you," I said.

"Happy birthday!" He smiled, and then he walked back

toward his beige Nissan.

I shut the door and opened the small note affixed to a plastic stick in the middle of the bouquet. It read:

For my girl.

Eighteen roses, for your eighteenth birthday. See you soon.

Love you, Tyler
P.S. Open the notes app.

What did that mean? I stared at the box for a few seconds, dropped the card, and tore off the brown packaging. Inside was a glossy-white box with a shiny silver apple on top. I squealed, pulled out the iPhone, and slid the button to unlock the screen. When I tapped the yellow note icon, a list of entries waited for me:

I love you.
Hope you like it.
Check your music app.
I'll see you soon. Just a little longer. You'd better answer when I call :)

My cheeks throbbed from the smile plastered on my face. I exited out of the app, pressed the music icon, and then checked the playlist he'd made. The first song was, 4 Non Blondes, *What's Up?*

Laughing out loud in the silence, I pressed play, and then I scrolled through hundreds of songs. He'd stocked it with all kinds of music: classical, pop, a few country songs, alternative, everything I could imagine. I exited the app and pressed the green phone icon. His number was the only one programmed. I touched it and held the phone to my ear.

"I see you've gotten my present," he answered. "Happy birthday."

"Thank you so much."

"Welcome to the modern age," he said, sounding pleased. "You have a hand-sized computer next to your ear. Enjoy. Google something, ask Siri any question – she's at your service. Please set up an email account, okay? You really need to get with the times."

"I'll do it right after we're done," I said, sounding like a giddy little girl. "I love you."

I could hear his smile. "I love you, Elsie. I can't wait to see you."

Three weeks after Dad died, I walked in the kitchen on a Friday afternoon. Mom stood in front of the sink, staring out of the window at the dirt driveway that led to the barn. Tears poured down her face. I leaned against the counter on the opposite side of the room. An albatross of sorrow pressed down on her shoulders.

Apprehensive about speaking, I softly asked, "Are you all right?"

"Oh." She spun her head, pressing her palm to her chest. "I didn't hear you."

Even her senses had dulled. She always heard everything.

"What are you thinking about?"

"Your dad, and just... " Her words trailed off.

If she wanted to tell me something, she'd keep talking.

Sometimes she'd tell you, sometimes she wouldn't. I waited. She shrugged, picked up her coffee cup, and went to her room. Mark walked in from work as her door clicked shut. We made eye contact. Bonded siblings, he read the worry on my face, then glanced at Mom's room.

"Is she okay?"

"She won't talk, and I'm afraid to push. I haven't seen her smile since the funeral. And I don't think those smiles count."

He started to empty his lunch box in the trash. "She hasn't gone back to work."

"What's she doing, then? Doesn't she need the money?"

"Dad had some life insurance, ten grand or something, but Grandpa wrote her a check." He spun around and eyed me. "Grandma doesn't know that, though."

"That's weird. She doesn't ask for money."

He opened the fridge and started rummaging through the drawers. "I didn't say she asked. He just gave it to her." He tossed a few grapes in his mouth.

"It isn't like her to skip work."

He shrugged. "She just lost her husband."

"Obviously. But she's usually so strong."

"She's tired of being strong." He grabbed some cookies off the counter, started to pop one in his mouth, then stopped. "It's different for her than it is for us. Yeah, I've cried about it, but it's not the same. They *loved* each other." His emphasis on the word "love" surprised me. "I miss Dad a lot, don't get me wrong, but she feels like she's dying inside. She told me herself."

"I've read about the five stages of grief. Be warned... anger is one of them."

"Ah. I can take it." He waved his hand. "We've duked it out before."

We laughed. He seemed happy to be able to take the brunt if she needed to blow. I felt even closer to him after our laughter faded. After all the bullshit we'd put each other through, he'd become one of my best friends.

"You haven't told me, have you and Megan been going out?"

His cheeks flushed. "Yeah. She's pretty cool."

"Well, we love her."

He flashed a big grin and turned to scrounge for more food.

A few nights later, I got off the phone with Tyler and went to the bathroom before bed. The hallway was dark, except for the light from under Mom's door. When I came back out, muted sobs made me turn left. I had to help her somehow, at least be there to listen if she wanted to talk. I tapped on her door and pushed it open without waiting for her answer.

I hadn't been in the room since the weekend Dad died. I wasn't exactly fond of the space anymore. She'd changed the curtains and bedspread, making it warm and cozy instead of an improvised hospital room. She didn't want company, but I sat on the edge of the bed anyway.

"Hi," I whispered.

"Sorry you keep finding me like this."

I looked down at her Victorian, floral quilt. "I don't mean to intrude."

"You're not. I'll get past this at some point, right?"

"There's no time limit. I can't imagine how much you miss him."

"You have no idea... I know you're hurting, but you have your whole life ahead of you. Make the most of it."

Her words stung, as if she'd been thinking irrational thoughts. "Your life isn't over."

"I know." Her voice cracked as she looked up at the ceiling. "I'll get there. I just don't feel it right now. I feel like part of me had died with him." She broke down and sobbed in her hands. Tears filled my eyes. Moments passed, and then she continued, "I keep waking up in the middle of the night, and I can feel him next to me. Such a cruel trick of the mind. I swear he's here. I can feel him under the covers, his warmth, his smell. I even heard him breathing one morning. But I open my eyes, or reach out to touch him—nothing. Of course, he's not there. Within seconds, my world crashes in on me." Her tone shifted to mock satire with an edge of anger. "It's a great way to start the day. If I could just get that to stop, then maybe... I'll want to get out of bed. But right now, I'd rather sleep. At least he's in my dreams."

"I wish there was something I could do."

"Thank you, but I have to do this one alone. How's school going?" Her tears faded, and she sat straighter. "Have you heard from Memphis College of Art?"

"No. I'm hoping to hear something soon."

"You will. How's Tyler?"

"We talk a lot more. He runs Nationals next weekend." Then, I remembered that Mom and I hadn't talked much. "I never told you about breakfast with his crazy grandmother!"

"You saw her?" she said, shocked. "What did she say? She'd better not have been rude."

"Of course, she was!"

I told her all about Mrs. Vaughn's empty threats, and then we gossiped for over an hour about the old woman and the years Mom had spent in her mansion. I'd missed her – my mother's bright smile, eyes the color of my cobalt vase, and most all, her contagious laugh.

Chapter

37

The Friday before Thanksgiving, I was backing out of the driveway to go to school and dumped my coffee on my lap. A creamy, sticky mess all over my jeans and the center console. After I cleaned myself up, and the car, I jogged through the front doors at school, fifteen minutes late. Before second hour, I smashed my middle finger in my locker, and then it pulsed and throbbed all the way through a math test that I undoubtedly bombed. Tyler and I played phone tag all day, back and forth we called, leaving voicemails and "I love yous." Plus, Emma had the flu, leaving me solo in the hallways and at lunch.

Worst of all, right before the two-fifty bell released me from Hardin County's hell hole, Mrs. Sanchez, the school counselor, called me into her office. Shiny black hair pulled in a low bun, she wore layers of draping fabric: deep reds, oranges, yellows, and browns of an Aztec pattern evocative of her native Central American heritage.

I sat down in the leather chair across her desk. She leaned forward on her elbows and peered over the rim of her cherry-red reading glasses. Her lips pressed in a hard line as she let out a slow exhale, her concerned, caramel-colored eyes affixed to mine. I'd seen that look before. Another lecture for being late to school. Just give me the detention and get it over with.

"When exactly did you apply to MCA?" she asked in a curious voice as devoid of a Southern accent as mine.

Her question took me off guard. "Um... early August."

"Elsie." Her brows creased with disappointment. "You were too late. I'm sorry. They didn't accept your application."

I deflated in the chair. Of course. A day late and a dollar short. The story of a Richardson's life.

I scanned the cramped office instead of looking at her. Warm and welcoming, one wall was lined in bookcases overflowing with titles. A small window behind her lit an elongated bureau stacked with papers, file folders, a Christmas cactus, and several wooden framed photos of her family. My chest tightened. *Fuck.* If I looked at her, I'd cry. Rejected. Vetoed. Bam—the door slammed in my face.

"All you have to do is reapply in the spring," she said. "Don't give up. You're a fantastic artist. Did you apply elsewhere?"

Devastated inside, I slowly inclined my head. "School of the Art Institute of Chicago and a few others," I murmured, my mouth suddenly dry.

Her high, arched eyebrows lifted. "Good, good."

I shrugged. "I don't know why I had my heart set on MCA, but I did."

"You have plenty of time and more than enough talent. Just reapply earlier this time. Who knows? You could still hear from the others."

After a few more words of encouragement, I hightailed it out of her office, gathered all of my stuff from my locker, and headed to the parking lot. Tears burned my eyes. I pulled my phone out of my book bag and glanced at the screen. *Tyler. Missed call. Shit!*

I spotted the Honda in the second row. Quickening my step, I took a long stride over a parking curb. An abrupt tug at my foot and my leg jerked backward when my shoelace caught a stray piece of rebar. My stomach lurched, and my phone flew out of my hand. Plunging forward, I extended my arms. *Bam.* I slammed the ground, hands and knees skidding in the gravel. My book bag flipped over my right shoulder, dragging me down harder. Dust billowed, lime grit dug in my palms and knees, stinging and burning in the open flesh.

"Fuck!" I pushed off the ground, scrambling to my feet.

A freshman girl with dark brown hair looked over her shoulder and started giggling. Fuming, I grabbed my phone and hurried to the car.

The brief moment of isolation faded fast as I jerked open the console and grabbed a napkin to wipe the blood from my hands. Fat, heavy tears rolled down my cheeks. I sniffled a grotesque chunk of snot, a horrific gurgle in the back of my throat. Humiliated, palms stinging, I wiped the blood and pulled out a few small shards of rock. When the bleeding slowed, I checked my phone to make sure I hadn't cracked the screen. A scuff on the corner, but nothing serious. I slid the icon for the voicemail open.

"Hey, Elsie," Tyler's low drawl hummed my ear. "I'm headin' to the airport, so I won't be able to call you for a bit. I'll try again when I get there, okay? I need to talk to you before I compete tomorrow. So... Answer. The. Phone," he stressed each word, and then he chuckled. "Love you. Bye."

Fuck! I slammed the steering wheel with the side of my fist, making my palm sting more. What a shit day! Nothing had gone right. Missing his calls hurt worse than the scrapes in my skin. I started the ignition and threw the car in reverse. Hopefully, Mom was home. I needed to vent. I needed a hug. What a stupid, stupid mistake. Late application? I felt like a total jackass.

As I drove toward Morris Chapel, I worried that Mom wouldn't listen even if she was home. She'd been distant and quiet the past few days. Talking on the phone behind closed doors, quick, one-word answers like she didn't want to engage too long. She'd stopped locking herself in her room, but the time she spent away from home, I still wasn't sure about.

Twenty minutes later, still agitated and shaking, I stepped inside the house. Mom walked into the living room from the kitchen, wiping her hands on a dish towel. Mark sat in the recliner, watching ESPN.

"Why are you home?" I asked him.

He kept his eyes on the TV. "Off early."

"Works out well." Mom moved across the living room toward the front door. "Have a seat Elsie, I need to talk to both of you."

What the hell now? I sighed, set my book bag on the floor, and pulled my cell phone out of my back pocket, setting the device on the coffee table. Eyes fixed on her, I sat on the couch.

She had a bomb. A big red button in one hand with a pointer finger ready to press. I couldn't take another ambush.

Not today. Run. No, hear her out...

Mom paced in front of the door, staring at the floor. Pace, turn, pace.

"Okay, guys. Here's the latest: McAllister sold the house." A deep breath. "And I've been offered a job at the University in Urbana." She sped up her words and turned our way.

I cringed. Had she completely lost her mind?

Mark puffed out his chest, nodding in agreement. I wasn't convinced he agreed in light of Megan. After a quick assessment of his reaction, seething, I turned to Mom.

"Why would you do that? You know how I feel!" I sprang to my feet. "You can't pull me out of school now! I only have three weeks left!"

She held up a palm with pleading eyes. "Listen. I talked to your principal. She said we can work it out. You'll still graduate early."

Recoiling, my cheeks burned. "You called her? You haven't even talked to me!"

Mom said something, but I didn't hear what. I didn't want to hear her. *Traitor.* She'd sided with her parents—turned her back on me. Blood rushed my ears. Her lips moved some more, a muted jumble of words. I clenched my teeth.

Don't speak. You'll regret it, Elsie. Horrible thoughts ran through my head: *Fuck off—I hate you—I'll run. Run now! Sprint as fast as you can!*

Mom paced back and forth, intentionally blocking the front door. Moments of silence passed. She spun and locked her eyes on mine.

Run, the voice said.

"Don't." Mom's tone was full of warning. She knew me too well.

LIFE HAPPENS ON THE STAIRS

Run, it said again.

"Elsie," Mark huffed. "Come on, now. Don't be stupid."

Stupid? *Run!* The voice screamed.

I pivoted, sprinted to my room, and pushed open the back door. Jumping off the steps, I dashed across the yard toward the abandoned house. Blinded with fury, I darted to the left, pushing through the thicket alongside the road. I broke through the dry brush into a forest of cedars, needled branches weaved a dense web above, filtering out the light. Within minutes, I rounded the back of the house, moving through the weeds to the cracked brick sidewalk. I yanked the back door open and quietly pulled it shut behind me. Heart accelerating, pounding clear to my throat, I gasped and squeezed my eyes shut.

I couldn't look at her. I had to run.

I opened my eyes, squinting to adjust to the darkness. The two-story house was shrouded in an overgrowth of scotch pines, oaks, and sycamores. I reached for my back pocket. *Damn it, no phone.* I froze and absorbed what light I could, listening in the darkness. Nothing but the breeze stirring the leaves outside, rustling the rickety old house. Silhouettes began to reveal themselves: the door frame, a dark hallway, the edge of the kitchen counter. Bearings in check, I moved forward, feet crunching dirt and rubbish covering the floor. When I stepped in the kitchen, I quickened my steps, turned left into the living room, and made a beeline to the Victorian couch. Inhaling the smell of red dirt and the musty upholstery, I hugged my knees to my chest, buried my face in my arms and cried.

Betrayed. Mom hadn't even talked to me. I wasn't a child. A pain of guilt stabbed me.

I'd just reacted like a little brat, though. *Damn it.*

My whimpers disturbed the silence in the room. I didn't like the sound. I coughed and let out a low growl. Sucking in a deep breath, I straightened.

A muted, golden glow flashed in the window at the far end of the room, then quickly faded as a car drove around the curve outside. As time moved on, the traffic outside became more intermittent and then eventually stopped. It was late—well after nine. Mom would freak out when I went home. My stomach rolled. I still couldn't will myself to move from the couch. Hugging my knees tighter, I'd barely moved a muscle for hours.

Creeeeaaak... I flinched. What was that? Sitting upright, my ears tingled at the sound of soft footsteps moving through the house. Mr. Smith's grimacing leer flashed in my mind. Fear rippled through me. A beam of fluorescent light illuminated the doorway to the living room. I curled tighter, peering over my knees.

All six-foot-two of him stepped through the entrance.

Tyler.

He held up his cell phone, brightening his sharp features. My heart leapt.

"Tyler!" I jumped to my feet and ran into his arms.

"Elsie—" Trembling, he hugged me tight, then gently pushed my head back, and kissed me. Slow at first, tender, longing, his desire uninhibited as he parted my lips, kissing me deeper. I melted into his embrace, exhilarated to feel his touch, the smell of his woody scent, the way he said my name, voice laced with fear. For a brief moment, I forgot that I'd run. He brushed his face against mine, rough stubble grazing my cheek.

"I've been worried sick about you," he whispered.

How did he even know? He was supposed to be on his

way to Indianapolis.

He let me go and stepped back. My elation to see him dwindled within seconds. He ran his fingers through his hair, dark eyes ominous in the glow of the cell phone's flashlight. I took an equal step back, defenses rearing from the serious look on his face.

"What are you doing here?" I asked apprehensively, unsure if I wanted the answer.

"I'm here to illustrate what a promise looks like."

"What the hell does that mean?"

"You promised," he stated with an underlying tone of accusation. "You swore you wouldn't do this again. And you have. I promised to keep your hiding place a secret. And I have. Which one of us is right?"

Another step back, I cocked my head to the side. "You condescending *asshole*."

"Oh. That's nice," his voice low, laced with contempt.

I had to watch my mouth. I'd say awful things under pressure. Not only did I run and hide, I had a tendency to be like a wild animal backed into a corner when someone found me. I had no idea why I reacted that way, no reasonable justification. A genetic flaw, I suppose. And in the past, Dad had been the one person who could persuade me to calm down.

Glancing at Tyler, I sat down on the couch, dust billowing from the worn cushions. I coughed and waved my hand in the air.

Tyler walked slowly toward me as he focused on his phone, texting.

"There," he said. "Claire knows you're alive."

He set the phone on the coffee table. The flashlight cast a bluish-white halo on the ceiling and elongated shadows crept across the floor. Tyler's eyes looked even darker in the dim light. The windows rattled, a cool draft cut through the stale air. Shivering, goosebumps rose on my skin. He sat down at the opposite end of the couch, stretched out his long legs, and draped his arm across the back. I glanced at him. Unshaven, I'd never seen him with a light beard – sexy as it was – and he was wearing a light-blue button-up laid open with a white T-shirt underneath. He made me ache inside. His dark gaze met mine. My heart skipped.

Sublime. He'd break me if I looked at him any longer. I turned and stared across the room. This wasn't his concern. I felt violated, like he'd listened in on a private conversation. How did he even know I'd run?

"Did Mom call you?" I asked, staring forward.

"No. I called you. She answered in a complete panic. When she told me you ran, I drove out of the airport parking lot and headed here."

"That's insane Tyler," I said, irritated. "Tomorrow's Nationals. Why would you do that?

"We've already covered that. The answer I'm dying to know is, why would you do this?"

"I'm pissed! She wants to move." My heart accelerated, and I spoke faster. "I didn't get accepted to MCA, and I've had a horrible day. Sorry, this has nothing to do with you."

"What-the-fuck-ever," he stated. "You lied. And I'm starting to wonder if this is a defense or a genuine problem."

I whipped my head toward him and glared. "What the fuck does that mean?"

"Lying." He let the word roll off his tongue.

"I am not a liar."

"You lied to your mom for six weeks." He spoke like a lawyer drilling a witness. "You broke a promise. You didn't tell me about your dad's death. Not exactly a blatant lie, but could be classified as one of omission." He glanced at his watch. "I have twenty-five minutes before I have to leave. I've already rescheduled my flight to Indy. What exactly do you propose?"

"I didn't ask you to come here."

"I didn't say you did." The room went silent. I pushed my hands through my hair, staring at the dusty floors. He took a breath and continued, "If you'll run and hide from them, what are you going to do to me when we have problems? That *will* happen. Everyone has problems. Are you going to run—hide—lie? I've been asking for you to trust me," he sighed. "Maybe I'm the one with trust issues."

"You think?" I pitched my voice higher, confirming my sarcasm. He let his head fall back with obvious annoyance. I tensed and quietly said, "This has nothing to do with you."

"Mm... " a cavernous hum rose from deep in his throat. "Maybe not today, but what about in six months—a year? Hell, how about in fifteen years? Will you decide to run then?" He paused, and then he said with a pleading voice, "Reassure me... please."

I wanted to explain, but the words stuck in my mouth like peanut butter fixed to my palate. The resentment I felt toward Mom and now him overrode all logic. He waited. I leaned forward and rubbed my palms together. Even his gentle appeal couldn't cut through the force field of anger shielding me.

Another huff from the opposite end of the couch. "It will never work between us if I have to guess what's on your mind. Please. Tell me."

"This is bullshit." I stared at my hands, unwavering from my stance. "I'm here because I'm pissed at Mom. It has nothing to do with you."

"Beyond disrespectful."

Motherfucker. Another jab.

"Much obliged, Mr. Vaughn," I exaggerated a Southern drawl, while fluttering my lashes. "Forgive me for being so forward. A lesson in my manners is always a pleasure."

"I'm not kidding."

I slumped back on the couch. "What do you want from me? Another promise? Are you keeping track of my fuck-ups?"

"Can't you see how much this hurts everyone? Elsie, help me understand!"

Tears filled my eyes. "I just can't go home right now. I needed time to think."

"You can't go to your room? Shut the door, and have your *'time to think'* where everyone knows you're okay?"

I pressed my lips tight and said nothing.

"Why are you shutting down like this?"

"You called me a fucking liar."

"No, I didn't. I was merely making a point. Elsie, I love you. But you've got to grow up."

"Get the fuck away from me!" I yelled.

He recoiled, a pained look crossed his face. "You are completely irrational right now."

I lifted my eyes to his. "Fuck off."

His lip curled into a cold scowl. Slowly standing, he grabbed his phone from the coffee table. "You know what? Fuck you," he said in a low, contemptuous tone. "You know your own way home. I suggest you go back."

I squeezed my eyes shut. His footsteps moved further away. Moments later, the screen door slammed on the other side of the wall. I imagined him walking across the overgrown lawn.

My arms and legs shook with fury. Fuck him. I'd stay on

the couch until I died.

The muted slam of a car door. I opened my eyes to the yawning void of darkness. The low hum of his Mercedes purred to life outside. My blood ran cold, panic surged through me.

What had I done? I jumped to my feet. *No, no, no, no! Don't leave. Oh God—no!*

I sprinted across the dark room, grabbed the threshold to the kitchen, and spun into the hallway like a slingshot. *Don't go!*

I burst out of the screen door and turned right in the overgrowth toward the forgotten driveway. Just as I rounded the corner of the house, his silver Mercedes sped down the country road toward Morris Chapel. Sprinting forward, I stopped at the asphalt. The full moon reflected off his rear window, its silver back end shimmering in the cool light before the car rounded the corner and disappeared behind the hill.

The hum of the engine echoed through the calm evening until the purr ebbed, leaving only the sound of the wind rustling the leaves and a distant mockingbird singing in the moonlight. Tears soaked my cheeks, dripping down to my shirt. As I walked home, the cool breeze chilled my wet face. I wiped my nose, feeling sick to my stomach.

Stupid, stupid. I'd stomped all over him. *Fuck off?* Why had I said that? Cruel, cold, unforgivable words.

Minutes later, I stepped inside the house, shaking with fear and regret. Mark and Mom were waiting in the living room.

"It's about time," Mark announced with a smack to the arm of the chair.

"Where's Tyler?" Mom asked. "He wouldn't tell me

where to find you, and insisted on coming himself." She shook her head. "I can't imagine how fast he drove. Is he coming inside?"

"He's gone. I blew it." I sniffled, unable to arrest my breath. "You don't ever have to worry about me running again. I'm sorry. I ruined everything."

She stared at me with her arms crossed. "Glad to know someone finally got to you."

Her poignant words stung deep. She turned and disappeared on the other side of the wall, footsteps pattering toward her room.

Mark and I made eye contact.

"Tyler was freaking out when he got here." Mark's contorted look of betrayal ripped another pain through me. "Whatever you did to run him off... you're an idiot. The guy fucking loves you."

He pushed out of the chair, went straight to his room, and clicked the door behind him.

Alone again. I gasped, but my throat was locked tight. Sucking in breath after breath, I thought I'd die inside. My stomach rolled as acid filled my throat. Darting to the bathroom, I fell to my knees in front of the toilet and vomited.

Chapter

38

The next ten days were hell. I'd been set back two months. All the pain I'd felt after Tyler left for school came rushing back, only this time, I owned it. I'd created my own circumstances. I sat on my bed staring at my phone. It hadn't vibrated, buzzed, hummed, dinged, rang—nothing. I'd called him every day, sent six text messages, and left eight voicemails. Nothing.

Mom poked her head in my room. "Are you almost done packing?"

"Yeah. Just a few more things, then we can tear down my bed."

"Okay. Have you heard from Mrs. Allen?"

"Yeah. I can take finals tomorrow."

"Good. All the teachers assured me they'd help."

My chest felt like it weighed a thousand pounds. "Yep."

"You still haven't heard from him?"

"Nope."

"Hang in there," she said before she closed my door.

Sure.

The next day, I came home from finals and scrounged up a manila envelope out of the hutch. I wrote on the front in black permanent marker: **Vaughn, 857 Jamerson Rd. Collierville, TN**, and slid Tyler's iPhone inside. Less than twenty-four hours until I left Tennessee for good. I couldn't take the temptation to call him again.

At eight the next morning, we stopped by Woodrow and Ruby's and said goodbye. Tears. Hugs. More tears. One last hug, then Mark, Mom, and I hit the road in separate vehicles. Mark led our convoy in a Ryder truck to start anew, and we headed North.

When we stopped in Mount Vernon, Illinois to get gas, I stopped by a post office to mail the envelope. Before I sent it, I wrote a note that said: *Unconditionally?* I slipped it inside, then sealed it tight. There. Maybe he'd get the point.

A week later, we'd settled in a small, three-bedroom, yellow farmhouse on County Road 400 in the middle of a barren, snow-covered field. After a few days, I started receiving letters forwarded from Morris Chapel, offering the chance to attend several colleges. Every time I read one, the possibility that I could study filled me with hope, but all of the universities were in Tennessee, and I couldn't even think about the state without tearing up.

Mark holed up in his bedroom which was an add-on to the back of the house. I stayed in my small, eight-by-fourteen room off the kitchen. Mom would come home from work and fall asleep in the recliner or crash in her bedroom at the front of the house every night before nine. We found a new routine without flinching. Each of us torn inside with our personal sorrow. Mom—Dad. Me—Tyler. Mark—Megan.

The long nights were haunting. I wanted to feel better, but more than that, I wanted to move on. As I lay in the silent darkness, I couldn't stop beating myself up. Over and over, I repeated the night at the abandoned house. The way Tyler pleaded with me and how I refused to give in. How terrified he was when he first showed up. The way he kissed me... I'd sacrificed everything for nothing, acted like a fool, and look at where it had gotten me – alone. In Illinois, anyway.

"Why are you so stubborn, Elsie?" I grumbled to myself, then I flopped on my side and cried myself to sleep, once again.

December fourteenth, I was standing in the kitchen, washing dishes, staring past the blue-and-white checkered curtains at the frozen cornfield. Cold, wet, frigid Illinois. I'd never warm up to the flatlands. Flatlander by birth, it didn't matter, my heart would always live in the rolling hills of the Tennessee River Valley.

The back door swung open and Mom ran inside, waving a manila envelope.

"I forgot to check the mail yesterday. It's here!"

I froze. "Okay... give me a second."

Trembling, I willed myself to dry my hands with the dish towel. The only school I hadn't heard from was the School of the Art Institute of Chicago. My last hope. I could move to the city and forget about the past six months of my life.

Please, let it be good news. I craved the idea of a loud city, somewhere to blend and be more or less invisible. She shoved the envelope in my hand. I stared at it for a moment.

Tyler. Chicago had never crossed my mind until him. An aching pain rolled through me.

"You're killing me," Mom said. "What are you waiting for?"

"I'm scared." I exhaled. "I'd set my hopes up too high."

"Elsie... I know the past few weeks have been hard. Don't let a broken heart stop you."

I pushed back the threat of tears. "You're right."

Slowly sliding my finger under the flap, the paper split at the seam. I pulled out the letter, heart thumping in my throat.

Dear Miss Richardson,

It is our pleasure to inform you that you've been chosen for a full scholarship.

"Oh my gosh, I got it!" I shouted.

"I knew you would!"

She grabbed me, and we screamed, jumping up and down in the middle of the kitchen.

A full ride. They'd offered me tuition, fees, and housing. My portfolio must've knocked their socks off. I'd never felt so high on life.

After our celebration dance in the middle of the kitchen, I

leaned against the counter and reread the letter.

"Mom, I can start in January. Are you okay with that?"

"Why wouldn't I be?"

"I don't believe you."

She let out a nervous laugh and flushed. "Why?"

"Because you're answering my questions with questions."

Shaking her head, her bewildered expression went flat. "Dad would be so proud of you."

"I know," I said, gently. "I've never questioned that. But are you proud of me?"

She snapped to attention. "I don't have the words to tell you how proud I am. Elsie, I'm in awe of you. I've never had the courage to be the person you are. Whether you're running for dear life or making the most beautiful picture I've ever seen, you have everything inside of you that I wish I could've been."

Tears filled my eyes. "Mom. You still can."

She gave me a weak smile. "We'll see. It's not about me right now. Enjoy your moment. Seize your opportunity and make the most of it."

I walked across the room and wrapped my arms around her. She held me tight.

"Now, you have a date tomorrow night," she said. "And I think it would be a great time for you to go check out the city."

I pulled away. "What do you mean? What date?"

"Didn't you tell me a few months ago that Tyler bought you tickets for a Bears game?"

I shrugged. "Yeah. But why would I go?"

"Because you need to see him. You need the closure before you start school."

"I pissed him off." I took a sharp breath. "He hasn't even let me apologize."

"Maybe you can work it out."

"He won't show."

"What if he does?"

"I've never driven in the city."

"It's not that hard. Just follow I-57 to the Dan Ryan and exit downtown. You're going to have to get used to it." She smiled. "You'll be living there in less than a month."

Butterflies fluttered in my belly. Chicago. Me in the city, living downtown, studying at one of the best art schools in the country. I *could* check the area out.

"Can you come with me?" I asked.

"I have to work Tuesday morning." Her eyes were sympathetic. "You know, I still have Tyler's number. You could always try to call him."

"I'll think about it."

The hole inside me pulsed like an abscessed wound. What if he did show? What would I say to him?

I thought of his words the day he gave me the tickets, *"Promise me you'll be there... Death is the only excuse."*

Nothing had gone as we'd planned and this was my last chance to make it right. If he didn't show, at least I'd know I tried. Mom was right, as always, I needed the closure so I could finally move on.

Chapter

39

April... Six Months Later
Chicago, Illinois

I jogged across Michigan Avenue to Madison Street. Morning traffic in full bustle, everyone hurrying to work, horns honking, tires screeching, rumbling machinery, repetitive beeps from trucks moving in reverse. I loved the sounds of the city. The lights. The energy. No crickets. No snakes. And most of all—freedom.

Running up to my apartment complex, I finished my work-out by taking the staircase instead of the elevator, all the way to the sixth floor. Within minutes, I unlocked my door and stepped in my efficiency apartment which SAIC provided for scholarship students. I loved my tiny, twelve-by-sixteen space. In the corner, I kept my easel and paints, papers scattered along the wall next to stacks of canvases and prints. I had just enough room for a futon couch and an old trunk which I used for a coffee table. I pressed the start button on my coffee maker. The north wall was covered with my favorite paintings and drawings, not an inch of plaster could be seen. The east wall was all windows where I loved to sit and watch the traffic on State Street.

I pulled off my jogging clothes and climbed in the shower. By the time I'd finished getting dressed, the coffee maker beeped. I poured a cup and looked around my little apartment. My heart sank. I had to move out in a month. Mom wanted me to come home for the summer, but after living in the city, the idea of being in the flatlands of corn and beans sounded like torture. If only the scholarship covered housing in the summer, too. Move in. Move out. Move in. Oh, well. That was college life.

Taking a sip of stout, black coffee, my navy-and-orange coffee cup made me think of the night of the Bears game...

Tyler was standing outside Gate A, dark eyes watching me walk toward him. Heart racing, I took deep breaths as I moved closer. It didn't help that he stared at me with no smile and his arms crossed. The sight of him felt like a dagger was being shoved through my chest. Crowds of people walked past, laughing and chattering, ready to watch the game. I held my breath as I stepped in front of him.

A light stubble covered his face again. It was almost like his alter ego stood in front of me. Dressed in a sweatshirt and jeans with no coat in the middle of December, his icy stare was as cold as the breeze rolling off Lake Michigan.

"Well, I see you're not dead," he said.

Of course, he remembered those words. I returned his unamused stare.

"I'm here to illustrate what a promise looks like."

A hint of a grin. "You are a girl of your word." His melodic drawl was like candy for my soul. I couldn't let him break me. He ran his right hand through his hair and said, "I reckon this is a little awkward."

"You ditched me."

"You dumped me." A frosty smile. "I got a cryptic note and an iPhone? What was that?"

"Your parting words were, 'Fuck you.'"

"I believe my last words were, 'I suggest you go back.' You told me to fuck off."

"Whatever. I tried to call you for ten days," I said. He looked down, cheeks filling with color. I held out the envelope he'd given me months before. "Here. Enjoy the game."

He ignored the tickets, taking my hand, instead. A tingling current ran up my arm. I craved his warm touch. A gust of wind moved his cologne through the air. His scent. I yearned to be in his arms. I wanted to bury my face in his chest and forget all about our mistakes. I jerked my hand. His grip gently tightened.

"You don't understand." His voice shifted from defensive to pleading.

"I understand perfectly. I pissed you off. I made a stupid mistake, and you wouldn't even let me apologize."

"I don't need an apology. I need... "

"What?" I snapped. "You aren't going to stomp on my heart again. I can't take it. The past month has been complete hell."

"I... I was testing what life was like without you." He winced, like he felt a sharp pain. "I real—really don't like the guy I am right now."

He stuttered. Tyler never stuttered or stammered. His hand trembled, holding mine. He hadn't been taking care of himself. His eyes were sunken and the scruff on his face was an obvious sign that he didn't care. Where had my strong, confident Tyler gone?

"Sorry to hear that." I said, softening my tone as I looked away. Only the sounds of the crowd lingered for a few moments. Cautiously, I lifted my eyes to his. "You said you loved me unconditionally."

His intense gaze brightened. "I do."

"Well, you've got a terrible way of showing it."

I pulled my hand away. He let me go this time. The crowd cheered in the background. People were ready for Monday Night Football, *and I was ready to leave. Pivoting, I started to walk away.*

Boom! Boom! Boom! Explosions of fireworks echoed above. The stadium roared. Tyler's warm touch grasped my wrist after a few steps. I spun around. Orange and blue sparkles crackled in the sky above us, casting shadows over Tyler's striking features.

"Elsie, please. Don't go—"

Honk! Tires squealed outside of the apartment on State Street, snapping me back to reality. I flinched. Coffee splashed on my arm. *Shit.* I grabbed a dish cloth and wiped it off, then glanced at the clock. Seven-fifty. *Oh crap,* class will start in ten minutes. I hurried around, slid on my shoes, grabbed my bag, and headed out the door.

By eleven-thirty, my stomach wouldn't stop growling, and the longer Ms. Allston droned on about Art Nouveau, the heavier my eyes felt. Finally, she said her parting words.

"Now, shoo." She waved her hands like we were annoying her. "Go make some art."

When I stepped outside, I took a deep breath of the cool,

spring air. The wind blew through the streets off of the lake, washing away the smell of fuel and exhaust fumes. Even the city couldn't resist the clean birth of Spring. I headed north toward Starbucks.

"Elsie, wait up!"

I turned around. Sarah. Good. I needed to talk to her about the exhibition tomorrow night. Sarah and I weren't like a lot of the students at SAIC. We wore jeans and T-shirts, no tattoos, and kept our hair natural. I loved how her Julia Roberts smile and eyes had a way of putting everyone at ease. Compared to the people who thought art belonged all over their body, as well as their work, she helped me not feel out of place.

She caught up with me and we started walking.

"Is Ms. Allston's class a drag or what?" she said.

"No doubt. I need caffeine after that." We stopped at the corner and waited for the signal to cross. "I have my piece ready for the exhibit. I can run it by the studio this evening."

"Good. I was worried you were backing out."

"No. I had to do some touch-ups."

"Is any of your family going to make it?"

"No. My mom has some conference she has to go to." The light changed, and we started across the street. "And my brother lives too far away."

"What about your dad?"

"He passed away last October."

"Oh. Sorry to hear that."

I opened the door and we entered Starbucks. People stood shoulder to shoulder, various shades of black and gray suits waited in line. Loud chatter competed with the song *Heartbeat* by *The Frey*, blaring from the overhead speakers.

Tyler. I remembered the night when he had stayed at my

house, and we'd listened to it.

"You okay?" Sarah asked.

Loud voices, machines grinding coffee, clanking of metal. A deep voice yelled out, "Number eight-six!"

I shook off my thoughts. "Of course."

"Isn't your brother getting married soon?"

"Yeah, in August. I'll be in a wedding one weekend and moving back the next."

"Where's it at?"

"Nashville. He met a girl when we lived in Tennessee. What's funny is he hated it there, but he moved back within months because of her." I laughed. "But Megan's really sweet. She's already like a sister to me."

"Can I help you?" a petite, red-headed barista asked Sarah.

"A large mocha latte." She paid the girl and stepped away.

"For you?" the girl asked me.

"Large, mocha Frappuccino, please."

"Three dollars and seventy-two cents."

After I paid, we stepped aside to wait for our order.

"Hey, Dad wants me to go out to dinner tonight," she said. "Wanna go?"

Sarah grew up in Evanston, within walking distance of the lake. Money was no object, and she frequently took long shopping sprees downtown. The last thing I wanted to do was listen to her dad go on about his job as the chief editor at the *Chicago Times*.

"Thanks, but I have some things I want to work on tonight."

"We're going to the Cheesecake Factory... " She raised her eyebrows like I wouldn't be able to resist. "Dad's buying."

"That's sweet of you, but not tonight."

She shrugged. "Your loss."

Three men, wearing different shades of gray, tailored suits walked past me. A cedar-laced, woody scent filled the air. I glanced over my shoulder. Was he here? The last guy stepped out, blocking the view of the other two men. I shook my head and turned back to Sarah.

It's Dior, *Elsie.* Plenty of men wore *Dior* cologne, especially in downtown Chicago.

"Why are you so tense?" Sarah asked.

"Sorry. Just can't stop thinking about someone."

"Oh, really?" She grinned. "Andrew?"

"Yuck. Hell, no."

"He's totally into you."

"He's covered in tattoos. And I'm a bitch to him."

"He likes that." She frowned.

"Number ninety!" a deep voice called out.

Sarah grabbed her drink. A few minutes later, they called my number.

Outside, the noise shifted back to the hum of the city – screeching tires, honking horns, buzzing machinery. I took a swig of the mocha and coffee all slushed together in the icy drink.

"I'm gonna head home," I said. "I'll drop off my painting later, okay?"

"Sure. I'll be at the studio until six."

My cell phone rang. I grabbed it out of my back pocket. Mark.

"Hi!" I answered.

"What'cha doing?"

"Nothing. Just headed home. How are you guys?"

"Oh, we're good. Swimming in wedding shit. Don't you

have an art show tomorrow?"

"Yep. You gonna drive up?" I joked. "Starts at six."

"Sorry, sis. Mom told me she couldn't make it, either. Just wanted to wish you luck. "

I stopped at the crosswalk. Cars sped past, blowing my jacket open.

"Aw, thanks. How's Megan?"

"Great. She got a job at the hospital. They want to send her to school to become an RN."

"Oh, that's cool. How about you?"

"I was accepted to Tennessee State! I'm also going to try out for the football team. Maybe I can be a walk-on."

"I'm so happy to hear that, Mark! Good for you. You really deserve it."

Chapter

40

April 25th
Gala Exhibition for 1st and 2nd Year Students

I gazed at the sign outside the studio, taking a moment to gather my nerves before I went inside. My first art show. I'd worn a simple, dark blue, Indian cotton dress – and finally, after months of waiting, I had an occasion special enough to wear my black Louboutins. With my red bottomed shoes boosting my confidence, I pulled the brass handle.

You've got this. That's what Dad would've said. *You got this, Elsie.*

Stepping inside, the open space was constructed of red brick walls and weathered plank flooring. Paintings were hung in gallery fashion, and pedestals displaying sculptures from ceramics to marbles were strategically placed for people to observe from every angle.

Sarah stood in the corner by an installation of shattered glass. I cringed. Shattered glass? *How dumb.* The girl who decided to break glass and call it art had a dark approach to life, from her Marilyn Manson wardrobe to the constant frown on her face. Someone had evidently shattered something inside of her. *Huh.* Maybe it did make sense.

"Elsie," Sarah called out.

She wore classic black slacks and a cream, button-up blouse. Her long brown hair fell in locks over her shoulders.

"You look great," I said.

"You, too." She smiled. "Love the dress."

"Thanks."

"Have you looked for your painting yet?" She pointed at the other end of the room. "Hopefully someone will buy it."

"That would be cool."

We started across the room. I'd submitted a drawing of a staircase. Inspired by the tessellations of MC Escher and a quote from Martin Luther King Jr. about faith, I'd drawn the piece with pastel and charcoal – a curving staircase shrouded in an ultramarine background. Some of the steps were cracked, one had an ominous black hole, others were bright and shiny-looking, and the final step faded to black, reinforcing the need to have faith to take the next step. I called it, *Life Happens on the Stairs.*

"I really love it," Sarah said. "What's your inspiration?"

Tyler.

"Um... A quote from Martin Luther King and a conversation I had with an old friend."

"It turned out great. Kind of dark and haunting. How

much are you asking?"

"Five hundred. I could use the cash," I said. "But there's a part of me that hopes it doesn't sell. That's kind of why I priced it so high."

She snorted. "You're in Chicago. That's chump change."

As the evening moved on, I stuck close to Sarah and watched the crowd. She introduced me to a few of her associates who promoted all the studios in the city. By nine-thirty, my head was spinning with all the opportunities and different conversations. I grabbed a drink and walked over to my painting.

Looking over the abstract print beside mine, I saw vivid primary colors fighting for attention – the polar opposite of my dark pastel. I stepped back and tried to look at my work with fresh eyes. I should've shaded more in the corner. Oh well, too late now.

I sensed someone step behind me. Inhaling an earthy, cedar-laced scent, I smiled.

"This painting screams Tyler and Elsie symbolism," a low, Southern drawl whispered in my ear. "You should re-name it 'Tysie.'"

I giggled. "A ship name for my painting?"

"You should consider it."

I turned around and wrapped my arms around Tyler's neck. He pressed his lips to mine, squeezing me tight. Taking a step back, I had to admit my man looked beyond gorgeous. He was wearing a white dress shirt, top two buttons undone, dark gray dress slacks tailored perfectly to his long legs, and polished, black Italian leather shoes.

The night of the Bears game, I couldn't say no to him. My urge to run had been destroyed when he'd left me, and I would never run again. As the fireworks faded above us, he had begged me to stay, then pulled me into his arms and kissed me with such desperate passion, I fell in love with him all over again. We didn't go to the game. Instead, we walked through the city streets, talking and mending our wounds until we almost froze to death. After retrieving our cars, I went back to the Hilton Hotel with him and we ate dinner in the restaurant.

When I told him I'd been accepted to SAIC, he let out a sigh and said, "Thank God. I just confirmed I'd go to Northwestern. The stars are finally lined in our favor."

We stayed up all night, making plans and daydreaming. A month later, we had both moved to the city. He lived five blocks away from me in an obscenely priced high-rise apartment. I moved into my efficiency flat, content and happy, especially now that he was only blocks away. We'd meet in the mornings and jog, then head our separate ways for the day, spending most evenings at one or the other's place. Once again, I liked our private world, and I kept it all to myself. Not even Sarah knew about him.

"I'm glad you made it," I said. "I missed you this morning. I hate jogging alone."

"Sorry. I had to talk to my professor before class." He stepped back and looked me over. "You're absolutely stunning."

"Not so bad yourself." I gave him a quick kiss. "Happy birthday! Congratulations. You're no longer a teenager."

"Thank you." He smiled, inclining his head. "Are you ready for some dinner?"

"After you humor me and look at all our hard work."

"Fair enough." He glanced around the room. "I've already purchased a piece, but I'll take a look at some of the others. Certainly not that shattered glass shit. What the hell is that supposed to be?" He smirked, staring at the installation.

"Wait. What did you buy?"

He turned back to me. "I need artwork for my apartment." He nodded over my shoulder, raising an eyebrow. "Do you really think I'm going to let someone else have our metaphor?"

I pointed at the painting. "I'll give that to you. I'm not taking your money."

"Money? Elsie." He shook his head. "My money is your money. It's a wash."

I sighed. "We aren't there yet, Tyler."

"Yes, we are." His eyes sparkled under the lights. "I'll prove it to you." He took a step away from me. "May I have everyone's attention?"

The chatter in the room faded as people turned to see who was talking.

I bristled. *What the hell was he doing?*

"Thank you." Tyler nodded to the crowd. "This will only take a moment. I'm Tyler Vaughn, and this is my lovely girlfriend, Elizabeth."

I narrowed my eyes at him for saying my real name. No one knew me as Elizabeth.

"If you don't know Elsie's work, please refer to the most beautiful piece in the room, over there in the corner." He shook his head. "Not sure why it's tucked back there, but I can pardon the mistake." His honeyed accent sounded imported amongst the Chicago crowd.

Sarah looked at me with a "What the hell?" look on her face. I shrugged.

"Regardless," Tyler continued, "the reason I've solicited your attention is because this amazing girl, right here, is the love of my life." He turned to me, took a step forward, and bent down on one knee. "Will you please give me the honor of spending the rest of my life with you?"

A princess-cut diamond ring appeared between his fingers. I held my breath at the sight of the sparkling solitaire.

"I love you more than life itself," he said. "Please, be my wife. Come live with me. Let me be the person you want to come home to every night."

A gasp in the background. Another person said, "How beautiful... "

Tears filled my eyes. "Yes... I would love to be your wife."

He nodded with that soft look in his eyes that I loved, and then he slipped the ring on my finger. The room erupted in applause. He stood and cupped my face with both hands.

"I can't tell you how happy this makes me."

"Me too, Tyler. I love you."

"And I love you. May I kiss you in front of a room full of strangers?"

"Anytime."

And that's what he did.

Acknowledgments

First and foremost, I thank God for everything in my life and for giving me a spirit of determination.

To my husband Jerrod, thank you for enduring the years of me lamenting over a project that you've believed in from the beginning, and your unconditional love for over 20 years.

Emily, my dear sweet girl, thank you for reading the book seven times and helping me stay sane. Without you, I'd have given up years ago.

To Joey for your constant encouragement and curious questions. You're going to write one someday too, my love.

Angie Ruwe, my dear friend, thank you for never giving up on my dream with me and for all your prayers.

Carrie Write, you've been with me for years, supporting my crazy ideas, thank you for always being there for me.

Nancy Hill, Cece Ruwe, Hailey Watts, Cora Hashbarger, Laural Collins, Rita Jackson, Jessie Latham and Jamie Smith, thank you for being my first readers, some of you had to trudge through the first draft. You're brave souls.

Rita and Bill Collins, my second Mom and Dad, thank you for all your love and support over the years, and for reading, too.

Kim Stanhope, big thank you for being a first reader and editing a massively bloated story. I think you'll really love this version.

Sage Lundquist, thank you for your insightful thoughts

and suggestions, it means a lot to me that you believed in this story.

A big thank you to my muffin-chucking, critique partner extraordinaire, Anne Spurgeon. The story wouldn't be what it is today if I hadn't found you.

Bea Pavia, you and Anne were blessings set in my life. Thank you, Bea, for your editing and encouragement that this *is* a story worth publishing.

To my writers' group, *Penmark Writers*, you've all been amazing on this journey.

A special thanks to Sabrina James, who not only loved LHOTS, but also interviewed me on Red Dirt Roots Radio, alongside her mom Jeri James, well before I was published.

A big shout out to Harley in Texas! Thank you for all of your support, brother, can't wait until the day I meet you and your family.

I owe the world to my mom, Barbara Rothermel. You've always been my loudest cheerleader and solid rock. Thank you for your love, and understanding that I borrowed pieces of our lives to craft a story that really isn't us at all, but rather, my therapy through fiction.

Thank you to my brothers, Pat and Marty Rothermel. I love you both, and remember, this is just a work of fiction, relax.

To all of my writer family online and in our writers' group – Soulla, Jackie, Alex, Henry, Melisa, Aaron, Anne Marie, and Susie. You've all kept me going, and I can't wait to meet all of you.

Finally, a huge thank you to the *Breakthrough Novel Awards* and the judges, The Book Khaleesi – Author Services and Eeva Lancaster for making my dream come true. You've made this story what I've always dreamt it would be. Thank you, Eeva, from the bottom of my heart!

About the Author

Amy J. Markstahler lives with her husband and two children near the banks of the Salt Fork River, just outside Urbana, Illinois. In 2016, she was the 3rd Place recipient in the Linda Howard Award of Excellence, and in 2018, she won First Prize in the Breakthrough Novel Awards, both for Life Happens on the Stairs, her first novel.

If she's not writing or hanging out with her family, you can probably find her on the porch with one of her many cats.

Visit Amy at **www.amyjmarkstahler.com**
On Twitter: @Ajmarkstahler
On Facebook: @ajmarkstahler

Made in the USA
Middletown, DE
19 May 2020